S HE LOOKED UP, HER TEAR-FILLED EYES MEETING HIS. Her voice shook. "What do you mean?"

"Right now your brother has no idea who took you. We were careful to leave no trace. Odds are he thinks the Danes responsible. But soon I will send word to him of where you are and he will come. If he thinks you a captive, abused, perhaps dead, honor will demand that he give battle, and he will perish. But if he finds you safe, honored, content, then he will accept the alliance he should have accepted months ago. All will be as it should be."

"You mean he will agree to give me to you in marriage?"

"No, I mean he will accept our marriage. If you truly want to save his life, you will let him find you my wife, not my slave."

She paled. "I cannot marry without my brother's approval."

He had expected this and was prepared for it. "If you wait for that, he will die before he can give it. We will burn his body, as is our way. He will not even reach your Christian heaven. But who knows, perhaps Odin will welcome him into Valhalla for by all repute he is a mighty warrior. But not mighty enough to survive the trap I have set for him."

"Oh, God," she whispered, and with no warning at all pulled back her fist and slammed it straight into his jaw.

FOR

M

FOR ALL THE YEARS AND
ALL THE LOVE

Dream
OF ME

Josie Litton

Bantam 🦃 *Books*

New York Toronto London Sydney Auckland

DREAM OF ME / BELIEVE IN ME

A Bantam Book

Bantam paperback edition / October 2001

ISBN 0-553-58436-7

Published simultaneously in the United States and Canada

Bantam Books are published by Bantam Books, a division of Random
House, Inc. Its trademark, consisting of the words "Bantam Books"
and the portrayal of a rooster, is Registered in U.S. Patent and
Trademark Office and in other countries. Marca Registrada. Bantam
Books, 1540 Broadway, New York, New York 10036.

PRINTED IN THE UNITED STATES OF AMERICA

OPM   10   9   8   7   6   5   4   3   2

Chapter

ONE

MIST RISES FROM WATER MADE INKY BY moonless night, swirling over the shingle beach where waves curl gently, drifting up the cliff side fragrant with purple gorse, slipping through chinks in the palisade walls of the great fortress called Holyhood.

Nothing stirs save for a stray rat nosing at kernels dropped from a grain sack hours before. A cat crouches on the timber wall . . . waits . . . leaps. . . .

At their posts, the guards nod, negligent in their duty. Within, the great hall rings to the snores of the garrison.

In a private chamber at the top of the innermost tower, a young woman murmurs in her sleep, turning her petal-soft cheek against a scented pillow, restless as her dreams.

. . . The cat sits, delicately disassembling her prey. A whisper of wind troubles her fur. She looks up, frozen by the swift, silent shape that cleaves the mist.

In the curved dragon prow of the war ship, a man watches the keep slip by. His eyes cold and deadly as the ice floes of the north whence he comes, he takes the measure of the fortress whose fate he has already decided.

The silent, deadly shape of the vessel vanishes back into the mist. The cat returns to her meal. The young woman, asleep in the high tower, cries out softly but does not wake.

THE WOMEN WERE THE FIRST TO SEE THEM. A GROUP had gone down to the stream to wash clothes. They were chatting happily among themselves, talking of men and children, children and men, when one looked up, peered through the rising dust, and rose slowly to her feet. A fine shirt she had labored long to make for her husband to wear on holy days fell to the ground. She pressed a hand to her mouth to contain the scream that nonetheless emerged, half choked but all the more urgent for it.

The other women stopped. They looked at her first, then followed the direction of her eyes. One or two others let out little exclamations of shock and distress, but quickly enough they quieted. Not one made a sound, and they hushed the babes they had brought with them to the riverbank. The silence was broken only by the tread of horses and the soft clank and creak of men in saddles.

Sir Derward came slowly, his back iron straight, relishing every prancing stride, every moment, every gaze. Behind him, the patrol rode in two lines, single file. Between them, watched every moment by two dozen pairs of alternately astounded and wary eyes, came the prisoners.

They were six in number including the leader, few enough against four times that number, unarmed, their hands tied before them and roped together at the neck. They should have been—and surely were—helpless.

They terrified.

Not one was less than six feet in height, and the tallest, the leader, was at least four inches taller than that. Their shoulders and chests were massive, surely far too broad and heavily muscled for any normal men. They wore short tunics and were bare legged, their limbs like sinewy tree trunks.

Most were bearded although the leader was clean-shaven, his face hard and lean, his skin burnished, midnight-black hair hanging to his shoulders. His gaze was sharp and clear as it swept beyond the women to the open gates of the fortress. They were grim-faced, hard-eyed, wolf-souled men, and the leader was the most frightening of them all. Yet they were captive.

Incredibly, amazingly captive. The patrol was past before the women thought to raise a hesitant cheer. They grabbed up their babes and their wash, following swiftly behind, not wanting to miss a moment of this.

A guard lounging against the gate stared slack-jawed at what approached and called a ragged warning. Heads appeared on the palisade, a group formed near the gate, parting swiftly as the horses neared. Work stilled as word spread and the inhabitants of Holyhood dropped what they were doing to come see what none of them had ever thought to witness.

Captive Vikings. Men straight out of nightmares led roped and helpless into their own Holyhood. By their own Sir Derward, for whom none had spared an appreciative thought until this very instant. It was a spectacle to stun, to be savored around the winter fires into distant years, told and retold to children yet unborn.

Their cheers, no longer hesitant but full-throated and heartfelt, rose to heaven, passing on the way the high tower at the center of the keep, drifting by the open windows from which the scent of drying herbs floated, and causing the young woman within to look up curiously.

"What is that, Miriam?"

The old nurse paused in the midst of tying bundles of fragrant grasses together and cocked her head. "The people sound very excited, milady. Would you like me to find out what has happened?"

Slender, white hands laid a final rosebud inside a small press, screwed the lid on tightly, and set the press carefully aside. "If you would. I'd still like to get the oils done today."

Miriam nodded, stood, and left the room. The Lady of Holyhood continued her work.

W OLF HAKONSON TOOK A LOOK AROUND THE CELL into which he and his men had been thrust, nodded slowly, and sank down on the damp stone floor, stretching his long legs out before him. His men, ever vigilant to his mood, grinned. They sprawled out and relaxed.

"Damn," one-eyed Olaf muttered. He glanced at Wolf and sighed. "It's ten pelts I owe you."

"It is," Wolf agreed. His good humor was increasing steadily and he was hard-pressed to conceal it. But conceal it he must, for they were all clearly visible through the crossed iron-lattice windows on the double wooden doors that secured the cell. The room was large for a dungeon and he suspected it was more commonly used for storage, as it no doubt would be again when the harvest was brought in. In the meantime, it served as a prison for the Vikings.

Vikings caught unaware beside their apparently trapped vessel, run aground on a sandbar. Vikings too far from their weapons to offer resistance. Vikings who had surrendered with scarcely a murmur.

The mere thought almost made him burst out laughing. Truly Odin had blessed him with the rooster-brained Saxon in charge of the patrol. Scarcely had he seen so pride-blinded a man.

It would have been the work of minutes to disarm and kill the lax Saxons. He and his men had done the same and more enough times to be confident of the outcome. But that would have left Holyhood yet to be taken. Its garrison was large, if poorly led. Its walls were high. The Wolf valued the lives of those who followed him too much to risk them unnecessarily.

Besides, his chosen method brought not merely defeat and loss but profound insult, perfect to his purpose. He was mulling that over, his thoughts grimly occupied, when a clatter outside interrupted him. His eyes narrowed as he beheld Rooster Brain, accompanied by an audience of several knights, approaching the cell.

"Bold Vikings!" Sir Derward sneered. "The terror of the north!" He threw back his head and laughed, an oddly shrill sound more suited to a nervous girl. The men with him laughed too, perforce.

"Never have I seen such cowards," Derward exclaimed, his cheeks flushed, warming to his subject. "They yielded like women. Indeed, I think perhaps they are women! Viking women would be great hulking things, wouldn't they?"

More laughter greeted this witticism. Derward put his hands on his hips and paced back and forth before the bars gloating at his captives. "God's blood, you are pathetic specimens of men, to muster no resistance at all. Was not one of you eager to sup in Valhalla this night? Or did you have the sense to know not even your craven gods would welcome the likes of you?"

The man beside Wolf stirred. "No," Wolf murmured, his lips scarcely moving. The man stilled.

"You'll rot in here," Derward continued. "You'll weep and beg for food. You'll fight over a rat's carcass. You'll watch each other sicken and die, and you'll pray for death. But it won't come quickly—oh no! The enemies of Lord Hawk die slowly. You'll curse the mothers who gave you birth before your ends come."

When this, too, failed to raise any reaction, Derward's flush darkened dangerously. He clamped his hands on the iron bars, his mouth twisting. Little flecks of saliva showed at the corners of his lips.

"Mayhap I'll put you to fight each other for the amusement of my men. Whoever survives will have a little food, live a little longer. Which one of you will be the last to die?" His eyes swept over the men in the cell, coming to rest at last on Wolf.

"You," he said, not a question. He stared at the man who, even seated on the floor of a cell, his hands still bound, exuded deadly strength and calm. For just an instant, Derward's eyes flickered. "Why didn't you—?"

Whatever thought he'd been about to pursue went unspoken. The door opened again at the top of the stairs leading to the cell. A shaft of golden sunlight penetrated the torch-lit gloom. And there, in that light, stood a woman.

Wolf rose in a single, lithe motion. He moved toward the bars, the better to see her. The sun revealed little, only a dark silhouette, but he could make out that she was tall for a woman, willow slim, and graceful.

Her voice came floating through the doorway, low, soft, melodious, a voice to entice a man or soothe a child. It reverberated through him like a deep, inner caress. He was shocked to realize that he actually shivered.

"What is this, Sir Derward? Why are these men being held?"

The knight stiffened, hands dropping to his sides. His color paled, then returned in a rush. "They are Vikings, milady," he said in a voice that was almost steady. "Their vessel ran aground and they were caught scarcely a mile from here."

"Did they offer you resistance?"

"No, milady. They surrendered at once, afraid to fight us."

"I see. Then you don't actually know that they intended any harm?"

Derward took a deep, shuddering breath, fighting for calm. Wolf heard it and felt an instant's wry sympathy for him. "They are Vikings, milady," the knight repeated.

"We welcome merchants from the northlands. Is there reason to believe these men are not like them?"

"These are no merchants," Derward protested. "You've only to look at them." Again, that flicker in his eyes as though a thought stirred weakly.

Wolf moved quickly, closer yet to the bars, distracting him. He needn't have bothered, for just then the Lady Cymbra came fully into the light and for the space of several heartbeats no man thought of anything at all.

Distantly, Wolf heard the collective intake of breath from the others in the cell, but he was too riven by his own surprise. The world abounded with stories, few of them even remotely true. One held that the renowned Hawk of Essex had a sister, Cymbra by name, who was likely the most beautiful woman in all of Christendom, a woman of such loveliness that her own brother hid her away lest men fight to possess her.

Wolf had long since dismissed that tale, assuming it most probably meant she was no more than middling pretty. Now confronted by the reality and the slow, stumbling recovery of his own reason, poor thing that it had become, he stared at her.

Chestnut hair shot through with gold tumbled in thick waves almost to her knees. Her eyes, blue as the sea beneath summer sun and thickly fringed, were set in an oval face of damask perfection. Her nose was slender and tapering above full, rose-hued lips that were moist and slightly parted. Her body, full-breasted with a wand-slim waist and hips perfectly fashioned to a man's hands—to his hands—moved closer, as though drawn by his will alone.

She was perfect—exquisitely, absolutely perfect. She looked like a statue come to life, scarcely a real woman. A real woman would have some imperfection, however slight, something to indicate her humanness. Had a speck of dirt ever touched this ethereal creature? Had a hair ever fallen out of place, a spot appeared on that perfect skin? Did she ever sweat, curse, strive, yield? Was she as much a stranger to passion as she appeared?

She needed messing. The thought sprung full-blown in his mind. He could think of a great many things he wanted to do to the Lady Cymbra, and he supposed some of them were rather messy, but he might have framed it differently.

Not that it mattered. Grimly, he reminded himself, his course was set—as was hers. She had chosen it the moment she rejected the offer of marriage that would have sealed a pact that could bring peace to thousands. That she had done so in terms chosen to sting any Viking's pride merely confirmed her fate.

He would possess her utterly—this proud, unfeeling woman who put selfishness and vanity above all else. He would strip away that pride, crush that will, and enslave her to the passion that was suddenly a raging torrent within him. And he would enjoy every vengeful moment of it.

Cymbra felt the touch of the slate-gray eyes that studied her so boldly and could not repress a quiver of shock. She felt moved in some strange, predatory way she could scarcely credit. Worse, pleasure flicked at the edges of her mind. Astounding. She had never experienced anything like that. Under other circumstances, she might have explored the sensations and the man who evoked them, but he awakened an anxiety within her that made rational study impossible.

Instinctively, she took refuge in the habit of a lifetime, repressing all emotion and concentrating only on the task at hand. Such serenity was her only defense against the pain of a violent, turbulent world, and she depended on it utterly.

Softly, but with iron determination, she returned her attention to the hapless Derward. "I understand that you are responsible for the safety of this keep, but I am responsible for the welfare of the people within it. *All* the people. These men must have food, water, blankets, and medicine, if needed."

"Milady! No one will give them such things. They are savages, brutal animals. It isn't safe for anyone to get close to them."

Silence reigned for several minutes. Wolf scowled, wondering if he had misunderstood her words, as he surely must have. Why would she have any concern for their welfare, this unfeeling woman willing to perpetuate war rather than sacrifice her precious self? Why would she care if they rotted and starved? Indeed, why wouldn't she rejoice like all the others?

And why, while he was tormenting himself with questions that had no answers, didn't Derward simply tell her to let him do his job and be done with it?

"You are right," she said at length in that so-soft voice. "It is a failure to ask others to do what one is afraid to do oneself."

He saw her take a quick breath. She wasn't so untouched by feeling, merely determined to avoid showing it. That realization brought him up short as she walked to the bars and looked at him directly.

Her chin lifted. In flawless Norse touched only by a slight, musical accent that instantly delighted him, she said, "I wish to speak with whichever of you is the leader."

His answer was a deep rumble that reverberated against the stone chamber. "I am the leader."

She blanched just a little, as though not happy to have

confirmed what she had already suspected. But she did not back away by so much as an inch.

"I have food, water, blankets, and medicine for you and your men. But to give them to you, I must open the cell door. Will you give me your word not to harm me?"

"You would take the word of a Viking?"

Her chin lifted even higher. Her cheeks pinkened. He watched, fascinated, as she bit her lower lip and was filled with an overwhelming desire to soothe that offended portion of her.

"I would take the word of a leader who cares for the welfare of his men."

Her perception surprised him. Could she possibly know that he would give his life to protect the men sworn to him? Watching her with the respect and wariness he would award a previously unencountered force of nature, he said slowly, "I give you my word."

Sir Derward and several other knights protested, but she was not to be denied. They were effectively helpless against her, Wolf noted, for clearly none was willing to touch her. That was good. Perhaps he wouldn't have to kill all of them. It was preferable to leave men alive who could speak of how they had been undone.

Yet neither would any oblige her by opening the cell doors. Without hesitation, she did it herself. It was a struggle and he winced to see the effort demanded of those slender hands, but she persevered until at last one of the iron bars rose and she was able to open half of the double door.

"These need to be oiled," she said over her shoulder at Sir Derward. "So do the hinges on the palisade gate." So mundane a subject, matter-of-factly mentioned, stripped the moment of whatever menace it should have possessed. He wondered if she made a habit of disconcerting men in that manner and suspected that he already knew the answer.

All his men were on their feet, watching her relentlessly. He swept them a quick, warning glance that none misinterpreted.

Mine.

They knew it and kept a careful distance from her, but they couldn't contain the urge to stare. Nor could he blame them.

Cymbra looked quickly at the other men and as swiftly looked away. She concentrated on the leader. He was more than enough to manage. Except for her brother, she had never seen as tall a man or one so powerfully built.

Interestingly, captivity didn't seem to trouble him. She could scarcely imagine how Hawk would be in such circumstances; probably taking the cell apart with his bare hands. But not this man. He appeared the very soul of calm and reason.

"Are any of your men wounded?" She was standing close enough for him to smell the faint honeysuckle scent of her skin and feel her warmth. For an instant, his senses reeled. He had to remind himself that she was only a woman, and an enemy at that.

"No."

"Good." She turned and gestured to an older woman who remained outside the cell. The woman's dried-apple face was creased with fear. Her eyes never left her mistress as she handed over the pile of blankets she held.

Cymbra said a soft word to her and turned back to the cell. She began to give him one of the blankets, realized his hands were still tied, and frowned. "You cannot remain like that."

He waited, not moving, curious to see what she would do. After a moment, she put down the blankets, removed a small knife from a sheath at her waist, and approached him. "Please," she said, gesturing to the ropes that bound his wrists.

He held out his hands to her. She looked at them,

then up at him very quickly before returning her gaze to the ropes. The knife was only middling sharp, or perhaps he had to make allowance for her lack of strength. She had to saw for several minutes before the ropes finally parted.

They stood almost touching, his hands free, her knife easily within his reach. She looked up again, their gazes locking and he saw, quite clearly, that she knew her own vulnerability. Understood it full well, yet was trusting him to keep his promise not to harm her.

"Thank you," he said quietly. Rubbing his wrists, he took a step back.

She nodded and, with her eyes averted, handed him a blanket. But she didn't stop there. Instead of leaving the rest for him to distribute, she handed one to each of his men after first cutting through his bonds. She did so silently, and he saw that she did not look directly at any of them, but her simple act of aiding—and thereby acknowledging—each man was one more surprise.

That done, she turned back to the old woman, who had used the time to fetch a basket and ewer. These too she handed through the open cell door under the watchful gaze of the guards. Cymbra set them down near Wolf, then straightened. Her hands were folded in front of her. He wondered if she did that to keep them from shaking.

"I will return in the morning," she said, waiting until he acknowledged this with a nod. The moment she stepped back outside the cell, the guards leaped forward and slammed the door.

The clang of the metal bar falling back into place still echoed off the stone walls as Cymbra said, "Sir Derward, I would not care to learn that these men have been harmed during the night. I would be most displeased. Do you understand?"

The knight took a breath, fists clenched at his sides. "Aye, milady."

Rooster-brained he was but still not so great a fool as to tempt himself beyond endurance. Scarcely had the Lady Cymbra vanished up the steps than Sir Derward did the same. He left only a pair of guards to slump back against the wall, eyeing their prisoners glumly.

No one moved in the cell until, after several moments, Wolf gestured to the basket. "We may as well eat."

The men gathered around, finding bread still warm from the ovens, rounds of golden cheese, plump apples, and several roasted hens. Better yet, the ewer held good ale, plenty for all of them.

"A feast," exclaimed Magnus, the youngest of the group. He helped himself to a crisp-skinned leg and sat back with a sigh of pure contentment. With his mouth full, he said, "This is amazing, isn't it? Did you *see* her?"

Swallowing a hunk of cheese, one-eyed Olaf grinned. "That's not a woman. That's a goddess come down to earth."

That did it. Everyone had to comment then.

"Those eyes . . ."

"That hair . . ."

"That mouth . . ."

"That body—"

Silence suddenly descended and quick glances were cast at Wolf. He tore off a piece of bread and shrugged. "We go as planned."

No one disagreed but he saw the flickering looks that passed man to man, the silent thought expressed that perhaps the Lady Cymbra—as kind as she was beautiful—did not deserve the fate the Wolf intended for her. It made no difference. His will would be done.

His will. What was that now? He had come wanting vengeance, believing it fully deserved. Now . . .

Now he wasn't sure. She was vastly different from

anything he had expected. She surprised him. She made him feel uncertain. No one had made him feel like that in a very long time. He didn't care for the experience.

He had promised not to harm her.

Aye, that was a complication. Of course, the lady's idea of what was harm could be very different from his own. He'd just have to persuade her to see things his way.

Sharp teeth tore at the soft, warm, fragrant bread. A wolf's smile flashed in the dim light of the cell.

Chapter

TWO

CYMBRA LEANED BACK, RESTING HER HEAD against the rim of the leather tub, and sighed deeply. Warm water lapped at her limbs. The scent of herbs sprinkled in the bath teased gently at her nostrils. The soft crackle of the fire and Miriam's quiet movements were the only sounds in the chamber. For the first time in far too many hours she could relax and, just perhaps, gather her thoughts.

What thoughts they were! She knew very little of Vikings except that they seemed to be of two types—merchants and raiders. Despite her claim to Sir Derward, she didn't really suppose that the difference was questionable.

The prisoners didn't look like the sort who would want to sell her a few lengths of cloth. Yet neither had they behaved as the brutal killers and despoilers that Derward had branded them.

Authority was very weak in parts of England, with the result that the Danes had seized control over broad swaths of land. They were poised to seize even more, and might if men like her brother didn't succeed in stopping them.

Which made these Vikings . . . what? Even as she told herself it wasn't her problem to solve, her mind could not resist turning over the puzzle. Nor could it keep from drifting irresistibly to the leader, the tall, heavily muscled man with the midnight-black hair and the icy gray eyes.

No, that wasn't quite true. His eyes weren't always icy. There had been times when they brushed her like white-hot fire.

She didn't want to think about that, mustn't think of it. Her body felt oddly heavy, especially between her legs, where a hot, moist sensation was building. She glanced down, surprised to see that her nipples were peaked, and flushed. Quickly she rose from the bath and seized the drying cloth Miriam had thoughtfully laid nearby. With that wrapped around her, she felt a little calmer.

Seated by the fire, she murmured her thanks as Miriam began to brush out her hair. As always, the motion soothed her but she stopped it before very long. Miriam's hands were sore now more often than not, and the unguents Cymbra made for her didn't always take the pain away completely. Gently, she laid her hand over the old nurse's.

"I'm sorry I worried you today."

Miriam sighed. She sat down beside the young woman who had been her charge since the tender age of three days, when Cymbra's own lady mother had passed beyond the veil of this world. She loved Cymbra dearly but she didn't pretend to understand her in the slightest.

"You terrified me." She shook her head in bewilderment, sparse strands of gray hair escaping from beneath her wimple. "How could you do such a thing? Much as I hate to say it, Sir Derward is right; Vikings are animals. They could have killed you without a second thought."

"What should we do then?" Cymbra asked softly. "Kill everything we fear? If we do that, others will fear us and seek to kill us in turn. It will never end. One cruelty begets the next endlessly."

The old nurse shrugged. " 'Tis the way of this world. No man can change that, and certainly no woman can."

Cymbra sighed and rose, standing before the copper brazier that dispelled the evening's chill. Her shoulders and arms were bare, the cloth barely covering the swell of her breasts. She shivered slightly. "Perhaps not, but still I must try. There is too much pain."

Miriam cast her a quick look. "You never speak of that anymore."

Both women shared a memory of the very young Cymbra, screaming and screaming, unable to explain what was wrong. It happened many times . . . when a stable boy cut his foot on a scythe, when a kitchen maid was scalded with water, when a warrior died of a wound that would not heal.

That had been the worst, going on for days until finally Hawk had drugged her with the juice of poppy brought from far lands and sat, holding her in his arms, through an endless day and night, his face grim as he decided what had to be done.

Holyhood became her sanctuary. Safe within it, she learned how to control what was at once gift and curse. Miriam didn't know how, could only dimly imagine the struggle Cymbra had waged. She'd won in the end, though at great cost. Now she could care for the injured and ill, even for the dying, without making their pain her own. She felt it still, Miriam was sure of that, but she managed to keep it apart from herself. Usually.

"There is nothing to speak of," Cymbra assured her with a smile. She drew the cloth more closely around herself and stared into the flames, but instead of seeing them she seemed to see only midnight-black hair, burnished skin, and eyes the color of slate. She shook her head, impatient with herself, and dropped the cloth, reaching for her bed robe.

"Go to your rest, Miriam," she said as she wriggled the garment over her head. Emerging from the mass of gossamer linen, she tugged her hair free—no small task in itself—grinned, and gave the old nurse a kiss. "Heaven knows, you earn it putting up with me."

Clucking a denial Miriam did as she was bid. When the door had closed behind her, Cymbra stretched her arms far above her head, standing on tiptoe, and made a small sound of contentment as more of the tension eased. She needed to sleep yet felt oddly energized, as though the day had lasted minutes instead of hours.

Tomorrow word would come from Hawk about the fate of the prisoners. She drew her brows together as she wondered what her brother would decide. Likely he would have them brought to him at Hawkforte to judge them for himself. She would never see the gray-eyed man again. Not that it mattered, couldn't, shouldn't matter. Why then did she ache?

Thought of sleep fled. She glanced around the chamber that had been hers most of her life. There near the brazier was her needlework, awaiting her hand. There, too, was the chest holding her medicines and precious manuscripts. Her lute was on a table next to the wooden coffer that held her paper, pens, and inks. All manner of distractions beckoned but she could not settle on any of them. Instead, she opened the door that led out onto the tower walkway just beyond her room. The night was cool but she felt unaccountably warm. The perimeter wall of the tower came almost to her shoulders. Her modesty was well protected as she stepped out, clad only in her night robe.

Protected surely from anyone on the ground. But not protected from the man who stood in the shadows of the walkway, watching her every movement. Wolf gazed at the play of light and shadow over her exquisite form and fought for the self-control that always before had been as natural as his next breath. No more.

Having scaled the tower, a simple feat, only to find the old woman in the room, he had waited, unable to tear his eyes away as Cymbra bathed, rose from the tub, draped herself in that ridiculously thin cloth. Then, as if to finish him off, discarded it in favor of a bed robe that couldn't have protected her from a balmy breeze, much less from his eyes.

In the northlands, people dressed sensibly—or not at all. She would have to adjust to that.

And rather more than that.

The men he had sent into Holyhood the preceding day disguised as merchants had done their job with expected precision. The guards outside the cell lay unconscious, bound and gagged. So, too, the guards on the palisade wall. His men kept vigil by the great hall just in case Derward or any of the others arose, but there was slim likelihood of that. They were all snoring deeply.

That left the Lady Cymbra—completely unprotected.

She was close enough for him to touch, a vision of pale beauty caressed by starlight. He smelled the fragrance of her skin, felt the brush of a strand of her hair lifted by the night wind. He heard her sigh, saw the rise and fall of her breasts as she breathed deeply.

It was more than any man could be expected to bear and he had no intention of doing so. Still, he was oddly loath to disturb her peace. She would know little enough of that in the days—and nights—to come.

Cymbra looked out over Holyhood, her sanctuary and prison both. An uncharacteristic impatience filled her, a longing for something she could neither define nor deny. Such foolishness. She was the Lady Cymbra, sister of the Hawk, and a healer. She had a place where she belonged and work that was her life. In all that, she was blessed.

Why then did she yearn for more? She was like a child wishing for the moon, rather than a grown woman who should know better.

She had to be sensible. It was late, she would go inside, lie down, and in time she would sleep. Morning would come, the prisoners would leave, life would go on. Yet she lingered a moment longer, gazing out at the walls of her home. Holyhood's walls, where Sir Derward's guards pretended to watch, nodding over their spears, their dark, drowsing shapes so well familiar to her that she scarcely noticed them—save when they were gone.

Gone. Cymbra stiffened suddenly. She leaned forward, staring. There was no mistake. She scanned every part of the palisade that she could see, and not a guard was in sight. Holyhood's security was more gesture than reality, but never before had there been no guards at all. Something was wrong.

Very wrong.

Vikings.

Hawk would have been taking the cell apart with his bare hands.

The gray-eyed man was so calm.

So unconcerned.

From the wrath of the Norsemen preserve us, oh, Lord.

She turned, already running, meaning to call the alarm.

Running . . . straight into steely arms and a merciless hand that slammed down over her mouth. Hot, piercing terror tore through her. She struggled with desperate strength but uselessly. In an instant, she was lifted high against a rock-hard chest and felt herself being carried through her room, down the winding steps of the tower, out into the night.

"Be silent," Wolf said implacably. "If you scream,

anyone who comes will die." He looked down into her
eyes to see if she understood. She did. He released her
mouth so she could breathe more easily but he did not
lessen his hold on her or slow his stride. She was dimly
aware of other men moving alongside them, more in number than the prisoners had been, swords gleaming. She
caught a glimpse of the gates of Holyhood standing open.
Then the fortress was behind her and there was only night
and wind. And fear so great it threatened to swallow her.

WOLF GLANCED DOWN AT THE WOMAN IN HIS ARMS.
Her pallor worried him, as did her silence. She
hadn't fainted as he'd thought she might but she was un-
naturally still. Her eyes were very wide and he felt her
heart beating like the wings of a frantic bird against his
chest. Yet she had conquered her fear when he warned her
it would mean death for others.

He understood nothing about her—not her kindness
to captive Vikings, not what he had heard her say to
Miriam about the cruelty of the world. She was utterly beyond his experience.

It wasn't supposed to be that way, he reminded himself again. She was supposed to be a captive woman taken
for vengeance. She was supposed to suffer for the insult done him and the willingness to condemn innocents
to continued war. He'd had her fate all planned. And
now . . .

She was probably cold. He'd have to do something
about that. Ahead, he saw the gleam of starlight on water
and the dark shape of the dragon prow. The rest of his
men—those hidden from Derward, who was too blessedly
stupid even to wonder how six men could have managed
so large a vessel—were already at the oars.

Wolf waded out into the water, hardly noticing as it
lapped around his legs. Young Magnus was right beside

him. Wolf directed a single, warning glance at him and handed Cymbra into his arms.

Magnus had the great sense not to speak or move, to give absolutely no indication that he was capable of any feelings whatsoever. He might have been holding a sack of wheat.

In an instant, Wolf was on the deck and had retrieved her. Magnus let out a relieved breath, dunked all the way under the water, and came up grinning. Wolf shot him a wry look as he turned toward the hold.

He took the ladder down and straightened, his head just clearing the deck. The hold ran the length of the vessel but was separated into several compartments. Aft was the space used for storing supplies including weapons. Adjacent to it were the men's quarters, although they used them only in the worst weather, generally preferring to sleep on deck.

Toward the bow was an area most often used for booty or trade goods. It was empty now save for a single thin pallet. Wolf frowned when he saw it. He had intended that the Lady Cymbra's conditions be deliberately harsh at first, the swifter to break her will and make evident her dire circumstance.

Now he was reluctant to leave her there even for the short time needed to get clear of Holyhood. Still, he had little choice. Until their escape was made good, his first duty was to his men.

Laying her on the pallet, he grasped her chin and forced her to look directly at him. "Don't move," he ordered, then released her and deliberately pushed her down farther. She said nothing, merely stared up at him from the silken fall of her hair and the soft, floating cloud of the bed robe, making him think she was either too afraid to say or do anything or was merely being sensible. Either way, he was satisfied—for the moment.

He went back on deck, thinking this had turned out to be even easier than he'd hoped—save, of course, for the complication of the woman herself and her refusal to be what he expected.

CYMBRA LAY STILL FOR SEVERAL MOMENTS, UNMOVing but for the rapid rise and fall of her shallow breathing. The molten heat of terror had fled, replaced by paralyzing cold that owed only a little to the cool night air and her thin garment. She had never been so frightened in her life. Or so angry.

Gratefully, she concentrated on the anger. As she sat up, her hair caught beneath her and tugged her scalp sharply. The small pain was welcome, further focusing her thoughts.

How dare they? How *dare* they? To penetrate Holyhood by trickery, take her from her very own chamber, and depart with contemptuous ease. What manner of men did such a thing?

No, not men. Man. She did not doubt for a moment that the leader was responsible, the very same man who had told her she would not be harmed.

Her own stupidity shamed her. Sir Derward was a vain and brutal man whose mind was darkly twisted, redeemed only by the instinct for self-preservation that had kept him from ever crossing her. Her opinion of him had not changed but she recognized now that it had blinded her to even the possibility that he might, on some occasion, be right.

How many lay dead in Holyhood because of her arrogant foolishness? She thought of the guards on the walls and near the cell, and her eyes filled with tears. Hastily, she rubbed them away. Crying would avail her nothing. With each passing moment she felt the powerful surge of the vessel moving farther and farther away from Holyhood. From the only safety she had ever known and from the people she must now, more than ever, succor.

Quickly, she stood. Her eyes had adjusted to the darkness in the hold. Chinks in the deck above admitted a tiny amount of light, just enough for her to make out the shadow of the ladder leading above. She climbed it swiftly, holding up her bed robe so that she would not trip. The hatch was closed. She took a deep breath and pressed both her hands against it.

Mercifully, it gave readily and without a sound. She spared a moment for the sour thought that the Viking war ship was kept in better repair than Holyhood's defenses. Then the cool night air touched her and she thought of nothing at all save escape.

The same thought was on Wolf's mind. He had taken his place at the oars and was pulling along with the other men, the powerful muscles of his back and shoulders flexing rhythmically. The sea was calm, the wind with them. Very soon they would be beyond even the chance of pursuit.

Not that it was likely anyone would try. No doubt Holyhood slumbered still. Their escape wouldn't be discovered until morning, when it would be too late to do anything—except to inform the Lord Hawk that his sister was gone.

Wolf smiled, imagining the reaction that would earn. At the very least, the Hawk would rage at being so contemptuously defied. If he truly cared for his sister, he would be rightly tormented by thoughts of her fate. Sir Derward's remaining days on earth were likely to be extremely unpleasant.

He felt no regret at that as he put all such considerations aside and concentrated on the task at hand. Or at least he tried to. Thoughts of the lady below intruded despite his best efforts to ignore them. Her beauty still

stunned him even as the mystery she presented itched at
his mind. Soon enough, he determined, she would yield to
him and then he would have the true measure of her.

For the moment, he decided, it was good that she was
afraid. It would make her more pliable, more easily bent
to his hand. In time, he would reassure her that her fate
would not be quite so dire as she feared. She was bound to
be thankful for that. He could think of all sorts of ways
she could show her gratitude.

He was smiling again, a feral smile of purely male anticipation, when a slight motion on deck caught his eye.
He stared, first uncomprehendingly, then in disbelief, as
the hatch slowly rose.

Wolf stopped rowing. Paired with him, old Olaf
glanced over to see what was wrong. His gaze followed
Wolf's and his single good eye widened but he did not
slow his pace. Nor did any of the other men who saw what
was happening. They kept right on rowing, although
more than a few felt a moment's relief that the lady wasn't
their problem.

Wolf sat back, his hands lying loose on the oar, and
watched. A head appeared where the hatch had been, followed swiftly by slender shoulders and then all the rest of
her as she moved, almost flowed really, across the deck toward the railing.

Shock roared through him. He had realized her panic
but never had he thought she would be driven to take her
own life. Horror filled him as he surged across the deck,
seizing Cymbra just as she was about to go into the inky
water.

She fought, far more earnestly than she had on the
tower when he'd had the advantage of complete surprise.
She lashed out with hands and feet, trying both to kick
him where it would do the most good and to scratch at his
face. All the while, she twisted, struggling to loosen his
hold.

He tightened it instead, cursing under his breath, and hauled the clawing, biting termagant back down the ladder. Flinging her onto the pallet at his feet, he stood with his legs braced apart, hands fisted on his hips, and glared at her in righteous male outrage.

"What in bloody hell were you thinking of? Do you value your life so little that you'd throw it away?" He was furious at her, actually shaking at the thought of her dying, wanting alternately to strangle and to caress her.

Incredibly, she seemed heedless of her peril. Tossing hair out of her eyes, she glared at him. "What do you care for my life, Viking?" On her exquisitely lovely lips, the word was a curse. "You invade my home, kidnap me, and expect me to just accept my fate? No!"

He should have seen it coming, should have at least anticipated it, but he was still so stunned by her words that he wasn't prepared when she leaped up and tried to run past him, seeking again to gain the deck and the water beyond. She almost made it.

At the last moment, Wolf's hand lashed out, closing on a length of gossamer linen. It tore with a rending sound that reverberated against the walls. He tightened his grip implacably, tearing the cloth farther, dragging her toward him, no thought in his mind but controlling this woman, forcing her to his will. The ruined garment fell from her body, leaving her naked to his gaze.

They both froze. Neither moved through the space of several heartbeats until finally Cymbra made a low sound of despair and wrapped her arms around herself, turning away from him. She lost her balance and began to fall toward the rough inner wall of the hold. Wolf didn't hesitate. He caught her and lowered her back onto the pallet. She curled on her side, drawing her legs up, the veil of her hair her only concealment.

He stared at his hands on her—dark and rough against the pale smoothness of her skin, hard, callused

hands more accustomed to holding a sword or an oar—
and had to force himself to pull away. His breathing was
ragged, his heart hammering against his ribs, as he stood.
He closed his eyes for a moment, inhaling deeply. When
he looked at her again, he had regained some small measure of control.

"I understand now why your brother kept you locked
up," he snarled. "You'd drive the sanest man mad."

She didn't move, didn't speak, but he saw her stiffen.
With a curse that would have scorched the ears of the
most hardened warrior, Wolf turned away. He climbed
back up to the deck, slammed down the hatch, and
slipped his sword through the braces to lock it in place.
"Damn woman," he muttered.

Pulling hard at the oars, his men grinned.

CYMBRA LAY TREMBLING ON THE PALLET. SHE KNEW
she had to get up, had to do something to save herself, but her legs felt too weak to hold her. The comfort
she might have taken in the knowledge that at least she
had tried to escape was scant indeed.

All she'd done was worsen her situation. She was
naked, trapped, held prisoner by a Viking warlord—she
wasn't going to lie to herself anymore about what he really
was—and utterly helpless.

Her stomach clenched at the thought of her likely
fate. She moaned and pulled herself into a small, defen-
sive ball, an utterly futile gesture if there ever was one.
She had heard the tales about women taken by Vikings.
No wonder he presumed she'd been trying to kill herself. It was the more merciful death.

Nausea swept over her. She was not so innocent that
she didn't realize the horror that might await her. *Might?*
What tiny fragment of hope remained to make her think
there was even a chance of something better?

He hasn't hurt me.

Oh, that was absurd. How could she even think such a thing? He was a Viking, a marauder, a savage straight out of a nightmare. She should have listened to Derward, should have had more sense, should—

She'd hurt herself struggling against him, true enough. Her whole body ached, but now that she forced herself to think about it, he'd actually held her rather gently. Even when he tossed her down on the pallet, he'd already lowered her most of the way first.

He'd torn off her clothes.

Accidentally?

Cymbra shook her head in amazement. She couldn't believe she was actually arguing with herself about the Viking's actions. Her situation could hardly be worse, yet here she was making excuses.

Oh, yes, it could have been worse! He left. He didn't rape or brutalize me in any way.

No, he'd just left her to freeze to death, naked in the hold of his ship. She was a raving fool to think anything of him but the worst. She was going to die horribly. If she had any sense at all, she would use whatever time she had left to pray.

She tried, she really did, but the familiar, comforting words wouldn't come. It was hard enough just to keep from screaming. She pulled herself up far enough to crouch in a corner, shivering, trying very hard not to cry. She wanted to die with courage and before her mind was crushed by pain she could not bear.

So deep was she in anguished reflection that Cymbra didn't hear the hatch open or the footsteps approaching. She had only the briefest moment to realize she was no longer alone before something very large and furry dropped over her.

An animal.

She screamed and started up, trying to shove it off.

"Stop that," Wolf said. He crouched beside her, clasping her flailing hands, his deep voice oddly soothing. "It's a cloak." Patiently, as though she might still not understand, he added, "To keep you warm." He paused, then said dryly, "And to protect your modesty."

A cloak. Not an animal. Slowly, Cymbra ran her fingers over the fur. She couldn't see very well, Wolf himself was little more than a very large, dark shape, but she could feel the luxurious warmth that enveloped her. She had never felt anything so enticingly soft. Fur it was, but not of any common sort.

"Ermine," he said as though he'd heard her thoughts. "From the lands of the Russka."

He'd brought her an ermine cloak.

Truly, she didn't understand this man at all.

"Thank you," she said with dignity.

He sighed, a long drawn-out sound of male endurance. "Listen to me." He waited to make sure she was doing just that. He was very close; she could feel his heat, greater even than that of the cloak, and had a quick, shocking thought of being covered not by ermine but by that big, long, hard-muscled body.

"Obey me and I will not hurt you."

Glad of the darkness that hid her fiery cheeks, Cymbra curled farther into the warmth of the cloak. With honesty, if not great sense, she said, "I'll try."

When he did not reply to what another man might have taken as less than full obeisance, she gathered her courage and looked at him directly. His eyes were really more silver than gray, at least in the filtered starlight. She had the odd sensation of having seen them before, somewhere, sometime. In a dream, perhaps.

So softly as barely to stir the air, Cymbra murmured, "Who are you?"

He rose, standing very tall and powerful above her, cast in shadow and stone. She felt those silvery eyes touching all along the length of her body. In the still darkness, broken only by the lapping of deep water against the hull of the dragon ship, his voice was like velvet drawn over granite. "Wolf Hakonson."

Cymbra gasped. Her senses reeled. Surely God could not be so cruel? Yet, even as she struggled not to believe, she knew the truth of it. Indeed, it all made a strange kind of sense. Who else could he be?

Who but the most feared Viking ever to come out of the northlands? The man before whom even the Danes trembled. The mighty warlord known the length and breadth of England by the name he had earned in blood and fire—the Scourge of the Saxons.

And she was his prisoner. Wrapped in ermine and still oddly unhurt, at that moment Cymbra knew herself truly to be beyond hope. She could think of only one more question to ask before fate closed around her.

"Why?"

Chapter

THREE

THE LADY CYMBRA'S REACTION TO HIS NAME was most satisfying. Yet Wolf was disappointed all the same, wishing she wouldn't indulge in the ploy of pretended innocence. Somehow he'd expected better of her. But then, he had to remember that she was only a woman.

He went down on his haunches beside her and, without thinking, reached out a hand to brush a stray tendril of hair away from her face. Incredibly soft hair. It went with the incredibly soft rest of her. Thoughts for another time.

"Why have I done this?"

She nodded, her gaze locked on his. "Yes, why?"

He would be patient. She would learn soon enough that her woman's games would not work with him. "Why did you reject an honorable offer of marriage that would bring peace between our peoples and aide in our mutual defense against the Danes?"

Her mouth dropped open. He really didn't want to think how those lips would feel yielding beneath his own, admitting the hard thrust of his tongue, but he thought of it all the same and it had the predictable effect.

"I did what?"

"You heard me." He spoke more sharply than he'd intended but there was a limit to his tolerance. Best she learn that, too. "You said that you would never consider marriage to a filthy Viking savage."

She blinked slowly, long lashes lying against her pale cheeks. When they lifted again, her eyes were steady. "I never said that." She seemed genuinely offended.

"What did you say then?"

"I said nothing. I never heard of any offer of marriage."

He frowned. She sounded utterly sincere. It was possible, just possible, that she was telling the truth. Wolf shrugged. "Then your brother said it. He replied on your behalf."

"No." There was no artfulness to that, no strategy. She just blurted it out. "Hawk wouldn't do such a thing."

He sat back, regarding her with undisguised skepticism. "Really?"

"Yes, really. First, he would have discussed any such offer with me and he did not. Second, even if he decided that such a marriage was not advisable, he would never have answered you in such terms. My brother wants peace."

It was good that she trusted her brother, even if such trust was sadly misplaced. Regretting the need to disillusion her, but determined all the same, Wolf drew a parchment from beneath his tunic. "Can you read?"

She gave a short, jerky nod. "Yes, can you?"

"I certainly had no difficulty reading this." He handed over the parchment, then rose and used flint to light an oil lamp in a small, stone-lined recess near the pallet. "Promise me you won't try to set fire to the ship," he said as pale, flickering light cast a circle over them both.

Her mouth tightened. She held the parchment up and scanned it quickly.

"Do you recognize the hand?" Wolf asked.

"It isn't Hawk's."

"He writes?" Wolf was surprised. Few men did, even those of noble birth. He had learned himself because he saw no reason to trust others with essential information.

Cymbra nodded. "It isn't widely known but Hawk actually considered becoming a monk when he was younger."

"What stopped him?"

"Something about women." She went back to her study of the document. "He writes his own letters to me but he does use scribes for some correspondence. It's possible that I wouldn't know all their hands."

She was honest in that at least. Pleased, Wolf pointed a finger at the seal on the bottom of the parchment. "Is that his?"

Cymbra stared at it long and hard. Slowly, with the utmost reluctance, she nodded. "It does appear to be."

Wolf took the parchment from her, folded it again, and slipped it back into his tunic. "Then these are his words."

"No, they are not! I can't explain how his seal comes to be on this parchment, but I know beyond any doubt that Hawk would never have done something like this." Again, she said, "My brother wants peace." By the light of the small lamp, her eyes looked shadowed with dread. "But what you have done will bring war."

"Perhaps." He gave no hint that he felt the slightest regret. Rising, he snuffed out the flame between his fingers, plunging the hold back into darkness. "We'll see. For now, you should get some sleep."

"Sleep?" She sounded incredulous.

He couldn't keep the amusement from his tone. "Yes, sleep. You lie down, relax, close your eyes."

"I can't possibly sleep."

"Then perhaps we can find some better use for this pallet."

"I'm almost asleep now."

He laughed, unable to stop himself. The lovely Lady Cymbra had more courage and nerve than he had ever thought possible. She was a fascinating, enticing bundle of contradictions. He would relish the taming of her. Indeed, he couldn't remember when he'd looked forward to anything more.

In high good humor, he left her and returned to the deck, where he stretched out beneath the stars. Shortly after that, the Wolf, too, slept.

CYMBRA GAZED OUT OVER THE EXPANSE OF GRAY-blue water, tugged the ermine cloak more closely around herself, and sighed. Wind filled the sails, but the men were not relaxing. They strained at the oars until the dragon ship seemed to fly across the sea.

During the night, the world had narrowed to the vessel alone amid the seemingly endless expanse of sea. From where she sat in the bow, the iron-riveted deck stretched at least fifty feet to the fearsome dragon prow. A single mast rose from the massive oak block fixed at the center of the keel, rigged with the square sail emblazoned with the emblem of the wolf.

The men sat two to an oar on benches on either side of raised planking laid down the middle of the deck. Most had stripped off their shirts and rowed bare-chested beneath a pale sun wreathed in clouds. The only sounds were the creak of the rigging, the occasional grunts of the men, and the slap of water against the sides of the vessel where the shields were hung.

How many miles were they from Holyhood? Certainly more than she had ever been before, for she had never even been out of sight of land. Amid the vastness of sea and sky, Cymbra felt lost and insignificant. The wound of worry for all those left behind throbbed incessantly. Again and again her thoughts returned to her brother and the survivors of the Viking attack. With every breath she drew, she felt their pain. After a lifetime of training herself to stand apart from her emotions, the conflagration within her was like staring into the sun.

And yet, for all that, she could not deny a strange, unsettling sense of . . . what? Surely not excitement? Even less exhilaration? She could not possibly be taking pleasure in the sudden shattering of her well-ordered life, could she? Beneath the veil of her lashes, she glanced at the man responsible at once for her peril and for the only possible hope of ending it.

Wolf had directed her to the bow when he brought her up on deck in midmorning. He sat nearby, one hand resting on the rudder, which he steadied occasionally. At first light, when she was still in the hold and just barely awake, he'd brought her food and water. That consideration emboldened her to ask for something to wear besides the ermine cloak, only to have him blandly tell her there was nothing. Not a tunic or a shirt, not a length of wool or linen, that she might put between her skin and the soft, sensual, seductive fur.

She didn't believe him; there had to be *something*. But she sensed that he wanted her to argue and she wouldn't give him the satisfaction. Nor would she talk to him. She'd had time during the night to think over her situation. As fear eased, resentment grew. Even if Hawk had sent that reply—which he absolutely had not but *even if*— that was no excuse to risk plunging into war. Surely there could have been some further diplomatic effort?

Good King Alfred, bless his name, was always saying that war should be the last resort, not the first. Not that the scion of Wessex ever hesitated to wield a sword when needed, but at least he paused long enough to see if there might be an alternative.

But not Wolf Hakonson. Oh, no; at the first hint of

insult, the Wolf rose from his lair to see what havoc he could wreak.

"Typical man."

"What's that?" Wolf asked. After hours of silence, he was delighted to hear a sound from her even if he couldn't make it out.

Cymbra started. She hadn't realized she'd spoken aloud. "Nothing," she said quickly and resolutely returned her gaze to the sea.

He shrugged, as if indifferent. Then, seeing where her attention was directed—instead of to him—he said, "You might not have drowned right away. Sharks could have gotten you."

There, he had her attention. She stared at him dumbfounded. "I'm an excellent swimmer and we were still within easy reach of the beach."

She hadn't meant to take her own life. She'd actually thought she could get to shore. She was wrong, of course, but he was relieved all the same. He didn't like to think she preferred death to him. A man had his pride.

"You'd never have made it in the dark."

"We'll never know, will we?"

He sighed, not really wanting to irk her. She was a surprisingly bristly little thing, rather like a hedgehog he'd had as a boy. The thought made him laugh.

Her eyebrows rose eloquently. "I amuse you?"

"I was comparing you to a hedgehog I used to have."

He was joking. He had to be. She'd never been compared to a hedgehog or anything remotely like it in her life. Truth be told, she was most commonly said to resemble a swan. That was nonsense, of course, but still . . . "You think I look like a hedgehog?"

"I think you act like one." She was talking to him. A victory. He leaned back at his leisure and surveyed her. "But I suppose you could be said to look like some furry animal. You have a great deal of hair." She had the longest, softest, most enticing hair of any woman he had ever seen. He yearned to feel those silken tendrils over his body, to twine his hands in them and ease her ever closer until—

"On my head," she pointed out. "Not all over." Too late she realized the trap he had led her into and flushed. If he said one word about having seen her naked . . . And for that matter, just what *had* he seen while he was lingering outside her tower chamber, waiting to commit his nefarious deed?

"Hmmm," Wolf murmured and smiled. He gave his attention back to the rudder. The morning wore on.

The sun was high in the sky when Olaf brought them food. He handed it to Wolf, not so much as glancing at Cymbra.

"She's got your cloak," he observed.

"I gave it to her."

"I suppose you'll have a new one from those pelts I owe you."

"I might."

Olaf grimaced. "I shouldn't gamble against you. You always win."

"It was a decent enough bet. We might not have gotten in so easily."

Cymbra couldn't resist. She waited until Olaf had gone, then asked, "What bet?"

Wolf shrugged. "Olaf bet me ten pelts that I couldn't just walk into Holyhood and take you out. He thought we'd have to fight."

They'd gambled on the success of his trickery. No doubt they'd also gloated over it. She remembered her thoughts the previous night and could not conceal her bitterness.

"You don't consider killing all those guards fighting? No, I suppose it wasn't. With so little chance to defend themselves, it was just murder."

He looked at her as though she were daft. "Little

chance? They were warriors who were supposed to be able to defend *you*, much less themselves."

"They also had families, wives and children! What do you suppose will happen to those poor souls now?"

He stared at her flushed cheeks and the angry glitter in her eyes. She really was magnificent. Still much too perfect, though. He really would have to do something about that. "I suppose that depends on how merciful your brother decides to be."

Her brow furrowed. "What do you mean?"

"I mean—" He realized that his teeth were clenched and forced himself to relax. The damn woman wasn't going to irk him like this. "We left the guards bound and gagged. Aside from sore heads, they should be fine."

Cymbra wondered if she'd misunderstood him. She hadn't spoken Norse much since learning it from an elderly monk who lived at Holyhood for several years before passing on. Brother Chilton had devoted several decades of his life to bringing the word of God to the pagans of the northlands. He'd told her a great many stories about them. She shivered at the grim memories.

"I'm surprised you would hesitate to kill anyone."

A muscle worked in his jaw. "A filthy Viking savage wouldn't have any such qualms?"

"I didn't say that!"

He clearly didn't believe her. Being thought of as a liar was a new experience for Cymbra; people tended to take her at her word. She stared at him, wishing she could convince him and at the same time wondering why she should care.

THE NEXT SEVERAL DAYS REPEATED THE PATTERN OF the first. Each morning, Wolf brought her food as well as water for drinking and washing. She suspected she got more than her fair share of the latter but couldn't bring herself to refuse it.

When she was ready, he escorted her up on deck. The weather stayed fair and she was glad to be out of the hold, but the silence and utter boredom grated on her nerves. The men, including Wolf, spent hours at the oars. They seemed inured to physical hardship and spared themselves nothing. Not one of them was without an array of scars that made Cymbra wince to see. Undoubtedly they had all been marked in battle, but she suspected that at least some of the scars came from the ordinary occurrences of a harsh life.

Having never before been exclusively in the company of men, Cymbra couldn't help but be curious about them. Men were very different when they dealt with women, she observed—or perhaps only with women of her own class, she couldn't be sure.

In either case, among themselves they were taciturn, saying little, but startlingly blunt when they did speak. She tried very hard not to eavesdrop, but in the confines of the ship that was really impossible. After having her ears reddened several times, she was surprised to find herself becoming accustomed to the men's frankness. She also learned when to avert her eyes, for the men were as matter-of-fact about their bodily needs as they were in their speech.

Wolf was the only one who spoke to her, and he did so rarely, usually only at the midday and evening meals. He did not mention his reasons for taking her again, nor did he give her any indication of what her fate would be. Cymbra considered asking, but her sense of vulnerability remained so great that she preferred not to know his answer. It was enough to dwell with her confusion over his claim that those left at Holyhood were unharmed—please God let that be so!—coupled with her continued dread

about her brother. Barely would she begin to contemplate
Hawk's likely reaction to her abduction than she would
shy away from it as though from the fury of a storm. She
loved her brother dearly, just as she held him in great respect, but she knew him to be a man of implacable
strength and a will capable of ruthless violence. Much as
she longed for rescue, she did not even let herself pray for
it, knowing as she did the bloodbath it would bring.

Yet for all that she could hardly claim that her confinement was horrible. Another pallet had been added to
the first so that she had a comfortable enough place to
sleep. Except for the fresh-caught fish cooked over small,
contained fires, the food was either dried or salted, but it
was so ample she couldn't finish it. Aside from the lack of
clothing other than the ermine cloak, she was denied
nothing.

A captive woman amid a Viking war band, her worst
problem was boredom. That and worry over what her
brother must be thinking—and planning.

On the seventh day at sea, just when Cymbra thought
she might break down and weep if something didn't happen to interrupt the unending sameness of the hours,
something did. She was seated as usual in the bow, her
face lifted to the sun, her mind drifting, when a gull glided
by on the wind. She straightened up, watching as the bird
circled the boat.

One of the men threw a fish head into the water. The
gull swooped, caught its bounty, and swallowed it whole.
A short time later, a second bird appeared and was duly
fed. Not long after that, Cymbra glimpsed the slight rise
along the eastern horizon that she had expected since
sighting the first bird. *Land.*

At the prospect of their journey's end, her calmness
vanished. She cast her mind ahead, trying to imagine what
awaited her. The Norse merchants she had met were
pleasant enough but merchants naturally made them-

selves congenial, the better to attract business. Brother Chilton, who had actually lived among the Norse, had painted a very different picture of them. A picture lit by fire, drenched in blood, imbued with hideous pagan practices too dreadful for him to describe in more than the most general terms.

Was that why she had been left unharmed this long? Did the Wolf intend some truly terrible fate for her beyond her capacity to imagine? The color fled from her cheeks as she fought the sudden return of all her fears.

Wolf saw the change in her and was surprised by it. He would have thought her glad to have the voyage over soon. But on reflection, he realized why she might well feel differently. Deliberately, he had given her no indication of his intent, preferring to let her dwell on the possibilities. She was, he had concluded, an intelligent woman, sensible enough when the time came to weigh alternatives and pick the one that was best for all concerned.

With a start, he realized that he was beginning to trust her, at least in some ways. That wouldn't do. She was a Saxon, a valiant but unpredictable race that had seemed bound for extinction in England until Alfred rose in the west to lead them against the voracious Danes. Well and good, but a people shouldn't be so dependent on a single leader for their survival. Certainly, his were not.

At the thought of his people, his mood lifted. As always when he had been away for even a short time, he felt a deep, irresistible yearning for the land of his birth. Soon now he would see the smoke rise from his own hearth and be content. But first they would make landfall, stretch muscles stiff from the days at sea, and hunt fresh meat. He was sick of fish.

Cymbra felt the slight change in course and stared ahead at the land they were rapidly approaching. She saw a coastline that sloped low to the sea, thick with pine forests and dotted with innumerable rivers and bays.

With a flush of surprise, she realized that she'd expected something very different—ice floes, unscalable cliffs, a dreary and threatening aspect. This place was . . . beautiful.

The men bent to their task, their bodies moving as one, powerful and also strangely beautiful. Wolf had given over the rudder to old Olaf and taken his place at an oar. He was stripped to the waist, wearing only close-fitting trousers and boots of soft leather. Cymbra stared at his broad, tapered back, the muscles flexing powerfully with each sweep of the oar. His long, corded legs were braced before him, his black hair swaying over the massive sweep of his shoulders. He glanced around to say something to the man behind him, his grin flashing in the bright sunlight. She looked away quickly, finding it oddly difficult to breathe.

The shore seemed to fly toward them. Cymbra saw a golden curve of beach and here and there small islets dotted with gulls and the gray, rounded shapes of basking seals. So swift was their approach that she had scarcely a moment to realize they were about to make landfall when Wolf shouted a command, the oars were suddenly raised, and the stone anchor and its iron chain splashed into the water. The vessel shuddered once and settled into place, swaying gently on the swell.

Several of the men took up weapons and shields and waded to shore. Others busied themselves securing the oars and furling the sail before they joined the rest.

Cymbra eyed the expanse between the vessel and the beach. She longed to dive into the water as the men had done, but the ermine cloak would weigh her down dangerously and going without it was out of the question.

She glanced at Wolf, who had been busy off-loading supplies to some of the men, and was surprised to find him watching her. His eyes were narrowed with amusement and, lest she be left in any doubt of his mood; the corners of his mouth twitched.

"Planning to sit there all day?" he asked pleasantly.

She turned her back to him. Addressing the water, she said, "*If* I had something sensible to wear, I could wade in like the rest, or swim."

"Oh, that's right, you're a good swimmer."

When he said nothing more, her anger rose. She felt painfully alone and vulnerable. There was no sign of a settlement or habitation of any kind on the pristine, golden curve of beach, and she had no idea why they had stopped there or what might happen to her now. Suddenly her throat was very tight and she felt horribly close to tears.

Before she could say or do anything, Wolf lifted her into his arms, adjusted the cloak around her, and strode to the railing.

It was old Olaf's turn to play blind, deaf, and dumb. He held her until Wolf was in the water, no longer than a heartbeat. Clasped high against a rock-hard chest, Cymbra was carried up the beach and deposited gently near where the men were making a fire.

For just a moment Wolf lingered beside her, his hand touching her shoulder in a gesture that was oddly reassuring. Then he turned away and reached for his weapons.

"I've a taste for meat tonight." He called several of the men to him, gave instructions to the rest, and ran easily up the beach, out of sight.

Cymbra got up after a while and stretched her legs. She found some needed privacy behind a thick clump of bushes, then walked a little farther. It occurred to her that she could just keep on walking, and she wondered how far she would get before the men came after her.

Or perhaps they wouldn't. How could anyone pursue an invisible woman? She smiled at her whimsy and decided not to tempt fate. Her decision was confirmed a short time later when she returned to the camp site. Olaf looked up from the pot he was tending on the fire, met her gaze, and nodded once in acknowledgment. Not quite invisible after all.

She sat down again on the sand, wishing she could stretch out as the men were doing, and felt her stomach rumble as a tantalizing aroma wafted by. Olaf was taking herbs from a small bag at his waist and adding them to the pot where water simmered. As she watched, he sniffed, considered briefly, added another pinch, and appeared satisfied.

"What are you using?" she asked.

He looked startled that she would speak. The other men stiffened, although they were careful to look anywhere but at her. She thought Olaf might do the same but finally he cleared his throat.

Concentrating his attention on a stick of driftwood he was carving into a simple ladle, he said, "Salt, parsley, sage, and one or two other things for me to know."

She smiled, unable to hide her pleasure at simply hearing a voice directed to her. Walking over to the pot, she took a sniff. "Caraway seed and . . . black pepper."

The men grinned. A couple even looked her way when she added, "You're expecting rabbits then?"

Olaf shrugged, doing his best to appear unimpressed but not entirely succeeding. He took turnips, some pearly white barley, and a head of cabbage from a sack and began adding them to the pot. "Not much sense going for something bigger when we'll only be here the night."

Having had that particular question answered, Cymbra decided to try another. "Just where is here?"

He looked surprised that she didn't know. "It has no name. It's just a spot Wolf likes, with good anchorage and hunting."

"Do you live near here?"

He might have answered but just then one of the men called out. Wolf and the rest of the hunting party were returning.

Rabbits it was, skinned, gutted, sliced up, and deposited in the pot. Cymbra wondered why they just didn't skewer them for roasting over the fire, but when the dish was ready and she took a taste, she understood. Olaf would have been king of any kitchen.

By the time the meal was over, the long summer twilight had settled over the land. Cymbra watched the gulls and petrels fly to their rests. A thin sliver of moon shone against the pale sky. The breeze picked up a little but it was still pleasantly cool.

The men were settling themselves for sleep, talking quietly among themselves. With a little start, she realized that she was more aware of their feelings than she had been before. Despite the close quarters of the boat, they had kept themselves very much apart from her, not acknowledging her existence by so much as a glance. Her conversation with Olaf, brief though it had been, had relaxed the barriers between them just a little. Instinctively, she took refuge behind the sheltering walls of her mind, but not before she felt the men's mingled contentment and anticipation as they thought of home.

A sense of melancholy rippled through her, a longing for all that she had taken for granted and might well have lost forever.

Being on the edge of tears all the time was very tiresome.

Wolf stood. He dusted the sand off himself and held out a large, sinewy hand. "Come."

Cymbra's throat closed. She considered refusing, but what would be the point? They both knew he need make only the slightest effort to force her obedience. She took a deep breath, fighting for calm, and stood, but wouldn't give him her hand. He looked at her chidingly but didn't insist. Instead, he began walking up the beach. Fighting the urge to comment on his nature, his parentage, and his grasp of the most basic courtesies, Cymbra plodded along behind him. Her bare feet sank into the damp sand. Keeping the cloak closed around her was awkward and keeping up with his long strides was even more difficult.

Wolf didn't spare her so much as a glance. He kept going until they were a good quarter-mile from the beach. When he finally did stop, it was with so little warning that Cymbra ran straight into his back.

She might as well have gone into a wall. Her breath left her in a rush and with it went her restraint. She glared at him. "Is there some point to this?"

He looked tempted to laugh but instead took something from a sack he was carrying, placed it in her hand, and pointed at a clearing beyond the nearby trees. "I thought you might like a bath."

A bath? They were in the wilderness with no sign of even the smallest habitation, and he was talking about a bath? The possibility tantalized but she quailed inwardly at the thought of submerging herself in the icy runoff of a glacier. "I don't really—"

"A hot mineral bath." His hand on her shoulder, he directed her gaze to the wisps of steam rising between moss-draped rocks. When she moved closer, she saw that the rocks framed a small pool simmering gently with the earth's inner fire.

A bath. A real, hot, luxurious bath.

With soap. At least she thought that was what the small block he'd handed her was supposed to be. Though it was far from her own lovely honeysuckle and lavender soaps, she held it like a precious gem.

"Thank you," she said, "a bath would be wonderful. I won't be long."

"Take as much time as you like." Wolf flopped down

on the ground nearby, stretched out on one side, and propped his head in his palm. The position gave him an unfettered view of the pool.

Cymbra's hand tightened on the soap as she fought the urge to hurl it at him. "I should have known."

"Known what?" he inquired mildly.

"That you wouldn't do something just to be kind."

"A bath isn't kind?"

"It isn't if I'm expected to take it in front of you."

He raised an eyebrow in seeming bewilderment. "Why would it bother you to take a bath in front of me?"

He was toying with her but she refused to let him see how much that troubled her. "Why? Because it's immodest and improper. No decent woman would do such a thing. Surely, Viking women don't—"

"We Norse are much more sensible about such things. We enjoy our bodies and aren't burdened by absurd feelings of shame."

"How very nice for you." Determined to return to the beach, Cymbra began to go around him. The clasp of a powerful hand around her ankle stopped her.

She had not even seen him move, yet he had reached beneath her cloak and caught her before she could even guess his intent. His fingers were long and warm. She could feel the callused tips moving lightly over her skin.

"Let me go."

"No." He tugged gently, forcing her to move closer. His hand slid up her leg, over the slender calf to the back of her knee and slightly higher.

Cymbra froze. No one had ever touched her like that. She was shocked, stunned, and afraid. Not of him, although she was sure that would come. No, her fear was of herself and her response to him. Beneath his hand, following the path of his touch, pleasure exploded through her. A moan rose in her throat. She bit down hard on her lower lip, fighting to suppress the sound, and failed.

Chapter

FOUR

WOLF WAS ON HIS FEET INSTANTLY. HE grabbed hold of Cymbra and shook her lightly. "Stop that. You've made yourself bleed."

Tiny droplets of crimson shone on her lower lip. She seemed unaware of the small hurt and was staring at him in bewilderment.

Anger, not at her but at himself for provoking the situation, made his voice hard. "Go take that bath. You need it."

Stubbornly, Cymbra shook her head. She was very pale but she faced him unflinchingly. "No, I won't."

Wolf knew only one answer to such defiance: punishment. His word was absolute among his people, proof of their understanding that disobedience was but one step from chaos, the monster always lurking just beyond the edges of a man's hearth, waiting to devour the unwary, the unlucky, and the just plain foolish. In a world where strength ruled, he had never hesitated to enforce his will. Until now.

Instantly wary but curious, he tried a different approach. "Your fears are misplaced, lady."

He glanced at the glorious tumble of her chestnut hair, resisted the urge to stroke it, and said, "I prefer my women to be blond."

Taking a step back, he shifted his gaze to her chest. "As well as somewhat better endowed."

Irrepressible Loki would be slack-jawed with awe. A masterful liar, the god of mischief was said to appreciate the skill wherever he found it, even in humans. Truly, he would wrangle Wolf's admission to Valhalla for this alone.

The look of amazement on Cymbra's lovely face almost made him burst out laughing, a tendency he was experiencing all too often in her presence and one out of keeping with his stern, harsh life. He just barely managed to maintain a look of utter sincerity. "Men do have varying tastes, you know."

She acknowledged this with a small nod although she still looked thoroughly perplexed. Cautiously, as though testing unknown waters, she asked, "You don't find me attractive?"

He was hard-pressed not to break down in mirth. No doubt all her life people had told her how beautiful she was. Her stunning appearance must have shaded every encounter she had ever had. He doubted that anyone, at any time, had ever treated her as just another person.

"Oh, you're not ugly or anything," he assured her, and felt Loki on his shoulder chuckling and urging him on. "It's just as I said, different men have different tastes in women."

Cymbra thought that over. She had very little knowledge of men and their tastes. She knew only that every man she'd ever known, with the sole exception of her brother, stuttered and stammered through their dealings with her—when they were capable of speech at all. Not even old Brother Chilton had been immune.

She hated being set apart and treated so differently, made so continually aware of how she looked and the effect it had on people. She had wanted so very badly to be ordinary.

And now she was? At least to this man?

She looked at him narrowly, trying to sense any duplicity, but he merely returned her gaze innocently and gestured again toward the pool. "It's getting late. I would like to get back to the beach sometime tonight."

Cymbra flushed hotly. Moments before, she had stood beneath his hand, riveted by pleasure so intense as to make her cry out. And now he was telling her very plainly that she was nothing more to him than a nuisance.

Fine. At least she would be a clean nuisance.

Her nerve almost failed her when she reached the rim of the pool, but she kept her back to Wolf, took a deep breath, dropped the ermine cloak, and plunged into the water. The shock of it made her yelp.

"Are you all right?" Not waiting for an answer, he was already coming toward her.

Quickly she held up a hand to fend him off. "I'm fine; it's just a little hot."

More than a little, but after the initial shock, the heat seeping through her was incredibly relaxing. She felt the strain of the days at sea, with all the attendant fear about her fate, melting away.

Delighted, and considerably more confident since she'd noted that the mineral-laden froth of the water effectively concealed her, she laughed.

"This is wonderful. I'd heard about baths like this but never experienced one before." With a happy smile, she reached out for the soap beside the pool and began to lather it over her bare arms and shoulders.

Wolf stifled a groan. The glimpse he'd had of her slender, tapered back, high, rounded buttocks, and glorious legs just visible behind the swaying curtain of her magnificent hair had pushed him right over the edge. He was achingly hard, his blood pounding hot and thick, his body demanding relief.

He flopped back down on the ground, stared at the thick bulge in his trousers, and muttered, "Stay down, you damn fool."

"What's that?" Cymbra called.

Wolf rolled over, wincing as he did so, but he forced himself to smile. A man stupid enough to let a woman know her power over him might as well put his cock on a leash and invite her to lead him about by it.

"Nothing." Taking deep breaths between his teeth, he silently berated his joyfully heedless member, that part of him disconnected from all thought, reason, and common sense.

When no amount of reprimand had the slightest effect, he forced himself to focus on the most mundane, boring thoughts he could muster—recalling the tedious, seemingly endless merchant accounts he had to go over periodically, going down them item by item, summoning mind-numbing detail until slowly, resentfully, his body quieted.

Only then did he look at Cymbra again. She had finished washing her hair and was preparing to leave the pool. Wolf silently blessed the impulse that had made him bring along a drying cloth for her even when he was tempted to leave it behind. Rather than risk yet more humiliation, he averted his gaze while she emerged, dried off quickly, and wrapped the ermine cloak around her.

"I'm done," she said softly. "Thank you. It was wonderful."

"I'm glad you liked it," Wolf muttered. Never mind the agony of frustration he suffered, she'd had a nice bath. There had to be some fairness in this. At the very least, he could damn well get clean.

"Sit down," he said. When she looked puzzled, he stood and stripped off his tunic. "It's my turn."

Cymbra's eyes opened very wide. In the dim twilight he couldn't be absolutely sure but he thought she blushed. Good, she deserved to be discomfited. Her calm, serene air was immensely annoying to him. He wanted her as hot and straining, as mindless and needful as she had made him. But he wasn't going to get it, not now at least, not if his plan was to work as smoothly as he wished.

"I'll go back to the beach," she said, turning to do so.

"Sit down," he repeated implacably. To his astonishment, he added, "It's getting dark. You could trip and fall, or lose your way."

Why was he explaining his orders to her? Frustrated at his inability to control himself where she was concerned, Wolf yanked off the rest of his clothes and dived into the water.

Cymbra gave a faint gasp and sank to the ground. The quicksilver glimpse she had of him before she averted her eyes burned into her memory. His shoulders were magnificent, sculpted of taut muscle; his back broad and sharply narrowing to his waist and hard buttocks; his legs long, corded with sinew, the whole of him formed so beautifully as to steal her breath away and overwhelm her with soul-shattering yearning.

It wasn't fair. She hadn't meant to look at him. It had happened just by accident, as though her body had developed a will of its own. A will that was expressing itself in all sorts of shocking ways. Her nipples ached, and there was a dampness beneath the curls at her cleft that owed nothing to the bath. Her thighs felt unaccountably heavy and weak, as though they would fall open at the slightest urging.

Sweet heaven, what was wrong with her? Was she so base that the mere sight of a man's naked form could fill her with such hot, urgent yearning?

Well, not the *mere* sight. In all fairness, there was nothing *mere* about Wolf Hakonson.

Shocked at the waywardness of her thoughts, Cymbra was horrified by a sudden, unexpected urge to giggle. Her well-ordered defenses, the fruit of desperate need and a lifetime of effort, were collapsing around her.

She was helpless to contain her emotions or protect herself from them in any way. She should have been repelled and frightened, but instead she felt positively giddy, as though she stood on the top of a great precipice, about to launch herself into space.

What a temptation it was to find out if she really could fly.

But, of course, she couldn't. If she was so foolish as to forget that for a moment, she and her wayward emotions would be crushed on the unforgiving rocks of reality.

Determined to remember that at all costs, she concentrated on looking anywhere and everywhere but at the pool. This part of the northlands—whatever part it was—had some aspects in common with Essex, but she noted there were far more fir trees with only a few birch and none of the oak and chestnut she knew.

The difference gave the surrounding forests a darker and rather more ominous appearance in the fading light. Still, they were quite lovely in many respects, and if she could only concentrate on them entirely, she could ignore what was going on only a few yards from where she sat.

Unfortunately, she couldn't shut off her hearing as easily as she averted her eyes. She was vividly aware of every splash of water, every sound of movement, imagining Wolf running the soap over himself, washing that magnificent body, rising from the pond, imagining—

It was fortunate that the air was cooling so rapidly, otherwise she would have been unbearably hot in the ermine cloak.

"Ready to go?" She looked up. He was standing right beside her, dressed again in his tunic and trousers.

Droplets of water clung to his thick, ebony hair. He looked very aloof and stern, very watchful.

Piqued by his ability to hide his emotions when hers felt rubbed raw, Cymbra took the hand he offered with a calm she did not feel. Lean, hard fingers closed around hers, evoking a deep shiver of pleasure. She ignored it stalwartly, stood, and, with a nod as regal as any queen's, tried to pull her hand free. Instinctively, his hold tightened. He looked surprised by his reaction and released her immediately. But he still wasn't above having the last word.

"Don't get too far ahead," he said pleasantly. "These woods are full of wolves."

Wolves, sharks, Vikings, what difference did it make? She was tempted to ask but thought better of it. Still, she didn't precisely go racing off without him. They returned to the beach together.

The men were already asleep around the fire, or discreetly pretending to be. Wolf lay down and pointed to the place next to him. When Cymbra didn't spring to obey, he merely shrugged and rolled over. Soon he, too, appeared to sleep.

She hesitated, suddenly feeling overwhelmed with fatigue and just slightly ridiculous. Her captor had made it absolutely clear how he felt about her. Whatever he intended, he was hardly likely to be overcome with lust at this late date.

Telling herself that the sting she felt wasn't from her battered pride, Cymbra finally stretched out on the still-warm sand. Her last thought was of the phantom motion of the dragon ship gently rocking her to sleep.

TWO MORE DAYS THEY SAILED, FIRST EAST INTO THE rising sun, then north. The land changed as craggy hills appeared and pressed in close to the shore. A few

farms were scattered along the narrow band of flat ground
beside the water, their fields stretching up the hillsides.

Once, Cymbra saw a gaggle of children come running
through a field of golden barley, waving to them, their
brown legs churning over the rich, black earth. The men
waved back and the children's happy shouts were heard
far out across the water. After that, it seemed as though
the mood on board was at once lighter and more tense as
the men counted down the hours to home.

Cymbra slept poorly that night, and the next day
anxiety gripped her. She sat in the bow, watching the
passing shore for any sign of their destination. Toward
midday, they approached a cluster of islands and shoals
that at first glance appeared to be impenetrable. Wolf took
the rudder and the men rowed more slowly as they carefully made their way through a narrow channel strewn
with huge boulders on either side.

The channel opened up suddenly into a large bay of
deep blue water perfectly reflecting the sheltering hills
that rose above it. At the far end of the bay, protected by
both land and sea, was a sizable settlement.

Several hundred small and medium-sized buildings
were clustered close together, smoke rising from the peaks
of their thatched roofs. In between were lanes filled with
carts, people, and animals. Within the town, several large,
open areas apparently served as marketplaces. Farther
out, three large stone piers reached into the bay. From the
one closest to the town, the shore had been faced in stones
so as to create a continuous dockage for shallow-draft vessels. Above the town, commanding a sweeping view out
over the bay, was a hill fort surrounded by an earthen
berm dotted with watchtowers. The whole created the impression of a bustling, prosperous trading settlement well
protected by nature but far from dependent on it for its
defenses.

As Cymbra gazed at the town, her anxiousness steadily

increasing, the deep, drawn-out blast of a signal horn sounded from the shore, followed swiftly by another and another. Watchers on towers along the curve of the bay had spotted the dragon ship and its wolf-emblazoned sail. They called again and again, their tones reverberating off the nearby hills, joyously welcoming the adventurers home.

By the time the vessel drew up beside the largest pier, men, women, and children lined the dock, waving and shouting. The men on board waved back, spotting loved ones in the crowd, calling assurances that all had gone well and all returned safely.

Before the anchor was dropped, Wolf leaped across the space between the vessel and the pier, and clasped hands with a man the crowd had parted to admit. Cymbra hid a gasp when she realized that the man was equal to Wolf in size and had something of the same look about him, although his hair was more brown than black. His features bore the pallor of recent illness and he moved with some difficulty, but he grinned broadly, and the pounding he gave Wolf's back would surely have felled a lesser man.

Just then the man said something that made Wolf frown and reply curtly. Whatever he said drew the man's attention to the vessel and to Cymbra. She felt his gaze on her and turned away, suddenly unbearably self-conscious. She was vividly aware of her nakedness beneath the cloak. The crowd pressed ever closer, the din of their voices ringing in her ears. She wished suddenly that the journey had not ended, that she was still at sea, where time had seemed to hang suspended.

Wolf stepped onto the deck again and came toward her. The crowd, its attention caught, fell silent. Hundreds of pairs of eyes turned in her direction, followed swiftly by a low, avid murmur of speculation.

Her cheeks burned and her stomach lurched. She could feel their curiosity, their conjecture, feel the whole dark, roiling surge of their emotions flowing over her, pulling her down, making it impossible for her to breathe or endure.

She couldn't let this happen. She had to find the courage and strength to face with dignity whatever lay ahead. Desperately, she fought to shore up the inner walls that protected her from the tumultuous, chaotic world of feeling. If she could only make them strong enough, retreat far enough behind them. If only—

"Come," Wolf said, and before she could reply, he lifted her into his arms.

"I can walk," she protested. She wasn't absolutely sure she could, or how far she would get if she attempted it, but pride demanded that she try.

He shrugged his massive shoulders and kept right on going, off the vessel and onto the pier. "I prefer to carry you."

And that, as it seemed, was that.

Wrapped in ermine, cradled in the arms of the Wolf, Cymbra entered the great Viking port of Sciringesheal.

S O MUCH FOR DRAGGING HER NAKED AND RAVAGED IN chains through the streets, Wolf thought ruefully. When he'd set sail for Holyhood, his only intent to avenge the insult done him and his people, he had at least entertained the notion of such a punishment for a woman he believed richly deserved it. Instead he carried her wrapped in a cloak fit for an empress, his care of her a silent but eloquent signal to his people of her status.

The crowd parted before them. He saw their shock, indeed their astonishment, and ignored it. Word of who she was would spread quickly enough. Without lessening his stride, he walked straight through the town, the crowd closing up behind and following.

The gates in the berm were opening as Wolf approached. He acknowledged the men who greeted him but still he didn't slow, continuing across the flattened top of the hill, past the various workshops and barracks, the stables and pens, the kitchens and the great hall, until he came to a building set apart from the others.

This was a spacious, single-story residence built of fragrant fir planks. Intricate, entwined designs were painted in vivid blues, reds, and yellows around the door and windows. Above the door, sheltered by the overhang of the pitched roofs, hung two crossed axes, ancient symbol of the jarl's authority.

Wolf kicked open the door and entered, stooping slightly to clear the lintel. He straightened and looked around with satisfaction. All his life he had known the communal existence of a true Norseman, sharing food, quarters, hardships, and victories with his people. But when the council confirmed his succession to the chieftainship of his clan, he had allowed himself what was to him the ultimate luxury—privacy.

He crossed the single large room quickly and set his captive down on the immense bed hewn of birch trunks and covered with wolf pelts. With regret, he released her and stepped back.

"The women will see to your comfort, lady, but they have little experience with such as you. If you want something, ask for it."

Her eyes were the most remarkable shade of blue. When they widened as they did now, he could imagine drowning in them.

He left without another word, and did not breathe easily until he closed the door of his lodge behind him.

C YMBRA SAT ON THE HUGE BED AND LOOKED AROUND. The chamber's barbaric splendor struck her at once.

Weapons and banners adorned the walls clear to the peaked ceiling. An elaborately carved table and two chairs stood near windows that commanded a magnificent view of the bay. Several equally elaborate chests were placed against the walls.

On the table was a pair of iron scales, the kind she had seen used to weigh coins. Nearby was a beautiful set of glassware, an ewer and several goblets of teal blue glass trimmed with silver. Everywhere she looked she saw small—and not so small—touches that bespoke the owner's wealth and power. Even the bucket meant to hold water was decorated with bands of beaten bronze.

She was still contemplating all this when the door opened and several women entered. Two of the three were quite tall and appeared to be a mother and daughter. They wore pleated linen petticoats visible beneath tunics with richly embroidered hems. The tunics were secured at their shoulders by carved brooches. The older woman wore an additional brooch pinned to her tunic. From it dangled a chain holding a pair of shears and several keys. Both had long hair, the older woman's gathered at the crown of her head and allowed to fall in a thick swatch, while the younger was in braids adorned with silk ribbons.

The third woman, who was an inch or two shorter than Cymbra, was darker of mien and dressed very differently from the two others. She wore only a tunic of rough, gray wool that came midway down her calves. Her black hair was gathered back with a leather thong. It was this smaller woman who gave Cymbra a quick, shy smile as she set down the tray of food she carried.

"Lady," the older of the tall blond women enunciated slowly and precisely, "the Lord Wolf has directed that you eat and bathe." She paused, waiting to see if the stranger among them understood proper language.

"Thank you," Cymbra said softly, offering a silent prayer of gratitude for Brother Chilton and his command of Norse. "What are your names, please?"

The women exchanged quick glances of surprise at her use of their language.

"I am Marta, lady," the older woman said, drawing herself up even straighter. "This is my daughter, Kiirla." As an afterthought, she said, "And this thrall is called Brita."

Cymbra looked at the smaller woman more closely. She knew the word *thrall* but wasn't absolutely clear as to its meaning. There was no real equivalent among her people. "Thrall?" she asked.

"A slave," Marta explained. She gestured to Brita. "Fetch the mistress's bath water."

As the young woman hurried to obey, Cymbra frowned. The Saxons held slaves, but they were generally prisoners of war who would be reclaimed by their own side or people guilty of some crime who were freed after serving a time of labor. With rare exception, they were treated decently. It wasn't unusual for a slave, once freed, to remain in the community, many having married and settled down even while still technically in servitude. Judging by Brita's poor clothing and Marta's manner to her, slavery among the Norse was much different.

Or perhaps this was just an isolated case. Cymbra cautioned herself not to leap to any conclusions even as she wondered at her status. As a captive, was she also considered a thrall? If so, she was certainly being treated far differently than Brita.

The younger woman returned bearing two steaming buckets of water. She set them down and went out again, then returned with a shallow leather trough and a bucket of cool water.

"The Lord Wolf said you were accustomed to this way of bathing, lady," Marta explained. "He said the heat of a proper sauna would likely be too strong for you just now." The pursing of her mouth indicated what she thought of such weakness.

Cymbra looked at the trough doubtfully. It was far too small to hold her and she had no idea how she was supposed to bathe in it.

"Come, lady," Kiirla said, darting a quick glance at her mother for approval. "If you will stand here—"

Following the young woman's gestures, and guessing at what was intended, Cymbra stepped into the trough. She hesitated when Marta held out a hand for the ermine cloak but steeled herself and gave it up. Marta looked her over very frankly, her eyes hardening. Kiirla looked startled and quickly looked away. Brita kept her eyes averted as she mixed the water in another bucket, tested the temperature, then nodded to Marta.

The task of hauling the water had been left to the slave, but pouring it over Cymbra was Marta's privilege. She made a thorough job of it, but when she took up soap and a rough cloth, Cymbra insisted on doing the rest herself. She was shivering by the time she finished, there being no heat in the lodge. Apparently it was not considered necessary in summer, although by Cymbra's standards the air was decidedly cool.

"Now you will eat," Marta directed when Cymbra was dried and wrapped in a sheet. She indicated the table. "Please to sit, lady."

Cymbra sat. Brita gave her another shy smile as she removed the cover over the tray, revealing a carved wooden plate holding slices of smoked fish, bread, cheese, and a handful of lush, ripe blackberries. A cup of equally rich design was filled with milk.

As Cymbra ate, she gazed out the windows at the town below. She saw the dragon ship riding at anchor, the water of the bay sparkling around it.

Other vessels docked nearby also had high, curved

prows, but these had not been carved into the nightmare symbol of the Norse raiders. They also appeared to have wider keels, which made her think they were merchant ships kept for peaceful use.

The people in town seemed to have returned to their normal tasks. The lanes were busy once again and there was a fair amount of activity in the marketplaces. On the hills beyond the town, goats and sheep grazed. So large were the flocks that they were spread out all the way to the tops of the slopes.

Contemplating the obvious prosperity and power of the Wolf's holding, she ate as much as she could, finishing just as Brita dragged a large chest through the door. Neither of the other women made an effort to help her. Cymbra was about to do so when surprise stopped her.

"That's mine." It was her very own chest, the one she had used for years and had last seen in her chamber at Holyhood what seemed a lifetime ago.

"Yes, lady," Brita said as she straightened.

Marta shot her a hard look, instantly silencing her. "The Lord Wolf also directed this be brought to you, lady. It contains your belongings."

Slowly, Cymbra walked over to the chest, knelt beside it, and opened the lid. On top was a small wooden coffer bound in iron. She lifted it out with great care, hardly daring to believe what she held. "My medicines," she said softly.

Setting it aside, she explored further and found in short order her needlework, her lute, her pens and papers, her manuscripts, and a very fair selection of her clothes. All neatly, indeed meticulously, packed, so that nothing had suffered the slightest harm during the voyage.

The same voyage wherein the Wolf had insisted there was nothing for her to wear save the ermine cloak he had given her.

Her fingers tightened on an over tunic of topaz silk,

one of her favorites. She caught herself quickly and smoothed the fabric before it could wrinkle but could not contain a soft mutter of anger.

"Lady?" Marta queried.

"Nothing," Cymbra said. She drew garments from the trunk and began to dress quickly. "I was merely commenting on Lord Wolf's thoughtfulness."

Brita hurried to help her. Cymbra gave her an encouraging smile and, when she was done, thanked her. That earned another frown from Marta.

As Brita tidied up from the bath, Kiirla combed out Cymbra's hair.

"I have never seen hair of such length, lady," the younger woman said. The words were admiring but the tone was not. There was an underlying catch of envy and disapproval. As though to emphasize it, she tugged the comb rather harder than was needed. "It must trouble you greatly to care for it."

Cymbra winced. "Not really. My maid, Miriam, always helped and—" She was suddenly swept by longing for her dear old friend.

At the thought of the worry that kind, gentle woman who had raised her must be suffering, Cymbra's cheeks flushed. What was she thinking of, to be lolling amid barbaric luxuries when her friends and family despaired of her fate? For the length of the journey, she had held off her protests and her questions. But the journey was over now, they had come to their destination, and it was time for her to face whatever might lie ahead.

She stood up and straightened her shoulders. With regal coolness, she said, "I wish to speak with Lord Wolf."

Marta was startled but recovered quickly and shook her head. "You must wait for him to summon you."

Nine days on the ship. Nine days of waiting and wondering. Nine very long, very frustrating days.

"No," Cymbra said and walked out of the lodge.

Chapter

FIVE

I'M NOT SURE I UNDERSTAND. EXPLAIN TO ME again how this captive woman you were bringing back to suffer a horrible but undeniably deserved fate was transformed into a pampered princess to be surrounded by every luxury and consideration."

Wolf scowled at the man across the table. He was the same man who had come to greet him on the pier. They were seated in the great hall, a timber building several hundred feet long with a center hearth large enough to hold an ox.

The walls were lined with sleeping recesses covered with blankets and furs, used by those of Wolf's men who were not settled with their own families in the fort or the town. Shields, weapons, and banners hung from the rafters. Trestle tables were set up around the hearth, with the largest of these, where Wolf sat, slightly raised so as to be visible throughout the hall.

A few servants moved about, beginning preparations for the evening meal, but otherwise it was empty save for the two men at the head table.

Wolf raised his drinking horn, took a long swallow

of ale, and scowled at his brother. "She's not what I thought."

This cursory explanation earned a grin from the man known from the ice caves of the frozen north to the souks of Byzantium as Dragon.

"I only caught a glimpse of her before you spirited her away. What sort of woman is she?"

Wolf thought for a moment, then shrugged. "Gentle. She brought us food and blankets while we were being held prisoner. Later that night I heard her telling her old nurse that there was too much cruelty in the world."

Dragon's eyes narrowed. "If she thinks that way, why did she refuse your offer of marriage?"

"She says she didn't. She claims she never heard about it."

"Then the Hawk . . ."

"No, she claims that isn't so either." Wolf's mouth tightened derisively. "Her brother wants peace, so she tells me."

Dragon's brows rose nearly to his hairline. "Well, he'll have a chance to prove it, won't he?"

Wolf grunted agreement and returned his attention to the ale. He knew he was just postponing the inevitable, but a man could be pardoned for taking a bit of time to collect himself. In aid of that, he had another long swallow.

Over the rim of the ale horn, he saw his brother's attention lock suddenly on the far end of the hall. His mouth dropping open, the Dragon rose.

Wolf did the same, quickly, and put a hand on his brother's shoulder. Dragon met his eyes in blank amazement.

"She . . ."

"I know." Wolf sighed. "Believe me, I know." He turned, aware of what he would see yet not truly prepared for it. Cymbra in the dim light of the cell at Holyhood was exquisite. Wrapped in the ermine cloak, she was lovely. Naked in her bath and in the hold, she was . . . He would not think about that.

Now, here in his hall, dressed in a simple tunic of indigo wool girded at the waist, with long, form-fitting sleeves and a chastely high neck, she was gut-wrenchingly beautiful. Her glorious hair tumbled free, unhindered by veil or circlet. Her cheeks were in high color and there was an unmistakable light in her eyes as she came toward him.

She could be Frigg, he thought—so far as he was capable of thinking at all—the wife of Odin himself and a power to be reckoned with in her own right. Certainly, Frigg must favor her for all that she was Saxon born. How else to explain a mortal woman with the physical perfection of a goddess?

A serving boy with the ill-luck to be walking across the hall at the moment she appeared went straight into a pillar. Another tripped over his own feet and sent a tray of bowls clattering to the floor. Both picked themselves up slowly, still staring. As were the few others in the hall, including one who ought to have known better.

Wolf moved deliberately, interposing himself between Cymbra and his brother. He caught Dragon's eye again, his message unmistakable for all that it was silent.

Dragon sighed. He hesitated but sat down again. Bluntly, he said, "Did we not share the same sire, I would fight you for her. Best you know that. Others will feel the same and be unhindered by the bonds of brotherhood."

Wolf did not begrudge such frankness; on the contrary, he welcomed it. Not for a moment did he pretend that the woman he had stolen was other than an immense temptation to any man who set eyes on her. No wonder her brother had kept her locked away. With hindsight, he had to applaud the Hawk's good sense.

"I would like to speak with you," Cymbra said, her

voice meltingly soft despite her obvious anger, her slight accent delightful as always. She spared Dragon only the briefest glance. All her attention was on the Wolf.

Who duly noted that and was pleased. His brother was thought an inordinately handsome man and enjoyed vast success with women. Yet Cymbra appeared oblivious to him.

"By all means," Wolf said pleasantly. "But not here." He took her arm and steered her toward the front of the hall where wide doors stood open to admit the summer breeze. She went impatiently, brimming with words as yet unuttered.

He did not stop or speak again until they had climbed the berm near one of the watchtowers overlooking the bay. He waited then, letting her catch her breath, the silence dragging out between them until finally she couldn't stand it anymore.

Facing him directly, her hands clenched at her sides, she said, "You must realize what you have done. My brother will come after me and there will be a war. Surely you can't want that?"

When still Wolf did not respond, Cymbra burst out, "You must let me send word to Hawk that I am safe!" She paused, staring at her captor, as coldness moved through her. He made no move to calm or reassure her, no effort at all to allay her worst fears. Indeed, his very silence seemed to confirm them. She could delay no longer the question that had been uppermost in her mind since the moment at Holyhood when steely arms had first closed around her: "What do you intend to do with me?"

Her courage pleased him but he was careful not to show it. Shrugging, he said, "Better you ask what I intend for your brother."

Cymbra paled. "What do you mean?"

Wolf raised an arm, long of bone, weighted with

muscle, perfectly crafted to wield a sword or lance as it did so very often. He pointed down to the beach. "Your brother will die there."

The rays of the setting sun spilled like blood across the water. Cymbra gasped and put her hand to her throat. "*Why?* You have no reason to kill him."

"He who is not my friend is my enemy. I gave your brother the chance for peace. I offered him an alliance against the Dane who plagues us both. His answer was a mortal insult."

"He didn't . . ."

"Enough! He will come for you, and when he does, he will die. I will have one less enemy in the world and the insult done me will be avenged."

He grasped her shoulders, deliberately allowing her to feel something of his strength, and forced her to look down at the crimson-lit beach. "Right there, Cymbra, that is where your brother will breathe his last. His life's blood will soak that sand. His last sight will be of these walls."

"No!" A sob broke from her as she tried to wrench free of him.

Wolf tightened his hold implacably. He pulled her hard against him, his hand clasping the back of her head to press her face to his chest. Softly, almost caressingly, he said, "Unless you prefer a different fate for him."

She looked up, her tear-filled eyes meeting his. Her voice shook. "What do you mean?"

"Right now your brother has no idea who took you. We were careful to leave no trace. Odds are he thinks the Danes responsible. But soon I will send word to him of where you are and he will come. If he thinks you a captive, abused, perhaps dead, honor will demand that he give battle, and he will perish. But if he finds you safe, honored, content, then he will accept the alliance he should have accepted months ago. All will be as it should be."

"You mean he will agree to give me to you in marriage?"

"No, I mean he will accept our marriage. If you truly want to save his life, you will let him find you my wife, not my slave."

She paled. "I cannot marry without my brother's approval."

He had expected this and was prepared for it. "If you wait for that, he will die before he can give it. We will burn his body, as is our way. He will not even reach your Christian heaven. But who knows, perhaps Odin will welcome him into Valhalla for by all repute he is a mighty warrior. Just not mighty enough to survive the trap I have set for him."

He held her then as the storm swept through her and knew that she was truly seeing what he had conjured not merely with words but with the steel-stark truth of his intent. For if she refused, what he had promised would come to pass as surely as they stood there above the empty beach with the stars winking on overhead.

"Oh, God," she whispered, and with no warning at all pulled back her fist and slammed it straight into his jaw.

T HE NIGHT THROBBED TO THE RHYTHM OF GOATSKIN drums and bone clappers. Birch flutes joined in, adding a lighter, teasing play, all combining in a robust, joyful tune that reverberated to the star-draped sky and the swollen moon hanging low to the earth.

Men, women, and children milled about, their faces aglow with excitement. Cooks swirled around the fires, working frantically. Servants scrambled to finish setting up all the extra tables, enough for a crowd far too large to be accommodated even in the great hall.

Wolf looked around slowly. What he saw pleased him

well. For a wedding feast prepared in a matter of hours, instead of the weeks that were normally required, he could find no fault.

Absently, he rubbed his jaw, caught himself doing it, and grimaced. She hadn't actually bruised him; he'd checked in a silvered reflecting glass Dragon had brought from the East. But there was no denying that his gentle bride had a surprisingly solid punch when she was riled.

With hindsight, he supposed that as marriage offers went, his had left something to be desired. Promising to kill her brother if she didn't become his wife probably wasn't the surest way to win a woman's heart. But damn it, it wasn't her heart he wanted. It was her obedience. And her body. Oh, yes, definitely her body.

Tonight she would be his. The formidable self-control he had exercised on the voyage would no longer be needed. He would sate himself fully in the beautiful witch. By morning, she would be simply a woman.

That didn't mean he wouldn't value her and treat her kindly, only that he would no longer feel the hot, dazed hunger she triggered in him. He would be himself again, in control.

But first there was this marriage feast to get through.

"Nervous?" Dragon asked as he emerged from his lodge behind Wolf. He grinned challengingly. "If you're not feeling up to it, brother, I'd be happy to—"

"Exactly how eager are you to feast in Valhalla this night?" Wolf asked pleasantly.

Dragon laughed and raised his hands in mock surrender. "Not quite that eager. The lady is yours and welcome to her." He glanced at Wolf's jaw and smiled broadly. "Gentle. Isn't that what you called her?"

Wolf flushed slightly. Dragon noticed too much. "She will learn," he said with utter confidence. That there might be any difficulty with her doing so did not occur to him. She was, after all, only a woman, Frigg-favored or not.

"Well then," Dragon said, "there's no reason to delay."

Together they walked into the large, open area where the crowd had assembled. They were seen almost at once and a great cheer went up. People pressed forward to greet their jarl and his brother, both warriors of great renown, and to offer their congratulations to Wolf on this happy occasion.

In the midst of much back-slapping and ribald jest, Wolf kept an eye on his lodge. He was just about at the point of going to fetch her when the door opened and Cymbra emerged. He couldn't be absolutely sure but he thought she had some help from Marta, who appeared to give her a little shove. He smiled grimly at the sight of his reluctant bride, then he simply smiled.

She was still wearing the indigo-blue tunic but had added a veil of translucent silk over her hair. Around her neck, no doubt placed there despite her objections, was a golden torque emblazoned with the wolf's head; the gleaming eyes were made of clear white stone said to have come from the fabled lands at the southernmost end of the world. More than anything else, the torque was an unmistakable sign of his possession. Cymbra certainly understood its purpose, for her fingers closed around the gold metal and even as he watched she tugged at it angrily.

Wolf grinned. He couldn't help it, her spirit pleased him. Not for the first time, he considered what a delight taming her would be. His patience suddenly gone, and determined that this not take a moment more than it absolutely must, he strode through the crowd and met Cymbra before she could take more than a few steps from his lodge.

She saw him coming and stopped abruptly. Her breath caught. He was dressed far more luxuriously than she had ever seen him, in a tunic of rich black velvet stretched tautly over his massive chest and close-fitting trousers of soft leather. The thick mane of his ebony hair was freshly washed and swept back from his high forehead. Bands of gold shone at his wrists, and around his throat he wore a larger version of the wolf-emblazoned torque her fingers were worrying.

The anguish she had suffered since he told her of his plans to kill Hawk, and the humiliation she felt at her utterly uncharacteristic lapse into actual violence, gave way before a strange surge of excitement. She tried to deny it but it flowered swiftly, pushing aside all else. Without thought, she held out her hand. His own closed around it with gentleness that surprised her. She was drawn with him into the crowd.

At the center of the large open area within the berm stood a tree. It was a very old ash with gnarled branches that stretched far out as though in loving embrace. Before it stood a man who appeared almost as old. He was simply dressed in a robe of unbleached homespun and he smiled as Wolf and Cymbra approached.

"This is Ulfrich," Wolf said. "He will say the words for us."

"He is a priest?" Cymbra asked.

"We have no priests in our faith. He is a wise and holy man."

Perhaps Ulfrich saw her perplexity, for he said gently, "You are new to our ways, lady. Please allow me to explain." He gestured a gnarled hand toward the tree. The people drew closer, falling silent as the music died away and only the deep, gentle voice of Ulfrich remained.

"Such a tree stands at the center of every Norse settlement. It represents Yggdrasil, the world tree with roots reaching into the netherworld and branches reaching to the sky. From the branches of Yggdrasil, the great god Odin hung for nine days and nine nights without food or water, giving of his life's blood in sacrifice. On the ninth day, as he was dying, he looked down and beheld the runes, givers of divine knowledge. Through them, he was reborn so that his wisdom may be shared by all mankind."

Ulfrich reached out, took their joined hands, and held them in both of his. "Wolf Hakonson, you have come to declare before all that this woman is your wife. You must pledge to protect and care for her, to shelter her beneath your roof, to share all you have with her, and to give her children. Do you agree to this?"

"I agree," Wolf said quietly.

"Cymbra of Holyhood, do you agree to be wife to this man, to keep his home, bear his children, and guard his honor throughout your life?"

Her throat tightened. It was all so very different from what she had ever imagined. Not that she had thought much about marriage. So long as Hawk did not speak of it, she saw no reason to concern herself. But she had assumed that if she ever did marry, she would have the blessing of the Church. Although she did not doubt the sincerity of this pagan ceremony, it was just that—pagan. And it left her longing for something more.

Yet she was a woman of courage and sense, not to mention of deep, unnamed yearnings she could no longer deny. Quietly, she said, "I agree."

Ulfrich nodded solemnly. He accepted a gem-encrusted goblet offered by a young boy, poured honeyed wine into it, and handed the goblet to Wolf. "Drink then to seal this bond."

Wolf raised the goblet to his lips. He was about to drink when he hesitated, lowered the goblet, and instead handed it to Cymbra. He did not release it but held the goblet steady as she slowly set her mouth to it and tasted the sweet, tangy liquid sliding down her throat. When she raised her head, he turned the goblet, set his mouth where hers had touched, and drank deeply.

The crowd roared its approval, but Wolf held up a hand before the well-wishers could engulf them. "One thing more," he said. He glanced at Ulfrich, who nodded and stepped back. From the crowd came a tall, thin man in a monk's simple brown robe. At Cymbra's startled look, his gentle face creased in a smile. "I am Brother Joseph, my lady. I have the honor to bring the word of the Lord to these good people."

"I didn't know you had a priest here," Cymbra said, looking at Wolf.

He shrugged, as though it was of no account. "Brother Joseph is just passing through. It is a Norse tradition to give hospitality to travelers."

"I have been passing through for three years now," Brother Joseph said with a smile. "Lord Wolf is most generous—and patient—with his hospitality."

"Perhaps I always knew I would have a use for you," Wolf suggested with a grin. "Proceed, Brother Joseph. The night grows no younger."

The young monk nodded. Quietly, he said, "You must kneel."

They both did so, Cymbra still stunned by the sudden fulfillment of her wish. Had Wolf truly anticipated that this would be important to her and granted it without her even asking? Or was he simply astute enough to use her faith as one more way to bind her to him irrevocably?

"Holy Father," Brother Joseph said, "we beseech Your blessing upon this couple united in marriage. May You who gave Your only Son for the salvation of mankind shine Your great love upon this man and woman, light their way in this world and make their life together a gift of joy to one another and all who know them. In the name of the Father, the Son, and the Holy Ghost"—his hand moved above them in the sign of the cross—"I declare you husband and wife."

There was no containing the crowd then. They surged forward, the men hoisting Wolf on their shoulders as the women did the same with Cymbra. As the music resumed in a fury, they were carried around and around the tree until at last, breathless and laughing, the crowd deposited them in their seats at the high table. As others found their places, and the servants darted forward to fill cups and bowls, Wolf leaned over and covered Cymbra's hand with his own.

"Are you all right?"

Was she? She really didn't know. She was dazed and very uncertain. And yet . . . Her eyes drifted to the place on his jaw where her fist had landed. Again she felt a tremor of shock at her own behavior.

There was no mark but at the very least she must have stung his manly pride. Yet he had said nothing of it to her, offered no recrimination and inflicted no punishment. Dare she hope he thought her small attack in some way deserved?

Slowly, less sure of anything than she had ever been in her life, Cymbra nodded.

THERE WERE PROPRIETIES TO BE OBSERVED. PEOPLE expected certain things. Rituals were important, serving as they did to strengthen a community. Wolf reminded himself of that yet again. It didn't help. He was rock hard, his blood throbbed more fiercely than the music, and he burned with a fire that threatened to consume him.

Cymbra, by contrast, seemed to be enjoying herself. Dragon was being charming, curse him to an eternity of icebound hell. His brother had started in on yet another story; he appeared to have an endless supply of them. Had he not been born to a warrior, no doubt he would have been a skald.

Wolf had a sudden, unbidden glimpse of his brother as a storyteller, going from holding to holding, keeping alive the great sagas of their people. He wondered for just a moment if Dragon might really have preferred that life.

As for himself, he had never given any thought but to the life he had. A life of duty and responsibility, often harsh, sometimes outright savage. But for all that, a life not without its compensations.

The most obvious of which sat at his right side, attending to Dragon's tale, her lips slightly parted and her eyes rapt with interest. She looked perfectly content to remain there all night. That impression was confirmed a few minutes later when Dragon concluded his story, or tried to. At once, Cymbra asked, "What was the name of the giant who challenged Odin to race?" Truth be told, she had no particular interest in a story that under other circumstances would have genuinely enthralled her. Indeed, she could think of scarcely anything save the terrible danger to her brother and the equally momentous step she had just taken to try to allay it. But Dragon was unexpectedly kind, reminding her yet again of her own brother and the kindess Hawk had so often shown her. Reminding her, too, of how reluctant she was to submit herself to the man so rightly called Wolf, who now possessed absolute authority over her.

Dragon smiled at her gently, as though he sensed the direction of her thoughts and sought to soothe them. "Hrungnir, who was foolish enough to believe his steed faster than Odin's own Sleipnir, the most magnificent of stallions."

"Surely they must have had many adventures together. Will you tell us of them?"

"Well, there was the time Odin rescued a warrior named Hadding from his enemies. He wrapped Hadding in a cloak and took him up on the saddle in front of him. As they rode, Hadding peered out from between the folds and saw to his astonishment that they were galloping over the open sea, Sleipnir's hooves pounding the waves just as though they were stone."

"Extraordinary," Cymbra said. "Does Odin make it a habit to rescue warriors?"

"Those he favors. Those he does not are often favored by Frigg, Odin's wife. These two are generally at odds over something or other." Dragon cast a quick glance in his brother's direction and grinned broadly. "Of course, that's not unusual in marriages."

Wolf waved away the slave attempting to refill his drinking horn. He'd drunk little this night and all but ignored the lavish feast. Neither food nor drink would satisfy the appetite raging within him.

"I've always thought," he said, looking hard at Dragon, "that most of Odin and Frigg's problems come from interfering relatives."

"And I," Dragon shot back, "have always thought Odin doesn't appreciate Frigg enough. She is, after all, the most beautiful, most courageous, and most clever of women . . . of goddesses, that is." He leaned back in his chair, still smiling, and added, "Maybe she's just too much for him."

Cymbra frowned, finding all this talk of gods and goddesses difficult to follow. She gathered that Odin was supreme among the Norse deities, and she had been startled by the story of his death and rebirth with its obvious parallels to her own faith. But it seemed very odd for him to have a wife and for the two of them to have all-too human problems.

Then, too, she was struck by the exchange between Wolf and Dragon, redolent as it was of unspoken messages. She glanced from one brother to the other. Dragon appeared in high good humor although she felt beneath it the lingering pain of the wound responsible for his limp. She wondered what care he had received and if he would be willing to talk with her about it. But there was little time to think of that before she was caught by the hard intensity of Wolf's gaze.

A small shock ran through her. Throughout the feast she had deliberately kept her attention from him, focusing on anything and everything else in an effort to remain calm. Now, for the first time, she saw the mysterious hunger in him and the savage battle he was waging to contain it. A battle she also saw, all too clearly, that he was about to lose.

Wolf raised a hand. A servant materialized at his side. He gave instructions, and the man nodded before hurrying off. A moment later, Marta appeared.

"It is time, lady," she said to Cymbra.

There certainly was no point asking time for what but Cymbra was tempted, just briefly. Pride rescued her. She'd already delayed as long as she possibly could, encouraging Dragon to tell story after story. Not that they weren't fascinating, but all she'd really managed to do was heighten Wolf's impatience. Now, she would have to face that.

Her throat was very dry as she stood. For an awful moment, she feared her legs were too weak to hold her. She took a deep breath, fighting for calm, and moved away from the table. The crowd saw her and raised a lusty cheer, thumping their drinking horns loudly on the tables. Their ribald comments made her cheeks burn.

She stumbled slightly and might have fallen had Wolf not reached out a hand to steady her. Their eyes met. She saw the raw lust still in his but beneath it something else, stronger even, more enduring, something that made her breath come just a little easier.

She moved away and Marta was there with several other women, hurrying her along. Behind her the music soared.

Iron lamps filled with tallow and set on long, pointed tips stuck into the floor cast eerie shadows over the walls of Wolf's lodge. Shapes were distorted and too large.

Cymbra shivered as she finished using the water brought
for her to bathe and quickly dried herself.

She could still hear the laughter and excitement of the
crowd in the distance but inside this chamber of barbaric
luxury it was very quiet. The silence of the women, the
absence of any gentle banter or reassurance, reminded
Cymbra how much she was a stranger among them.

The covers of the vast bed were turned down and
sprinkled with the petals of wild roses. Sheaves of freshly
cut barley were twined around the roughly hewn posts.
Her clothes were taken away and she was left only in a diaphanous gown, not her own, embroidered at the hem and
collar with ancient runic symbols.

The other women took their leave, casting hooded
looks of speculation at her and at the bed. Marta remained
to comb out her hair.

"The gown is a gift, my lady I intended it for Kiirla
but it is too fine now for that."

"I don't understand. Why too fine?"

"She will not make as good a marriage as I had
hoped."

It took Cymbra a moment to understand what Marta
was saying. When she did, she turned in her seat and
looked up at the older woman. "You wanted Lord Wolf to
marry your daughter."

Marta shrugged. She continued brushing out
Cymbra's hair. The flames of the tallow lamps continued
to cast shadows. "I did and I didn't, lady. Certainly the
honor would be great, but she is my daughter and I love
her."

When Cymbra said nothing more, waiting her out,
Marta added, "You are young and far from home. Were
your mother here, she could . . . warn you. Perhaps prepare you, so far as it is possible to prepare."

She paused, came around in front of Cymbra, and

leaned down so that their eyes met. Marta's were wide in apparent sincerity yet curiously flat.

"He will hurt you, lady. All the women he lies with say it. He is built more like a stallion than a man and he cares not what pain he inflicts."

She straightened and resumed her brushing. "Why should he care? He is jarl and his word is law. No one will interfere with anything he does, not even if you scream loudly enough for all to hear."

"That's enough!" Cymbra jumped up, wrestled the comb from Marta's hand, and tossed it onto the table. "You are done here. Go."

The older woman's demeanor changed abruptly. She sneered at Cymbra. "Oh, yes, give orders, act the fine lady, but we all know what you are, nothing more than a thrall like Brita. If your brother weren't who he is, you'd have been taken already by every man here. The Lord Wolf has to marry you but he cares nothing for you. Nothing! You are less to him than dirt and that's how he will treat you."

She flounced out the door and slammed it behind her. Cymbra stood frozen in place, her whole body trembling. Slowly, she sank down, her legs giving way beneath her, until she was sitting on the floor, her arms wrapped around herself and her face buried against her knees.

Chapter

SIX

WOLF SHUT THE DOOR FIRMLY BEHIND his noisy, boisterous escort. He shoved the iron bar in place across it lest the drunken revelers prove to have more enthusiasm than good sense. A few of the more persistent remained outside, calling encouragement and lewd suggestions, but he ignored them.

He turned, his silvery eyes scanning the chamber. When he failed to see his bride, his first thought was that she had fled. Anger was already surging through him when a faint movement drew his eyes to the woman huddled in the shadows.

"Odin's blood," he muttered and started toward her. Cymbra looked up, the pale oval of her face framed in a torrent of silken hair, and pressed her lips tightly together. He needed no great sensitivity to know that she was fighting a desperate battle against raw fear.

"Cymbra," he murmured, worry overtaking the hard, thrumming lust he would not have thought anything could supplant. Lifting her carefully, offering a silent prayer of thanks when she did not resist, he carried her to the bed and sat down with her on his lap.

For a time, he did nothing more, merely rocked her as gently as he would a child, had life offered him the opportunity to do such a thing. His big hands felt clumsy when he began to stroke her back but she relaxed a little under his touch, and that encouraged him.

Finally, she looked up, met his eyes bravely, and said, "I'm an idiot."

Her statement so shocked him that he laughed, the sound itself a further shock. He was consumed with hunger for her, randier than he could remember being since boyhood. Such hot, driving need had nothing to do with laughter. Or did it? Thinking on it, perplexed, he squeezed her a little tighter. "No, you're not. It's natural to be nervous."

That had to be it. She was a virgin bride confronted by a husband she hardly knew and had every reason to think was an enemy. She was bound to be frightened. But then, damn it, why hadn't Marta and the others said something to reassure her? They were all married women, Marta herself the widow of the very warrior who had trained the young Wolf. He'd sent them with her precisely so they'd do whatever it was women did under such circumstances. Distantly, he thought of Marta pushing her daughter his way a time or two, but he had never given that the remotest consideration. Perhaps she had, though, in which case . . .

"Did your mother ever speak to you of these things?" he asked gruffly.

Against his shoulder, Cymbra shook her head. "She died when I was born."

"Your nurse?"

"Miriam never married. She doesn't . . . think much of men."

She took a breath, steadying herself. "But you mustn't

think me ignorant. I am a healer. The workings of the body are no mystery."

"Perhaps not." He didn't believe that for a moment. Despite whatever occasional kindness she'd shown the sick, he would have bet coin enough to build a dragon ship that she didn't have the remotest idea of what really passed between a man and a woman. Still, this didn't seem like the best time to tell her that. Better she discover it in the doing.

"That's good," he crooned, stroking her hair, drawing her a little closer. She gave a small sigh and snuggled on his lap. He managed not to groan but it was a near thing.

"So much has happened . . ." she said.

Wolf lifted his eyes to the ceiling, fighting for control, praying for patience. Women seemed to need to talk under circumstances where any man would have the sense to keep his mouth shut, or find a better use for it.

All the same, she was his wife. He had made promises to her before Ulfrich and the others. And she had made him laugh. That had to count for something, so unusual was it. He tilted her chin up, requiring her to look at him. "Don't tell me you feel confused and frightened just because your entire life has been turned upside down and you find yourself in a situation where you never imagined you could possibly be?"

She blinked in surprise, which pleased him. He liked the idea of being as unexpected to her as she was to him. It righted the balance between them.

"Well, yes," Cymbra said softly, "as a matter of fact that's exactly how I feel."

"What an odd coincidence. So do I."

She straightened up slightly and stared at him. "You do? How can that be?"

His reluctance to talk forgotten, he found himself doing exactly that. Ideas he had just barely thought, never spoken, took word. "No one around here talks about peace. Even my brother, who has wits beyond any man I've ever met, seems to think war is inevitable. But I got the notion things ought to be different, and try though I did, I couldn't ignore it. So here I am, a warrior turned would-be peacemaker. You have to admit that sounds a little odd, and as though it weren't enough, now I find myself married . . ." his eyes swept over the length of her, "to you."

"What's wrong with being married to me?"

He started to laugh again but caught himself quickly. A man didn't want to do that kind of thing too often. "Let's just say you affect me strangely."

She shrugged lightly. "Oh, well, as to that, you do the same to me."

She shouldn't have said that. He'd been all right up until then, holding on to his self-control, mustering patience, trying his damnedest to give her whatever she seemed to need. But now . . .

He looked down again, his gaze drifting over pale, rose-hued skin clearly visible through the sheer fabric, sweetly delicate curves and long, perfectly formed limbs. His hands shook with the need to touch her . . . all of her . . . now, this instant, without any more of the maddening delay made suddenly intolerable by the knowledge that she desired him, too.

He fell back across the bed, drawing her with him. Cymbra gave a little gasp at their sudden change of position and tried to sit up. Wolf rolled atop her, covering her completely with his hard, lean body.

"Hush," he murmured, his mouth tracing the delicate curve of her jaw, down her slender throat to the sweet hollow between her collarbones. Blood pounded in his veins. Hot, driving lust surged through him, making him heedless of all else. "Everything will be all right . . . let me . . ."

He ran out of words. If he'd tried to continue, he would have been reduced to grunts. Swiftly, holding his weight above her, he clasped her face between his hands and took her mouth, parting her lips for the hard, driving thrust of his tongue. He was going too fast, knew it, couldn't stop.

The touch, sight, scent of her, the breathless little gasps she gave, overwhelmed him. He'd held himself in check too long, wanted her too much, and his control was sizzling away like water on hot stone.

He grasped handfuls of the diaphanous gown and pulled it up, baring her exquisite legs, the nest of downy curls between her sleek thighs, the chalice of her hips, her tiny waist. . . . His vision blurred, a red mist moving over all. She twisted beneath him, pushing against his shoulders, and tore her mouth from his. "No, wait—"

He heard her but from a distance and against the great roar of his blood surging through him. The words were mere sounds, meaningless. The Wolf was not to be denied.

The delicate fabric tore as he yanked it over her head. Heedless, he tossed the remnants onto the floor and ran his hands over her in blatant, raw possession. "Mine," he rasped, and pushed a heavily muscled thigh between her legs, forcing her open to him.

He was reaching to free the hard, throbbing length of his shaft from the fawn-soft trousers when awareness of what he was doing suddenly washed over him like an icy wave. He froze, staring down at her pale face and fear-wide eyes.

Shock knifed down his spine, so great as to cause the hair on the nape of his neck to rise. Never in his life had he lost control like this with a woman, and she his wife and a virgin. If ever gentle care was needed . . .

And he knew all that, understood it to the marrow of his bones, yet still had been swept away by lust unlike any he had ever known. Or at least had come very close to that.

Truth be told, for just a moment he would have given almost anything to be in bed with a practiced whore. The thought passed as quickly as it had come. As did the next, darker still, the wish that she really was only a captive, a slave of no account, even though he never used such women.

But she wasn't, and he wouldn't have wanted that for her under any circumstances, much less merely for the swift satisfaction of his savage need.

He pressed his forehead against the pillow beside her and groaned. She lay very still, small and fragile, so vulnerable against his vast strength. With a deep, shuddering breath, he forced himself to move to his side but he couldn't bear to let go of her entirely, and drew her into his arms.

She trembled and brought her legs tightly together but didn't try to pull away. Despite her fear, honor refused to let her forget that she had made promises to this man. She had accepted the blessing of the Church. She was his wife and there were things she simply couldn't shirk.

He was breathing very hard, his massive chest rising and falling rapidly. Tension radiated from him. Slowly, Cymbra lifted her head and dared a peek at her husband.

His eyes were closed but he certainly didn't look at peace. On the contrary, his features were tightly drawn, and a pulse beat in the hollow of his lean, burnished cheek. Her gaze swept lower, past the thick column of his neck and broad sweep of his shoulders, and a very strange sensation stirred within her.

The times she'd seen him bare-chested and the one glimpse by the pool had merely whetted her curiosity. Astonished though she was by her feelings, she was too inherently honest to deny them. Her gaze drifted down the long, muscled length of his torso to—

Cymbra's cheeks flamed. With some difficulty, she murmured, "I . . . uh . . . thought you didn't find me attractive."

Wolf opened his eyes a slit, followed the direction of her gaze, and winced. "I told you that, didn't I?"

She nodded solemnly.

"I lied."

Cymbra sat up a little farther, acutely conscious of her nudity. She was blushing from head to toe and was grateful for the concealment her hair provided. "Why?"

He sighed, a deep rumbling she felt all along her body. "I thought it would make you feel safer."

Her last fear that Marta's horrible words might be true vanished. He was a proud, strong, even arrogant man bred in a violent world and accustomed to absolute obedience. But he had never hurt her, despite ample opportunity and—she admitted deep inside—at least some provocation.

And he was her husband.

Tentatively, she touched the tips of her fingers to his chest. He stared at her, not breathing. Emboldened by his stillness, she laid her palm against him. A frisson of shock pulsed through her at the sensation of rock hardness covered by warm, smooth skin.

"Cymbra . . ."

She heard the warning rasp in his voice, but far from being discouraged, it only emboldened her further. "It doesn't seem fair," she murmured.

He fought for breath, a fascinating sight made all the more so when she noticed that his hands were clenched into fists digging into the bed. "What doesn't?"

"Your being dressed and my being . . . not."

CYMBRA'S HEAD ARCHED BACK AGAINST THE PILLOWS, her hair spilling in disarray around her. Her body bowed as though drawn taut in the hands of a master archer. A delicate blue vein in her throat throbbed. She cried out, half sob, half scream, and dug her fingers into the massive shoulders of the man who loomed above her, a dark, powerful, naked presence dominating her with ruthless intensity.

His hands moved over her breasts, the callused thumbs rubbing against her distended nipples, filling her with a terrible, burning ache for something she could not define. She writhed helplessly when he suckled her, drawing hard, then laving each nipple with his tongue before his teeth closed on it, bringing her again to the very edge of pleasure-pain. Never had she imagined her body capable of such sensation—or such terrible need.

And he had only begun.

Wolf raised his head and looked with grim satisfaction at the beauty beneath him. Through the hot, surging roar of his hunger, he dimly thought that this was fairness, a redressing of the imbalance that had existed between them from the first moment he'd glimpsed her in the cell at Holyhood. He had not drawn a free breath since. Astonished as he was by her power over him, he also deeply resented it.

Before this night was done, their positions would be reversed. His lust would be satisfied or at least so eased as to be the nearest thing, whereas hers— He smiled and slid his hands down her sleek flanks, cupping her buttocks, squeezing, and feeling her muscles clench in response.

He would leave her so dazed with pleasure, so primed for arousal, that she would be utterly willing, pliant, and obedient. Exactly as she should be. So resolved, he moved farther down her body, savoring every exquisite inch, and lifted her to his mouth.

Cymbra gasped. Even through the molten haze of pleasure he had unleashed, she was stunned by the sudden daring of his caress. She couldn't believe he would touch her there . . . and in that way. The intimacy of it shattered her even as pleasure mounted to unparalleled heights.

He probed her lightly with his tongue, drawing out her most sensitive nub, and stroked her relentlessly as she twisted helplessly in his hands, her satiny skin covered with a dewy flush. Not satisfied with that, he delved farther, probed deeper, maddening her with his touch.

His claiming of her body, so absolute and irrevocable, shocked her deeply. He left her no place to retreat, no way to deny him anything. She fought to do so, instinctively seeking to keep some part of herself intact, but still he pursued her.

A harsh groan broke from him, relief mingling with victory, as he was rewarded with the nectar of her arousal. Swiftly, he moved up her trembling body, covering her mouth with his own. He kissed her deeply, repeatedly, his hands moving over her, spreading her thighs wide, positioning her for him.

Cymbra felt the probing pressure, massively thick, steel hard. Instinctively, she tried to pull back, but he was holding her by the hips, preventing her from moving except by his will. She gazed up into his gleaming eyes and knew that he would wait no longer.

"Hold on to me," he ordered gutturally and released her just long enough to place her hands on his shoulders. The solidness of his strength was oddly comforting to her. She clung to him, left with no choice but to trust that he would not hurt her too much, as the pressure continued to build. A burning sensation filled her. She cried out but did not let go of him.

Wolf's features were harshly contorted, his breath coming fast, as he fought to hold on to the last shreds of his control. His warrior's spirit screamed for relief.

The exquisite anguish of restraint threatened to consume him as he forced himself to move slowly, entering her little by little, giving her at least some chance to adjust to his size. When he felt the barrier of her virginity, he gazed down into her eyes, pools of indigo wide with fear

but lit, too, by what he prayed was the dawning of fulfillment.

"You are mine, Cymbra," he said harshly. "Never
forget it."

He took her mouth, swallowing her scream at the
same time as he tore through her maidenhead. She struck
out instinctively, her fists pounding against him, but he
held her fast, waiting until the initial shock passed.

"Easy," he murmured, "easy . . . hush, love, it will be
all right." He kissed her tears away, whispering words of
comfort, hardly knowing what he said, until he felt the
slight relaxation of her body easing around him.

Slowly, watching her intently, he moved within her
but not thrusting, not yet. The hard, broad tip of him
flexed, stroking a place within her she had never known
existed, and the world came undone. After the initial
pain, there was nothing except wave after wave of sensation, carrying her higher and higher, the crest seemingly
endless.

She cried out, her hips lifting even as her body tightened, drawing him even deeper within her. Wolf's harsh
shout joined her own. The exquisite milking sensation
undid him. He erupted within her in a hot, surging jet
that seemed to go on forever.

When the spasms of his release finally lessened, he
was slumped against her, his lungs working like bellows,
his body sweat-slicked, the smell of sex lingering in the air
around them. Slowly, Wolf raised himself on his forearms.
He stared down at his wife.

Cymbra's eyes were closed, the thick lashes fanning
against her delicately flushed cheeks. Her lips, slightly
swollen from his impassioned kisses, curved in a small
smile. She looked supremely . . . content.

He groaned and flopped over onto his back, any further movement being impossible. Long moments passed
before he was aware of much of anything save the utter sa-

tiation of his body. He looked at Cymbra curled at his side. The silken curtain of her hair alternately concealed and revealed her perfection, but hardly offered her much in the way of warmth.

Lest she become chilled, he used what little strength had returned to pull the covers over them both. She murmured her thanks and snuggled closer to him. At the touch of her silken limbs, or perhaps it was the honeysuckle scent of her skin, or maybe the brush of her breast against his arm did it, or —Whatever the cause, his manhood stirred in instant response, tentatively but with obvious enthusiasm. Wolf groaned, torn between astonished wariness and reluctant pride.

Cymbra stiffened. "Is something wrong?" She couldn't meet his gaze, swept as she was by mingled shock and embarrassment at her unbridled response. But still she was his wife and must be mindful of his welfare. Especially since he had been so thoroughly attentive to her own.

"Not at all," her husband murmured. What could possibly be wrong? Never mind that his grand plan showed every sign of having failed, at least so far as giving him back the control he had always taken for granted before this earthly goddess came into his life. He was hardly the sort to give up; the battle between them was only just begun.

Yet neither could he give vent to the hot, surging lust that, incredibly, burned anew in his veins. She was too untried, too delicate. If he took her again before she had time to recover from this first joining, it would be nothing more than abuse.

With a half-stifled groan, he rolled out of the bed. There was some satisfaction in his wife's quick, wide-eyed glance in his direction before she promptly ducked her head back down, but it really didn't help much. Smothering a sigh that would have shaken the rafters had he uttered it, he went to the basin of water left out on the table, dampened a soft cloth, and returned to the bed.

As he pulled back the covers, Cymbra tried to grab hold of them. "What are you doing? Don't—"

"Be quiet," he said gruffly and sat beside her. Ignoring her startled response, he shoved the furs to the foot of the bed and forced a hand between her legs, which she had tightly clenched. "I want to be sure you've stopped bleeding."

She opened her mouth to protest further but before she could do so he applied just enough pressure to her knees to force her legs apart and quickly placed the cloth gently against the juncture of her thighs. She had bled, and he who had waded through rivers of gore on un-counted battlefields winced to see it, but it had stopped. As had all thoughts of taking her again so soon.

He tossed the cloth onto the table, pulled the covers over her, and got back into bed. She remained very stiff, shocked no doubt by his frank speech and action. She needed to learn that he would have his way with her, for she was no more—or less—than his property. But in the meantime . . .

Wolf sighed and gathered his wife to him, ignoring her efforts to hold herself apart. Although sleep beckoned, he forced himself to stay awake, gently stroking her back until she relaxed.

Her breathing had grown slow and deep when he reflected that merely getting married had been a great deal more trouble than he would ever have expected. However, now that he had Cymbra safely wedded—and bedded—that was bound to change.

She was a gently reared girl, schooled in the duties of a lady. After tonight, she'd make a nice, quiet, docile wife, exactly as he had expected. He was quite confident of that, he told himself groggily. There was no doubt about it. No doubt at all.

Chapter

SEVEN

MARRIAGE," WOLF SAID GRIMLY, "IS SUP-
posed to be for a man's convenience. A wife
exists to ease his burdens, keep his home,
and give him children. There's nothing un-
reasonable about any of that, is there?"

Thus appealed to, Dragon looked thoughtful for a
moment. "I suppose it's worked out that way a time or
two. But from what I can see, generally it's the women
who call the tune."

"That's ridiculous," Wolf snapped. "Men are stronger
and wiser. We are calm, capable of reason, not ruled by
emotion. Obviously, the gods meant us to be in charge." As
though to emphasize his conviction, he swung his long
sword high over his head and brought it straight down
at Dragon.

His brother grinned, leaped back, and parried with
his own weapon. The clash of steel rang across the training field. Here and there, men stopped their activities to
watch this battle between two supremely powerful and
well-matched opponents.

"Mayhap," Dragon said, his breathing little altered

despite his exertion, "but the average man left to his own devices goes from woman to woman, enjoying himself. He doesn't worry particularly about the roof over his head, or even so much about the crops in his fields, or indeed whether or not he has any fields."

He slashed the air in front of Wolf as steel struck steel again. "If he wants to pick up and go adventuring, he goes. He enjoys his life and doesn't concern himself too much with the future. But let a man get a wife and all that changes. He's got responsibilities then and she damn well makes sure he knows it. The bull is yoked, whether he wants to be or not."

Dragon shook his head decisively and thrust at Wolf again. "No, marriage is a woman's creation. She gets a man to protect and provide for her and her children. A man gets—what?"

"Children he knows are his own?" Wolf suggested, parrying his brother smoothly. Offhand, he couldn't think of anything else.

Dragon laughed. "Aye, they might be, but I've known many a wench who didn't let her bed grow cold when her husband was away, and if she happened to get a babe in the bargain—" He plunged again, from a different angle, aiming to slice Wolf's legs out from under him.

Wolf grinned at the strategy and moved almost too swiftly to be seen, coming up behind Dragon and forcing him to turn.

"Who do you think dreamed up all those stories about gods sneaking into unsuspecting females' beds in the dead of night or waylaying them in forest glens?" Dragon asked as he swung at Wolf's head. "No man ever thought of that one, let me tell you. Women are damn improvising when they need be."

"Do you never think to marry then?" Wolf asked as they locked swords.

"Me? Perish the thought. Oh, I wouldn't mind a quiver of sons, but I need no marriage for that, only a willing woman or two or three." His grin flashed white against burnished skin. "And there's no lack of those."

"You said yourself, you wouldn't know the get was yours."

"I can count to nine as well as you. Besides, a man's got to know how to keep control of a woman, not give her an opportunity—or a need—to go wandering off."

Wolf's eyes hardened. "And when a woman's beautiful as the morning, tempting as a river of gold?"

"Then the man better be damn good with a sword, brother, damn good indeed."

Wolf grunted, dug his feet into the soft ground, and knocked Dragon off balance. His brother landed hard on the dark earth and shot him a rueful smile. "Not bad, Lord of Sciringesheal, not bad at all. But shouldn't marriage have dulled your sword just a little?"

Wolf sighed, sheathed his blade, and offered a hand to help Dragon up. They had dueled often over the years and stood even in number of wins. Their conflict was saved for the practice field; in all other matters brother stood stalwartly beside brother.

Wolf trusted Dragon as he would never trust another man, and he knew that trust was returned in full. Still, he was glad their combat was over for the moment. He was worried about the wound Dragon had suffered and its aftermath.

"Not this marriage," he said as they walked to the barrel of cool well water set in the shade. Wolf took a ladle, poured it over his sweat-streaked head, and sighed. "I swear, she hasn't missed a chance to irk me."

"Your sweet, gentle bride?" Dragon laughed. "But I see her everywhere, brother, interested in everything, inquiring about all manner of things. She obviously takes her responsibility to run your household seriously. I swear, in the scant two days you've been married, she's been in every corner of this stronghold."

Wolf grimaced. His brother spoke the truth. Cymbra was a veritable whirlwind, seemingly busy everywhere at once, now in the weaving shed, now in the dairy, back and forth to the kitchens, the dying vats, the smithy, and on and on and on. The woman didn't stop moving from dawn to dusk. And she had an opinion about everything, a suggestion, a different notion of how this or that should be done.

Worse yet, she seemed to need no help from him at all. She had only to murmur a few words and people stumbled over each other to carry out her wishes. Well, not all people. Marta looked like she'd swallowed a mouthful of brine whenever she was near Cymbra. Some of the other women, those he vaguely knew to be Marta's friends, seemed to be following her lead.

A frown darkened Wolf's face. The last thing he needed was a war among the women. The mere thought of that sort of thing made any sane man yearn for a long sea voyage.

He'd heard about an island found only a few years before, west of the Irish Islands, a wild place with mountains that ran with hot mud, barren landscapes that appeared not of this earth, immense mineral streams bigger than any seen in the Norse lands, but also with beautiful fjords and bays, and rich earth for growing or pasture. People were settling there already and more were likely to go. Not only that, but there were rumors—whispers really coming from wild-eyed Irish monks—of an even vaster land yet farther to the west, beyond the setting sun, a land they said had no end.

A sensible man could take off if he liked, but a leader didn't have that luxury. He had to do what was best for all. And that, Wolf decided, was to stop this problem with his bride before it could go any further.

"She's just settling in," he murmured. "That's all it is."

Dragon laughed. "Who are you trying to convince, me or yourself?"

Wolf's only answer was a grunt. He strode off in the direction he'd last seen Cymbra, only to discover that she was nowhere to be found.

"I have no idea, my lord," Marta said with cold pleasure when Wolf finally broke down and asked her if she knew where his wife had gone. Emboldened by his obvious annoyance, she added, "If you don't mind my saying, the Lady Cymbra seems a very headstrong individual, perhaps the result of an overly privileged upbringing."

Wolf did not appreciate hearing any criticism of the woman whose behavior, after all, reflected most directly on him. But he had to admit, if only to himself, that Marta might have a point. Cymbra's brother appeared to have given her virtually free rein to live as she pleased. Perhaps it wasn't really her fault that she didn't defer as she properly should, but she would have to learn. And damn fast.

He hurried to the stables, determined to find his wayward wife.

L OOK," CYMBRA SAID. "HOREHOUND." SHE EASED THE small plant from the earth, keeping its roots intact, and nestled it in the palm of her hand. "I had no idea I'd find it here. It's wonderful for coughs and inflammations of the lung." Smiling, she carefully tucked it away in her sack along with the several dozen other plants, mosses, and lichens she had already found.

"It's amazing how much you know," Brita said shyly. After several hours in Cymbra's company, helping her find and collect herbs, the slave had lost some of her reticence. "My mother had a little skill at healing, but nothing compared to what you know. How ever did you learn so much?"

Cymbra hesitated. As always when speaking of such things, she chose her words with care. "I became interested in healing when I was a child. My brother was very kind and arranged teachers for me."

"You were fortunate. I, too, had a brother. . . ." Brita looked away quickly.

Pain rose in Cymbra, the pain of loss, of fear, of anguish almost too great to be borne. She forced herself to breathe slowly and steadily, not fighting it for she knew by hard experience that there was no point, but separating herself from it, erecting a shield that allowed her to acknowledge the pain without being crushed by it.

In the midst of that pain, she had a fleeting thought of the message Wolf must surely send soon, if he had not already, informing her brother of her whereabouts. She was torn, wanting to reassure Hawk of her welfare and having him see her thus, yet dreading the confrontation to come between husband and brother. A shiver moved down her spine even as she turned away from her own anguish to soothe Brita's.

"I'm so sorry."

The gentle touch of her hand on Brita's startled the girl. They knelt together on the mossy hillside beyond the keep. Around them, the day glittered, bright with sunlight, soft with the balmy breeze of summer. Brita blinked hard and rubbed a hand across her cheeks. "It was a long time ago now."

"How long?"

"I was taken in my twelfth year." As though a dam had broken and released its torrent, she could no longer avoid speaking of what had happened to her. "My family lived near the coast of Ireland, beside a place we call the

Mountains of the Morne. They aren't as big as the mountains here, not at all, but we thought of them as mountains all the same."

Her eyes filled with memories both sweet and savage. "We'd heard rumors about the Norsemen but none of us had ever seen them until they came of a sudden just two days after Easter. The men fought but there was nothing anyone could do."

A heart-wrenching sigh escaped her. "I don't even know if any of my family survived. The last I saw was the smoke rising from our burning homes. I was taken many days to a large town and put in a pen there with many other captives, then sold. Eventually, I was brought here. That was five years ago."

She paused and looked at Cymbra. "There have been times when I thought of dying but our faith forbids it. I was a sheltered girl and just presumed that I would have a home, a husband, children. Never would I have believed that instead I would be a slave, a thing of no account, to just be . . . used without thought or care." Her lips trembled. She lowered her head quickly. "Forgive me, lady, I did not mean to burden you."

Cymbra did not feel burdened. She felt enraged by what had happened to Brita. As well as she knew that the world was filled with suffering, it was impossible for her simply to accept it. Her spirit rebelled. She had no choice but to fight with everything in her.

"There is nothing for you to be forgiven, Brita. Rather it is for others to ask your forgiveness." She put an arm around the girl and hugged her gently. But there was no gentleness in Cymbra's silent resolve that the situation would not be allowed to remain as it was.

She was just considering how she would speak to her husband about it when the sound of hoofbeats interrupted her thoughts. Both women looked up to see a large, black stallion bearing down on them at high speed. Brita jumped to her feet and drew Cymbra with her. "Run for the keep, lady! I will try—"

But her protectiveness was both misplaced and futile, as both women realized a moment later when the rider came into view. "Wolf," Cymbra said, relieved yet also annoyed that he would frighten them so.

Really, what was the man thinking? He had barely spoken a word to her in two days, had hardly even acknowledged her existence since their wedding night, despite her valiant efforts to be a good wife. So she had resolved as she said her marriage vows and so she was determined would be the case no matter what difficulties she might have to overcome. Not only was she sworn before God to do so, but on the success of this marriage might well rest the hope of peace between their peoples. She could not possibly fail, yet as she watched the Scourge of the Saxons come riding down on her like a thundercloud, she could not help but wonder if perhaps she had taken on too daunting a task. Normally she was the most even-tempered of women, but something about her Norse husband brought out feelings she had never known and threatened to shatter the serenity she still sought as a familiar shroud.

Wolf looked from his errant wife to the slave at her side. He pointed at Brita. "Go."

The girl paled and her whole body shook but, incredibly, she did not obey instantly. Instead, she looked at Cymbra. "Lady?"

Without taking her gaze from the infuriated male astride the immense horse, Cymbra said softly, "It's all right. I just want to have a word with my husband. You go on."

Brita dared a last, frightened glance at the mighty jarl and hurried off. Wolf glowered at his wife, the slave's disobedience diminishing to nothing as he took in Cymbra's glowing beauty, the fire in her eyes, and her unmistakable look of annoyance.

His gaze narrowed. She was annoyed? *She*? Odin's blood, what right did she have to be annoyed about anything? Hadn't he been the soul of gentleness and consideration, denying himself these past two days to avoid hurting her again before she was healed? Hadn't he suffered mightily, lying awake beside her at night as though stretched out on a rack? To the point where he could scarcely concentrate on his duties and was questioning his own sanity because he could think of nothing but her?

She was annoyed?

He swung out of the saddle in a single, lithe motion, hooked the reins over a low-hanging branch, and advanced on her. To his satisfaction, she took a quick step back, but only a small one. Hands on her hips, she glared at him.

"You're trampling the plants I was about to collect."

He stared at her dumbfounded. She was talking, and he could hear her plainly, but she made no sense. She should have been doing anything possible to placate him, instead of rattling on about—"Plants?"

Summoning patience, Cymbra explained. "There is no herb garden. I looked, I really did, and I can't find any sign that there's ever been one. So it has to be started, and these plants"—she gestured to the sack on the ground beside her—"are a beginning."

She wanted a garden? She had come out of the fortress unguarded, alone except for a female slave, and without having first secured his permission, because she wanted a *garden*.

He took hold of her shoulders and shook her hard. "This is not Holyhood, wife, and you are not the pampered sister of an overly indulgent brother who damn well should have known better. This is a hard land and we are a hard people. Your little luxuries and privileges are a thing of the past. You will learn to do without them, as you will also learn to—"

He was about to instruct his wife in the absolute necessity of obeying him at all times and in all ways when she stared at him blankly and, to his utter astonishment, burst out laughing.

"Luxuries?" Cymbra repeated. She knew she was being rude to laugh but this was just so blatantly, typically, mule-headedly male that she couldn't contain herself. "You think a garden is a luxury? A garden, at least the kind I have in mind, is an absolute necessity if people are to be healthy."

She gestured down at the sack. "The plants are God's blessing upon the earth, proof that He truly cares for His children and wants us to be well."

When her husband failed to respond with the interest she felt he ought to have shown, Cymbra faltered slightly. She was extremely aware of his powerful hands on her shoulders. He had stopped shaking her after scarcely a moment but he was glaring at her most fiercely. Perhaps he just didn't understand. . . .

"I told you I am a healer," she said gently. "I have my medicine chest and am grateful for it, but eventually the supplies in it will have to be replaced as they are used up. These plants and others I expect to find are essential to that."

"You think to dose people here?" When her silence confirmed his suspicion, it was his turn to laugh. He let go of her, threw back his head, and roared. Birds scattered from the overhanging branches. His horse started and pawed the ground nervously.

Grinning broadly, he gazed at his naïve little wife. Damn, but she was beautiful standing there in the golden sunlight, her hair only thinly covered by a veil, her skin satiny smooth and begging to be touched.

Sternly, he reminded himself of his duty. She was only a woman and a stranger at that; he would have to explain things to her very clearly. "We are not weak like the Saxons who need such cosseting. Our remedies are few—fire on a wound if it won't heal, knife to a limb if it must come off—but sufficient for us. We don't expect to live to old age, indeed the thought horrifies us. A man seeks to die with his sword in his hand so that he may enter Valhalla. Anything else is what we call a 'straw death,' unnatural and the path to extinction."

Color flooded Cymbra's cheeks. His callousness horrified her, but it also confirmed what she had noticed in her two days of exploration. The people of Sciringesheal did look robustly healthy for the most part, but that worried rather than reassured her. It suggested that anyone who was not in peak health simply perished.

"And what about a woman suffering in childbirth or an ailing child?" she demanded. "Do they just give up and die? What about those who do live to an old age even if they do not want to? Are they denied comfort in their final days? I can't believe that all your people are so ignorant and cruel!"

Indeed, she knew better, for Brother Chilton had told her of Norse women, crones he called them, who he claimed consorted with the devil to brew potions of great power. Although she would never have said so to him, Cymbra suspected he had misunderstood what the women were about and that they were merely healers like herself. But there were none such as that here. Perhaps it was because the Wolf's keep was so purely a male domain, with the women relegated to positions of servitude.

"I am a healer," she said again stubbornly. "I cannot ignore the suffering of others." Although she held her head high and regarded him steadily, inside Cymbra quaked. She could not imagine what she would do if her husband forbade her the pursuit of her life's calling. If she was forced to live among these people, to feel their pain without being allowed to help them, she would shrivel and die.

Slowly, Wolf surveyed her. He could see this was very important to her although he didn't understand why. He supposed it had something to do with her overly tender nature—the same nature that had prompted her to take the insanely stupid step of entering the cell with him and the others in order to help them.

He remembered that, seeing her as she had been then, and acknowledged the great courage it had taken for her to act as she did. Courage he could not help but admire. Now that he thought of it, perhaps it wasn't such a bad thing for a woman to be so caring. There might even be some benefit to it.

"I suppose there would be no harm in your caring for the women and children." He surprised himself, making such a concession so quickly, but it was a small thing really. They were weaker and not expected to have the same strength or stamina as warriors.

Cymbra felt relieved but was far from satisfied. Silently, she vowed that before too long her arrogant brute of a husband would not only acknowledge her contribution to the welfare of his people—all his people, men included—but would thank her for it.

"It's a beginning," she said, and when he frowned she added quickly, "I will need an assistant."

Wolf rolled his eyes. Whatever else she was, his wife was not timid about getting what she wanted. He wondered suddenly what it would feel like to be the object of her desire and almost groaned when he instantly hardened in response.

"An assistant?"

"That's right. Someone to help me gather herbs, prepare medicine, care for patients." Cymbra pretended to think. "It would be much easier, of course, if I could find someone who already knows something about healing. Let's see . . ." Her face lit. "Brita told me that her mother was a healer in Ireland. She would be perfect." That was exaggerating what Brita had said, but under the circumstances Cymbra wasn't about to quibble.

Wolf shrugged. He gave his slaves no thought and had virtually no contact with them. They might as well have been invisible to him. "You are mistress here, the directing of the household is your affair. Do as you like."

The glowing smile she bestowed on him made his heart lurch and his body harden even further. It occurred to him that they were alone, some distance from the town and the keep, and that the two days just past should have been ample time for her to heal. At least he hoped like hell that they had been because he wasn't going to be able to wait any longer.

"You know, wife," he said as he advanced on her, "it is much easier to wring concessions from a man when he is in a pleasant frame of mind. In the future, you might remember that."

His sudden change of manner, and the light that had sprung up in his silvery eyes, surprised Cymbra. She didn't know what to make of either.

There was no escaping the fact that her husband was an extraordinarily handsome man. He possessed immense strength tempered by grace, and when he smiled, as he was doing now, he fair stole her breath away. She had an all but irresistible desire to touch him, to trace the hard, chiseled lines of his face, caress the thick strands of his ebony hair, measure the breadth of his shoulders and trail her fingers down his granite chest to—

Cymbra flushed and reached down for the sack. She clutched it in front of her as though it might offer some scant protection, not from him but from the extraordinary waywardness of her thoughts.

Wolf's smile deepened. He reached out a large, sinewy

hand and took hold of the sack. Cymbra refused to let go of it. A tug-of-war ensued, one-sided to be sure and of foregone conclusion. Steadily, relentlessly, the Wolf pulled his wife toward him.

"Perhaps you'd like me to show you what's in here," she ventured nervously. "Each plant is unique. Their properties vary tremendously. Why, I could spend hours just explaining to you how—"

"Be quiet." Wolf closed his arms around her, not harshly but preventing any possibility of escape, tipped back her head, and claimed her mouth with ruthless thoroughness. He had thought to dominate her, to bend her to his will, but the moment his lips touched hers, his intent changed drastically. He wanted only to lose himself in her, to know again the incredible sense of completion she had given him on their wedding night, and to bring her to the same.

Swiftly, allowing her no chance to protest, he drew her down to the moss-draped ground. Her sack was laid aside, her mantle swiftly following. He kissed her brow, the curves of her cheeks, the delicate line of her jaw, his hands wandering at will over her, tangling in the thick mass of her chestnut hair, stroking the high, firm curves of her breasts, sliding down to grasp her tunic and bare her long, slender limbs.

Cymbra cried out softly. He meant to bed her right here and now, where there *was* no actual bed and where anyone might come along at any moment. Worse, she couldn't find it in her heart to object. On the contrary, after two long days of being without his touch, she was on fire for him, eager to experience again the delights he had shown her.

She pulled at his tunic, trying to get it up over his head. When he obliged her, baring his powerful chest, she gave a sigh of pure pleasure and pressed her palms against

him, feeling the crisp, tickling sensation of the dark hair
that spanned the great distance between his flat, male nipples before tapering down in a thin line that vanished beneath his trousers.

Her senses whirled as she refused to let herself think,
or doubt, or hesitate in any way. She had waited long
enough for him to regain his male stamina and who knew
how long she would have to wait again? Best to avail herself of the moment while she could.

Wolf grunted in surprise at her eagerness but wasted
no time taking advantage of it. Her gown laced down the
side. He made a brief, halfhearted attempt to undo the
laces, gave up promptly, and ripped them apart. Her scent
and heat enveloped him. Clasping her breasts in his big
hands, he squeezed lightly, moving from one to the other,
suckling the rose-hued nipples that tightened at his
slightest touch. At the same time, he thrust his iron-hard
thigh between hers, pressing against the center of her
womanhood.

Far in the back of his mind, he knew that he should go
slowly. She was still so new to the act and he hated the idea
of hurting her again. He prayed for patience as he reached
down between her legs, his fingers probing through the
silken nest of curls, stroking between the delicate folds. A
heartfelt groan broke from him when he found her already
hot and wet, ready for him. Later, he told himself, he
would think about the meaning of that. For now, he could
not think at all.

Freeing his engorged length, he hesitated just at the
entrance of her, gazing down into her beautiful, flushed
face. Her eyes were smoky with desire, her mouth curved
in a smile of unmistakable delight. A surge of tenderness
washed through him, different from yet somehow allied
to the hot, driving passion that had him nearly mindless.
He was vividly aware of her not merely as a woman, not

even simply as his wife, but as Cymbra, a unique, enticing, mysterious individual his spirit called out to as surely as did his body.

What little control he had left snapped and he drove within her, seating himself in a single, powerful thrust. Clasping her hips, he held still long enough to give her some time to adjust to him. When her inner muscles clenched slightly, tentatively, he was lost.

He struggled to hold on to some degree of gentleness, but it was consumed in the red, raging mist of need. He plunged into her again and again, her soft cries and clasping hands urging him on and on, until the spasms of her release ignited his own and he surrendered to her in a long, jetting rush.

When next he knew anything at all, Wolf found himself slumped on top of Cymbra, their bodies still joined and faint aftershocks of pleasure still reverberating through him. Slowly, he withdrew from her and touched his knuckles lightly to her face. She opened her eyes and gazed into his. He was relieved to see that she was as disoriented as he, but her vision cleared quickly and she smiled.

"I truly had no idea of this," Cymbra admitted. The self-consciousness she had felt earlier was gone. While she was still amazed to be so at ease with him under such intensely intimate circumstances, she supposed it merely meant that she was becoming accustomed to him. "There is so much power and beauty in it," she said softly and stroked his cheek, letting her finger trail over the sculpted line of his lips.

Wolf caught her finger between his teeth and bit down just enough to wring a playful yelp from her. He felt absurdly happy. At that moment, he was utterly delighted with his Saxon wife, and indeed, his life in general. "I'm glad you think so."

The soft rumble of his voice made Cymbra quiver.

"It's not always like this, is it?" She hastened to answer her own question. "I mean, it couldn't be, or people would never do anything else. Perhaps it's just as well that men need time to recover."

That seemed a sensible arrangement on nature's part, for truly, were it not so, she failed to see how the world could possibly go on, so distracted would everyone be.

Wolf raised an eyebrow. "Excuse me?"

She wasn't sure what he meant at first but divined it quickly and gave him an understanding smile. "Two days seems hardly any time at all. Does it usually take longer?"

A moment later, as she saw his expression, she wondered if she had been too frank. As a healer, she was accustomed to thinking about the human body without shame or restriction. But perhaps it would have been better in this case to keep her thoughts to herself.

Too late now, for her husband was looking at her most peculiarly. Wolf's eyes darkened. He flopped over onto his back, stared up at the sky as though seeking something there, then propped himself on an elbow and gazed at her.

"You thought I needed two days to recover from making love to you?" The corners of his mouth twitched.

"Oh, please, don't think I meant that as criticism. On the contrary, I realize you're unusually . . . uh . . . that is—" Floundering, she tried to hide her face in her hands.

Wolf wouldn't let her. He moved over her again, pulling her hands down and securing both of them with one of his. "I'm unusually what?"

Damn it, he was enjoying this while she was beginning to feel embarrassed clear to her toes. "Strong, unusually strong."

He smiled, stretching her captured hands above her head, his gaze settling on her breasts. With his free hand, he played with her, stroking her nipples lightly, repeatedly, until her hips arched and she moaned. Pleased by her response, he released one of her hands and guided it down his body to close her fingers around him.

Cymbra's cheeks flamed even as her eyes flew to his face in bewilderment. Keeping her hand firmly in place, he said, "Sweet wife, I let you sleep untouched for two nights in deference to your virginal state when first I took you. Be assured I feel no such restriction now." As though to express its eager agreement, his cock hardened yet further beneath her touch, the velvety tip nudging her palm like a playful animal wanting to be petted.

"Oh, my," Cymbra murmured. Caught in helpless fascination, her body responded in kind despite its recent satiation. Lying back against the welcoming earth, she drew her husband to her.

Chapter

EIGHT

H ER LUTE WAS BROKEN. CYMBRA STARED
at the splintered fragments of wood and
tangled strings on the table beneath the
windows that overlooked the harbor of
Sciringesheal. Slowly she picked up the ruined instrument
and turned it over in her hands, as though somehow her
touch might heal it. The lute was beyond hope of repair.

She had played it for Wolf just the night before, after
they had left the great hall and sought the privacy of their
lodge. The memory of that and what had happened immediately afterward in the great bed they shared was most
pleasant, but this discovery cast a shadow of pain over it.

Someone had done this deliberately. There was no
other explanation. The lute had been fine when Cymbra
last saw it scarcely an hour before. In that time, there had
been no reason for anyone to enter the lodge.

She had been busy elsewhere and Wolf was out all day
hunting with the men. Brita, who, in gratitude for her new
position had insisted on taking on myriad duties, including tidying Cymbra's quarters and caring for her clothing,
had been with her mistress. While they were all so

occupied, someone had entered the lodge, smashed her lute, and left the pieces where Cymbra would be sure to find them.

A shiver moved down her spine. The wanton act of destruction carried a message she had no difficulty understanding. Since returning with Wolf the previous day, astride his great horse, she had been aware of a heightening in the resentment of Marta and some of the other women.

Her full mouth tightened when she remembered how the older woman had looked her up and down, taking in the mantle Cymbra held clutched about herself to conceal the disarray of her clothing, the bits of moss and grass caught in her hair, and the high color of her cheeks. All this no doubt made it perfectly clear what the jarl and his Saxon wife had been doing during their absence from the hill fort.

Wolf hadn't seemed to notice anything amiss but gave her bottom a pat, grinned, and went off to rejoin his men. Cymbra beat a quick retreat to the lodge, where she bathed and dressed before reappearing.

Her first priority had been to seek out Brita and inform the young woman of her new duties. She'd had no time to think of anything else, much less notice what Marta and the others might be up to. Now, reflecting on it, she realized she should have made the time.

So long as the Wolf took no wife, Marta had enjoyed a position of power and respect among the women. She wore the keys to the keep's storage rooms as the visible symbol of her authority. As yet, Cymbra had not asked her for them. She had thought to ease her way in, win the trust and if possible even the affection of the people before asserting her rights. Truth be told, she had also hoped that Wolf might notice the problem and simply order Marta to turn the keys over to her.

She should have known better. Let a chunk of dirt fall

from the protective berm around the fortress, let a fragment of rust appear on a weapon, let a man take an instant
longer to react on the training field, and Wolf would know.
But anything that smacked of the purely domestic he ignored completely.

She had noticed that he appeared oblivious to what
he wore, what he ate, what the temperature was, and all
manner of other concerns related to simple comfort. In
that, he was very much like her brother, Hawk, who had
precisely the same tendencies. She was far too wise to
think her husband would ever change. To go to him with a
problem he would think of no consequence would mean
belittling herself. So, too, it would mean failing at her self-
appointed task to be a good wife, a task she was desperate
to accomplish. If Wolf and his people could truly accept
her, if she could truly make a place of honor for herself
among them, Hawk would be far more likely to accept
both her marriage and the alliance that must of necessity
go with it. That she might also wish to please the husband
who had unleashed such unexpected feelings within her
was a possibility Cymbra did not wish to contemplate.
Confused, bewildered, and still deeply worried about her
brother, she shied from her emotions as she had always
shied from those of others.

Before such thoughts could run away with her, she
walked swiftly out of the lodge, across the field, and into
the great hall. As expected, Marta was there, directing the
servants in preparation for the evening meal. Trestle tables were being set up and wiped down, benches put in
place, and large platters of fresh-baked bread distributed.

Cymbra walked directly up to Marta and held out her
hand. "Give me the keys."

Around the hall, all activity stopped. The women
stared at Cymbra.

Marta looked her up and down very deliberately and
sneered. How bold she was when there was no one she

feared about, Cymbra thought. That would change, and soon.

"You think because you satisfy the jarl's lust you should have the running of this place?" Marta asked. She raised her voice enough to be heard by everyone in the hall. "Any whore can spread her legs for a man. It means nothing." Around her, the women tittered.

"The keys," Cymbra said again. She refused to give Marta the satisfaction of seeing her angered. "Then you will remove yourself from here and not return until I have given you permission to do so." Lest there be any misunderstanding, she concluded, "You are a vindictive and destructive person. Until you change, you are not worthy of trust."

Marta's face darkened. "How dare you! You are nothing and less than nothing! Kiirla should have been wife to the jarl and would have been had he not been forced to wed you. If you think for one moment that gives you any rights—"

"Forced?" Cymbra raised her brows. "Are you saying that Lord Wolf was *forced* to do something not of his own choosing?"

The women glanced at one another nervously. One or two even smiled slightly, suggesting that Marta was not without critics herself.

Reckless as she was in her prideful folly, even Marta knew when she had gone too far. Quickly, she tried to recover. "You twist my words! The Lord Wolf is a great leader who does not hesitate to sacrifice himself for the well-being of his people. However, that changes nothing where you are concerned."

"The keys. This is the last time I ask. Hand them over now or I go to the Lord Wolf." Cymbra spoke with deceptive softness. "We both know there is much for me to tell him."

Marta paled slightly, perhaps remembering her intemperate remarks to Cymbra on her wedding night, but she did not give way. "My husband was foster father to the Wolf, the man who first placed a sword in his hand and taught him how to use it. You are nothing but a Saxon captive wed for political gains. Which of us do you think he will believe?"

Cymbra wondered that herself but she did not show it by so much as a flicker. "I have no doubt that my husband will do what is right."

For just a moment, Marta wavered. She saw before her a young woman of glowing beauty, a woman whom recent days had transformed from innocence to awakened sensuality. So, too, had she seen the look on the Wolf's face when he rode back into the hill fort holding his wife in his arms. Never had a man appeared better satisfied, or more tender.

It was well enough to think that this would pass, for men tended to lose interest in that which they possessed. But this enticing Saxon witch might have unexpected powers. Perhaps she truly had been sent to tame the Wolf.

"He will not appreciate your involving him with any dispute among the women," Marta said sensibly enough. "Men hate such things. If you knew more about them, you would understand that."

As one, the other women nodded. This truly was wisdom.

"Moreover, he will wonder why you seek to sow discord among his people. He will remember that you are of enemy stock and he will consider what harm you wish to do."

The line was drawn. Marta would not yield the keys despite Cymbra's threat to go to Wolf. Nay, not threat, for it had to be a promise. If she did not act on it, she would be disparaged among his people for all time.

She almost regretted saying what she had, for she truly dreaded the thought of involving her husband. Now, she had no choice but to ask for his help.

She left the great hall and did not return until it was time for supper. Wolf had come back from the hunt but gone directly to the sauna with several of his men. Cymbra did not see him until she came to the high table.

He was already seated, laughing with Dragon over some sally the latter had just made, but the sudden lapse of conversation that always seemed to accompany her appearance alerted him. He broke off and rose, pulling out the high-backed chair next to his.

"Prompt as always, my lady," he said with a smile. More softly, for her ears alone, he added, "And as beautiful."

She flushed, pleased by his praise but nervous, too, at the thought of what lay ahead. As she took her place beside him, Dragon lifted his goblet to her.

"Greetings, sweet sister, and thank you."

"Thank me? Whatever for?"

"For inducing in my brother so good a mood that he cursed only mildly when we failed to find a boar and had to content ourselves with stag."

"You don't care for venison?" Cymbra innocently asked her husband.

Dragon grinned at the chiding look his brother shot him. "Oh, he likes it well enough," he answered for Wolf. "But he prefers the contest with a bad-tempered boar. Although in all honesty, I've wondered a time or two if he might not rightly feel some kinship with such a beast."

Cymbra dared a quick look at her husband. He merely rolled his eyes. "Ignore him, sweetling. Dragon has always believed wives were to be avoided at all costs. It pains him to confront evidence of his misjudgment."

"It's true," Dragon said, sighing deeply. "You've upset my whole understanding of how the world works.

Rather than go back and begin again, I've decided to regard you as a unique exception."

"I see," Cymbra said although she didn't really. It
was enough that her brother-in-law seemed to approve of
her. That was a beginning. Now, if she could only make as
much progress with the several thousand other people at
Sciringesheal . . .

"If you do like venison," she ventured, "I have a wonderful recipe. Perhaps you'd like to try it."

Wolf had no interest in the intricacies of preparing
food. It was enough if it arrived at the table reasonably hot
and not entirely raw. But he was inclined just now to
please the beautiful wife who had pleased him so greatly.
"Do whatever you'd like with it," he said magnanimously.

Cymbra had the opening she needed and hesitated
only a moment before taking it. She could see Marta at
one of the lower tables, watching her with narrowed eyes,
and was aware that she was an object of attention for
many of the women scattered around the hall. Most of
them looked at her unkindly but Brita and the other female slaves dared to offer her small smiles of support. Her
throat tightened with nervousness but she forced herself
to speak calmly and pleasantly.

"I would be delighted to do so, my lord. Unfortunately, lacking the keys to the household storage, I cannot
obtain the spices needed to make the dish."

It took Wolf a moment to realize that there was a significance behind her seemingly casual words. A vague
sense of disquiet stirred in him, as though something he
should have done but hadn't itched at his memory.
Distantly, he recalled that women in charge of households
always wore keys. Indeed, a gaggle of good wives at market could be heard some distance off by their jangle.

He frowned. Why hadn't Marta simply turned the
keys over to Cymbra after the wedding? For that matter,
why hadn't Cymbra simply asked for them rather than

employ this transparent subterfuge to involve him in what she should have handled for herself?

His eyes drifted over the hall. Among the men, all seemed as it should be. They were eating, drinking, talking, laughing, fingering their knives, and generally behaving normally. But the women . . . Sensible male dread stirred in him at the sight of their averted eyes and alternately smug and tense expressions.

Lest the situation go any further, he caught Marta's eye, noting as he did that she was watching him intently, and beckoned her to him. She came promptly and smiled. "Lord?"

"Give the household keys to my wife, Marta. She is mistress here now and they are hers by right."

The older woman's smile deepened. With a kindly look at Cymbra, she said, "Of course, my lord." She unhooked the keys from her belt and handed them to Cymbra. Returning her attention to Wolf, she said, "I hope you don't mind, my lord, I thought it best to wait until her ladyship decided to take up her duties."

Cymbra inhaled sharply. She did not thank Marta for the keys or acknowledge her in any way. Wolf disliked that. He had known Marta all his life and she always seemed to do her job well enough.

"Thank you, Marta," he said, feeling compelled to make up for his wife's silence. "I'm sure my wife is aware of your wisdom and experience, and will depend on you to help her."

Marta's face softened yet further. So moved was she that her eyes glistened. "You are too kind, my lord," she murmured, and with a deep bow withdrew from the high table.

Cymbra sat frozen, hardly breathing, her hand so tight around the hard metal keys that they dug into the soft flesh of her palm. She had underestimated Marta. The woman must have realized that in a direct confronta-

tion, Cymbra would win. Marta had turned the tables on
her effectively, and in the process made it impossible for
Cymbra to carry through on the second part of her promise, namely to remove Marta from the household until she
changed her behavior. Now, by her husband's own word,
she would not be able to do that.

Wolf said little to her through the remainder of supper. He gave his attention to his brother and the other
men of rank who were privileged to share the high table
with him. Late into the evening, when the meal was
finished and the more serious drinking begun, a skald
stepped forward. The assembly hushed, settling comfort-
ably into their seats in anticipation of the stories they
would hear.

At first, Cymbra was drawn into the great epic the
storyteller unfolded. He did not offer its name for it
seemed well known to all save her. The tale began in the
dawn time of the world when a Seeress spoke.

> In the beginning, when Ymir lived, there was
> neither sand nor sea. The earth was not there, nor
> the sky—there was only a gaping chasm, with
> grass nowhere!

In the night-dark hall lit only by torches that flickered in
the summer breeze entering through the great doors left
open at either end, Cymbra felt an ancient stirring deep
within herself and shivered at it. So she imagined men and
women had gathered beside fire since time immemorial,
finding comfort and protection in one another, holding off
the unseen monsters of the night until day could reclaim
the world.

The skald's voice, deep and sonorous, rose to the high
timbered roof. Smoke curled and sparks flew from the
huge logs dying down now to embers. The tale continued
as Odin and his brothers created the world and all things

in it, including man. The mighty god Thor battled giants, and the purest of the gods, Baldur, was murdered.

So caught up was she in the tale that Cymbra only gradually realized that the tone of it was changing. The cock of Valhalla crowed, followed by another "soot red" bird of Hell. The watchdog Gram bayed and tore free of his bonds. The watchman Heimdall let loose a blast from his signal horn. The great world tree, Yggdrasil, trembled and catastrophe was unleashed upon the earth. Men descended into depravity. Mercy became unknown.

Images of fire and death filled the hall. Men perished in vast numbers, homes and hearths vanished as though they had never been. The sky caught fire and split in two. Evil was unleashed and walked the earth. *Ragnarök* descended, the twilight of the gods.

One by one, Odin and his brothers gave battle and one by one they died. The sky turned black and the stars were extinguished. The world was utterly destroyed.

The skald's voice fell away. Cymbra waited for the storyteller to resume, sure he would say something more, offer some hope, but he had nothing to add, nor did anyone else seem to expect it. Slowly, the silence of the hall was punctuated by a deep, rhythmic banging.

Still caught in the hideous visions of the tale, Cymbra looked around dazedly as first one, then another of the warriors brought his drinking horn down hard, thumping the scarred tables again and again in full-hearted approval of the despair-ridden tale.

The skald smiled, bowed, took his seat. More ale was poured. Conversation resumed.

"What was that?" Cymbra murmured. She spoke so faintly that for a moment she thought no one had heard. But then Wolf turned to her quizzically.

"That is *Völuspá*, the Seeress's Prophecy, our greatest epic. It explains the origins of the world and foretells its end. You have never heard it before?"

She shook her head. "The world just ends like that, with the triumph of evil? There is no hope?"

He shrugged as though the notion surprised him. "Some say the world will be reborn and the cycle begun again but with the same end. Always there will be the battle between good and evil, and evil will win as death always wins, but the gods and man will always rise to try again."

"It doesn't seem . . . futile to go on like that, over and over, with no chance for anything better?"

The moment she spoke, Cymbra regretted her words. She understood that her husband's faith was different from her own, and she did not wish to appear disrespectful. But what she had just heard appalled her almost as much as his ready acceptance of it.

"I forget how soft you Christians are," he said matter-of-factly. "You have a child's need for a happy ending."

Stung, Cymbra forgot about tempering her response. "Or you might say that we simply have more faith in our Creator."

He shrugged. "Yet your own tales tell of a great battle between good and evil at the end of the world, don't they?"

"But evil doesn't win! The Savior comes again in triumph and the world is reborn as the Kingdom of God."

Wolf looked unimpressed. "It's a nice idea," he allowed. "Brother Joseph speaks of this 'Prince of Peace.' I have trouble respecting a man who goes like a lamb to his own slaughter."

"He wasn't just a man, he was—and is—the Son of God. And he didn't die, he was reborn as all of us shall be reborn through God's love."

"All well and good, but I haven't noticed that Christians are any more peaceful than anyone else—on the contrary. At least we Norse live by the teachings of our faith. We don't pretend to be better than we really are."

"And at least we Christians aspire to something better," Cymbra snapped. "We don't just accept an endless cycle of violence and death."

Fire-lit shadows danced against the shield-emblazoned walls. A servant poured golden ale into Wolf's drinking horn. He raised it, took a long swallow, and eyed her narrowly. "I warned you this is a hard land and we a hard people. You will do well to remember that."

When he said nothing more, but turned from her to speak to Dragon, Cymbra remained seated stiffly in her chair.

Time passed. Wolf did not speak to her again. At length, she rose and left the hall. Outside in the cool night air, she paused. The smoke had burned her eyes. That was the only reason there were tears in them.

She went through the darkness to the lodge, where kindly Brita had lit the lamps, left water still warm to the touch, and turned down the covers of the great bed. Cymbra slipped beneath them certain she would not sleep. Visions of a bloodred sky splitting open to pour forth demons were bound to keep anyone awake. But she hadn't counted on the exhaustion of the long day.

She woke, some unknown time later, to the touch of callused hands stroking the satiny skin of her inner thighs. Heat ignited instantly within her. She moaned and reached out to her husband. In the darkness of the night she could see very little, but she was vividly aware of him covering her along every inch of her body.

He spread her legs wider and moved between them. She had scarcely a moment to draw breath before he thrust into her, rearing back to thrust again and again, quickly, remorselessly. His possession was so abrupt, and with an edge of roughness to it, that Cymbra felt the stirrings of fear, but she had no time to think of that before her body, already so perfectly attuned to his, responded helplessly.

The pleasure built and built, became unbearable, and suddenly, without warning, release was upon her. She cried out, moaning his name against his sweat-dampened skin. His answer was a guttural rasp as he drove even harder and deeper, taking his own satisfaction.

Scant moments later, he moved off her. Cymbra felt curiously stunned and bereft. The suddenness of his possession, his silence throughout, the lack of gentle caress, all made this time different from any other time between them. She reached out across the bed, seeking some small comfort and reassurance, but he had moved too far away. She encountered only empty space and the chill air of the Norse night.

Chapter

NINE

WOLF LOOKED UP FROM THE WEAPON
he was sharpening, saw his wife returning
through the open gates, and scowled.
Gloriously beautiful as always, she was
still paler than she should have been and there were faint
violet shadows beneath her eyes. The stubborn wench
was wearing herself out.

In the week since Marta had turned the household
keys over to her, Cymbra had risen each day before the
first hint of light, dressed quickly, and hurried about her
duties. Wolf, who had never been one to lie about in bed,
was damn tired of waking up alone. Especially when he
invariably did so with a powerful desire for his Saxon
beauty and no way to slake it before nightfall.

He ran a finger over the blade, confirmed its sharp-
ness, and set it aside. Rising, he walked in the direction of
the mounted escort that had accompanied his wife and
was now drawing rein in front of the stables.

Cymbra had wanted to go into town without being
surrounded by armed men who looked inclined to kill as

easily as they breathed. Wolf took that as further proof of
her foolishness. Not that he actually believed anyone in
Sciringesheal yearned for the savage death that would be
his if he so much as looked wrong at the Wolf's woman,
but he had to allow for the effect of her extraordinary
beauty on even the sanest man.

The escort, six grim-faced warriors well blooded in
battle, nodded to him. He returned their silent greetings,
pleased to see that none was so ill-disciplined as to actually look in his wife's direction. It took more effort to select the best men and train them solidly, but it always paid
off in the end.

He raised his powerful arms, lifting Cymbra from her
saddle before she could attempt to dismount. She started a
little in surprise. Smiling, he slid her down the long length
of his body but did not let go of her even after her feet
touched the ground "What have you bought now?"

Caught within the circle of his arms, she tipped back
her head and looked up at him. That he was her husband
still amazed her. That she could touch and be touched by
him as though that were the most ordinary part of life was
astounding. After living untouched for so many years, the
sudden intimacy left her feeling as though she had walked
from a dark room into brilliant sunshine—bright, glorious, seductively warm, and yet a bit painful, leaving her as
yet unsure of how she truly felt about it. She was doing
her very best to hold on to her hard-won serenity but increasingly she knew herself to be losing the battle. And
never more so when she was like this, so vividly aware of
the warmth and strength of the man who held her. Aware,
too—no, too aware—of her tremulous response to him.
All the same, pride drove her to conceal the dishevelment
of her senses he so effortlessly provoked. "Cloth for the
servants' new tunics," she said briskly, then reminded
him, "you did say I might."

That was true, he had. Cymbra was meticulous about asking his approval for every purchase she made. Although he was astounded by the sheer variety of *things* she thought necessary, he couldn't find it in himself to refuse her. And after all, he had to admit that from what he had seen so far, everything she bought had a practical use.

Moreover, judging by the coin she was spending, she was a champion haggler. Of course, that shouldn't surprise him. The poor merchants who had to deal with her were probably startled to discover they hadn't just given their goods away for one of her smiles.

He couldn't quite remember how but she'd made the idea of new tunics for the servants sound sensible. Something about people taking more pride in their work when they were better garbed, and something else about the reflection on his own consequence. He'd only been half-listening, distracted by the subtle play of light over the damask curve of her cheek.

"You're working too hard," he murmured, still holding her close against him.

She didn't try to pull away but neither did she soften as he would have liked. "There is much to do," Cymbra said. It was a simple statement yet replete with her deepest concern that she would fail to be a good wife, a bringer of peace to her people and his, and that all of this, all the bustle of ordinary life, would explode suddenly into devastating violence and lives would fall like so much discarded chaff upon the hard-packed floor of the winnowing shed.

"How many servants are there in this keep, how many slaves?" When she would have answered, he stopped her with the light touch of a finger on lips he would far rather have been kissing. "Never mind, I know you know. My point is that I fail to see why you think you have to do everything."

She could have told him—about the flour spoiled

with salt, the watered ale, the pots improperly cleaned, the many and sundry small acts of sloth—or sabotage— that were making her days a constant trial. But pride wouldn't allow her to complain.

There had been no further confrontations with Marta. The older woman was merely a silent, unsmiling presence hovering over all, a continual reminder that the outcome of this battle was yet to be decided.

Brita did everything possible to help and had managed to enlist the support of the female slaves. But all the other women did the absolute minimum and did that as poorly as they dared. The food served in the hall was hardly edible by Cymbra's standards.

She was astonished—but wearily grateful—that Wolf apparently hadn't noticed. Still, she wondered how much longer she would be able to keep beating her head against what increasingly seemed an immovable wall.

Her decision to outfit the servants in new garb was intended partly to correct the obvious deficiency in their clothing, but she hoped it would win her some small degree of support. Without it, she feared she would flounder.

Even now she felt compelled to hurry off to the kitchens to make sure there would be something served at supper that wasn't either rotten with maggots or still moving of its own accord. But Wolf's arms close around her kept her from doing so.

"Enough," he said, his voice low and rasping against her ear. "There are other duties you have neglected."

She opened her mouth to protest the injustice of that, only to stop when his smile stole her breath. Dragon was supposed to be the charming one in the family, but in Cymbra's opinion her husband beat him easily.

She was just about to relent—and gladly so—when she caught sight of Brother Joseph hurrying toward her across the field. The look on his face made her forget her own inclinations.

"I'm sorry," she said quickly. "I promised Brother Joseph I would . . . pray with him." Before Wolf could react, she ducked under his arm. Looking back over her shoulder, she said, "It shouldn't take too long, not more than an hour or so—". The fierce scowl her husband shot her made Cymbra decide she had nothing more to say.

Wolf watched her go with mingled chagrin and what felt suspiciously like disappointment. He had come to realize in the past week that Cymbra was very devout, for she prayed daily with the monk. Had Brother Joseph not proven himself over the previous three years to be a man of rigorous self-denial, including unwavering celibacy, Wolf would have hesitated to allow him so much in his wife's company.

As it was, he was trying hard to reconcile himself to this part of her life that apparently meant so much to her. Whether or not he would succeed remained to be seen.

AFTER HER GLANCE BACK AT HER SCOWLING HUS-band, Cymbra did not dare look at him again. She intercepted Brother Joseph and quickly drew him off to the weaving shed.

"Dame Mikal's pains are upon her," he said with great agitation. "She begs you to come quickly."

Cymbra nodded. The woman was wife to one of the Rus merchants who traded so often in Sciringesheal that he had built a house in the town. She was expecting her first child and had approached Cymbra, through the monk, earlier in the week.

Nor was she alone. Barely had the first rumors about her healing skills begun to spread, aided no doubt by Brita, than people began asking for her help. So far, they were all Christians, but she hoped that would change soon.

Having assured Brother Joseph she would go at once,

she hurried to the lodge and gathered up her supplies. Back outside, she sought Wolf. When she could not find him, she went up to one of the men of her guard.

"Do you know where Lord Wolf has gone?" she asked.

The big, hard-faced warrior looked down at the ground, then up at the sky, then to either side, anywhere but at her. Curtly, as though unsure that he should speak to her at all, he said, "To the river. To swim."

Cymbra thought briefly of going after him but time was rushing past. Besides, his absence might be a blessing in disguise. The man was so damnably protective, there was no assurance he would let her go.

She murmured her thanks and walked away in the direction of the kitchens, but before she reached them she turned a quick corner that took her out of sight of the men on the field. Removing a plain gray cloak from her bag, the same kind of cloak worn by many of the servants, she put it on, raised the hood over her head, and walked straight out through the open gate. Consoling herself with the thought that Wolf would surely understand, once he knew the circumstances, she made her way back down to the town.

As it turned out, Dame Mikal's time had not come, she was merely experiencing the false pains that could easily be mistaken for the real thing by first-time mothers. Cymbra sat with her for an hour or so, long enough for the pains to end and not return.

"I am so sorry, my lady," Dame Mikal said when she realized she was not in labor. Her Norse was slow but fluent, accented with the rhythm of her native tongue. "I should never have asked Brother Joseph for you until I knew for sure."

"Not at all," Cymbra assured her. "It's much better to be on the safe side." She laid her hand gently on the young woman's swollen belly and smiled. "You have a fine, strong child, but I suspect he—or she—will wish to remain within you several weeks yet. However, if you experience pains again, please call for me. Babies have been known to surprise people."

Her gentle reassurance calmed the Rus woman, who clasped her hand in gratitude. So, too, did her husband, who had returned rapidly from an expedition into the hills to meet with the fur and amber traders whose goods he bought.

"We cannot thank you enough, my lady," he said huskily. His gaze on his wife, he said, "My Nadia should be home safe with her own mother but she insisted on coming with me. Glad though I am to have her near, I worry for her safety birthing a child in this harsh place."

"It is hard to be far from home," Cymbra agreed. She still missed Holyhood although she tried very hard not to think about that, or indeed of what lay ahead when her brother realized what had happened to her.

Most especially, she tried not to think about the inevitable day of reckoning and how she would bring about the peaceful reconciliation between her husband and brother that she was determined to effect.

"However," she continued, "women have babies here all the time. You mustn't worry."

She left the small house a short time later, reflecting on the couple's obvious devotion to each other. Unbidden, the question rose in her mind of how Wolf would feel once she was with child. That she would be was not in doubt given her husband's obvious virility. It was even possible that she might be already.

A smile tugged at her mouth as she touched a hand very lightly to her belly. If life was there she didn't know it yet, nor was she likely to early on, for her body had never been particularly regular in such things. But when there was . . . She didn't dare hope he would show the same care as the Rus trader, yet she couldn't help but wish for it all the same.

Cymbra had little opportunity to consider this before she slipped back in through the stronghold gates, returned her cloak and medicines to the lodge, and hurried off to check on preparations for supper. She was crossing the open area in front of the great timbered hall when she saw a crowd had gathered.

Even as she stepped closer to see what drew them, a dark wave of pressure overtook her. She heard a buzzing in her ears as though a swarm of insects had suddenly surrounded her. Panic rose in her as her heartbeat accelerated wildly.

Desperately, she fought against the sensations that threatened to overwhelm her, taking deep, steadying breaths as she frantically summoned up the vision of the wide, high, sturdy wall within her that she had learned to build stone by stone over the years.

When she could finally proceed, she walked slowly and carefully toward the crowd. Before she could see what lay beyond, what she heard confirmed her worst fears.

A man was tied to the punishment post a short distance to the side of the timbered hall. His tunic had been stripped away, leaving him naked to the waist. Long, red welts darkened his back.

As Cymbra watched, her lips pressed tightly together to contain the scream that threatened to break from her, a guard positioned behind the man raised a black leather whip. It coiled like a snake, lashed through the air, and struck with a harsh crack. The man cried out and arched against the pain, straining at his bonds. The guard drew the whip back, raised it once more, and delivered another savage blow.

Watching impassively from the side, his face a mask, Wolf raised a hand, signaling the guard to stop. The man slumped against the post, unable to stand upright, blood trickling from his wounds. Instinctively, Cymbra took a step toward him.

At that moment, Wolf saw his wife—and in the same instant realized what she intended. He grasped her arm and yanked her back against him. "Do not," he said.

She stared at him in disbelief. "You can't mean that. He's been punished for whatever he did. Surely, that's enough." So shocked and sickened was she that she paid no heed to the startled looks of the crowd, their attention diverted by this new spectacle. Wolf, to the contrary, was keenly conscious of the avid gazes directed at the jarl and his defiant wife.

"He stole a man's plow and another's horse," Wolf said through gritted teeth. "Had he not been caught, the thefts would have robbed two families of their livelihood. For such a crime, he is lucky to get off this lightly."

Cymbra looked again at the man who now appeared unconscious. What she saw sickened her. His back was a mass of wounds. She judged he must have been lashed at least several dozen times. Bile rose in her throat. She spoke with loathing.

"Lightly? He's been all but whipped to death. You must let me care for him."

Wolf did not answer, but walked away, the crowd parting before him. He still grasped Cymbra's arm so that she was compelled to run alongside him. When they were some distance from the post, he stopped.

Without releasing her, he said, "He will hang there until morning. It is part of his punishment. If Odin wills and he lives through the night, Ulfrich will see to him. You are not to go anywhere near him. Is that clear?"

When she remained silent, glaring at him, he tightened his hold on her arm. "And you are never again to question anything I do." He paused. "At least not among our people. If you have some comment to make, do so when we are private. Is that also clear?"

Distraught though she was, Cymbra could not miss the significance of what he had just said. He was insisting on her absolute obedience and respect—in public only. Much as she wanted to hold on to her anger and disgust at what she had just witnessed, she could not quite do so in the face of so great a concession.

Slowly, not taking her eyes from her husband's stern features, she said, "I am not accustomed to such things. This is . . . difficult for me." It was the closest she had yet come to revealing the truth of herself and the strange curse/blessing that had shaped her life. What would he think of her—this man of such grace and strength—if she told him how very different she truly was, even to the extent of suffering the pain of others? Their ills, their torments, their wounds and scars, all their afflictions could overtake the outward beauty he saw and twist it into a hideous thing of endless suffering. *If* she did not find some safe place for her gift in the suddenly changing landscape of her life.

"I know that," Wolf, who did not know at all, replied. His voice gentled. "You lived a very sheltered life at Holyhood. I am sure that even among your brother's people, such punishment is common."

Cymbra could not contest that. Indeed, she suspected it was one of the reasons Hawk had chosen to shelter her from the ways of her people.

"I wish there were another way," she said quietly. He had loosened his grip on her arm but not let go. His fingers moved gently over her skin, stroking her.

"You are too tender-hearted." His tone robbed the words of any sting. He bent his dark head and lightly brushed his lips down her throat.

"Are you hungry?" he murmured, tracing the curve

of her cheek to nuzzle her just behind the lobe of her ear where he knew her to be exquisitely sensitive.

A tremor ran through her. *Hungry . . . food . . . supper.* She was supposed to have done something about that but she couldn't seem to remember— "No," she whispered, as he clasped her hips, moving her against him, letting her feel his need.

He raised his head, silvery eyes faintly mocking. "No?"

"No, I'm not hungry . . . for food."

His beautiful, hard mouth curved in the intimate smile that never failed to make her knees go weak. "Good." He was pleased, arrogantly so, for having been able to distract her from her duties. He was also relieved, for there had been a moment, just then, when she seemed on the verge of saying something . . . serious, something he did not especially wish to hear. Life should be simple, elsewise it could not be controlled. Most especially, he wished no complications with his Saxon bride. Controlling her was vital for the peace that was his greatest dream and, too, for his pride as a man.

Cymbra gave a little yelp as the ground gave way beneath her feet. Swept into the Wolf's strong arms, she was carried in long, swift strides across the field and into their lodge.

The jarl and his wife did not appear at supper that eve. They left the timbered great hall to their retainers, servants, and slaves. Dragon, realizing before the others did, broke out in hearty laughter and raised a cup to his absent brother.

It was as well there was good ale to drink, for the food was truly appalling. Even the normally oblivious men grumbled a bit before getting sensibly drunk.

WOLF DREW A RAGGED BREATH AGAINST WHAT felt like a band of metal constricting his chest, and continued the slow, skilled caress that was relentlessly driving his lovely wife to madness. He watched, fascinated, as her head tossed back and forth across the pillows. Soft cries broke from her and a fine sheen of perspiration glistened on her creamy skin.

Their first coupling, scant minutes after gaining the lodge, had been as hasty as it was fulfilling. With the worst of his urgency slaked but his desire only heightened, Wolf was doing what he had not managed to do since their marriage. He lingered over his wife, savoring her beauty and her passion, exploring her body with gentle thoroughness, drawing out her pleasure until she dug her nails into his shoulders and cried his name.

"*Wolf!*"

He laughed, a raspy sound of male triumph, and moved up her body, taking her mouth, his tongue thrusting possessively even as he guided himself into her. She tightened around him reflexively, the pleasure of this most intimate caress so intense it teetered on the edge of pain. He groaned and moved within her, unable to hold back any longer, driving them both to wave after wave of release.

Afterward, holding his wife in the crook of his arm, with her head resting on his shoulder and her hand lying just above his heart, Wolf reflected that there was much to be said for lingering. He chuckled softly.

Cymbra raised her head and looked at him uncertainly. "What?"

"I'm meditating on the virtue of patience."

It took her just a moment to realize what he meant. Fiery color moved over her face. She sighed elaborately and reclined against him. "Oh, *that* was patience."

Wolf stiffened but only until he heard her teasing tone. He smacked her bottom very lightly. "Perhaps it was not enough. Would you prefer for me to draw out your pleasure even longer?"

She ran a long-fingered hand up his thigh, her nails

scratching him just enough to send a quiver along his spine. "Perhaps you would like to consider how a woman might take vengeance for such a thing."

"Vengeance? My sweet, gentle, *obedient* wife?" His wolf's eyes widened in mock astonishment.

"No," Cymbra said dryly. "The wife you actually have." And proceeded to show him just what she meant.

It was very late when next Wolf stirred, surpassingly content. Never had he expected his bride of scarcely a week to prove his match in passion *and* control. In the end, it had taken every ounce of strength he possessed not to simply throw her on her back and satisfy the burning, raging lust she unleashed in him.

He had held on, if only barely, and been rewarded finally by the sight of his exquisite Saxon beauty slowly lowering herself onto him inch by rock-hard inch, her face a vision of delighted discovery as she began to move, tentatively at first, then with growing confidence. The hushed lodge seemed still to reverberate with their cries of pleasure.

He was drifting from such pleasant thoughts to even pleasanter sleep, when Cymbra stirred. Wolf's eyes flew open with just a hint of alarm.

"About being hungry," she said. She sat up, tossed her glorious hair out of the way, and stretched languidly. "I am now."

"Hungry?" Incredibly, impossibly, the sight of her made him stir again. It was true then; a man's cock really would try to kill him. "For food?" He sought distraction more than clarity. If he stared at the pale aureoles of her breasts much longer, the shadows of her ribs, the exquisitely graceful curve of her hips and thighs—

"We missed supper," she reminded him with a winsome smile. Displaying energy he could not help but resent, she left the bed and began to dress. "You stay where you are. I'll just go over to the kitchens and get something."

Wolf scowled. The sight of his bride traipsing about in the middle of the night to fetch a belated meal because he was too drained to crawl from his bed would have the watch so consumed with guffaws as to virtually invite an invader to walk right past them. By morning, everyone in the hill fort, the town, and the smallest settlement miles distant would know that the mighty jarl had been bested by his bride, if only in the sweet combat of the marital bed.

Nor would it stop there, for the jokes would spread on the sails of merchant ships, repeated from the golden palaces of Byzantium to the ice-encrusted huts of the wild Lapps until the veritable world itself rocked with laughter at the expense of the mighty Lord of Sciringesheal.

"I'll go with you," he said. He dragged himself from the bed and began pulling on his clothes.

The kitchens consisted of several small buildings set a short distance from the great hall. One held a deep, straw-lined pit into which leather buckets of milk were lowered to be kept cool. Here, too, cheese was made, the whey separated out, milk churned for butter, and eggs stored for use. Nearby was a smokehouse where fish and meat were hung to absorb the scent of slowly burning fires fed by charcoal, apple wood, and occasional handfuls of seaweed. The largest of the buildings contained the main work area as well as storage for grains, flour, spices, and ale.

Her hand clasped in Wolf's, Cymbra unlocked the door with one of the keys on her belt. A low fire still burned in the hearth at the center of the kitchen. The light of its embers and the moonlight streaming through the open door were enough to see by.

A heartbeat later, she wished for deepest darkness.

The kitchen was a shambles. Dirty pots and trays had been left where they were dropped. Food, abandoned on the worktables, already smelled in the summer warmth. Even as she watched, horrified, a rat glanced up from his meal, stared at her boldly, and shuffled off at no great haste.

She dropped Wolf's hand and walked farther into the disaster. Fury filled her as she beheld the blatant message from Marta and the other women. She closed her eyes, struggling for self-control, only to open them when she felt her husband watching her.

"I'm sorry," Cymbra said, her voice choked with tears. "Obviously, I've made a mess of things."

He looked around the room and back at her. His expression was unreadable. "Has this been going on all week?"

Although he spoke mildly enough, Cymbra wasn't fooled. She was certain her husband was coldly, furiously angry at her, as he had every right to be.

Not attempting to defend herself but determined only to tell the truth, she replied, "It hasn't been this bad. As long as I've been there to watch them, at least some things get done properly, but tonight—"

"Tonight they took advantage of your absence."

She dropped her head, shamed. "I'm afraid so."

He came to her, closing the distance between them until they stood so near she felt his breath. Still, she couldn't bear to look at him. Clasping her chin, he forced her head up. "You asked Marta for the keys."

It wasn't a question, but Cymbra nodded stiffly, as best she could in his hold.

"She refused them and organized the other women against you."

"Not all the women. Brita and the other female slaves have done everything they could."

"Because they, like you, are strangers here and know what that can mean."

He paused, compelling her to meet his gaze. "What happened on our wedding night?"

Cymbra paled. He could not possibly know— "W-what do you mean?"

His grasp tightened implacably. "You appeared only a little nervous when you left the hall with Marta and the women. By the time I joined you, you were terrified. What happened?"

"Nothing . . . it was just so new and sudden, I—"

"Cymbra!" He made her name a warning. She didn't need more. Color returned to her face and deepened rapidly. "Marta said something about you hurting me." Quickly she added, "I didn't believe her, not really, but I felt very alone and—"

He let go of her so suddenly that she almost fell Barely had she caught her balance then he was out the door and striding across the field.

THE WOMEN WORKED BY TORCHLIGHT. Several knelt, scrubbing the floor, while others rubbed down the tables with sand, and still more cleaned the dishes and utensils. They labored in silence, watched over by their scowling menfolk, who no more liked being rousted from their beds than did the women but who stood foursquare in support of their jarl. Besides, the food really had been terrible.

The slaves were not permitted to help. Brita and the others, awakened by the commotion, were sent back to their beds and told to take the coming day for rest. They would do no work, not so much as the lifting of a broom, until the freewomen had restored all to rights.

Nor was Cymbra allowed to help. When she tried, Wolf pulled her away. He stood, silent and forbidding, until he was satisfied that the work was well in hand. Then he gestured to several of the guards who stood ready. They closed in around Marta, who gasped and tried to slip away but could not.

"Come," Wolf said and stalked off, leaving a small parade of wife, guards, and the curious to follow him into the timbered great hall. He sat alone at the high table and stared at the others. The silence dragged out until Cymbra truly believed she could bear it no longer. At length, the jarl spoke.

"Marta Ingridotter, you are the widow of a man who held my greatest respect. For that reason, I did not hesitate to give you the ordering of my household while still I lacked a wife. But you betrayed my trust by deliberately seeking to turn my wife against me and by refusing her that which was hers by right."

When the woman would have tried to speak, he cut her off with a look. The others shared glances among themselves. Clearly, they knew of the issue with the keys but the rest, how she had tried to turn Cymbra against her husband, was by far the graver matter and made all the more so for being mysterious. To sow such disharmony was to betray them all.

"You will leave Sciringesheal," Wolf went on implacably. "And your daughter with you." He ignored Marta's strangled cry. "You will make your home at the settlement at Oslofjord. It is within my holdings and the landsmann there is a strong leader. Behave properly and you will be fairly treated. Otherwise—" He shrugged, making it clear that Marta would be responsible for her own fate.

She was crying softly, her head buried in her hands. Wolf rose, facing his people. More had crowded in as word spread that Marta was being judged. Deliberately, he said, "This woman chose her path when she stood against my wife. Let all here know that and take lesson from it."

He looked slowly and directly around the room. To Cymbra, his gaze seemed to stare into their very souls. Whatever he saw must have satisfied him for he nodded finally. The crowd, silent and subdued, dispersed.

Marta and Kiirla were taken away to their quarters by

the guards. They would be given a chance to pack their belongings and say goodbye to whichever friends were brave enough to visit them. With morning light, they would be gone.

Alone with her husband in the great hall, Cymbra prayed for calm. All but overwhelmed by his swift and absolute support of her, she was nonetheless horrified by the punishment he meted out so unhesitantly.

In all likelihood, Marta had come to Sciringesheal as a young bride. Perhaps she had even been born and raised there. It was certainly the only home Kiirla had known. Now they were both to be cast out, forced to start over in a place where they would be looked down upon and where no one would have reason to offer them anything beyond the bare minimum needed for survival.

And all because she, the Lady of Holyhood, had not known how to win over her husband's people.

Cymbra straightened her shoulders. Through the open doors of the great hall, she saw the first gray rim of light above the horizon. There was very little time left.

"I am also to blame," she said quietly. "If I had better known how to—"

"Yes, you are."

Her husband's prompt agreement in the matter of her guilt brought Cymbra up short. She had thought to have to explain it to him, even persuade him to it, but it seemed that was not necessary after all.

"Your fault lay in your refusal to tell me the truth of the matter from the beginning." He came closer, looking at her, his voice emotionless. "I am master here. When all is said and done, nothing matters save my will. You thought to hold yourself apart from that."

"No!" She could not let him make that charge against her, for of that she was truly innocent. "I only wanted to be a good wife, to manage my duties for myself without troubling you."

Wolf was at a loss to understand why she had tried to keep the problem from him. Had he not been supremely gentle and patient with her, beyond any measure he would ever have thought himself capable of achieving? Was he not the very model of a kind, tolerant, even indulgent husband, whom she should have approached at the very first sign of difficulty? Well, no, apparently he wasn't, and that stung, making him wonder as it did what really went on behind those remarkable eyes as blue as the tranquil sea, yet hiding unknowable depths. What did she truly think of him, of their marriage, and, most important, of the crisis that would inevitably occur when her husband and her brother stood face to face for the first time? Would that meeting come over locked swords or raised drinking horns? The answer lay buried within her heart, as well shielded as the most impenetrable stronghold.

Spurred by such thoughts, he raised an eyebrow, silently reminding her of the trouble she had brought by not being troubling. "I think," he said consideringly, "you are too proud."

"Proud? Me? I am not—" That was outrageous. It was other people always appealing to her pride, telling her of her beauty and her skill, praising her to the skies until she had to fight back the urge to scream that she was only a woman like all the rest, frail as any other human.

"It is your pride that drives you to not want to disappoint people. To live up to what you imagine their expectations to be, whether those are at all realistic or not."

She stared at him, dumbfounded. A strange, undefined sense sparked within her, grew stronger, threatened to overtake her. She recognized it then, a sense of being invaded, as though he had reached straight into her mind. It was what she had seen him do with the others in the hall but far more so.

With a shock, she realized that he *knew* her. That

wasn't possible. She had kept too much hidden for too long. And besides, she was the one who knew what others felt, who could sometimes even sense fragments of their thoughts. Never was she the *known*. Until now.

Her mouth was dry. She had no idea how to respond to this, no experience in dealing with it. Slowly, she said, "It is proudful to care about duty?"

"Your duty is to me. To *me*." The emphasis was all the clearer for being so quietly uttered. "I require your absolute obedience and loyalty. I thought I'd made that clear."

Perhaps he was right and she was proudful, for she couldn't merely accept this. "I was neither disobedient nor disloyal when I tried to manage a purely domestic matter—a matter of women—by myself."

He leaned against his high-backed chair, seemingly at his ease, and regarded her steadily. "How did you try to manage it? What did you do?"

She hated this, hated feeling so exposed and having to defend herself to him. Nothing in her life had prepared her for it. But then the Scourge of the Saxons had provided her with so many new experiences.

"I thought it best to wait, to give Marta and the other women time to come to know and accept me. Under the circumstances, taking into consideration the surprise of our marriage and the fact that I am a stranger, it seemed best for all concerned."

He nodded, as though considering all this. She wasn't fooled. He had already made up his mind and was not to be swayed. "You did not think to discuss this plan of yours with me?"

"I did not think you would concern yourself with such matters."

"What prompted you to ask her for the keys when you did?"

Cymbra hesitated. She had never told him about the

lute. Now she supposed that would be another black mark against her. They were piling up too quickly, making her wonder if she had done a single thing right since her arrival.

Not looking at him, she said, "I found my lute destroyed. I believed Marta responsible because of her resentment of me. I went to her and demanded the keys. She refused to give them."

His eyes darkened but he still spoke with infuriating calm. "So you thought to trick me into solving the problem for you with that talk of venison?"

"It was not a trick!" He was making her sound like a terrible person, this man who had brought her to such ecstasy only a short time before.

"I wanted your help," she said, "and I didn't know how to ask for it directly."

"It's very simple." He came toward her, stepping from light into shadow, then light again. The grayness was growing brighter as the Norse summer birthed another day.

"You come to me." He took hold of her arms, placing them around his neck. "And you say, 'Husband, I need your help.' See, that is not so hard, is it?"

"And if you are away on the training fields or on a voyage? Or if you have other problems to solve? Or perhaps you are merely weary or preoccupied. I take none of that into account? I merely load my difficulties on you without thought?"

The corners of his mouth twitched. "Not necessarily without thought. You could, for instance, seek the right moment. You might . . ." He considered, searching for the most helpful suggestion. "You might take my boots off, for instance, rub my neck, see to my comforts, and then when my mood is at its best, tell me what you wish."

Despite herself, Cymbra felt the beginning of a smile. The heady rush of emotion she never failed to experience with this man left her disoriented. In moments, she had gone from resenting him to being charmed by his sudden teasing playfulness.

"I think it would be simpler to just take care of things myself," she said, but lightly, letting him know she didn't mean it. To be absolutely sure he got that message, she moved her hips delicately against him.

"Simpler," he murmured against her throat, "isn't always better."

Beyond the timbered hall, a rooster warbled full-throated greetings to the sun. Another quickly followed and another, their raucous calls resounding off the berm floating down the hill to join the cries of all the other roosters in the town heralding the morn.

For a few, giddy moments, the world seemed to consist only of their triumphant song. They sounded for all the world as though they believed they called forth the sun themselves.

EVEN CYMBRA—*PROUDFUL* CYMBRA, AS SHE REMINDED herself—knew better than to try to persuade the Wolf to rescind his order of exile. The best she could do was make sure that Marta and Kiirla had ample and more supplies to take with them to their new home. This she did as soon as she emerged for the second time that day from the lodge, hastily reordering her clothes and patting her hair into place.

Crossing the field to join his men a short time later, Wolf saw her loading the wagon that would accompany the women. He caught her eye to let her know he had seen, but he said nothing, not even when she looked back at him defiantly. She thought he even smiled a little but she couldn't be absolutely sure.

She was still staring after her husband, distracted by the hard, powerful beauty of the body so recently entwined with hers, when one of the guards approached him and spoke briefly. Wolf stopped, turned around, and headed in the direction of his brother's lodge. That surprised Cymbra, for she would have expected Dragon to be on the training field already, as he was every day. Looking around, she realized there was no sign of him.

She made her farewells to Marta and Kiirla. The former refused to look at her but the younger woman nodded calmly. She seemed more in possession of herself than Cymbra had ever seen her, as though her formidable mother no longer overshadowed her.

Gesturing toward the wagon, Kiirla said, "Thank you for all this. It is very kind, especially so under the circumstances."

"I wish you did not have to go," Cymbra said frankly.

"It is best," Kiirla replied. "This will be a fresh start for us and I think we need that."

"If the landsmann at Oslofjord proves unkind—"

"He will not," Kiirla said quickly. Her cheeks colored faintly. "As it happens, he is not a stranger. We met at the spring festival." She met Cymbra's gaze. "He has no wife. I spoke to my mother of him, but . . ."

Understanding dawned and with it came a wave of relief. Not for a moment did Cymbra doubt that her husband was fully aware of the marital status of the landsmann.

Still reflecting on Wolf's cleverness, she waited until the women, their wagon, and their escort departed, then went in search of him. She found him just emerging from his brother's lodge. Ulfrich was with him and the two were so deep in conversation that they did not notice Cymbra's approach.

"He is not telling the truth about the pain," the elderly wise man was saying. "It remains great."

"But the wound has healed," Wolf countered. His brows were drawn tightly together. "He has returned to training and seems to be managing well. Or he did seem to until today."

"He has concealed much and pushed himself very hard. This fever is the result. I am afraid that—" Ulfrich broke off and nodded to Cymbra with a smile. "My lady, we were just—"

"This does not concern you," Wolf interrupted.

"Does it not? Then I must have misunderstood when I thought you were talking about your brother's wound not healing properly and now bringing on a fever. How foolish of me to think that the sensible thing would be to bring in a healer."

Ulfrich puffed out his cheeks in dismay and took a quick step forward, interposing himself between the jarl and his wife. "My lord, I'm sure she means well. A woman's heart overflows with compassion, after all, and—"

"Proudful," Wolf said flatly. He ignored Ulfrich and continued to stare down his wife, or at least tried to.

"Sensible," she shot back. More gently, she added, "Do not tell me it is pride to acknowledge my own skill and seek to use it where needed. You said that I was to ask your help. All well and good, I will do so. But now you need my help. Will you not take your own advice and do what you know is right?"

Ulfrich glanced nervously from one to the other but both ignored him. Cymbra was too preoccupied trying to remember her concern for Dragon while her attention kept focusing on how magnificent her husband looked even if he was scowling at her—*again*. She longed to run her hands over his massive chest, to tease a smile from his lips, to take him deep within her body and feel his life pour into her.

For his part, Wolf could not help but notice how glorious his wife appeared with her eyes lit for battle and her cheeks flushed. He knew he ought to be concentrating on her defiance—*again*—and he did make a feeble attempt, but the cheerful stirring of his cock distracted him. This was really too much. He was a man and a leader, not a randy boy. He could not, would not, allow any woman to control him.

But he was also a brother and he could not forget that either.

"Dragon is a warrior," he growled, "not a weakling. He will not tolerate being coddled."

"That's good," Cymbra replied as she brushed past him and opened the door to the lodge. "Because if what I think is wrong is indeed the case, the last thing I'm going to do is coddle him."

Her face was set, her manner utterly determined, but she faltered slightly as she confronted the man sitting upright in the large bed. Dragon's glare was remarkably like her husband's.

"What is this?" he demanded, not of her but of Wolf, who had followed directly after her. Ulfrich came too, no doubt unwilling to miss anything.

"My wife," Wolf said, "has the notion that she might be able to help you."

"I need no help," Dragon said emphatically.

Cymbra looked at him with open skepticism. She saw a man of vast strength, as big and heavily muscled as Wolf himself, and no doubt in peak condition under normal circumstances. But these were not normal, as the pallor beneath his tan and the lines of strain around his mouth testified.

"When were you wounded?" she asked, moving nearer to the bed.

Dragon spared her one swift glance and returned his attention to his brother. "You can't be serious about this."

Wolf shrugged. "She has some skill. As yet I don't know how much, but perhaps she really can help."

"I am not some mewling infant to be cosseted by a

woman!" He started to rise, remembered he was un-clothed, and sank back into the bed with a curse that would have melted ice.

Cymbra ignored him. She laid a hand on his brow. Instantly, he yanked away. She moved as quickly, keeping her hand in place and firmly pushing his head back against the pillows.

"As I thought," she said. "Too weak to fight off a woman."

For just a moment, she feared she had gone too far. Wolf must have thought so too, for he took a step forward. After a tense moment, Dragon surprised them both by laughing, however faintly.

"Odin's breath, she's right," he said. He glanced up at her assessingly. "Do you truly know what you're about?"

"You will answer that for yourself," she replied. His skin beneath her hand was hot and dry. There was a too-bright light to his eyes that also bespoke high fever. But so far as she could tell standing near him, his breathing was clear. She intended for it to remain that way.

She turned to Ulfrich. "I will need hot water, lengths of cloth about this long and wide"—she indicated with her hands—"and my chest of medicines. Oh, and Brita to help me."

"What are you going to do?" Dragon demanded suspiciously after the older man hurried off to do her bidding.

"Bring down the fever first, then find out what has gone wrong with your wound."

"Nothing's gone wrong. It's healed."

"Do I need to, I will drug you and find out for myself."

"You wouldn't let her do that!" Dragon demanded of his brother.

Wolf sat in a carved chair, stretched his long legs out in front of him, and prepared to stay awhile. Doubtful though he remained about the rightness of all this, he could not help but hope that Cymbra might actually be able to help.

"Of course not," he assured Dragon. "I'd just hold you down for her."

Cymbra's Norse vocabulary expanded somewhat in the minutes that followed. She pretended not to notice. Ulfrich returned with Brita on his heels. After that, there was very little Dragon could do except scowl.

W OLF WENT INTO THE TOWN AFTER MIDDAY. Dragon's fever was down and he was asleep, with Ulfrich keeping watch beside him. Cymbra, who so far as her husband could tell appeared to need no rest at all, had bustled off to see to matters in the kitchens. With Marta gone, she intended to assure there were no further problems.

It was just as well she was occupied for he had matters of his own to attend to. He went alone and on foot but with no expectation of being unnoticed. On the contrary, when he settled himself on a bench outside a tavern with a fine view of the harbor, it was with every intention of being seen and duly noted.

He didn't have long to wait. Barely had the buxom—and *very* friendly serving wench—brought him a horn of ale than a man approached. Wolf recognized him as the captain of a Breton galley that plied the waters as far west as Ireland and north to Sciringesheal itself.

"Sit," he said, and gestured for another horn to be brought. When this was done, the man, Onfroi by name, nodded his thanks, took a long swallow, and said, "News travels on the wind."

Wolf accepted this bit of wisdom with due solemnity. "News and rumor both, my friend."

"Sometimes it is hard to tell the difference."

"But not for one as experienced as yourself."

Onfroi inclined his head in agreement. "Still, one hears strange things."

"Indeed?"

"For example, I made port a fortnight ago in Essex. No one there talks of anything except the disappearance of the Lord Hawk's sister. You've heard of her, of course? Her beauty is said to rival the moon's and it is whispered that she possesses strange powers. Her brother kept her locked away, sensibly enough. But her sanctuary was invaded and the lady herself taken."

Wolf raised his eyebrows with polite interest. "By whom?"

"Rumor says the Danes. The man who headed her garrison swore to the Lord Hawk before he died that they were invaded by an army of savage Danes, several hundred he claimed, who overran them despite their most valiant efforts."

"The Hawk believes this?"

Onfroi spread his hands. "Who knows? There is a bit of a problem in that apparently no bodies were found, or for that matter any evidence of fighting. One doesn't think of Danes as such a tidy lot, cleaning up after themselves as it were."

"True, one doesn't think of that."

"And then there's the old nurse who babbles about a handful of Vikings who were taken captive the same day all this happened but who somehow escaped."

Wolf finished his ale and sat back in the sun. Truly, it did a man good to rest a bit. Not too much though. "Does she say anything else of them?"

"Only that the Lady Cymbra had speech with them in their own tongue while they were being held."

"Since all Norsemen whether Dane or not speak essentially the same language, that is of little use."

"Apparently the Hawk thinks the same. It is said he has sent men up into the Danelaw to learn the truth of his sister's whereabouts. When he knows it, he intends to give battle and destroy the villain who dared to take her."

"A predictable enough response."

"Indeed. One might even think that whoever took her intends her brother to do precisely as he will."

"Or at least intends for him to try," Wolf said and smiled.

He tarried a little after Onfroi departed, drank a little more, spoke with several more men who happened, as it were, to come by. They told the same tale but added bits and pieces.

The Hawk was said to rage. He had sworn to flay alive the despoiler of his sister. Yet it was also claimed that he wanted her safe return at all cost, her life held even above honor. That was the hardest part to believe, and no sensible man would, for surely honor counted more than the life of any mere woman.

Yet, it was food for thought and Wolf did not mind chewing on it. Ordinarily, word of the mysterious Saxon beauty lately come to Sciringesheal would have been carried to the Hawk on the selfsame ships that brought news of his rage and its cause. But the captains who put into the rich port controlled by Wolf Hakonson were a wily lot. They had enough sense to hold the favor of the jarl who protected their profitable trade in high regard and not risk losing it. So it was likely they would say nothing, no matter how tempted they might be.

Soon, then, he would send word himself. He had delayed long as it was, telling himself that the stolen time with his bride was meant only to strengthen her conviction when she stood before her brother and swore to her happiness, thus sealing the alliance he had gone to such extraordinary lengths to secure. Yet did he also know himself prey to a yearning to postpone the inevitable moment of confrontation, whatever that might bring.

Wolf shrugged inwardly. The Hawk would come, and when he did . . . What would be would be. They would make peace or Valhalla would welcome a new warrior to sup in Odin's hall. That the warrior would be Saxon he did not doubt for a moment. Every aspect of the battle, if there was to be one, favored his own victory.

He had plotted this much before sailing to Holyhood, but now, in the aftermath of all that had happened, he had no choice but to think further. What he perceived did not please him. Cymbra loved her brother. If he died, she would mourn him forever—and hate the man who had killed him.

It shouldn't have mattered. Life was harsh, duty and honor were all. Men lived or died as the Fates willed. Still, there was nothing to say a man's destiny had to be rushed. It wouldn't hurt the Hawk to rage awhile longer.

Wolf tossed a few coins on the table for the ale and began walking back through the town. On the way, he made one more stop and was well pleased with what he found.

CYMBRA TURNED THE LUTE OVER IN HER hands reverently. The graceful curves of polished wood seemed to glow with a life all their own. She looked up at her husband through tear-misted eyes. "I cannot believe you did this."

Wolf shrugged. "I enjoyed hearing you play. It seemed a shame to miss that pleasure."

His casual manner did not fool her for a moment. He had obviously gone to some trouble, seeking out and choosing a magnificent instrument better even than the one she had possessed, then leaving it on their bed for her to find when she came in to change for supper. That he had followed in time to see her reaction could not be coincidence.

She managed a wobbly smile as the tears threatened to spill down her cheeks. Never could she remember a gift meaning so much to her. "Thank you," she said with simple sincerity.

It did not escape Wolf's notice that his wife cared more for the lute—the best of its kind to be had but still only a lute—than she had for the ermine cloak fit for an empress. That, too, pleased him. "Perhaps you will play for me later."

"Whenever you wish," she said, and raised herself on tiptoe to brush her lips against his.

They arrived late in hall after that, but at least they got there. All things considered, Wolf counted that a victory. He forgot it quickly, though, when the sight of Dragon's empty seat reminded him of problems yet to be solved. Cymbra saw his concern and touched his hand gently.

"He woke this afternoon and had some broth before going back to sleep," she said as Wolf pulled out her chair for her. "That is really best for him right now."

She did not add that the broth contained a sprinkling of herbs from her medicine chest guaranteed to assure Dragon would sleep untroubled by pain. She saw no reason to bore her husband with such details. The grateful look he gave her as he took his own seat convinced her she was right.

His even more obvious surprise and pleasure when the meal began furthered her confidence. Not that he didn't give the pike in cream sauce a suspicious look when it was set before him, but after a single bite any doubt he had vanished. The well-seasoned pork, rounds of herbed bread, peas in butter and wild mint, and delicately flavored squab that followed even brought a smile of approval from Olaf the one-eyed, who had been conspicuously absent from the hall of late, wisely preferring to prepare his own food until the crisis of the women was past.

That it was behind them was confirmed as uncharacteristic silence descended over the timbered hall. The usual cacophony of conversation, laughter, and insults was stilled while people ate . . . and ate and ate. At length, when there was scarcely a bone left to gnaw, a round of hearty belches and a burst of cheers acknowledged Cymbra's culinary success.

She welcomed it with a sigh of relief and relaxed for the first time since entering the hall, only to stiffen a little when she caught her husband studying her assessingly. The look on his face bewildered her. "What?"

"I'm just wondering if it was really your beauty that made Hawk hide you away or if he feared he'd never get his men to leave any table you provisioned long enough to fight."

His smile deepened until he was actually laughing. "I can just imagine his warriors waddling into battle waving haunches of goose or hurling a pie or two at their enemies. If nothing else, they'd certainly have the advantage of surprise."

That absurd image made Cymbra smile in turn, yet the very mention of her brother and battle sent a dark ripple over her pleasure. It was on the tip of her tongue to say something to Wolf about his threat to kill Hawk, but she couldn't bring herself to do it. The accord between them was still so new, and she feared somehow still fragile, that she preferred to let the matter lie.

Besides, she really didn't believe there was any chance that her husband and her brother would fight. Hadn't Wolf said that his first choice was an alliance with Hawk? She had only to convince her brother that she was happily, willingly married and all would be well.

Wolf watched the flicker of emotion behind his wife's lovely eyes and silently cursed himself for a fool. Why, in the midst of such harmony, had he reminded her of the shadow that lay over them? Granted, the matter was on his mind, but that was no reason to speak of it to her, even indirectly.

The problem was that she distracted him so easily, there were times when he hardly recognized himself. And he didn't care for that at all.

Still, it was difficult to nurture any resentment in the aftermath of the best meal he'd ever eaten, and even more difficult later, when his lovely wife, clad only in her glorious chestnut hair, sat beside him on their bed and played him to sleep with the lute whose giving had brought her to happy tears.

BY MIDMORNING THE FOLLOWING DAY, CYMBRA WAS close to tears again but for a far different reason. She had decided that Dragon Hakonson was the worst patient she'd ever encountered and she was on the verge of telling him so.

"If you do not do as I say," she enunciated slowly and clearly, "you will *never* fully recover. You will have to live with the results of this injury for the rest of your life."

His dark brows drawn together, his heavily muscled arms crossed stubbornly over his massive chest, the Dragon glared at her. "And what's wrong with that? It's how it should be."

Cymbra prayed for calm even as she glared back. "That may be the stupidest thing I've ever heard. I'm not sure, maybe it's only the second or third stupidest, but I think it really does have a chance at being first."

He started to speak, cut himself off, and stared at the wall, pointedly ignoring her.

"Fine," she said, "have it your way, but I'm not leaving. My husband has told me to see what can be done for you and that's exactly what I will do."

When he still refused to acknowledge her, Cymbra took hold of the fur throw covering the lower half of his body and gave it a good, sharp tug. Had Dragon's reflexes not still been so swift, she would have had him bare as a babe.

"By Odin, woman!" he roared. "Have you no decency at all?"

Pleased to get any reaction from him other than sullen silence, Cymbra settled for lifting the edge of the fur far enough to expose the ugly, puckered scar on his left thigh.

"I am a healer," she informed him as she poked at the long red welt. "If your modesty is offended, I apologize, but you really need not be embarrassed around me." She gave him a confident smile. "Perhaps it would help to just think of me as a man."

Behind her, Ulfrich had a sudden need to clear his throat. He coughed so heartily that Cymbra decided to fix him an infusion of black currant and comfrey. He sounded as though he needed it.

Dragon was looking at her most peculiarly. She supposed he was struck by her good sense.

"There now, you see," she said, "it's as I thought. The wound has healed on the surface but there is deep scarring below. The muscles and tendons are badly knotted. They must be exercised slowly and patiently to restore their vigor."

She frowned. "I don't wish to be critical, but whoever treated this wound did a very bad job of it."

"I thought the same," Ulfrich declared. He peered over her shoulder, recovered from his coughing fit but sounding rather hoarse. "Frankly, my lord, a blind man could have done better."

Dragon grimaced. "Since the care was my own and I was in rather a hurry to get it done, I don't think you should be so critical."

"Your own?" Cymbra was horrified. "There was no one to help you? How could such a thing have happened?"

He sighed, resigned to having to tell her the story. "I stopped in Jutland on my way back from Byzantium. Outside the market at Hedeby, I was jumped by half-a-dozen Danes. I killed them, of course, but not before one of them did this." He gestured to his leg.

"You killed all of them?" Cymbra asked, her eyes widening.

"They were brigands only, not warriors," he said, accounting it no great thing. "Were it not for a patch of mud I slipped on, none of them would have landed a blow."

"Where were your men?" Ulfrich asked. Unlike Cymbra, he was not surprised by the Dragon's fighting prowess.

"I was alone, having just visited a . . . friend."

Ulfrich chuckled. "Is it possible this friend had a husband who didn't take kindly to your presence?"

"I suppose," Dragon admitted matter-of-factly. "I didn't pause to ask the scum who hired them."

Cymbra schooled herself to take no notice of his frankness. She did spare a moment's thought for the sheer determination and courage it must have taken to treat such a wound alone. Had he not been able to stanch the bleeding, he would likely have died. She suspected he knew that but would never acknowledge it.

"Very well," she said briskly. "Tomorrow you will begin a regimen of baths, massage, and exercises. In addition, I will give you a tonic to drink thrice daily. If all goes well, within a fortnight you will be able to return to the training field but only for limited periods."

She smiled at him reassuringly. "I will explain all this to Wolf so that when you do return, he will know better than to overstrain you and set back your recovery."

A look passed between warrior and wise man. Ulfrich opened his mouth to speak, but Dragon forestalled him.

"Brew your tonic and if it isn't too vile, I'll drink it. But as for the rest—" He shrugged shoulders as broad as Wolf's own. "The fever is gone. I return to the field tomorrow, and if I get a whiff that my brother thinks me an invalid, he'll be the one whose wounds need tending."

Cymbra heard him out, smiled sweetly, and said, "The fever will return again and again until this wound has healed properly. If that happens often enough, you will be left impotent."

Dragon's jaw dropped. He stared at her. "That is not true." He looked to Ulfrich for confirmation. "It isn't, is it?"

"Alas, my lord, I am not the healer the Lady Cymbra is and have not her knowledge. Besides, how many men have survived a wound such as this to discover what the consequences of it might or might not be?"

"Of course," Cymbra interjected, "perhaps you don't really care. Perhaps prowess on the training field is more important to you than prowess in—"

"That's enough!" the Dragon roared. He was actually blushing, a sight that delighted Cymbra although she was not about to show it. "I cannot believe my brother married so bold a woman! You were supposed to be a sweet, gentle, docile maiden, not some termagant fit to ride with the Norns!"

"Who," Cymbra asked although she suspected she wouldn't like the answer, "are the Norns?"

"The Weird Sisters," Ulfrich explained kindly. As she continued to regard him inquiringly, he warmed to the topic. "They ride through the sky in blood-flecked armor, their wild steeds dripping hailstorms from their distended nostrils. Over battlefields, the She-graspers of Spears sound their mighty horns, shoot rays of light from their javelins, and select those warriors who will live or die."

Cymbra nodded. "Oh, *those* Norns." To Dragon, she said, "Consider me such if you will but it changes nothing. In a fortnight, you can be free of pain. By winter, you can be fully recovered. If—and only if—you do as I say."

"You would be well advised to do so," a cheerful voice pronounced from the lodge door. With an apologetic smile, Brother Joseph stepped within. "I hope you won't mind my coming by, Lord Dragon, but I found the bloodroot Lady Cymbra wanted and—"

"That's wonderful!" she exclaimed. "Wherever was it? You must show me the place."

"I will and gladly, lady," the priest assured her. To Dragon, he said, "The Lady Cymbra was kind enough to make a poultice that has immensely eased the aches in my joints. You really can put great store in her cures."

"How nice," Dragon muttered.

"What kind of poultice?" Ulfrich inquired.

"Oat, pansy, rue, and rosemary," Cymbra said. "It is necessary to first boil the oat to a good consistency, guarding against allowing it to become too mushy—"

Wolf entered just then, in time to see the two holy men listening intently to his wife while his brother lay in the bed and rolled his eyes heavenward. He had come, he told himself, merely to see how Dragon fared. Not because he had noticed his wife's woman near the kitchens and realized that Cymbra was alone with the man who had lured countless women into beds, hay ricks, and who knew where else.

The man was his brother and Cymbra his wife. He trusted them both. He just didn't like the idea of them being alone together and disliked even more feeling that way.

Now he felt a perfect fool. First, they weren't even alone, and second, Dragon looked far more inclined to strangle than to seduce her. That cheered Wolf immensely. "You seem in good hands," he announced.

"I'm never marrying," Dragon growled. He shot a pointed look at Cymbra. "Wives get above themselves far too quickly. A man might as well put a ring through his nose."

Wolf chuckled, feeling better and better. He wasn't sure how she had done it, but his sweet, gentle wife seemed to have the situation well in control. "So you'll be back on the field tomorrow?" he asked.

In the dead silence that followed, Cymbra took a step forward. She tipped her chin up until he thought her slender neck would snap, glared at him, and said, "I think I'll make a tonic for you, too. One with plenty of thyme in it *to clear the head.*"

By which he deduced that Dragon would be a while yet recovering.

S HE'S THE KEYSTONE OF A SAXON PLOT. ALFRED'S AT the bottom of it. He's sitting over there in Wessex right now laughing himself sick."

Wolf raised his head from the bench where he was lying naked and sweat-soaked and glanced at his brother. "I thought of that. If she really were, they'd have tricked the Danes into taking her."

Dragon groaned. He bestirred himself enough to toss another ladleful of water onto the heated stones, then flopped back down on his own bench and let the steam of the sauna engulf him.

This day had been his first back on the training field after a fortnight of torture at the direction of his sister-in-law. He'd been stretched, kneaded, pummeled, twisted, and goaded through a battery of exercises that made him speak longingly of the cheerful carnage of battle and the relative mercy of a swift death.

Even Wolf, inured though he was to the harshness of life, had to wonder at the devilish torments devised by his lovely wife. And yet, though it would choke Dragon to admit it, his leg was stronger. Wolf had confirmed that for himself in just the last few hours.

He scratched his chest lazily and stretched out farther on the bench. The wood was cool against his back and buttocks, at least in comparison to the intense heat of the sweat lodge. "You'd have more strength if you refrained from bedding a wench every night."

Dragon scowled through the pine-scented mist. "I'm just making sure, that's all."

"Sure?" Wolf peered at his brother and laughed. "You're joking. Since when have you needed to make sure?"

"Since your darling wife told me I'd be impotent if I didn't do as she said."

Wolf sat bolt upright, staring at Dragon in disbelief. "She didn't!"

"She damn well did. Smiled as sweetly as you please, and suggested I cared more about prowess on the training field than prowess in bed."

"Cymbra said that?" He was incredulous. Surely his brother had misunderstood. Cymbra, who was still shy about telling him what she liked, who would only whisper it to him, her lovely face flaming and her eyes unable to meet his. Cymbra, speak so bluntly and not to him but to another man? *Cymbra?*

Dragon grinned, pleased to have gotten back a bit of his own. "You tell her I said so and I'll come after you with an ax, but the fact is she's at least as smart as she is beautiful."

"That's a truly frightening thought," Wolf said and meant it.

There was nothing much to do after that except beat each other with birch branches and run naked into the icy river. In that same spirit of male conviviality, it was only sensible then to retire to the timbered hall, summon the skald and a vat of ale, and while the night away in drink and song.

"How long has it been since we got drunk together?" Wolf wondered aloud some unknowable time later. They were sitting on the ground in front of the hall, although he couldn't quite remember when they'd moved out there. The moon had set and the sky was a sea of stars, split almost in half by the vast silver river along which the gods rode to glorious battle.

"Too damn long," Dragon replied. "Ought to do this

regularly. Good Vikings get drunk." He thought for a moment, then added, "And pillage. We're supposed to do a lot of pillaging. People expect it."

Wolf nodded, pondering that as he might a childhood memory. "Times are changing."

"Perish the thought!"

"No, it's true, they are. Look right here with us." He waved an arm to encompass the hill fort and the town beyond. "How much pillaging do we actually do? I mean really? We fight when we have to—and we do it too damn much thanks to the bloody Danes and Saxons. But we're traders, brother. We make an honest profit—"

Dragon laughed. "A damn big honest profit."

"Nothing wrong with that but it's still trading. And there are other changes, too. You think Brother Joseph stays here because he likes the climate?"

"What's wrong with the climate?"

"Nothing, I'm just using it as an example. He's here 'cause people are listening to him. Hell, sometimes I listen to him."

"You do? Really? What's he say?"

Wolf frowned, wanting to get it right even if it didn't make much sense. "He says we're supposed to love each other."

Dragon mulled that over. He was silent for a while, drinking, then remembered what they'd been talking about. "He doesn't mean everybody, does he? Couldn't mean that."

Wolf started to shake his head, decided that wasn't a good idea, and shrugged. "I think he does."

His brother blinked at him owlishly. "Why?"

More thinking, then, "Something 'bout being the children of God and him sending his son to die for us."

"Sacrifice." Dragon nodded. This was something he could understand. "You don't allow those here anymore, do you?"

Wolf hesitated. Images slipped through his mind, stories his father had told him of men and sometimes even women and children sacrificed to the Aesir, the great gods. Nine times nine, they were hanged from the branches of trees, their blood soaking the ground for nine days. Sacrifice was still an accepted part of life but it was slowly dying out, replaced by a sense of—what? Other possibilities? Other hopes?

"I don't mind the occasional goat getting its throat cut," he said and emptied his drinking horn.

Later still, still singing, Wolf entered his lodge. Determined not to wake his wife, he put a finger to his lips and said "Shuush" loudly. That made him laugh, which he was still doing when he lost his balance and thumped into a table.

Righting himself, he stumbled in the general direction of the bed, but since it was moving—*Ought to talk to Cymbra about that, bed shouldn't be moving, least not unless I'm in it with her*—he missed and careened off back toward the door.

Sitting up in the bed, watching these antics with a tolerant eye, Cymbra shook her head in amusement. She knew well enough that men drank, often to excess, but she hadn't expected her husband to overindulge. Mayhap it was just as well that he let his iron control slip once in a while.

At least he was a cheerful drunk, singing again and still shushing himself. But if he kept on the way he was going, he was liable to break his neck. She left the bed, wrapped a blanket around herself, and retrieved Wolf from where he'd wandered off a short distance from the lodge. He blinked at her in surprise, then produced one of those devastating smiles that made her toes curl.

"Shymbra, *elskling*, I was jus' lookin' for you."

He had called her "sweetheart." How nice, even if he

did have to be drunk to do it. "I'm sure you were," she murmured. "Come on now."

He went, holding her hand, docile as a lamb until they were back inside, at which point he grabbed her and tumbled them both onto the bed. "Have I tol' you how beaut'ful you are?" he asked.

"Well, no, not in so many words, but you get the idea across." Pushing against his shoulders, she tried to slip out from under him. "Let me get up and I'll take your boots off."

He stared at her. "You will, really?"

"Absolutely." One more good shove and she was free, but only because he had rolled over onto his back. Lying there staring up at the ceiling, he said, "You're sush a good wife."

"Thank you." She went to the end of the bed, took hold of one boot, and began tugging. It gave but only slowly.

"I really didn't think it'd work out that way," her husband informed her.

"Didn't you?" The dead weight of his leg was making her arms ache but she kept pulling until finally the boot came free. She tackled the second.

"You bein' Saxon and all, thought there'd be problems. Then there's the way you look." He nodded sagely. "Tha's a big problem right there."

"I thought you decided you like the way I look."

He gave a sharp laugh. "Me and every other man, tha's the problem. Can't think straight when you're around. Can't think 'bout anything 'cept spreadin' your luscious legs and—"

The second boot came off, distracting him. She tossed it onto the floor and pulled the covers up over her husband. He tried to grab hold of her again but she deftly sidestepped him.

Wolf shot her a sulky look, for all the world like a child deprived of a favorite toy, and fell back against the pillows. A moment later, he was snoring loudly.

Cymbra considered trying to get back to sleep but she didn't feel tired. It would be light soon and there was much to be done. Humming softly, she dressed, tied her keys to her belt, and gave Wolf a last, fond look.

He lay with arms and legs akimbo, his big, lean body taking up most of the immense bed. A lock of ebony hair fell across his forehead. Thick lashes fanned out over his cheeks. In sleep, his features were relaxed, making him appear younger and much less formidable than the mighty Scourge of the Saxons.

Cymbra supposed that was how he had looked before life hardened him. The thought made her heart tighten.

She made sure he was well covered and dropped a light kiss on his brow before going to the door. Even then she couldn't resist a glance over her shoulder. Truly, she was the most fortunate of women, she couldn't have asked for a better husband.

Their marriage was going to be a complete success.

She was absolutely sure of it.

Chapter
TWELVE

THEIR MARRIAGE WAS A DISASTER. HE WAS an arrogant, unfeeling, insensitive brute of a Viking and she had been a fool ever to believe otherwise.

In the grip of such dire thoughts, Cymbra stared up at her husband and blurted out the first thing that came into her head: "You can't mean it!"

They were standing near the open gate in the berm surrounding the hill fort. Cymbra had just returned from the town, where she had treated a burn suffered by a young boy who strayed too close to one of the many open fires.

Fortunately, it wasn't serious and the boy would be fine. His gratitude at the relief of his pain and his parents' thankfulness had reminded Cymbra yet again of why she was a healer.

Or at least she was if she was allowed to be, and that teetered in the balance. Her heart lurched the moment she realized Wolf had returned early from visiting a settlement on the opposite side of the fjord. Seeing him crossing the field, bare-chested after a swim, laughing with

several of his men, Cymbra tried to make herself as incon-
spicuous as possible. But for some reason, the concealing
disguise of her plain gray cloak didn't work.

He came straight at her, his face hard and his manner
implacable. In an instant, he assessed the situation—cor-
rectly, damn him—and rendered his verdict.

"I can't go into town at all? Not even with an escort?
That's absurd! I'm not a prisoner here! I'm—"

His hands came down heavily on her shoulders,
abruptly stopping her. "You are my wife and a disobedient one at that. Or are you going to claim you did not
know that you were only to leave here with permission
and with an escort?"

Cymbra would have given just about anything she
had to be able to claim it but she could not. It was just that
in the past week the unbroken accord between them had
made her believe Wolf was coming to trust her. Now the
realization of how foolhardy she'd been to think any such
thing struck her hard.

"I could not find you to ask," she said, "and a child
was hurt. I could not wait."

"Then the child should have been brought to you
here." His lean, hard fingers moved against the coarse
fabric of her cloak. Were it not for his intimate knowledge
of her body, even to the graceful way she moved, he would
never have recognized her, so well disguised had she been
by the anonymous garment.

He scowled as a possibility occurred to him. "How
many times have you worn this, Cymbra? How many
times have you concealed your identity to evade my will?"

Unable to meet his eyes, she looked down. Her gaze
swept the broad, heavily muscled expanse of his bare
chest. She swallowed hard and stared hastily at the
ground, rubbing her foot in the dust. "Not often and only
when it was necessary."

His hands tightened again, compelling her attention.

The thought that she had defied him not once but several times sent a surge of anger through him. Had she been anyone else, there would be no question but that she suffer punishment sufficient to reform her ways.

He knew that was the proper response to such disobedience, knew it was his duty to impose such punishment to uphold the order and discipline vital to survival. As jarl, he was required to put aside his personal feelings and do as he knew was right. Yet, understanding that full well, he could not act as he knew he should.

Instead, he said, "It is not your place to decide what is necessary or not. My orders are to be obeyed in all circumstances."

A small voice of caution warned Cymbra that this was not the time to challenge him. Hadn't he said something to her about a man being more inclined to grant favors when he was in a mellow frame of mind? If she had any sense, she would seek to placate him, work whatever feminine wiles she possessed to get her own way.

Apparently, sense was not one of her great attributes.

"Even when those orders are wrong? Surely you don't believe I could come to any harm? No one in Sciringesheal is so foolish as to displease you."

He lifted an eyebrow. "No one? Only my Saxon wife, it seems." When she would have answered that, he forestalled her. "I have treated you with great patience and restraint from the beginning, and I continue to do so. Were that not the case, you would be punished right now for your disobedience."

He took hold of her chin and forced her to look at him. "Let us understand each other, *wife*. My word is law here. You will do exactly as you are told—exactly—or you will suffer the consequences. Is that clear?"

The color fled from her face, only to return with a vengeance. Her fists curled at her sides as her eyes blazed. "So I am not to use my own judgment even when I know it to be sound? I am merely to be the slave to your will? I am no thrall, *husband*. The very existence of such poor creatures disgusts me. So does the suffering I see around me that sometimes could be readily eased or avoided altogether. I understand what you said about this being a harsh land but I don't see why the harshness must be added to. It is no weakness to seek to make life better."

Several thoughts occurred to Wolf. Despite the fair—and more than fair—warning she had received, his wife was still defying him. She was actually angry at his dictate while seemingly unaware of the magnitude of the concession he was making by not punishing her at once.

"This life you hold so precious depends for its very existence on order." His hands tightened further on her shoulders and, for good measure, he gave her a little shake. "Transgress again and you will be punished, this I promise you."

Her lovely face tightened. Distantly, he realized that she was afraid, and he regretted that, but far more he saw her courage and admired it. "What will you do, *husband*?"

She said the word again, every bit as challengingly as before, but then everything about her was a challenge. "Tie me to the punishment post, whip me as you did that poor man?"

The very thought made Wolf feel as though he had plunged into the coldest sea. He wanted to shout his denial, gather her to him, comfort and reassure her. But he was a man and she a woman. The balance of power between them had to be maintained.

Slowly, he forced himself to smile. His hands slid down her arms, no longer cruelly demanding but caressing her. His smile became real when he saw the startled look in her eyes.

"How dramatic you are," he said. One hand held her firmly around the waist, the other slid lower. Without warning, he squeezed her buttocks hard. At her little yelp, he laughed.

"I would merely apply correction where it would do the most good. You might have trouble sitting down for a day or two, but you wouldn't suffer any permanent damage." He couldn't resist adding, "Except perhaps to your dignity."

He was going to drown in those eyes, so wide had they become. "You wouldn't dare!"

"Wouldn't I?" He softened his hold a little, deliberately stroking her. Had they not been in so public a place, he would have done much more. Briefly, he considered taking her the short distance to the stables.

They were deserted at this hour. His prideful wife might benefit from a swift, sweaty tumble in a hay-filled stall. The temptation was great but he stopped himself. That she would end by yielding to him fully he did not doubt. But at the same time he would be yielding to her and he could not do that, not now, if he had any hope of controlling her.

Instead, he gave her bottom a sharp swat. "Return to your duties, *wife.* My men and I labor hard this day. We expect a good meal at table tonight. See to it."

If the glare she gave him was anything to judge by, he would need the services of a food taster before he supped. He watched her go, then turned away only to stop abruptly at the sight that confronted him.

Dragon lounged against a wall nearby, arms crossed over his chest and a broad grin wreathing his face. He had the air of a man who has been well entertained.

"You waste yourself teaching the arts of war," he said as he walked over to join his brother. "You should be instructing the rest of us poor, benighted males in the proper management of the fair sex."

A lesser man would have quaked at the look the Wolf

shot him and the lip-curling snarl that accompanied it. "I trust your leg fares better than your wits."

Dragon made a show of flexing the limb and nodded pleasantly. "It fares well indeed, thanks to the ministrations of your gentle, *docile*"—the word made him choke with laughter—"wife."

"It isn't funny," Wolf said, shaking his head. "She endangers herself and doesn't even realize it."

"Does she? She's right, you know, no one in Sciringesheal would dare so much as to look at her wrong."

They walked some little distance back toward the training field before Wolf replied. "Men of all sorts come and go here. Not all of them are loyal to me."

"True enough, but none would rush to embrace the kind of death you would mete out. It isn't really *their* loyalty that worries you, is it?"

Wolf's face hardened. "Do you think to read my thoughts, brother?"

Dragon laughed. "A blind man could read them. It is the loyalty of your Saxon bride that worries you, although I don't really see why. She seems to have settled in well enough."

"Seems . . . aye, I suppose she does, but it is scarcely a month since we wed, little enough time to know her heart."

"Is that why you have yet to send word to the Hawk?"

"Are you so eager for battle?" Wolf countered.

"There won't be one. Hawk will come, Cymbra will tell him she is well and happily married, and, indulgent brother that he is—you can hardly deny he is *that*—he will accept what has happened and you will have the alliance you have wanted all along. What could be simpler?"

"Nothing," Wolf agreed though his voice held doubt. "Provided Cymbra plays her part."

"You doubt it? You think she means to play you false,

betray her marriage vows and slay her brother in the
process? That seems the far side of unlikely to me."

Put that way, Wolf's concerns sounded even more
outlandish than he himself knew them to be. Yet still he
had hesitated, letting the days—and the nights—pass
without summoning the Hawk.

Now in high summer when the fields shone gold with
grain it was difficult to accept that before too long winter
would descend over the northlands. Ice would clog the sea
channels and savage winds would destroy even the sturdi-
est vessels. Men would stay to their hearths, counting up
the bounty of the harvest, telling stories around the fires
and planning the adventures of the coming year.

If he did not act soon, not even the Hawk in all his
fury would be able to come for his sister. The matter
would have to wait months, well into the new year, until
the world gentled once again.

Wolf was tempted to let that happen. He could gain
more time to bind Cymbra to him in every way possible.
But to put off the day of reckoning meant leaving her to
worry over her brother's fate. He had seen that worry in
her eyes too often to pretend he didn't know how real it
was. When all was said and done, he could not do that
to her.

"Only a little while longer," he said, and added, lest
Dragon be disposed to discuss it further, "she is not yet
fully to my hand, but she will be and soon."

"If you say so." Dragon hesitated but he loved his
brother too much not to speak his mind. "Yet do I ask you
to consider that loyalty and obedience aren't necessarily
the same thing. One is freely given, the other too often
forced. It is for you to decide which you truly want."

"I want both. I expect both."

"Ah, well, then perhaps you should have wed a *docile*
Norse maiden."

Wolf arched a brow in blatant doubt. "Is there such a thing?"

"Not on this earth," Dragon conceded. "Which is why I'm safe from matrimony. The only wife I'd take would be a soothing little woman to bear my sons and rub my feet, and never give me a moment's worry."

Wolf stared at him for a moment before shouting with laughter. He couldn't help it, the specter of Dragon with such a creature undid him. And, not incidentally, went a long way toward restoring his good humor, which he suspected was the actual intention.

"Pray you never find her, brother. She'd have you dead of boredom before the bridal flowers wilted."

Dragon flung an arm around Wolf's shoulders. "Enough talk of women. I say I can throw a javelin ten paces farther than you can."

"Not even with Odin passing wind at your back."

They went off to settle the matter, but later, as he swam again in the river and watched the day's long twilight creep over the land, Wolf remembered what his brother had said. He frowned, considering the possibility that Dragon might be right. Perhaps it was impossible to have both Cymbra's unquestioning obedience and her loyalty as well. Perhaps to win her loyalty, he had first to give her his own trust.

It was a hard thought and one he did not accept readily. He was still considering it when he dried off, dressed in clean apparel, and made his way to the great hall.

HE DID NOT, AFTER ALL, NEED A FOOD TASTER. Cymbra greeted him with impeccable courtesy and no lingering sign of her earlier anger. Looking ravishing— and highly ravishable—in topaz silk, her hair set back from her face with jeweled combs but left free to tumble to her knees, she inclined her head slightly as he approached the high table where she awaited him. Firelight glinted off the petal-smooth curve of her cheek. He inhaled the faint lavender scent of her bath still clinging to her and felt himself harden in helpless, resented response.

"Good evening, my lord." They might have been distant acquaintances, so cool and calm was she. Her control provoked him mightily, particularly when contrasted to his own lack, but he was damned if he'd show it.

"My lady," he said, all civility. Smoke swirled from the cooking fire at the center of the hall. Children ran among the tables and benches, playing with the eager dogs. People gathered in companionable groups, chatting about the day's events. It was all very normal, very ordinary.

All but his Saxon wife, Frigg-blessed woman, at once bane and joy of his existence. Resolve flowed through him. He would teach her a thing or two about this game, having played it in courts of intrigue from black-watered Dubhlinh to treacherous Byzantium.

They proceeded to supper, which was as fine as any served in his hall since Cymbra had taken the keys. Nor did he deny himself the pleasure of telling her so, if only to see her veiled surprise at his graciousness.

"I've never had better haddock. Taking into account that I'm not particularly fond of fish, this is amazingly good."

She had eaten very little, only toying with her food. Now she dropped all pretense of interest in it and looked at him cautiously. "You don't like fish?"

"Not especially. I probably ate too much of it as a child."

A child? Her stomach did a slow tumble. The thought of a child like Wolf, a small, black-haired, gray-eyed mischief maker for her to love and nurture, swept over her with sweet longing. Her cheeks warmed.

"Why was that?" She was hardly aware of what she

asked, wanting only to distract him so that he wouldn't notice her sudden self-consciousness.

He lifted his horn of mead, drank, and set it down again in the curled iron brace made for that purpose. "There were times when we had no fodder for the animals and they had to be slaughtered. When the crops also failed, there was only the sea to keep us alive."

Cymbra could not mask her surprise. "I had no idea you endured such hardship."

He shrugged dismissively. "We were not always so prosperous. In my childhood, there was great disorder. Many holdings were raided repeatedly, ours among them. My father tried to protect us, but as often as not, our walls were breached. We had to run and hide while the raiders took whatever they wished and burned the rest."

Struggling to reconcile what he had just told her with the wealthy, powerful man he had become, Cymbra asked, "How did you go from that to all of this?" She gestured around the hall filled with the trophies of victory, gleaming gold and silver plate, vivid hangings, and, most important, happy, prosperous people.

He hesitated and for a moment she thought he would not answer. His expression was guarded. "In my twelfth year, raiders came again. This time both my parents and a good many others were killed. There was nothing left for Dragon and me. We went to sea."

Cymbra waited, thinking he would follow this matter-of-fact recitation with something more. When he didn't, she looked to her brother-in-law. "How old were you then?"

"I was eight."

"Weren't you afraid?"

"I was more afraid he might leave me." He cocked an eye at Wolf. "But he wouldn't have. After we buried our parents, we stood beside their grave. Wolf put his arm around my shoulders and promised me everything would be all right."

Cymbra's throat tightened painfully. Vividly she could see the two boys as they had been, one still a child, the other little more, setting out alone to face a dangerous and hostile world.

"You were lucky to survive."

"We did more than that," Dragon said lightly. "Wolf seemed to have a knack for figuring out which voyages to sign on with. He was big for his age and already handy with a sword, so he didn't have too much trouble convincing shipmasters to take him on. It was only after they thought they had him that he'd mention I came along, too."

The two men shared a grin over the memory. Cymbra marveled at it. A past that would have destroyed most people seemed only to have strengthened the valiant Hakonson brothers.

"We sailed the world," Dragon said, "or at least most of it. Everywhere we went, Wolf studied how people fought and how they defended themselves. The rest of us would be . . ." he sought a discreet term suitable for her tender ears, ". . . relaxing while he'd be making sketches of fortifications or having long discussions about the best way to smelt steel."

Cymbra eyed her husband skeptically. "Didn't you ever . . ." she paused, mimicking Dragon, ". . . relax?"

"My brother exaggerates," Wolf said with a chiding look at that worthy. The smile he turned on his wife was purely, breathtakingly male. "And I think you already know the answer to that."

Her cheeks flared. She looked away hastily, resuming her pretense of interest in her food. Indeed, she knew the answer too well, having been the recipient of skills he could not possibly have acquired examining fortifications or talking with blacksmiths.

"You really should eat," he said pleasantly. "Especially after going to so much trouble to prepare such a magnificent meal."

Recalling on what terms they had parted when he *ordered* her to see to supper, she replied tartly, "I assure you, my lord, I went to no trouble at all."

"Oh, but you must have. There's no reason to deny it."

"It is as easy to prepare good food as poor," she insisted, "provided just a little thought is given."

"You are too modest. Surely only a great effort could produce such a feast." He gestured to the array of rich dishes on the table.

"Not at all," she assured him. "Indeed, hardly any effort was required."

"I cannot believe that. The servants alone could never have managed this. You must have stood over them for hours, guiding their every movement, attending to every detail, and—"

"I did no such thing!" Cymbra burst out. She caught herself but too late and now she had to face his look of blatant amusement. Truly, he had baited the hook well, playing to her barely suppressed anger and her pride. She had to admit, he'd done it awfully well.

Dragon clearly thought so, although he was being very careful not to look at either of them. Nor was anyone else, as it seemed that every man, woman, and child in the great hall was suddenly intensely occupied with their own matters. Yet she knew they were full well aware of the tension between their jarl and his Saxon bride.

Tension that suddenly weighed down on her unbearably. She longed for a return of the accord they had so briefly known and dreaded the thought that such strife might instead be the pattern of their days together.

"Wolf—" she said tentatively.

"I thought you'd taken to referring to me as *husband*."

He said it in exactly the tone she had used, at once dis-
dainful and challenging.

Cymbra flinched and looked at him swiftly, but he
was smiling and there was a look in his eyes that took her
aback. "My lord—"

He leaned closer, so close that the breadth of his
shoulders and chest blotted out the light. She felt the
warmth of his breath, its touch sending tremors through
her. "I prefer my own name on your lips," he said, so
softly only she could hear him. He leaned closer still. "I
especially prefer it when you say it in certain ways . . . at
certain times."

Her face flamed. She felt confused, uncertain . . . and
excited. The cool restrain she had tried so hard to maintain was melting away as though it had never been.

Beneath it, and vastly more important, the walls she
had built around her emotions from earliest childhood
seemed to be dissolving. She had an image of them in her
mind as no longer solid and strong but fading in and out,
almost transparent.

The thought terrified her, for she knew too well the
devastating pain that could lie beyond them. And yet the
idea of being without those walls that were as much prison
as protection . . . To be truly free . . .

"What is it?" Wolf's eyes had gone dark as he
watched her. He raised a hand, lightly touching the backs
of his fingers to her cheek. "Are you all right?"

His obvious concern touched her deeply at that moment when she was so intensely vulnerable. She tried to
tell him she was fine but her throat was suddenly very tight
and a glimmer of tears clung starlike to her thick lashes.

Wolf cursed under his breath. He stood and lifted her
out of her seat in one fluid motion. Instantly, all conversation—and all pretext of disinterest—vanished. Every eye
turned on them.

"Lady Cymbra is weary," he said in a tone that

brooked no disagreement from her or anyone else. Holding her high against his chest, her silky hair spilling over his arms and down his legs, he strode from the hall.

Before he had gotten very far, Cymbra recovered sufficiently to protest, if halfheartedly. On a note of self-disgust, she said, "They will think me a weak-willed ninny."

He looked down at her but didn't stop. "They will do no such thing, but would you truly care if they did?"

The question surprised her. "Of course."

He did slow his step just a little then and studied her closely. The moon had risen. By its silver light, she looked gloriously pale. His body stirred, inevitably, but beneath the hard thrust of passion was tenderness he could no longer ignore. "Why would you?" he asked softly.

"Because your people are my people now. It's only natural that I would seek their good opinion."

A fierce pleasure rippled through him. *Her people.* Was it true? Had she accepted so much, so quickly, after being so badly begun? Dare he believe her?

Her worry over her brother must be even worse than he had thought, else how to explain her sudden fragility? Remorse filled him but with it came the steely determination to end her uncertainty soon.

Soon, very soon. But not this moment, not with the moon on them and the scent of her skin filling his breath. Not with their lodge only a few rapid strides away.

Wolf kicked the door open, passed beneath the lintel emblazoned with the crossed-ax symbols of his rank—and responsibility—and shut out the world. The shutters were open, filling the room with moonlight. The covers of the bed were turned down, revealing fresh linens he knew had been scented with herbs, a luxury he would have thought foolish were he not coming to realize that it was his wife's way to show her care in small, meticulous touches.

His wife. His beautiful, courageous, compassionate,

proudful wife whose hands had trembled when he spoke of the hardships of his youth and whose eyes had filled with tears when he reminded her of their quarrel.

Cymbra.

It came to him suddenly that he had known her only a few short weeks yet she was already far more important to him than he would have believed any woman ever could be. And not because of the alliance she represented. Something in her spoke to a part of himself he had barely acknowledged, the part that was not responsible brother, not resolute jarl, not deadly warrior or leader of his people or even seeker of peace but simply and supremely a man.

And he loved her for it. The shock of that roared through him. Love was weakness, vulnerability, a kind of madness that shredded reason and made the most sensible man a fool. He had always scorned it, denying its very existence, yet there it was, full-blown within him. He could no more root it out than he could tear out his heart.

The knowledge was a sweet agony, bringing him a furious pleasure. He dropped his arm from beneath her legs and, holding her around the waist, let her slide down the length of him until her feet just barely touched the ground.

She raised her head, a little startled. With ruthless thoroughness, he molded her to him, claiming and controlling. He held back nothing, gave her no quarter, but sought to establish his mastery beyond the shadow of a doubt.

She made a sound deep in her throat but he felt no fear in her, only feminine strength and need rising to match his own. Elation drove out resentment. He felt a sense of recognition, as though the very essence of him knew her in a secret, eternal way that surpassed the frail boundaries of life itself.

They undressed each other hastily, clumsily, without regard for the finer points of brooches and buckles, laces and garters. They fell across the fur-covered bed, limbs entwined, mouths seeking, amid hotly murmured words and soft, indiscernible sounds.

As so often happened, their first coupling was swift and fierce. Wolf eased her beneath him, his hands running over her, desperate to know her silken heat. She parted her legs. He hesitated, meeting her eyes, desire and doubt mingling in his.

"Please," she whispered, "I need you so badly . . . please. . . ."

He went into her carefully. When he was fully seated, he rose, the muscles of his powerful arms and shoulders bunching, and gazed down at her. Her lips were parted, her cheeks flushed. She looked well and thoroughly like a woman in the throes of passion, and it pleased him mightily to know she returned his desire in full.

"You are so beautiful," he said, swelling even further, "so exquisitely . . ." he moved within her, "so utterly . . ." again he moved and again, "so completely . . ." he thrust harder, deep and deeper. Her hips lifted to meet him. He caught her hands in his, their fingers entwining against the scented pillows. His mouth on hers, he groaned, ". . . a woman. *My* woman." The silken sheath of her body flexed around him as though acknowledging his claim even while making its own.

"So beautiful," she said as the first curling edges of hot, sweet pleasure took her. Her gaze locked on his. "So beautiful," she repeated, making it clear she meant him. He started to laugh at the notion but the pleasure was upon him as well, and he could only gasp. He was at the edge before he knew he was close to it, fighting to hold back, wanting to give her everything and more.

He let go of one of her hands and slid his own between their joined bodies, stroking her until she cried out, her head twisting on the pillow. "Don't stop, oh, please, don't stop . . ."

"I won't." He continued the caress as he drove again within her. Scant heartbeats passed before she convulsed around him, her exquisite body arching up from the bed, his name a cry on her lips.

"Wolf!"

He growled in response, rising above her, gripping her hips between his hands, driving harder and deeper yet until he, too, was taken, convulsed by pleasure so intense he lost all awareness of the world, of himself, of everything save the woman who clasped him to her, gently stroking his sweat-dampened back.

Such was the first time. Afterward, Wolf resolved to do better. Well, not precisely better. Just longer. He wanted to linger over her, savoring every inch of her. A man was a fool to waste such beauty and passion in hasty coupling.

Call him a fool, then, for he could not manage such restraint the second time, although by Odin he did try. Nor did he think he mistook the little laugh he heard from her afterward, as though she was mightily pleased by his lack of restraint.

He lifted his head then, from where it rested slumped against her lovely breasts, and eyed her narrowly.

"Amused, *wife*?"

Her delicious mouth curved in an enticing smile. "Well satisfied, *husband*."

"You think so?" He felt himself growing hard again. She felt it, too, and her eyes widened most gratifyingly.

"Wolf . . . ?"

"Hmmm?" He moved, as though to withdraw from her, but returned quickly enough when she clasped his buttocks.

He smiled down at her, gray eyes gleaming, and moved again. "Oh, is *this* what you want?"

It was and she made that clear enough to send them both whirling into a red mist of release before he found himself once again slumped against her, scant-breathed and lack-sensed. This time she managed not to laugh but he *knew*, though he had not the strength to raise his head, knew beyond doubt that she was smiling.

He woke later to feel her silken thigh thrown over his and the swell of her breast against his arm. Incredibly, that was enough. His cock stirred in cheerful anticipation. Wolf groaned and stared down the length of himself. His cock moved again, as if waving at him. He bit back a wry curse and glanced at his wife. She was asleep. He couldn't wake her. She was only a woman. She needed to rest, to recover from his manly attentions.

Her thigh moved, warm, smooth, slightly moist with the mingled essence of him and her. Tempting, testing, enticing. She raised her head, tossed back her hair, and smiled at him.

Would death in the sweet combat of the marital bed qualify him for Valhalla? he wondered. He imagined himself trying to make that claim before Odin and all the gods, thinking of how they would laugh. Ah, but he would have an ally. Frigg would welcome him. No doubt, she'd seat him right beside her.

"We used to sacrifice to Frigg," he whispered still later against his wife's sweet skin. "Mayhap you wish to revive the custom."

She laughed but, he noted, didn't deny it, and curled against him, her breath soft against his chest. He thought she slept and thought to do the same, until she stirred beside him. Slowly, she lifted herself, the curtain of her hair falling over them both. He saw . . . uncertainty in her eyes, hesitation, and something more. Fear? No, surely not that.

"I have been meaning to ask you," she said slowly, for clearly the asking was not easy. "You have not said . . ." In the dim light of the lodge, he saw her glance away and knew in an instant what she meant to ask. What must be uppermost in her mind, what he should have told her, what it was cowardice to deny and delay.

"No," he said suddenly. He cupped the back of her head, pulling her down to him. He would not let her go. Holding her close to him, feeling her soft lips on his chest, he said, "I have not sent word to Hawk, not yet."

Silence and then, shivering softly through it, "Why not?"

Why, indeed? He had never hesitated in battle, or on those occasions when he had to render judgment, or in any other arena of his life save this. What could he say to her? That he was as yet uncertain, that she was more than he had ever even dared to long for, that he was at some level deeply afraid?

He was man and jarl, husband and leader. He could not admit to his fears.

"I thought it best to wait. It may sound cruel now, but your brother will be more likely to accept our marriage if he has had some time to worry over you."

"He will be worried," Cymbra said softly, "very worried and very unhappy."

"I am sorry for that." He meant it. What was happening to him that he should be concerned over the tender feelings of a Saxon warlord who would joyfully dispatch him to Valhalla? Had he truly become so craven?

Her breath was warm and tempting as she relaxed against him, her slender form molding to his. The confession of his regret had carried the day, or at least the night. He said a silent prayer of thanks to Frigg, for he had no doubt the credit was hers.

Thus reassured, Cymbra fell into sleep as though off the edge of the world. He dozed again, the light sleep of a battle lull, and woke toward dawn feeling oddly energized. After a cautious look to be sure Cymbra did not stir, he pulled on a pair of trousers and took himself outside where he stood stretching in the pearl gray morn.

He felt good, *damn* good. Better, indeed, than he could ever remember feeling. What was it Dragon had said—a meek little woman to bear him sons and rub his feet? Wolf laughed. Better a temptress to alternately infuriate and dazzle him. A woman of strength and will to match his own, a true partner in his life as well as his bed.

The cool air, heavy with sea mist, caressed his bare chest. He brushed droplets away idly, chasing thoughts like stags over the hills. What else was it Dragon had said? That he would have to give Cymbra his trust before he could expect her loyalty? That sounded like an alliance between jarls, not a marriage, or at least not how he had always thought of marriage.

Mayhap he needed to think again.

Mayhap he needed to thank the Norns for gifting him with a woman of pride and courage, a fitting mate for a true Viking.

Mayhap he needed to go back inside, shuck his trousers, and make love to his temptress until she cried his name and clung to him in victorious surrender.

He was pushing the door open, already bending his head to enter, when he heard hoofbeats like muted thunder shattering the morning stillness. He turned and saw the rider racing up the hill toward the berm.

His hand fell away, his back straightened. He clenched his fists slowly, grasping air, feeling steel. Barechested, mantled in the aura of his rank, he paused just long enough to shut the door gently on his sleeping wife before he walked toward the gates and whatever summoned him from beyond them.

Chapter

THIRTEEN

SHELTERED BENEATH THE OVERHANG OF THE weaving shed, Cymbra pulled an edge of her cloak up over her head and watched the water drip from the thatched eaves of the great hall. It was raining. Again. She sighed and closed her eyes for a moment, drawing on the memory of sun. It seemed to have done nothing but rain ever since Wolf's departure a week ago. People were becoming concerned. If it didn't stop soon, the crops would be at risk.

She saw old Ulfrich slogging his way toward the hall and waved. Running out between the drops, she joined him. He smiled in welcome, pleased to see her.

"How is your chest?" Cymbra asked as they made for the hall together.

"Much better, thank you. That infusion of yours truly is a wonder."

She nodded, pleased yet still uneasy about him. But then she seemed uneasy about almost everything these days, dogged by worry over her brother, dread of what was to come, and a strange feeling of vulnerability she could neither understand nor deny. "You really shouldn't be out in this. Dampness isn't good for you."

He smiled again, patiently, and didn't reply. He didn't need to. She knew he had been in the fields and the woods beyond, reciting the prayers, making the sacrifices, doing what he could.

Brother Joseph had been doing the same but in the relative comfort of the small building Wolf had allowed him to make into a chapel. Two men, two faiths, working for a common end. She had to believe they would succeed.

The monk was already in the hall, seated by the fire. He jumped up when he saw them and quickly offered a stool to Ulfrich. Helping the older man off with his sodden cloak, he said, "Here, put this blanket around yourself. I've warmed it."

Ulfrich nodded gratefully and did as he was bid.

Steam and the scent of wet wool rose from Cymbra's cloak. She discarded it and kindly refused the blanket Brother Joseph offered her. "I was only out for a few minutes. You look as though you could use it yourself."

Belatedly, she noticed that he, too, was soaked through. His smile was a little abashed as he said, "I went out to the fields." At her surprised look, he added, "I am truly grateful to Lord Wolf for permission to have a chapel, but all of God's creation is his sanctuary. It seems fitting to walk among it."

Ulfrich inclined his head at this wisdom. He accepted a mug Brita offered to him and nodded at the Irish girl gratefully. She offered mugs to Cymbra and Brother Joseph as well, then hesitated before shyly taking the seat Cymbra offered.

"Brita has learned to make the infusion you are using," Cymbra told Ulfrich. She smiled at the girl. "She learns very quickly."

The Irish lass blushed at this praise and Cymbra

smiled again. But her smile faltered at the prickling sensation that stirred deep within her. For just an instant she was engulfed by the memory of Brita's pain and despair, then it melted away into relief and a feeling of safety. It was gone faster than a star streaking across a midnight sky but it served only to increase Cymbra's sense of unease. In the past, she would have been able to shield herself from such sensation. Now it came without warning, not even giving her time to try to distance herself.

Despite this, it pleased her greatly to see how much Brita had changed in so short a time. Garbed now in clothing Cymbra had given her, already showing the effects of better food and rest, she looked almost like a different person.

All the servants—and the slaves, for Cymbra refused to make any distinction—were newly garbed and were well pleased by it. They also seemed less aware or at least less concerned with who was slave and who was free.

As she glanced around the great hall, she saw others who had come in out of the rain, finding a corner, a bench, some convenient place to work and chat. There was an air of busy purpose and contentment. She was glad of it but not misled, knowing herself to be only one among many counting the days until the return of the jarl of Sciringesheal.

A shiver passed along her spine and she leaned closer to the fire, staring into the darting flames. Too well she remembered being awakened from the deep sleep of sensual exhaustion to see a huge, dark figure of menace, armored and helmeted, standing beside the bed.

Barely had she time to gasp than her husband lifted her to him. For just a moment she felt crushed by leather, steel, and the unyielding power of the warrior himself. Yet his kiss when it came was achingly gentle.

Against her mouth, he murmured, "I'll be back soon.

Take care of things here." Dropping her lightly back onto the pillows, he pulled the covers up and lingered just a moment longer to look at her.

Then he was gone, striding out into the too-bright light of what turned out to be the last fair day they were to have between then and now.

It was only later, after she had rushed to dress and hurried after him to find he was already gone, taking Dragon and two dozen men with him, that she learned what had happened. Ulfrich told her, as gently and kindly as he could: a settlement near the coast raided. The Danes suspected. The attackers to be hunted down, the deaths avenged. All in a day's work for the Norse Wolf.

Except a day had passed and another and another until now a full week had passed. Cymbra had begun to look toward the gates every few minutes, hoping against hope that she would see her husband and the others riding through them. At night she lay awake, tormented by memory and desire, aching for him. And fearing.

She told herself not to be absurd. He was a mighty warrior, proven in battle time and time again. He was to be feared, not feared for. Yet any man could make a mistake, a small misjudgment. Any man could die.

"My lady . . . ?"

Startled, Cymbra lifted her gaze from the fire to find Brita looking at her with concern. She realized the young woman must have spoken and she had not heard her.

"Is something wrong, my lady?"

"No," Cymbra said hastily. She managed a weak smile. "I'm fine, just distracted. Pray excuse me."

"You should rest more." Brita glanced over at Ulfrich and Brother Joseph, who were deep in conversation, then continued in a soft voice. "It's natural to feel tiredness. You don't eat very much either."

"I haven't had much appetite," Cymbra admitted.

"You know better than I that there are tonics to help with such upset. Gentle things that will do no harm."

Cymbra nodded, but absently, for just then she saw the Rus trader come into the hall. He stood for a moment, peering through the filtered light, before spotting her. He hurried to join the little group by the fire but he had notice only for Cymbra.

"Lady, I am so relieved to find you! My Nadia, her time has come! Please, you must hurry!"

Brother Joseph stood and placed a gentle hand on Mikal's arm. "Easy now, friend. Even I know babies take their sweet time, and you've thought this one was coming ere now."

"This time he really comes! And soon!" He looked to Cymbra. "My Nadia, she says, bring the lady quickly! Please, you come!"

Cymbra got to her feet, never taking her eyes from him. Her stomach clenched.

"I spoke with your wife just yesterday. She promised me she would come here at the first sign of labor."

"There was no time! Everything happened too swiftly." He faltered and she saw the fear in his eyes. "Please, lady, there is blood. Just drops but there should not be blood, should there?"

She took a breath, her lips pressed tight together. Brita caught her eye. A silent understanding passed between them. Cymbra exhaled slowly. She turned to Mikal. Gently, she said, "It's all right. I will come."

"My lady . . ." Ulfrich and Brother Joseph spoke almost in unison, one swiftly echoing the other. A glance at them was enough to tell Cymbra that they were well aware she was not supposed to leave the fortress. Did everyone know, then? Would anyone actually try to stop her?

"Dame Mikal must be brought here," Brother Joseph said.

Cymbra shook her head. "She can't be moved, especially not in all this mud. It's too . . ." She paused, seeing the trader's strained face. "It's too slippery."

Quickly, before anyone could object further, she turned to Brita. "Please, my cloak and the chest from beside the bed."

"Your gray cloak, my lady?"

"Yes, that one." The cloak would offer at least some concealment, in case anyone was tempted to stop her.

"I will go with you," Brita said.

Cymbra laid a hand on her arm. "No, I go alone."

"But, my lady—" This time it was Ulfrich who objected. "You should not be unaccompanied! One of us will—"

"No," Cymbra said even more firmly. She would not, could not, involve anyone else in this. Wolf's wrath, if it had to come at all, must fall only on her. Determined on that as she was, it took precious moments to convince Ulfrich and Brother Joseph that she meant what she said. Even so, she felt their unhappy gazes as she hurried from the hall.

Brita was even more stubborn when she met her with the cloak and medicine box. "You will need help, my lady," she insisted even as she donned her own cloak, preparing to go with Cymbra. "It is only sensible to take me with you."

Cymbra hefted the box in one hand and pulled the hood up over her head with the other. She was vividly aware of Mikal, standing nearby, bouncing from one foot to the other in his agitation. Gazing into the pale but determined face of the young Irish girl, she shook her head firmly.

"No, Brita, you absolutely will not come. You must promise me, as you value your service to me, that you will not think of following."

The girl hesitated, her expression making it clear to

Cymbra that was exactly what she'd planned to do if she was refused.

"Promise," Cymbra insisted. For good measure, she added, "Swear before God."

Brita looked heavenward as though seeking guidance, or perhaps just patience. "My lady . . ."

"No, I mean it. You must swear." Softly, she added, "And we both know why."

The two women, so different in upbringing and position, shared a moment of stark equality. Each knew herself to be vulnerable to the anger of a man. Each knew what defiance could bring.

Cymbra put out a hand and gave the girl a gentle shove back toward the hall. Brother Joseph was standing in the open door. He saw and came to Brita, taking her arm.

"Come, lass, Ulfrich could use more of that infusion."

Still staring at Cymbra, Brita looked in danger of crying. "I've never made it alone."

"But you're more than able to do so," Cymbra assured her. She added an encouraging smile. "Go on now. With this awful weather, there will be more in need of care. I'm relying on you."

That did the trick. Reluctantly, Brita went with the monk. Cymbra breathed a sigh of relief and joined Mikal. Together they passed through the gates and on down the road to the town.

Most people were inside. They passed only a very few darting along the rain-slicked stones of the wharves and over the wooden planks laid across the muddy lanes. Several ships rode at anchor, their decks empty and rain swept.

A heavy mist obscured the rocky islands that sheltered the harbor, making the entrance impassable to even the boldest. Waves slapped against the piers, driven by the wind coming off the sea. Cymbra tasted salt on her lips. She ducked her head down and concentrated on walking faster.

The wind gusted powerfully just as they reached the house of the Rus couple. Mikal thrust the door open and stood aside for Cymbra to enter. She took a quick look around, noting that everything was in good order save for the dishes, which still held remnants of breakfast and appeared abandoned on the table in the center of the room. Clearly, Nadia had been well enough to see to her housewifely duties until only a short time before.

"Through here," Mikal said anxiously. He parted a curtain leading to a small alcove behind the main room. Most of it was taken up by a large, richly carved bed covered by a mound of blankets and furs. Only Nadia's pale, distraught face was visible beneath them.

"Oh, my lady, I am so sorry! I mean to come to you but everything happen so quickly and I am—" Her voice caught. She held out a hand, instantly grasped by her husband, who hurried to her side. "I am afraid, my lady."

Even as Nadia spoke, Cymbra felt the woman's mingled terror and regret surging so powerfully that she almost gasped. The sudden realization that her usual defenses against the emotions of others were not working made her teeter on the edge of panic. She had to take several quick, deep breaths before she could respond calmly.

"It's all right, Nadia. I understand." She set down her box and removed her cloak, all the while grappling inwardly for some means of shielding herself. Slowly, her sense of the other woman's emotions receded.

When she was sure she was fully in control, Cymbra said, "Mikal, please heat some water."

He hesitated, gazing at his wife with deep concern. "Go," Nadia echoed softly. "The lady is here now. Everything will be fine."

He went, though not without a backward glance at his

wife. The deep love and worry in his eyes made Cymbra's throat tighten. But she showed none of that as she smiled again at Nadia. Gently, she drew back the covers to expose the mound of the woman's belly covered by a linen robe.

"Well, now, let's see how the little one is doing."

In the next few minutes, Cymbra carefully felt the baby's position and confirmed that the bleeding was slight. During that time, Nadia was swept by two powerful contractions. With each, Cymbra cautioned her not to yield to the temptation to push. When the water was ready, Cymbra washed her hands, then checked more thoroughly before finding what she had hoped.

"Your labor is strong and swift. This child is indeed eager to be born but you are not quite ready to bring him forth. Trying to do so now tears you and causes bleeding. That's already happened to a small degree but the baby is not in danger from it and you will heal."

This time Cymbra was ready. The wave of Nadia's intense relief swept past but not through her. While the Rus woman was yet buoyed by it, Cymbra helped her to stand. Holding on to her, she encouraged Nadia to walk back and forth across the room.

Mikal returned with yet more water and, after recovering from his surprise at seeing his wife on her feet, took over the task of helping her remain upright. Meanwhile, Cymbra quickly washed her instruments, covered the bed with a clean sheet, and warmed a swaddling blanket.

She had barely finished when Nadia bent double with the force of an even more powerful contraction. Her husband and Cymbra helped her back into the bed. Uncertain what he should do, Mikal made up his mind abruptly when he saw the plea in his wife's eyes. He took up his place at the head of the bed, holding her hands and offering her all the strength and courage he could give as she fought to bring their child into the world.

A child who was born moments later, sliding from his mother's body with a lusty wail that made Cymbra grin ear to ear. Quickly, she did what was needful for the baby, wrapped him in the blanket, and handed him to his parents. As they gazed in awe at the miracle they had wrought, she cared for Nadia, who was so caught up in the wonder of her son as to be oblivious to everything else.

With all as it should be, Cymbra relaxed a little and enjoyed the sight of the child. She joined his parents in exclaiming over his size, his thick head of black hair, and his obviously intelligent expression. When Mikal, bursting with pride, hurried off to make some broth, Cymbra encouraged Nadia as she put her child to her breast for the first time. The new mother jerked in surprise, her eyes flying to Cymbra's before she laughed shakily. "He certainly knows what he wants!"

"He's a strong, healthy child and will undoubtedly have an appetite to match. You must take care to get proper rest and eat healthy foods. I will prepare a tonic for you to drink now and I will send another daily for the next fortnight."

Mikal returned with the broth and Cymbra left the new family alone while she prepared the tonic. As she worked, she paused long enough to pull aside a wooden shutter and glance outside. It was still raining but not as much as before, yet the light was grayer. With a start, she realized that she had been so caught up in the drama of birth as to make time slip by with deceptive fleetness. Far more of it had passed than she had realized.

She was worried momentarily but then pushed that aside, reasoning there was nothing she could do about it. As it was, she wasn't free to return to the hill fort until she was certain that both baby and mother were doing well.

Even then, she cautioned Mikal, "Send for me if anything untoward happens whatever the hour." At his sudden frown, she added hastily, "Not that I'm expecting trouble. Nadia did extremely well and your son is very healthy."

Mikal beamed, both reassured and proud. But when Cymbra put on her cloak he sobered and began reaching for his own. "I will come with you, lady. You must not go alone."

"And you must not leave your wife and child. They need you." When still he hesitated, she said, "Mikal, tell me truly, who do you think would endanger me? Aside from the fact that no one is out in this foul weather, who should I fear?"

He had no answer for that and admitted as much. "I don't know, my lady, but it is the principle of the thing."

"Do you allow your wife to go about the town on her own?"

The mere thought of trying to restrict Nadia in such a way surprised him. "Of course, but—"

"Do you trust me less than her?"

"Certainly not! But, my lady, we both know that is not what this is about. You are guarded, protected, as a sign of respect."

She nodded, well understanding that. "Respect for my husband, not for me. Respect for me, or for any woman, would be to allow us to go about our lives unmolested."

Mikal spread his hands, not unkindly but in acceptance of what was. "You speak of a different world, my lady."

"Perhaps I do. Let us be practical then. Even in this flawed world, no man would risk the jarl's anger."

"Anger?" Mikal looked at her as though she had just described a howling wind that froze men's blood in their veins as though it was no more than a summer's breeze. "My lady, I most profoundly hope I am never so foolish as to incite such *anger*. Were I to do so, it is the last thing I would ever do." He shuddered at the very thought. "Save for dying, of course, and that would be a kindness."

Cymbra chose not to dwell on what exactly Mikal imagined her husband capable of doing. She was occupied enough with the sudden realization that the Rus trader had, all unknowingly, done exactly what he most feared.

Brother Joseph, Ulfrich, and Brita had obviously known of her husband's order that Cymbra remain in the fort, but Mikal had not known, nor had Nadia. Cymbra had told them only that Nadia should come to the fort when her labor began because everything needed to care for her was there. Pride, resentment, whatever had kept her from revealing that "everything" included herself, she who was as much captive as bride.

Horror filled her as she comprehended the extent to which she might have placed Mikal in danger. With it came even greater resolve that no one but herself would pay the price for defying the Wolf. If indeed there was a price to be paid.

Although she was by nature an honest and forthright person, it occurred to her that perhaps her husband need not know of this. She would return safe and sound. Why should he be troubled by something that was over and done?

Such thoughts sped her on her way. She checked once more on Nadia and the baby, reassured Mikal yet again, and took her leave. The light was fading rapidly as she passed out of the town and began to climb the hill to the fort. She was more tired than she had realized and the climb left her just a little breathless.

Near the top, she paused, looking ahead through the rain, and saw with relief that the gates were still open. Swiftly she passed through them and hurried, a gray shadow, through the rain until she came to the lodge she and Wolf shared.

With a sigh of relief, she went inside and returned her medicine box to its proper place beside the table. Removing the gray cloak, she shook it well before hanging it spread between two pegs set into the wall. The braziers were lit, warming the room and casting a cheering glow. She gave silent thanks to Brita, who undoubtedly had thought to light them.

For a moment she was tempted to crawl into the huge bed and go straight to sleep. But the churning of her stomach reminded her that she had eaten almost nothing that day.

It would be time for supper soon. In the meanwhile, she decided to look in on the kitchens and see how the meal was progressing. Perhaps she'd just grab a taste or two to tide her over.

Donning a dry cloak, she left the lodge, skirted around the timbered hall, and went down the short flight of stone steps into the kitchens. They were as crowded as she had expected at this hour.

A dozen or so women worked around several tables, preparing meat for roasting over the great fire in the hall, scraping fish, and peeling vegetables. Children helped stir simmering pots from which delectable aromas wafted. Other women were taking loaves of bread out of the brick ovens, placing them in baskets to be carried into the hall along with golden rounds of cheese and platters of bright berries.

Cymbra slipped in unseen and promptly made for the berries. She took several, popped them into her mouth, and was just savoring their sweetness when a sudden silence descended. Glancing around, she found herself to be the object of all eyes. One by one, the women stopped what they were doing, knives and spoons halting even in midair, and stared at her.

Suddenly aware of her berry-stained fingers, she tucked them behind her back and said self-consciously, "I missed midday meal."

No one replied, no one so much as moved. They might have been statues frozen in place by the breath of

an ice god. Except for the dawning looks in their eyes
of . . . sympathy, concern . . . fear.

Cymbra's heart pounded against her ribs. She swayed
slightly and put out a hand to steady herself against the
table. Too late, she remembered what she should have noticed before, and would have if she hadn't been so tired
and preoccupied with her hunger.

The lodge, the bed into which she had been so
tempted to creep, and on the foot of that bed, her husband's cloak left where he had tossed it.

The Wolf had returned to his lair. While she was
away, disobeying his most clearly expressed orders and
despite his clear warning of what would happen were she
so foolish to do so.

Yet even as she thought of that, she couldn't help but
be elated. He was back, he was safe. She was overjoyed . . .
and filled with dread. Tremendously relieved . . . and
deeply apprehensive. Even as she ricocheted between
contrary emotions, another joined the mix. She resented
being so worried when she should have been so happy.

She had merely done what was right. He should see
that and agree. She lifted her head, straightened her
shoulders. He would have to see; she would insist that he
do so. She would—

"*Out.*" The single growled command ripped apart the
unnatural silence. Pots dropped, knives fell from hands,
footsteps thudded. In an instant, the kitchens were empty.

Save, that was, for Cymbra, who turned to greet her
lord, her noble husband, the man to whom she had sworn
obedience. The enraged Viking who stood, feet planted
solidly apart, fists on his hips, glaring at her.

Chapter

FOURTEEN

THE FIRST SIGHT OF HER HUSBAND EMPTIED Cymbra's lungs and left them starved for air. Memory could not encompass the reality of him. Shorn of his helmet and leather armor, wearing only a simple tunic, he was yet bigger, harder, more massive, more virile even than she could recall.

He was also . . . grubby. He looked as though he'd slept in his clothes, which undoubtedly he had. He needed to shave, as his jaw bore the dark shadow of a week's growth of whiskers. His hair was unkempt, falling thickly to his broad shoulders.

He looked . . . *wonderful* . . . enraged . . . *exciting* . . . infuriated . . . *tantalizing* . . . dangerous.

"You—" He got out that much from between gritted teeth, no more. She couldn't bear to hear what he would say, what accusations he would throw at her—all unfortunately true but still intolerable. She had done *nothing* wrong, or at least not when weighed against the right she had also done.

"I had to!" Cymbra blurted. "A woman and child's lives were at risk. And besides," she hurtled on, determined to say it all before he could stop her, "Mikal knew nothing of your order. He's entirely innocent, as is Nadia. I'm the only one to blame, no one else."

She stopped as abruptly as she had begun and stood, her arms hanging at her sides, looking at him. Surely he would understand. She thought of all they had shared, the joy they had made together, and told herself he would never really hurt her.

"I warned you," Wolf said. He advanced toward her, his face implacable. "You had every chance to mend your ways. Too much chance, it now seems." He stopped, scarcely the length of a man away from her, and shook his head regretfully. "You leave me no choice, Cymbra."

She could have stood almost anything better than the disappointment in his voice. That and the intent stamped clearly in every inch of his bearing. He *had* warned her. She knew exactly what he meant to do.

No one had ever struck her. In all her life, she had never experienced any such thing. She knew full well how unusual that was, but that made no difference. Besides the physical hurt and humiliation, she truly doubted whether she would ever be able to forgive him for not understanding.

"You—" It was her turn. She searched for words and found none. There was nothing but hollow pain, pulsing within her, and the acid resentment of her anger spilling up and over any wall she could ever hope to build.

Her lips moved stiffly, forming each separate word with care. "Don't . . . you . . . dare."

He looked at her, she thought, as though at a horse that had suddenly opened its mouth and spoken. A woman daring to defy him must be as rare a beast. For just an instant he paused, but his intent did not waver. He continued toward her, speaking quietly with regret that in no way lessened his resolve.

"You will remember this, Cymbra, and then we will go on. You will not be so foolish again—"

That did it. The walls crumbled and all poured out. "Foolish? It is not *foolish* to help people in need! It is not *foolish* to trust in my own judgment! You told me—*told me!*—to take care of things here. Or perhaps you don't remember that, husband. Perhaps it is conveniently forgotten. Would you return to a dead woman and child, and me simpering that they died because I couldn't venture a quarter mile into a town? Would you have me live with that on my conscience for the rest of my life. *Would you?*"

No, not merely a horse that spoke. A pink one that sprouted wings, flew around the room, and sang. He looked so startled that she was almost tempted to laugh, just for a moment, before the urge to cry overtook her.

She'd be damned if she'd give him that. Oh, no! Instead, she'd give him Hardly knowing what she did, she reached across the table, seized the first thing she touched, and hurled it straight at Wolf.

The ball of cheese hit his chest with a hollow thud and fell to the floor, rolling away into a corner. He watched it roll, looked at her, and looked at the cheese again, now lying still and slightly dented. When he raised his head once more, the light in his eyes had changed. Gone was the ominous darkness. In its place was silver fire.

"The first time I saw you," he said, almost pleasantly, "I thought you needed messing."

"W-what?"

"Messing. You looked too perfect to be real." He glanced around almost casually before his gaze lit on a bowl on a nearby table. He picked it up, hefted it lightly, and tossed the contents right at her.

Cymbra yelped, more in surprise than for any other reason, and tried to jump back, to no avail; she was splattered with whey. The drippy, oozing stuff landed in her hair, on her cheeks, on the front of her cloak. She stared down at herself in disbelief. *"Why, you—"*

She picked up a honeycomb and threw it right at his face. It landed, stuck, and stayed there until he pulled it away.

"If that's how you want it, my lady—" He strode toward her, honey dripping from his face, and before she could move, caught her around the waist. "Far be it from me to deny you."

The world turned upside down. Cymbra landed in a pile of flour sacks. Instantly she tried to get up, but her husband came down on top of her, holding her trapped. He caught her flailing arms and pinned them down. His teeth flashed whitely. "Not so bold now, wife?"

She'd show him bold. She'd show him what a Saxon woman was made of. Frighten *her*, would he? Smear *her* with whey? She'd make him regret— Trying to gain leverage against him, Cymbra dug her heels into the sacks. Dug . . . and dug . . . and stopped digging abruptly as the fabric gave way and flour shot up, covering them both.

As the powder settled around them, she looked up into her husband's face, streaked with honey and coated with flour, and laughed. She couldn't help it.

He quirked an eyebrow. "This amuses you?"

Her response wasn't smart but it was honest. She nodded.

He held her eyes, smiling, looking oh so very beguiling as she remembered how worried she'd been for his safety and how truly glad she was, despite everything, that he was home. It was so silly of them to waste time like this. They had been apart for a week. They should be—

"Oomph!"

Milk poured over her, a sea of milk emptying from the bucket her insufferable husband had seized. She was soaked through, covered with whey, flour, and milk.

She was at a loss how to respond until her eye fell on a basket of eggs lying nearby. With unholy glee, she yanked away from Wolf, who was nearly doubled over with laughter, seized the eggs, and pelted him with them. Yellow yolks and runny whites matted his hair, dripped off the end of his nose, and turned the flour all over his tunic to glue.

She was on her feet, trying to scramble to the steps, when Wolf caught her by the skirt. She landed again in the torn sacks, briefly blinded by a new shower of flour. When her vision cleared, it was to see him over her, holding a handful of ripe berries descending right toward her—

—mouth. "Open up," Wolf growled. Dazed, heart pounding, she obeyed. He slipped one of the succulent fruits between her lips. Instinctively, she chewed and swallowed. He watched her intently.

Slowly, deliberately, the Norse Wolf fed his disobedient wife berries as they lay amid the shambles of the kitchen, stained, sticky, and dripping.

Until the berries were forgotten. Slowly, sweetly, their lips met. Cymbra moaned in relief, in need, in sheer pleasure. Wolf's beard rasped her delicate skin. His hands moved over her, possessive, urgent, yet controlled.

"Missed you," he murmured against her mouth. "So much."

"Mmm . . . the same . . ." She tugged at his tunic, shameless in her hunger for him. He pushed aside her cloak and raised her gown over her legs, bunching it at her waist.

"Someday," he muttered as he rose over her to undo the ties of his trousers, "I'm going to take my time with you."

"But not right now," she said, demand and plea together. She clasped his upper arms, her fingers digging into the powerful muscles. A sob of pure desire broke from her as he spread her legs and moved to join their bodies.

He was so big, filling her so completely, that for just a moment she felt too stretched, too invaded. But she adjusted quickly, her hot, silken sheath alternately tightening and relaxing around him. She was rewarded by his husky groan.

Moving within her, he whispered of how she felt to him, how he wanted her to feel, how he had thought of her when they were apart, what she did to him. His bluntness shocked and excited her. She felt herself spiraling out of control and clung to him even more tightly.

He raised her legs, clasping them around his hips, and drove even more deeply. She rose to meet him, her back arching, her head falling back to expose the vulnerable curve of her neck. He laid his mouth against her delicate skin, tracing the pale blue line of her life's blood down to where it disappeared beneath the gown she still wore. His teeth tore at the fabric, ripping it aside, freeing her breasts. Urgently, he suckled her, drawing her deeply, raking her lightly, the sensation teetering on the edge between pain and pleasure. Before it could tip over, he raised his head and took her mouth, his tongue thrusting with the same powerful, driving rhythm as his sex.

She was lost, the world shattering, every particle of her being resonating with the exquisite fury of her release. Yet still she felt his own when it followed swiftly, incredibly renewing and extending her ecstasy until nothing remained save sweet, soft oblivion.

GAZING DOWN AT THE FACE OF HIS WIFE, WOLF traced a finger carefully over the faint, half-moon smudges beneath the thick fringe of her lashes, and a little farther over the curve of her cheek, along the delicate line of her jaw, lingering on her rose-petal lips, now slightly swollen. He kept his touch feather-light, careful not to disturb her. A rueful smile tugged at the corners of his mouth. A man could do worse than to make his wife faint with pleasure. Much worse.

Tentatively, he sought the stinging anger that had struck him the moment he realized what she had done, anger he had struggled mightily to control even as he faced the grim but seemingly inescapable duty of punishing her. Only the faintest echoes of it remained and those were fading fast. He let them go gladly.

If he had failed in his duty, so be it. For once in his life, he was content and more than content to be only a man—and a husband. Cymbra's husband.

The sudden image of his wife as she had looked when she threw the cheese at him made him chuckle. No meek, docile little woman, his Saxon bride. No cloying, simpering female to make him long to go adventuring.

No wonder Frigg favored her. She had the spirit of a true goddess. For surely she had taken him like one, milking the life from him in a soul-shattering rapture he could still scarcely believe for all that he had experienced it. He could well believe that no god had ever climaxed as long, as hard, or as intensely as he had just done. She made him feel like he could conquer worlds, if only to lay them at her feet.

Something nibbled at the edge of his awareness, slowly distracting him from the pleasant contemplation of his wife. He glanced over his shoulder, seeking the source of the faint, dripping sound, and saw the upturned pitcher of water, no doubt spilled in their . . . contest. Yes, it would be as well if he thought of it that way. A contest between two superbly matched contenders, so well pitted as to assure that both emerged victorious.

Standing, he righted the pitcher, then looked again at Cymbra. She had turned onto her side, one bare leg drawn up, an arm resting over her full breasts. Escaped flour covered the sacks on which she lay and drifted over her skin. Traces of the whey still clung to her and there was a little stain from the berries on her chin.

He glanced down at himself, noting that he had fared worse still. Flour and egg clung to him along with the sticky honey. A deep laugh rumbled up from his chest. The master and mistress of Sciringesheal, coupling in the kitchen on flour sacks amid the wreckage they themselves had caused. He couldn't remember the last time he'd done something so inappropriate to his rank—or so pleasurable.

Grinning broadly, he lifted Cymbra in his arms. She stirred against him and blinked. "Wolf . . . ?"

He looked down at her, his smile softening, becoming tender. "I think the cooks would like the kitchens back."

She stared at him uncomprehendingly for a moment. "Oh, no!" Turning bright red, she hid her face against his chest. Yet was her muttered distress clear enough. "I can't believe we did this! What were we thinking of? The kitchens! Everybody will know . . . they'll—"

"Cymbra," he said gently, with utmost patience.

She peered up at him. "What?"

"They already know we lie together."

"Not in the kitchens! Not on flour sacks! Anyone could have come in and—"

He laughed even more at the sheer absurdity of that. "You're joking! They feared the worst and were glad to get as far from it as they could. When they realize what did happen, they'll be relieved."

"Maybe they won't realize. Maybe they'll think we talked and—"

She faltered, looking around at the kitchen. If Loki and his mischief makers had rampaged through it, it wouldn't have been in worse shape. Were that not bad enough, the clear imprint of where they had lain on the flour sacks made the outcome obvious.

She hid her face against him once more. Still laughing, he carried her from the kitchens. It was time, he decided, for his Saxon wife to experience another kind of pleasure.

He went into their lodge just long enough to get a few things, then carried Cymbra back outside and across the flat top of the hill to a beehive-shaped building made of rocks and set low in the ground. She lifted her head from his shoulder and looked at it in surprise. "The sauna? I haven't been in there yet."

"I know." He eased open the wooden door and stooped to descend the steps. "Any particular reason why not?"

"You'll laugh."

"That's bad?"

"You'll laugh *at me*. An old monk at Holyhood, Brother Chilton was his name, said only devils could endure the heat of the sauna. He thought it proved what Vikings were."

"You believed that?"

"Well, no, but I did take it to mean that saunas are extremely hot."

His smile returned. "They can be. We'll go a little easy." He bent closer, his lips brushing her ear. "This being your first time and all."

A shiver ran down her back. She knew he was only playing with her, deliberately inciting memories of their first time together, but it worked. If she wasn't careful, she would be clay in this man's hands.

Such large hands, honed for battle, callused by sword and rein, bronzed by the sun. Yet such careful hands as he set her on her feet in the center of the small chamber, lingering for just a moment on the curve of her hips before drawing away.

She looked around curiously. The stone walls narrowed to a small opening at the top of the structure.

Directly below it, in the center of the floor, was an iron firebox. A hole in the top of it directed the smoke to an opening in the roof. Around the vent lay several dozen smoothly rounded rocks of a size to fit into a man's hand. The floor beyond the firebox was covered with planks of polished wood. Other planks were set up as benches around the chamber. The air was just a little smoky, smelling mainly of pine.

Wolf bent down in front of the firebox and began feeding branches into it from the stack set nearby. Over his shoulder, he said, "Take your clothes off."

When the fire was going strongly, he went over to the door and pulled it shut, securing it from inside. With the faint remnants of twilight gone, the interior was plunged into darkness save for the red glow of the fire. Slowly, Cymbra's eyes adjusted until she could make out her husband taking his own advice.

He stripped easily, pulling off his boots, then drawing his tunic off over his head and dropping it onto a bench. His leggings followed quickly. Naked, he stretched without a trace of self-consciousness, the powerful muscles of his back and buttocks flexing. With graceful ease he returned to the fire, went down on his haunches, and continued feeding wood into the flames.

Cymbra swallowed against the fluttering in her throat and tried, without success, to look at something—anything—other than her husband's magnificent body. She moistened her lips, took a quick breath, and murmured, "Isn't that . . . uh . . . hot enough?"

He glanced up, saw that she was still dressed, and shook his head chidingly. The thick mane of his ebony hair brushed his massive shoulders. "You'll pass out if you don't get out of those."

When she still hesitated, he went to her and gently put a hand beneath her chin, compelling her to meet his gaze. "Cymbra, is something wrong?"

How to explain to him that she felt suddenly, almost unbearably self-conscious? He knew her so intimately and so completely that she felt she had no defenses against him. Life had schooled her to an inner world of carefully crafted serenity. He shattered all of that, plunging her into a turbulent sea of emotions in which she could barely stay afloat.

Why, in scarcely an hour she had gone from worry to fear to anger to passion and now . . . to what? She felt utterly drained yet oddly exhilarated. And very confused.

"Cymbra?"

She didn't answer, only looked at him. He saw again the shadows beneath her eyes, recalled his intention when he'd found her in the kitchens, and remorse pierced him. She had delivered a baby only a short time before. She needed rest and care, not yet more of his relentless passion.

"It's all right," he said gruffly. "You'll feel better when you're clean."

Encouraged when she didn't object, he removed her cloak, then gently, carefully did the same with the rest of her clothes. He was surprised to see the tear across the top of her gown, having been completely unaware of doing that. It hinted to him of the force that consumed him when he took her and he resolved, yet again, to hold it in strict check.

By the time she was naked, the sauna was well warmed. Or so he thought it. Cymbra took a breath, testing the air cautiously, and said, "It's very hot."

Sweat had begun to form on her lovely breasts. He ran a hand along her smooth, slick arm. "Are you uncomfortable?"

"No . . ." Her voice trailed off. She couldn't seem to do anything except look at him. He turned away to throw a ladle of water on the stones and she followed the movement of his big, perfectly honed body.

Her eyes, drifting over him, might have been her hands, so vividly aware was she of hard muscles bunching beneath smooth, warm skin. Steam hissed up suddenly.

"That's why we call it sauna." He drew her over to a bench, where he sat down and stretched out his long legs. "It's wet heat, not dry, better for the bones."

Beside him, Cymbra nodded. The dark, moist warmth of the chamber half-buried in the earth seemed to be seeping into her. The world beyond might have been as far away as the stars she could just glimpse glittering through the hole at the top of the roof. She took another breath, letting the scent of pine fill her, and felt her senses spin.

"Lie down," Wolf said. She heard him as though from a distance, yet she obeyed. He positioned her face-down on the bench, her head turned so that she could see the glow of the fire. She heard the faint sound of a vial being opened and a moment later smelled a tantalizing scent she couldn't identify.

"Patchouli," he said, "from the East."

A sigh of pure delight escaped her as his hands, slick with the perfumed oil, moved over her shoulders, down to the curve of her waist, and back up again. Slowly, methodically, he massaged away the tension and fatigue of the long day, the days of worry that had preceded it, and the largely sleepless nights.

With more oil in his palms, he went farther, lingering over the high, firm curve of her buttocks and along each slender, shapely leg. His fingers just grazed the sensitive skin of her inner thighs, making her squirm deliciously. Little whimpers broke from her, becoming outright moans when he dug his thumbs into the balls of her feet and flexed each toe separately.

Having attended ever so thoroughly to one side of her, he turned her over and smiled into her smoky gaze. "Feeling better?"

"Hmm. Do I get a turn?" The thought of running her oiled hands over every inch of his body made the sensation of liquid heat pooling within her even more intense.

"Maybe later." She watched, enthralled, as he poured more oil into his palms, rubbed them together to spread it evenly, then settled his hands on the curve of her waist. "Have I told you lately how exquisitely beautiful you are?"

She shook her head. "No, not since that night you and Dragon got drunk, but—"

"We weren't drunk. We were just a little . . ." He paused, looking for the right word.

"Sotted?" she offered helpfully. When that didn't seem to do, she tried again. "Grogged . . . scrooched . . . guzzled . . . toss-cupped?"

His laugh was rich and deep. "All right, we were drunk. It doesn't take that to get me to tell you that you're beautiful."

"There was a time when I was very, very tired of being thought beautiful. . . ." Her voice trailed off as he ran his hands up to cup her breasts, his slick thumbs rubbing over her erect nipples. A little moan caught in her throat. Helplessly, she felt her hips rise.

"Why did you feel that way?" he asked, continuing his ministrations.

"It . . . it just made things . . . Wolf, *please*—"

"Things how?"

"More complicated. *Please!*"

His teeth gleamed in the firelight. "Don't you know I always want to please you, Cymbra? Can't you feel that when I'm deep inside you? How I hold back, waiting for you? How I stroke deeper and deeper, touching you where you're most sensitive and—"

She writhed on the bench, caught by the dark, smoky sensation of his words and touch, turning to fire beneath his hands. Helpless.

And not helpless. She stroked his granite thigh, her fingernails raking him lightly. "A smart man might think that a woman would find a way to get back at him for playing with her like this," she reminded him.

"I am playing," he admitted without a flicker of remorse. "I love *playing* with you . . . touching you . . . discovering you—" His hands slid lower over her belly, moving between her thighs, his touch suddenly so soft she was scarcely sure she felt it until, abruptly, he thrust a finger deep inside her and rubbed his thumb tightly against her distended nub.

She came in a rush, her body bowing as seemingly endless spasms of pleasure seized her. They had just barely begun to ebb when Wolf lifted her off the bench. He sat down on it, placed her with her legs straddling his iron-hard thighs, and lowered her onto him.

"Your turn," he rasped, the cords of his neck standing out in high relief as he fought to keep himself from coming at once. His hands braced her back beneath the luxurious fall of her hair. Slowly, hesitantly, she began to move. She felt almost overly sensitized, overly filled, stretched to unbearable proportions. Almost, not quite. She clasped him fully, savoring the freedom to move as she would, drawing herself up almost completely before lowering herself again inch by delicious inch.

He groaned, his head falling back against the wall of the sauna. She saw the sheen of sweat on his burnished skin, the flexing of muscles and tendons in his massive shoulders. Saw, too, the hard glitter of his eyes as they met hers.

Again she rose, smiling now, lingering at the very tip before drawing him deep once more. Her mouth took his. She found his tongue, sucked it, bit his lower lip ever so lightly.

"I like this," she murmured, clasping his head between her hands, clasping him within, kissing him again.

Her breasts rubbed against his chest, her hips rose and fell faster, her tongue thrust deeper. She felt the big, smooth tip of him begin to pulse, felt him try to hold back, and deliberately contracted her muscles, compelling him to yield.

Her name on his lips was half blessing, half curse. He exploded within her, convulsing over and over, his powerful body slamming into the bench. Her own response came hard and fast. Their cries of pleasure drifted on the hot, perfumed air of the firelit chamber cupped in the palm of the earth.

Chapter

FIFTEEN

WHEN CYMBRA WAS NEXT AWARE OF anything at all, it was of staring at her husband in bewilderment. He had spoken, she thought she had heard him, but what he had said made no sense at all.

He was lying stretched out on one of the benches. She lay draped over him. From her position, she was just able to raise her head and look down at him, trying to see if he could possibly be serious. "The river? The river out there?"

He nodded, although it seemed to cost him. "That's how a sauna works. First you heat up with the steam, then you run outside and jump in the river to cool off. It's very invigorating."

Since he sounded rather hesitant himself, Cymbra couldn't help but laugh. "Oh, I'm sure it is. Go right ahead. Just leave me out of it."

"Truly, if you're going to have a real sauna experience, that's the way you should do it."

She raised her head higher and grinned at him. "I did

just have a *real sauna experience*. It might not be the usual kind but believe me, it counts."

On a sudden thought, she added, "And please, don't make me describe what would happen to you if you gave even the teeniest little thought to carrying me out of here and tossing me in that river."

He propped an arm behind his head, gazed up at her, and smiled. "Something terrible?"

"Something *excruciatingly* terrible."

"Too horrible even to speak of?"

"Much too horrible."

He flopped back down on the bench and ran his hands along her sleek flanks. "Well, terrible woman, since you have drained me of all strength, I suppose you're safe enough. For the moment."

They lay awhile longer, gathering themselves, before Cymbra murmured, "Besides, I have a much better idea."

She rose gracefully, stretched so that her fingers brushed the curving roof of the sauna, and lowered them to find her husband studying her appreciatively. With a flush, she searched among the items he had brought until she found one of her bars of scented soap.

Delighted, she appropriated one of the buckets of water beside the firebox and dipped in a finger to test the temperature. "Perfect." Lathering her hands, she began to wash herself.

Before very long, Wolf was on his feet, showing surprising resiliency for a man who claimed to have had all the strength drained out of him. "You shouldn't have to do that all by yourself." Ever helpful, he took the soap from her and ran it through his hands.

Slowly, gently—and very, very thoroughly—he washed her. With equal care and attentiveness, she did the same for him. They rinsed off by throwing ladlefuls of water at each other, laughing, until the laughter faded

suddenly. Wolf caught her to him, lowered her carefully
to the smooth plank floor, and loved her with his hands,
his mouth, his body, until nothing remained save raptur-
ous bliss.

Later still, after the embers in the firebox had burned
low and steam had long since ceased to rise from the
stones, the Norse Wolf carried his sleeping wife back to
their lodge. He nestled her beneath smooth linen and soft
fur, gathering her close beside him. In the final moments
before sleep took him, he felt an irresistible need to give
thanks for this woman who touched his very heart and
soul.

He had little experience with prayer other than before
battle when he offered sacrifices to Odin and afterward
when he offered up thanks for victory. This was different.
It didn't seem to have anything to do with Odin or any of
the others, not even Frigg, despite his undeniable affection for her.

Still, thanks were owed. His eyes were closing when
he thought suddenly of the Christian God, the strange
one without sword or thunderbolt. With only the cross
and the empty tomb. Strange God, dying and undying.
God not of endless battles but of one everlasting victory.

It seemed to fit somehow. He said his thanks and fell
asleep, his last thought that somewhere, somehow, someone had heard.

BRITA FINGERED THE CLOAK, LOOKED AT IT CLOSELY,
and glanced at Cymbra. Mildly, the young Irish girl
asked, "Would you happen to know what this stain is
from, my lady?"

From her perch in the bed, where she was eating the
breakfast Brita had thoughtfully brought—and trying not
to gobble it down, for she was *very* hungry—Cymbra did

her utmost not to blush. As casually as she could, she said, "Whey, I believe."

"Ah, of course, whey. And this would be—?"

"Milk. That one would be milk."

"That's fine then." Struggling not to smile, and not entirely succeeding, Brita put the garment aside. "We won't have any difficulty getting those out. Now, as for his lordship's tunic—"

"Honey," Cymbra blurted. "And cheese, possibly, and eggs. I really am sorry about the mess." She hoped it was understood she wasn't speaking only of the messy clothes that needed to be washed but of the much larger mess that had been made in the kitchens.

"Oh, no, my lady! There's no need for you to apologize. We're all just . . . Well, there's just no need, that's all."

Brita bundled the clothes away quickly, mercifully saying nothing about Cymbra's torn gown, and picked up a comb from the table beside the bed.

"Would you like me to tend to your hair while you breakfast, my lady?"

Cymbra plucked at a tangled strand ruefully. "The condition it's in, it might take through breakfast, midday meal, and supper. I really shouldn't sleep with it unbraided."

"These things happen," Brita observed, the very soul of tact. She sat down on the edge of the bed and began gently running the comb through Cymbra's knee-length tresses, beginning at the bottom and slowly working her way up. Her touch was so gentle that Cymbra winced only once or twice.

"Have you heard anything from Mikal and Nadia this morning?" Cymbra asked after she plucked yet another slice of warm, honeyed bread off the platter. She couldn't remember ever being so famished.

"Oh, yes, my lady. Mother and son are both doing very well and Mikal was especially delighted with the gift Lord Wolf sent. He said he had never seen such a fine drinking cup and would treasure it forever."

Cymbra smiled, delighted that her husband had found so swift and thoughtful a way to show that he held the Rus trader and his family blameless.

"That's good then. And everyone returned safely? There were no injuries?"

"None, my lady. But—" She broke off, suddenly very preoccupied with Cymbra's hair.

"But what?" When this was greeted only with silence, Cymbra twisted around so that she could see Brita. "What's wrong? What happened?"

"Nothing, I shouldn't have spoken. It is for Lord Wolf to say—" She dropped her eyes and concentrated again on the tangles.

Cymbra didn't persist. She had no wish to make the Irish girl uncomfortable. A feeling of apprehension grew in her, making her glad when at last she was dressed and able to leave the lodge.

Sunlight welcomed her. Bright, glorious, almost forgotten sunlight. The rain had stopped. The gray, leaden clouds were gone and in their place was a sky of pure cerulean blue dotted with just a scattering of fleece. As she stood with her face turned to the sun, savoring its warmth, Ulfrich hurried to greet her.

"Good morning, my lady! Isn't it wonderful? The crops are saved, the jarl is back, and everything—" He looked at her with a wise smile. "Well, everything is just fine!"

"Tell me your chest feels well and I will agree with you."

"It feels splendid, absolutely splendid. I could run rings around the young men here. However, as I have no wish to make them feel inadequate—" He laughed and

Cymbra joined him as arm in arm they walked across the hill top.

Brother Joseph caught sight of them and waved them over to the chapel. "Good morning, my lady . . . Ulfrich," he said with a smile. "Lovely day. Some of the children offered to find flowers for the altar and I thought I'd go with them." He exchanged a look with the older man, then smiled again at Cymbra. "Perhaps you'd like to come with us, my lady."

"What a splendid idea!" Ulfrich said. "We could all go. We could even take a meal with us, make a day of it."

"Wonderful!" Brother Joseph exclaimed. "Brita, perhaps you'd like to come, too."

Cymbra turned, surprised to see the Irish girl. For just a moment, she had the odd thought that Brita had followed her, although she could think of no reason why she would have done so.

"Oh, I'd love to," Brita said. "My lady and I could gather more plants for the garden."

"Then it's decided!" Brother Joseph said happily. "We'll all go. If we're going to make the most of it, I think we should set off immediately. Don't you agree?"

"Absolutely," Ulfrich said.

"Certainly," Brita replied. "In fact, why don't the three of you start with the children and I'll just follow right along after I've picked up the food. It won't take but a few minutes."

A stillness settled in Cymbra. She looked slowly from one to the other, seeing the eager faces of people who were her friends, yet in whom she sensed a certain strain.

"Haven't you forgotten something?" she said gently. "I'm not supposed to leave here without permission—and an escort."

"That's not a problem."

Cymbra whirled to find Dragon standing directly behind her. He had come up so quietly that she hadn't heard him. He looked very fit, well rested and at ease, with no trace of the pain that had plagued him for so long.

"I'll be happy to escort you," he said with a smile. "As for permission, I don't think my noble brother would begrudge you a day picking flowers."

"Excellent," Ulfrich said. "Then there's nothing to prevent us going. Let's be off."

"Wait." Cymbra took a long, level look at her brother-in-law. "*You'll* escort us . . . for a day of picking flowers?"

He shrugged shoulders as broad as Wolf's. "Well, I don't guarantee I'll actually pick any. I'll just keep watch, that sort of thing."

"And Wolf won't mind if I'm gone all day?"

"Of course not."

"I think I'll just ask him. Where is he?"

Dragon frowned. "In the hall but he's very busy and I'm sure he doesn't want to be interrupted."

"Really? What has him so occupied?"

The four of them—Dragon, Ulfrich, Brother Joseph, and Brita—exchanged glances. It fell to Dragon to answer her.

"Look, Cymbra, the thing is . . . we brought back prisoners, men who attacked the farmstead. . . ." He hesitated as though deciding exactly how much he would—and wouldn't—say. "They have to pay for it, that's all."

He fingered the hilt of the sword strapped around his lean waist, took a deep breath, and said, "It was actually Wolf's idea that you go pick flowers today. He wants you away from here."

The others had the grace to look just a little shamefaced at this revelation of their mutual deception, but they were still resolved.

"We'd best be off," Brother Joseph said firmly.

Still, Cymbra refused to budge. She looked from one to the other of them in astonishment. Finally, she addressed Dragon. "It was Wolf's idea? He started this?"

"He's only thinking of your well-being. You got so upset when that thief was lashed and he's—"

"The prisoners are going to be whipped?"

Dragon closed his eyes for a moment, summoning patience. He clearly wasn't experienced in dealing with recalcitrant women. Indeed, Cymbra had to wonder if he'd ever encountered one before in his whole life.

"They . . . killed people."

Devastation. Burning rubble. Bodies thrown about, some in pieces. Women spread-eagle on the ground, raped, killed. Children—

Cymbra reeled. The vision came without warning, so vivid that she could have sworn she smelled it. For a horrible moment, she feared she would vomit.

When the world righted, Dragon was holding her and cursing vividly. "Dammit, that's why you have to leave! Whatever *that* is, Wolf doesn't know, I sure as hell don't, and I'm not even sure you do. We have to get you away from here."

"She has the gift," Brita said quietly. She stood with her hands tightly clasped, staring at Cymbra. "I suspected it a while ago and now I'm certain. The great healers are like that, my ma always said. They can feel the suffering of others but they have to be able to protect themselves lest they be destroyed by it."

Dragon looked down into Cymbra's eyes, his own face grim. "Is this true? Can you feel what other people are feeling?"

"S-sometimes." She stepped away from him and forced herself to stand very steadily. The sudden exposure of her most deeply held secret was shock enough but the realization that others had sensed something different about her was an even greater surprise. She thought she had concealed the truth so well. What else had she been wrong about?

Fighting to hide her sudden panic, she said, "That's

why Hawk sent me to Holyhood. At first, he wouldn't allow anyone there who wasn't strong and healthy, and if
there was an accident, the person was taken away immediately."

"He expected you to live like that for the rest of your
life?" Dragon asked, astonished.

"I'm not sure what he expected. He was just trying to
protect me. But I got better. I learned, as Brita said, to
protect myself."

"You couldn't just now," her brother-in-law reminded her. "You saw something."

She flinched at the memory but stood firm. "It's true
that I haven't been doing as well lately, but I can't just run
away whenever something bad happens."

"You wouldn't be run—" Ulfrich said.

"Be sensible—" Brother Joseph entreated.

"Please, my lady—" Brita added.

Dragon shrugged. "This is all very interesting but the
jarl says you are to go pick flowers, so pick flowers you
shall. You can sort this out with him later if he's of a mind.
In the meanwhile, we've tarried long enough."

He took her arm, clearly intending to drag her if he
had to, only to find that she slipped between his fingers
like quicksilver.

"Cymbra!"

She heard him but she didn't stop. Holding her skirts
up, her long hair flying behind her, the Norse Wolf's
Saxon bride raced to the timbered hall.

H E SAT IN STATE, IN THE LARGE, HIGH-BACKED CHAIR
behind the high table. His tunic was gray trimmed
with gold. Gold bands glinted on his arms. He wore a gold
torque around his neck, the ends joined in a wolf's head
emblazoned with eyes of bloodred rubies.

He radiated power and authority. And no mercy whatsoever.

Cymbra stopped just beyond the large double doors. She stood, heart pounding, unsure of what to do now that she had done it.

She had disobeyed him—again.

But she could not be so weak, so craven as to be unable to face the reality of their lives. He was jarl, he carried great responsibilities. She was his wife, it was her duty to stand beside him and help him in any way she could. Not run away and hide.

Still, she could not bring herself to walk farther into the hall thronged with grim-faced men and only a handful of women. There were no children at all even though they normally went everywhere and were part of everything. With a start, she realized they had already been gathered up and removed. As she was supposed to have been.

So then the punishment would be very bad. All right, she could face that. The men had killed savagely. Wolf was right when he spoke of the need to maintain order lest chaos descend. In his own life, he had seen the terrible results when that happened. He had lost his parents, his home, almost everything save for his life and that of his brother.

A brother who was still bound and determined to carry out the Wolf's orders. Cymbra just managed to dodge aside when a grim-faced Dragon bore down on her. He stood, glowering at her like an enraged thunder god who, rather absurdly, was trying to be discreet.

"Cymbra, come with me now," he hissed from between clenched teeth.

She shook her head and edged farther away, staying beside the wall. Short of drawing everyone's attention to them, there was little he could do.

"Wolf!"

Apparently, Dragon didn't have as many qualms about drawing attention as she'd hoped. He strode right into the middle of the hall, faced his brother, and said in a loud, clear voice, "Your wife is here."

All eyes swiveled in her direction. But the only ones she cared about were silver gray and lit by fire.

Slowly, he rose. Slowly, he came to where she was standing, wishing for all the world that she could dissolve right into the wall. That being unlikely, she straightened her shoulders and mustered a smile.

"There seems to have been a misunderstanding, my lord. I don't think this is a good day to pick flowers."

His gaze raked over her. "Yes, I'd say there's been a misunderstanding. Let me correct it. *I* want you to go pick flowers."

"I think there will be better days to pick flowers whereas—"

"Do not argue with me." If he had spoken harshly, she might have been able to resist him. But his tone was soft, for her ears alone, with such gentleness as to bring tears to her eyes.

She blinked them back fiercely and blurted the fear that drove her, fear of what he might believe, what he might truly think of her. "I am not a weakling!"

"I never said you were. But you are—" He hesitated, uncertain.

Dragon caught his eye. "She feels the pain of others. That Irish girl calls it a gift."

Wolf's gaze locked on his wife, his own impenetrable. He appeared neither shocked nor surprised, merely curious. But then why should it be other when he knew her so well? "Is this true?"

"Yes, but it doesn't make me any less strong. I can still do all the things your wife should be able to do."

His composure broke. He stared at her dumbfounded. "*That's* what you're worried about? That you would somehow disappoint me?"

"How can I not if I am too weak and craven to stand at your side? What kind of wife is that for a jarl to have? People will say you made a mistake to wed me. Perhaps you will say it."

They continued to stare at each other for several moments. Abruptly, Cymbra gasped and lashed out, striking Wolf on the chest. "Don't you dare laugh at me!"

"I'm not . . . All right, I was. I'm sorry. It's just that how any woman could think . . . after last night."

Abruptly aware of their avid audience, Wolf caught himself. He cleared his throat and said loudly, "The Lady Cymbra, my wife, has requested to witness this judging. As I know her to be a woman of courage and strength, I agree."

Beneath the approving comments of the assembly, he murmured to Dragon, "At the first sign of trouble, get her *out* of here."

Grim faced, locked in their mutual determination to do right by one stubborn female, the Hakonson brothers took their places at the high table. Dragon held out the chair beside Wolf's for his sister-in-law. He positioned himself right behind her, prepared to carry out his jarl's orders with dispatch.

Cymbra sat down gladly, afraid her legs would no longer hold her. She could scarcely believe what she had done or how Wolf had reacted. Truly, he was the most princely of men, kind, thoughtful, understanding—

Ruthless. She bit back a gasp as the prisoners were led into the hall. There were five in all, large men and very fit, or at least they had been. Their arms were drawn behind them and chained to wooden staffs that ran across their backs. They were hobbled over, dirty, bruised, and cut, and showing clear evidence of having been dragged. Their mouths were cracked and parched, their eyes frantic.

They were men who teetered on the very edge of death
and knew it.

*Devastation. Burning rubble. Bodies thrown about,
some in pieces. Women spread-eagle on the ground, raped,
killed. Children—*

She had seen. She remembered. And she kept silent,
stifling the impulse to show kindness even in the face of
evil.

Wolf held up a hand. The assembly, which had been
yelling curses at the killers, became silent.

Into that stillness, his voice cut deep and hard. "You
fell upon the peaceful settlement of Vycoff. You slaughtered the men, women, and children dwelling there. You
showed no mercy, not to oldest or youngest. No crime had
been committed against you or yours. This was not payment for harm done, it was murder. For it, you will die."

Several of the men moaned, a few tried to hold out
their hands in supplication but were restrained by their
chains. One, the largest of them, looked at Cymbra. Weak
as he was, in pain, afflicted with hunger and thirst, facing
death, yet still his eyes widened at the sight of her. He
stared, unable or unwilling to draw his gaze away. Slowly,
he leered.

"The Saxon bitch."

His voice was hoarse, rasping in the silence. Yet were
the words unmistakable.

Pandemonium erupted. Several men rushed at him
and began to pummel him with their fists. He went down
but even so, through the tumult of bodies, he continued to
stare at Cymbra.

She refused to respond; not by so much as a flicker
would she acknowledge his presence. Dragon felt no such
constraint. He caught his brother's glance, nodded, and
wadded into what was rapidly becoming an enraged mob.
Pulling men away, he yanked the offender back onto his
feet.

Wolf had not moved. He appeared utterly unaffected. "This one merely seeks to hasten his own death," he told the crowd. "Do not oblige him."

Murmurs of understanding replaced shouts for blood. The jarl was wise, he saw what they had not. He was right, of course. Why should the scum die quickly? Let him suffer as was fitting.

Cymbra held herself very still. She heard what was being said, she could hardly fail to do so. Yet her mind reeled from the implications. Not only death, then, but slow death. And she had insisted on being present.

Instinctively, she sought the walls that had sheltered her for so many years, those she had built in her mind to protect herself from the too-violent world. But the walls were gone, vanished as though they had never been. There was nowhere to run, to hide, nowhere safe.

Her heart beat frantically. For a sickening, dizzying moment, she felt herself utterly open and exposed to every pain, every cruelty, every sorrow. It would destroy her. Yet scarcely had she thought that than another sensation seized her. She felt strong arms close around her, drawing her near, cradling her. Arms she knew very, very well.

Yet did Wolf remain unmoving in his seat, not touching her at all. Only looking at her. She met his gaze, saw the understanding there, and felt the terror ease from her like water flowing unhindered over smooth ground.

He was her wall now, her shelter, her protection. His arms were strong and they would never let her go.

She closed her eyes for a moment, savoring the sensation of being safer than she had ever been in her life. When she opened them again, she was calm, resolved, as ready as she could be for what was to come.

And Wolf was still staring at her.

He looked away, looked at the killers, looked at her again. Abruptly, he stood.

"Olaf!"

The old, one-eyed man Cymbra had become fond of on the voyage to Sciringesheal strode forward. He nodded to her and stood before his lord.

"Fetch the ax."

The crowd shouted its approval. Eager hands fell upon the killers, dragging them out of the hall, into the open area beyond. Ulfrich was there, looking grim and somber. Brother Joseph stood beside him, his head bowed. Between them was Brita, her face very pale, her eyes dark smudges, yet clearly determined not to desert her mistress at such a time.

Cymbra wanted to order her away, but her throat was too tight to emit any sound. She could only gather herself inward, praying she would not break, would not disgrace Wolf. She stared at the punishment post, remembering the thief who had been lashed and the horrible tortures Brother Chilton had told her about, those that would make a mere lashing seem as nothing. She braced herself for the wave of pain and terror that she knew would overwhelm her.

Yet still did strong arms hold her and did she know herself to be safe.

"These are not men," Wolf said suddenly. He made a sweeping gesture of contempt in the direction of the killers. "They are but carrion feeders, no better than offal themselves."

He looked around at the crowd, which hung on his every word. "A man does not soil his hands with offal."

The crowd murmured agreement.

Wolf glanced at Dragon and Olaf. Without warning, they dragged forward one of the men, thrust him down onto his knees, and yanked him across a wooden block that had suddenly appeared. In the space of a breath, Dragon took the ax Olaf proferred, swung it once, very high, and brought it down. A head rolled across the hard-packed earth.

The crowd gasped. Dragon didn't wait. He seized the second man and dispatched him just as quickly. Olaf finished the next two just as efficiently. That left the last, the one who had dared to insult Cymbra.

Wolf took the bloody ax from Olaf. With it dangling from his hand, he walked over to the man and gestured at the block. "Kneel, and when you do, know that only the value I place on my Saxon wife sends you from this life speedily."

The man stumbled to obey. The ax cleaved the air once more, singing its blood song as it went. The earth drank of the red river thirstily.

No one moved, no one spoke. There was only the wind from the sea and, borne on it, the distant cry of the hawk.

Chapter

SIXTEEN

O H, LOOK! HE'S YAWNING AGAIN." NADIA
gazed at her son in delight surpassed only by
his doting father's fascination. Oblivious to
them both, and to the gently amused Cymbra,
the baby produced a prodigious yawn, smacked his lips
together, squeezed his eyes shut, and drifted off to sleep.

"He's such a good baby," his adoring mother said as
she settled him into his cradle. "He knows just what to do
and how to do it."

"He's nursing well then?" Cymbra asked. There
seemed little doubt as to the answer, for the baby was already putting on weight, but she wanted to be sure Nadia
wasn't having any problems.

"Extremely well," the proud mother assured her.
"Why, you would think he was born knowing how to do it."

Cymbra decided against pointing out that he had
been born knowing exactly that. The new parents' happiness was contagious. She lingered awhile longer, enjoying
it, before taking her leave.

Back out on the street, she found Olaf leaning against
a wall, surveying the passing scene. He straightened, nod-

ding to her cordially. Several days before—shortly after
the executions—he had appointed himself her escort. At
least, she thought he had.

Given her husband's inclination to *arrange* things for
her, she couldn't rule out Wolf's having had a hand in it.
But Olaf really was the perfect choice for such duty, vastly
superior to the armed cordon of warriors Wolf had previously insisted accompany her. The older man had confided to her that he liked feeling useful, something that
didn't come easily for those past their prime.

"Surely Lord Wolf values your wisdom and experience," she had said when they spoke of the matter.

"Aye, he does but he's rare in that. Generally, the old
are only a burden to themselves and to everyone else as
well."

"But that should not be so! The old should be trea-
sured for what they can teach us about life. Without their
knowledge, passed on to us, we would always be starting
over."

"That's a way to think of it," Olaf agreed. "But think
of this, too. The northlands are harsh, unforgiving. Food
and shelter can be hard to come by. For many, there is little enough without stretching it to provide for those who
can no longer contribute."

She remembered that now as she glanced around the
busy street and beyond it to the even busier port. Everywhere was the evidence of the wealth of Sciringesheal,
wealth made possible by the power of its jarl. The houses
were sturdy and well appointed, the shops well stocked.
The people themselves were well dressed and amply fed.
They carried themselves with confidence and pride.

Beyond the streets, along the stone wharves, several
ships rode at anchor. They had arrived so recently that
cargo was still being unloaded. One in particular drew
Cymbra's notice.

It was different from the vessels of the northlands,

being broader in the hull and double-masted. The sides were painted in alternating bands of vermilion and gold. Brightly colored flags trailed from the rigging. She craned her neck a little to get a better view and noticed the dark-skinned men moving between the deck and the wharf.

"They've come a long way," she observed.

Olaf followed her gaze and nodded. "That would be the Moor . . . Kareem ben something-or-other. Hails from Constantinople. He's an old friend of Wolf and Dragon's."

Excited by the prospect of meeting someone from so far away, Cymbra did not tarry in the town but returned promptly to the stronghold. The gates were open and a steady stream of people hurried in and out. Some were bound for the fields where the harvest had begun. Others were off the vessels come to trade before the first blast of winter closed the northlands for another season.

Some of the crew from the Byzantine ship were clustered near the doors of the timbered hall, talking with several of Wolf's men in the polyglot tongue common to traders everywhere. The strangers broke off abruptly as Cymbra neared, and stared at her in the usual slack-jawed way she barely noticed anymore. A couple of those with quicker reflexes than the others began to move toward her.

Olaf growled deep in his throat and put a hand to the hilt of his sword but neither gesture was necessary. Scarcely had the newcomers taken a step than they were stopped by the local men. Cymbra heard the murmured words, warning and explanation together, as she hurried by.

"The Wolf's woman."

The newcomers froze in place like men who had just noticed they were about to walk off the edge of a precipice. They stepped back hastily, averting their gaze from the vision of their own deaths.

Cymbra entered the hall to be struck at once by a swirl of exotic colors, tantalizing aromas, and rich, male laughter. As always, her gaze sought Wolf. She found him standing at the far end of the hall near the high table. Dragon was with him and another man she couldn't identify but guessed to be the Moor.

He was a few inches shorter than either of the Hakonson brothers but very fit and richly garbed in a vermilion tunic that complemented his dark complexion and neatly trimmed black beard. He happened just then to glance toward her and his jaw dropped, but he closed it again with a snap, as though he might already suspect who she was.

"Ah, Cymbra, there you are." Wolf held out a hand, drawing her to his side. "Come and greet an old friend, Kareem ben Abdul. Kareem, this is my wife, the Lady Cymbra."

Their guest bowed courteously but without taking his liquid eyes from her. His smile was broad and appreciative. "The *legendary* Lady Cymbra, I would say, my friend, for surely her fame precedes her."

"You exaggerate, sir," she said softly, not in reprimand but in simple truth.

His eyes widened at the sound of her voice, leaving her to wonder what surprised him—that she could talk or that she would. Her thoughts were refocused abruptly when Wolf hauled her against him, an iron-hard arm wrapped around her narrow waist. She glanced up to see him, too, showing his teeth, with the suggestion that he was ever ready to take a chunk out of the other man.

Kareem held up his hands in the universal gesture of peace. "Be at ease, my friend. I honor your lady and you."

"But you understand I'm a bit sensitive on this score?"

"Oh, absolutely, what man wouldn't be? With your permission, perhaps the Lady Cymbra would care to examine the fabrics I've brought with me?"

While Wolf graciously allowed as to how he thought

that was a fine idea, Cymbra prayed for patience. She had just gotten her Viking husband to the point where she didn't actually have to ask for permission to go into the town—provided Olaf went with her—but now she needed his permission to look at fabrics?

"Perhaps later," she told both men briskly. "I'm going to see to supper."

Without waiting for a response from either, she nodded to the Moor, leveled a look at her husband, and took her leave. But not so quickly that she didn't hear a startled Kareem ask, "She *cooks*, too?"

Wolf laughed. "Like a dream."

"I'm happy for you, of course, but there's no fairness in this world."

Since they seemed determined to speak of her as though she were not there, Cymbra was glad enough to absent herself. She spent the remainder of the afternoon in the kitchens, showing the women how to make several dishes she had yet to serve in her husband's hall.

She had been planning to do that anyway. It had nothing to do with wanting to justify his obvious pride in her culinary skills, nothing at all.

By evening, almost the entire crew of the Byzantine vessel had arrived. As regular visitors, they were well known and heartily welcomed. Instruments were brought out and soon the rafters rang to song and story. In the midst of all that, news and rumors were exchanged, old acquaintances renewed, and plans made for the coming year.

Cymbra left the kitchens for a short time to bathe and change. She chose a gown of spring-green linen so finely woven as to seem almost weightless. It was embroidered with flowers at the hem and bodice and along the flowing sleeves. Because the evening was warm, she chose to do without an over tunic. Leaving her hair to tumble in waves to her knees, she secured it with jeweled combs at her brows, then hesitated for just a moment.

The gold wolf's-head torque her husband had given to her on their wedding day had remained in her jewel box since that single wearing. Now she took it out, feeling the weight of it in her hands. Before she could reconsider, she secured it around her slender throat.

Thus armored, she left the lodge and returned to the timbered hall.

S UPERB," KAREEM SAID. HE BIT THE LAST SUCCULENT meat off a plump chicken leg, tossed the bone on his trencher, and sighed. "I've never had a more splendid meal."

Devouring a slice of pork seasoned with peppercorns and saffron, Dragon paused just long enough to agree. "I used to think the best table I'd ever dined at was old Hakim Bey's in Alexandria. Remember him?"

"I do indeed," Kareem said. "A fine man, very fine. He had a fondness for almonds."

"But the honor goes to my noble brother now," Dragon continued with a grin. "Soon every fancier of fine food will have to be able to say that he's been to Sciringesheal or no one will take him seriously."

Wolf laughed, picked up a spear of wild asparagus, and chewed it thoughtfully. When he was done, he said, "I hope you carry a full cargo of spices, Kareem. For a man who used to consider that anything not still moving counted as food, I've become damn particular of late."

The Moor grinned broadly. "I boast the fullest possible assortment, my friend, including some brought from the farthest reaches of the world, islands beyond Cathay."

"I didn't know there was anything beyond Cathay," Cymbra said. She had been largely silent until now, content to listen, but this so sparked her curiosity that she had to speak. "Indeed, I will admit that I have heard some say even Cathay is a myth."

"Cathay is very real," Kareem said pleasantly. "I myself have met men from there."

Wolf nodded. He turned to his wife. "Cathay is real, sweetling. Kareem has met men from there."

She frowned slightly. Although an excellent wine from the vineyards of Sicily had been served, her husband had drunk very little of it and Kareem none at all, being forbidden by his faith. Yet did both men seem to be behaving . . . peculiarly.

Still, she was not about to comment on it. "How fascinating. Is it true that their eyes are shaped differently?"

"Indeed they are, being slanted and drawn up at the edges."

"Their eyes are slanted," Wolf told his wife, "and drawn up at the edges."

"They almost resemble the almonds Hakim Bey liked so much," Kareem added.

"Like almonds," Wolf said.

Cymbra stared at them. What strange performance was this? Why was her husband repeating what Kareem said as though she were incapable of hearing it?

"Do you also carry almonds?" she asked.

"Beautiful almonds as well as many other nuts. It will be my pleasure to bring a complete sampling tomorrow."

"He has all sorts of nuts, sweetling. You can try some of each tomorrow."

"And fabrics?" she asked.

"Dozens of different kinds—the finest silks, the most beautiful brocades, the sheerest linens—"

"Silks, brocades, linens," Wolf repeated. "The best of everything."

"Any animals? I have the most desperate craving for a pet monkey."

"Alas, no, they do not travel well."

"No animals, *elskling*, but I'm sure—" Wolf broke off

abruptly and stared at her. "Why would you want a monkey?"

He'd called her sweetheart again, and this time he was sober. She couldn't help but be pleased. "I don't actually. I just wondered how long it would take for you to stop repeating everything our guest says." She smiled at Kareem. "Your Norse is excellent and less accented than my own. I understand you perfectly."

"I am pleased your lady finds it so," the Moor said to Wolf.

Dragon laughed. He beckoned a servant to refill the goblets, then said, "I believe you are confusing Cymbra." After a quick glance in her direction, he widened his eyes with mock alarm. "In fact, I think you're annoying her."

"I am not annoyed," she said. "I merely seek to understand why Kareem does not address me directly."

"Because you are the property of another man," Dragon said cordially. "It is as unthinkable for him to speak to you directly as it would be for him to touch you."

"That's absurd!" Quickly remembering herself, she addressed the Moor. "I am sorry, I don't wish to be rude, but I have never heard of such a thing."

Wolf shrugged. "It is commonplace in the East."

"A very civilized place, the East," Dragon commented. When his sister-in-law glared at him, he laughed. His gaze fell to the torque at her neck. "You bristle at being called property yet you wear my brother's mark."

"I wear a bride's gift." Her eyes flared. "Or do you perceive no difference between a wife and, say, a horse?"

Dragon was seized by a sudden fit of coughing that, oddly enough, seemed to be contagious. It afflicted Kareem as well. Only Wolf appeared immune, and he seemed to be having a hard time keeping a straight face.

"Is it so absurd to say that a wife is different from that?" she demanded.

He shook his head until he was sure he could speak.

"No, *elskling*, of course it isn't." Whatever kindly thoughts she might have had for him as a result of that vanished in an instant when she saw his look of masculine amusement.

Abruptly, she realized what a wife and a horse had in common—both were mounted by a man. Her face flamed. Before she could react, Wolf moved judiciously to calm her.

"The ways of the East are different from ours but that isn't to say they are wrong. Wives are deeply respected, sheltered and protected, provided with every possible luxury. Surely that isn't so terrible."

"Quite right," Kareem affirmed. "The harem is a fine custom. There's a great deal to be said for it."

"What is a harem?" Cymbra asked. She'd come too far to back down now.

Before Wolf could reply, ever-helpful Dragon did so. "Where the women live, secluded from the world, seen only by their lord and master." He raised an eyebrow, inviting her reaction.

Kareem glanced from one brother to the other and stepped in hastily. "*All* the women of the household, old and young, mothers, aunts, cousins, daughters as well as wives, and the very young boys, too. It's a very spacious part of any residence with its own gardens, courtyards, fountains, and so on. Very pleasant, very nice."

"But the women are not allowed to leave there?"

"Oh, no, they can leave. They must only go veiled from the eyes of other men, of course, and with escort. That is all for their own comfort, obviously."

"I see." She glanced at Wolf and murmured, "However did you miss requiring a veil, husband?"

"There are other kinds of harems," Dragon commented. He ignored his brother's quelling look and went on cheerfully. "Remember Erik Leifson?"

"Dragon . . ." Wolf's tone of warning went unheeded.

"He had the villa just outside Constantinople, near the beach. Still does, as far as I know."

Kareem nodded. "Yes, of course I remember him. He is still there and doing extremely well for himself."

Dragon grinned. "I'm sure he is. Very generous fellow, Erik. Always wants his friends to be happy."

"I don't think this is—" Wolf began.

"Now there's a harem," Dragon continued blithely. "Erik isn't just a collector, he's a connoisseur." He sighed deeply, savoring memories. "There was a Circasian . . . incredible woman, had hair red as fire . . . and a Nubian with remarkably beautiful eyes who had trained as a gymnast and could—" He sighed again. "Remind me why we finally dragged ourselves away, Wolf, I forget."

"What I'm trying to remember is why I didn't leave you there," his brother muttered.

Dragon laughed. "You need me to liven things up?" As Kareen stroked his beard and chuckled, Dragon nodded thoughtfully. "All in all, I'd say the way of the East is better. A man always knows where his women are, at his beck and call, exactly as they should be. As for the women, they have no thought but pleasing their master and they're the happier for it."

Silence followed this ringing declaration. Wolf studied his drinking cup, apparently with an eye to crushing it. Dragon lounged back in his chair, well pleased with himself. As for Kareem, he made a manful effort to conceal his amusement but did not entirely succeed.

Cymbra folded her hands in her lap and smiled. With perfect pleasantness, she asked, "Tell me, my lord Kareem, do you carry any medicinals in your cargo?"

"Medicinals?"

"He's not sure what you—" Wolf began.

"I heard what he said." Cymbra smiled again, aware of all three men staring at her. For once, she was pleased to command male attention so effortlessly.

"Plants such as . . . oh, belladonna, for example. Or hemlock, thorn apple, monkshood . . . or oleander, Star of Bethlehem, castor beans . . . And then there's purple cockle, dwarf bay, flax olive, copse laurel . . ."

"Lady, those are all deadly poisons!" the Moor exclaimed, propriety forgotten.

She smiled sweetly—at him, at her dear brother-in-law, and most particularly at her husband. Lord and master, indeed!

"They are, aren't they, for all that most can also heal when used properly. And there are many more of them, all so easily mistaken for edible. A leaf here, a root there . . . why, the least carelessness on the part of a cook and . . ."

She sighed deeply but brightened as the servants reentered the hall. The men's eyes widened at the sight of the heavily laden platters being carried to the table.

"Oh, good," Cymbra said, "the next course." She looked around at the others innocently yet was there an unmistakable note of steel in her silken tones. "You *are* all still hungry, aren't you?"

HOURS LATER, LYING BESIDE HER HUSBAND IN THEIR bed, Cymbra was still inclined to smile. She would long remember the responses that had followed her little joke. Kareem looked at her as though she were some manner of being he had never seen before and wasn't sure he ever wanted to encounter again. Dragon was so startled he knocked over his drinking cup.

And Wolf . . . ah, yes, Wolf . . . her dear husband had stared at her for only a moment before breaking out in rich, hearty laughter. Yet she could not begrudge his amusement for with it came his obvious pride in having so clever a wife.

"I remember now why we left," he declared, "or at least why I did. Not a single woman there reminded me of Frigg." His gaze, both tender and ardent, left no doubt that such deficiency had been remedied.

So she reminded him of a goddess. That was rather sweet and certainly deserving of acknowledgment, such task as she set herself to perform very shortly after they retired to their lodge. If in the process she demonstrated that a man and a horse also had much in common, all the better.

But now she needed to sleep and couldn't, her mind still awhirl with thoughts, images, questions. . . .

Nadia's baby was wonderful. Cymbra's hand drifted to her flat belly. She'd love to have a child of her own. A dark-haired baby with gray eyes . . . a son or daughter for Wolf to adore as she knew he would, and other children to follow . . . please God . . .

The Moor with his dark, liquid eyes and ready smile, his talk of exotic, faraway places, of a different world where women were kept apart in silken bowers, secluded for the pleasure of a man . . . She could never bear that, *never*, yet there was a strange excitement in the thought.

Women intended solely for pleasure . . . Wolf had known such when he lingered in the villa by the Byzantine sea. A very generous man, Dragon had called their host, the collector—no, *connoisseur* of women. Red-haired Circasians, agile Nubians, and who knew what else . . . She had a sudden, too-vivid image of her husband, lounging on a couch, his long legs stretched out before him, lazily eyeing the beauties displayed for his selection.

Would he have chosen her had she been among them?

Stupid thought! He had chosen her, indeed come all the way to Holyhood to claim her.

For vengeance . . . for alliance . . . for whichever fate decreed when Hawk came.

Since the day of her marriage, she had stalwartly kept her thoughts from the terrible promise her husband had made. She had gone so far as never even to glance toward the beach he had sworn would be stained with her brother's blood.

She told herself she was merely being sensible. Wolf didn't really want to kill Hawk. He truly did want an alliance. All she had to do was convince her brother—when he came—that all was well and all would be.

All she had to do . . . When he came . . .

She made a small, involuntary sound of distress and turned over on her side. Huddled beneath the covers, her knees drawn up, she fought to restrain the tears that threatened to overtake her.

Fought, that is, until she felt the brush of a hand on her bare shoulder, the sudden sensation of strength hovering over her, and heard Wolf's voice, sleep roughened but instantly alert.

"Cymbra, what's wrong?"

Only a tiny sound, a small movement, yet somehow he had known at once that she needed him. Without waiting for an answer, he turned her into his arms and held her close.

"Did you have a bad dream?" he asked, stroking her back soothingly.

Not trusting herself to speak, she shook her head against his massive chest. He tried to lift her chin so that he could look at her but she resisted, burrowing closer to him. With a sigh, he lay back.

"Dragon didn't really upset you, did he? He was just teasing."

That surprised her enough to wring an answer. "No, of course not."

"Kareem then? He's a good soul, he wouldn't dream of offending you or—"

"No, not him either."

Wolf was silent for a moment. Slowly, he said, "Well, that seems to leave me. What have I done, *elskling*?"

"*N-nothing!*" Her tears broke suddenly, streaming down her cheeks and onto his chest. She sobbed convulsively, unable to stop, as her bewildered husband held her, alternately trying to calm her and demanding that she tell him what was wrong.

Finally, she brushed the tears away and looked at him. "I—I'm sorry. I don't know what's the matter with me." She paused a moment, sniffed, took a shuddery breath. "I'm fine, really."

He didn't answer, only looked at her before abruptly swinging his legs over the side of the bed and standing. Naked, he strode to the table beneath the window, poured wine into a jeweled goblet, and brought it to her.

"Drink this."

Obediently, she took a swallow, then another. He held the goblet for her until she indicated she'd had enough. Putting it aside, he sat down on the edge of the bed, took both her hands in his, and stared earnestly into her eyes.

"Now, *elskling*, would you *please* tell me what's wrong?"

He looked so . . . so rumbled, and concerned . . . and endearing with a lock of hair falling over his forehead and a night's growth of beard shadowing his jaw. He was a man others feared, a man of ruthless strength whose name was whispered with mingled awe and dread. Yet he sat there naked on the side of their bed in the middle of a night that had given him little rest and patiently pleaded with his wife to tell him what troubled her.

No wonder she loved him so much.

Cymbra gasped. Her hand flew to her mouth. She didn't merely desire Wolf or respect him or like him—although she certainly did all those things. She loved him—passionately, deeply, completely. Love that transcended all else, even life itself. Love taking her unawares, announcing itself already fully rooted within her, like a flower exploding to the sun.

"I love you," she said. The words spilled out—song, prayer, joyful shout for all that they were whispered. Three small words that said everything of who she was, who she would always be, what would always exist for them.

"I love you," she repeated as her happiness welled up, surging free and triumphant. "I love you!"

"I love you, too," Wolf said matter-of-factly. "But, *elskling*, I don't see why that should make you cry."

But it did, all over again, as she tried to absorb the incredible, astounding fact that *he* loved *her*. Wolf withstood it as well as any befuddled male could be expected to do. He stroked her back again, told her how wonderful she was, tried in every way he knew to calm her. When all that had no effect whatsoever, he gave up and resorted to a different strategy that required no words and worked far better.

But later still, when she slept at last, the Norse Wolf lay awake, holding his beloved wife in his arms and accepting what could no longer be denied: The time had come to snare the Hawk.

SEVENTEEN

A WEEK AFTER KAREEM BEN ABDUL RAISED AN-
chor and sailed out of the port of Sciringesheal,
Cymbra was still trying to find places for
everything he had left behind. It seemed as
though the entire contents of the Moorish vessel's cargo
hold had been transferred to the hill fort. She knew that
wasn't true—at least not quite. The residents of the town
had also made purchases, as had crews on other ships
happy to acquire such exotic goods to trade along with
their own.

Yet there was no denying that an extraordinary quantity of fabrics, spices, foodstuffs, and the like were now
hers to do with as she saw fit. Her husband, it seemed, was
an even wealthier man than she had realized. Several of
the chests in their quarters that were kept locked, and
which she had never bothered to inquire about, turned
out to be filled with gold coin, more than she had ever
imagined existed, as well as jewels of every description.

Nor was that the extent of it. Dragon possessed great
wealth in his own right. Together, the Hakonson brothers
maintained a trading empire that stretched from their

northern stronghold to the shores of the Mediterranean and even beyond.

When she expressed surprise at all this, Wolf merely shrugged. "A strong arm and a useful mind don't seem to go together all that often. When they do, a man finds more opportunity than he can take."

She knew he was being too modest. The *strong arm* of which he spoke was a fighting force feared throughout the world, and as for the *useful mind*, she already knew him to be keenly intelligent and perceptive.

So now here she was, surrounded by bolts of the most exotically beautiful cloth she had ever seen, the vivid colors of silks, satins, linens, and brocades glowing in the sun filtering through the open windows of the lodge to mingle with the barbaric luxury already present there. The fabrics covered the bed, the table, the chairs, and spilled over onto the floor.

Nor was that all. Set among them were intricate wooden chests banded with bronze and gold, containing within them drawer after drawer of fragrant spices. Cymbra opened one drawer and found sticks of precious cinnamon. In another were pungent mustard seeds. Still another held fragile threads of saffron in such quantity as to make her gasp, for this spice was the rarest and most costly by far. On and on the drawers went until she thought she must surely have enough spices to last her a lifetime.

"We will need a large chest for the kitchens," she said to Brita, who was helping her sort through everything. "Something sturdy and big enough to hold all these."

The Irish girl, who looked as dazed as Cymbra felt, nodded. "Something with a good lock on it, too, and bolted to the floor. The folk here are honest as the day is long but a stranger just passing through might be foolishly tempted."

This was good sense. A handful of spices, easily concealed, could buy a man more than he would see from a year of labor.

"We'll have to find a place for all this fabric, too," Cymbra said. "It can't stay in here."

Brita shook her head in wonder as she held up a length of deep blue brocade intricately stitched with silver swirls. The effect made Cymbra think of dancing stars weaving complex patterns across the night sky.

"Have you ever seen the like?" the Irish girl asked. "Or even imagined it existed?"

"I've seen some beautiful fabrics but never so many in one place at the same time. They are exquisite, but truly I don't know how we can possibly use all this. None of them are what could be called practical."

Brita giggled. She draped a link of apricot-hued gauze across the bed and said, "Oh, I don't know, my lady. That one looks very useful to me."

"Do you think women really wear such things?" Cymbra asked as she eyed the cloth. It was undeniably beautiful but even the thought of wearing it made her blush. Its purpose was so very evident.

"Indeed! When I was in Hedeby, I heard many a tale about women in the East and the things they do. Why, do you know some of them shave their pubes and put perfume there?"

"I wasn't aware of that." Brita's frankness surprised her but she couldn't deny that she was curious. Dragon certainly had fond memories of the East and she had no doubt her husband's were just as pleasant.

"And they rouge their nipples," Brita went on. "Some of them even have little tattoos of flowers and such like on their privates. Oh, and they have all sorts of toys—"

Cymbra coughed to cover her shock. *"Toys?"*

Brita laughed. "You'd be amazed. There are sheaths to make a man bigger so he feels more potent, some with nubs on them that are supposed to excite women even

more. There are little balls women can put up inside to excite themselves. And there are even bands men can wear
at the base of their cocks to make them stay hard and pro-
long their pleasure."

Cymbra stared at her in amazement so great as to
overcome her embarrassment. "People actually use such
things?"

"That and more, my lady. There are ointments to rub
on various places with various effects, elixirs of every sort,
incantations, magic incense, and on and on." She laughed.
"I know it all sounds unbelievable but it seems there are
no limits to people's imagination, at least not when it
comes to coupling."

"Apparently not." And to think she had believed herself knowledgeable about such matters just on the basis of
her few weeks of marriage. She eyed the apricot gauze
again. It was lovely and it did suit her coloring. Perhaps
she would just think about it.

There was little enough time for that, though, for
scarcely had she finished deciding what to do with all the
items than one of the serving women knocked hurriedly
on the lodge door and, at Cymbra's bidding, entered.

"My lady, his lordship wants you." She gestured toward the great hall.

Wondering what it was that could not wait, Cymbra
answered her husband's summons to find him in conversation with Dragon. Both men fell silent as she approached. They rose politely and Wolf held out a chair
for her.

"Is something wrong?" she asked, glancing from one
to the other.

They both answered at once. "No." "Of course not."

Dragon cast his brother a look she couldn't decipher
and sat back to listen.

"I've decided to invite the other lords of Vestfold to

assemble in Sciringesheal," Wolf said, "that we may meet together and talk over matters of mutual interest."

Cymbra swallowed her surprise and thought quickly. For such guests, there would have to be a great feast lasting several days and including only the finest of everything. It was quite an undertaking. She prayed she was up to it. Scarcely had she thought of that than she looked at her husband cautiously.

"When is all this to be?"

"The summons has just gone out. They will begin to arrive within the week."

"*A week?*" Only a week to prepare. "How many?"

Wolf shrugged. "There are the jarls themselves, their sons and retainers, the usual escorts and hangers-on . . . all in all, not more than a few hundred."

"A few hundred! In a week?" She stared at him in disbelief. She loved this man with all her heart. He was strong, protective, kind, utterly wonderful. Yet none of that stopped her from demanding, "Are you *mad?*"

"I told you she wasn't going to be happy," Dragon said. He looked pleased to be proven correct.

Wolf shot him a hard look but directed his attention to his wife. "There's nothing to be concerned about, *elskling.* You'll have all the help you need."

She stared at him unmollified. Typical man to say such a thing. She doubted he had given it any thought whatsoever. "Where will they sleep? What will they eat? How do you plan to keep them entertained when you aren't talking over these great matters, whatever they may be? Several hundred men who have to be fed, amused, and kept comfortable, and you give me only a *week?*"

"Easy, sweet sister," Dragon said with a laugh. "We begin today to build two temporary halls on the hillside that will shelter our guests. As for entertainment, there are few better than the hunt, which has the added advantage of providing food. But if you are still concerned, such word is already spreading that will bring ample . . . entertainment on the next tide. You need have no worry about that."

"Oh, good," Cymbra said. "Hundreds of Viking lords *and* every whore who can hie herself here. Truly, something to look forward to." She shook her head, then added, "It will take everyone in the town working together if this is to be as it should." Yet, even as she spoke, she felt a spurt of excitement at the prospect. She did enjoy a challenge and this promised to be a huge one. Moreover, she could not have conceived of a better opportunity to prove herself to her husband.

"You're the woman to organize it," Wolf assured her. "Buy anything you need, arrange everything as you see fit."

His confidence in her made Cymbra forgive the short notice, but she didn't stop worrying even as she hurriedly summoned the women together and began describing what must needs be done. In the flurry of activity that followed, she had very little time to think about anything except the endless details of the preparations.

And no time at all to be aware of the matter that concerned her husband far more than anything he would discuss with the other lords of Vestfold.

WHEN ARE YOU GOING TO TELL HER?" DRAGON asked several days later as he and Wolf rested beside the river after a cooling swim. Around them were scattered the remnants of the midday repast Cymbra had sent down—rounds of warm bread, ripe cheese, apples and berries in abundance, legs of chicken, partridge, and grouse, fallen upon eagerly by the hungry men who with Wolf and Dragon had labored long and hard to construct two very fine timbered halls that would house their guests. The finishing touches were still to be added but the major work was completed by dint of laboring through each day and far into the twilit night.

Nor was this respite to last long, for scarcely were the halls finished than it was time to begin bringing in supplies for the feasting. Soon the hunt would ride out, staying in the field day and night while relays of servants brought the kills back to the dozens of women and children mustered to deal with them. Stag, deer, and boar would fall before flashing spear and speeding arrow while the young boys set their traps for smaller game.

So, too, were the longboats putting out to sea, their great seine nets at the ready to bring forth cod and herring in abundance. The smoke fires would burn without cease. Great blocks of ice hauled from the river the preceding winter and kept packed underground would keep other foods well chilled. Some would be salted, some pickled. Several hundred Vikings would find no complaint for their stomachs' sake while the Lord of Sciringesheal hosted them.

The lord . . . Wolf's thoughts strayed back to his brother's question. Lying naked in the sun, letting the warm summer air dry him, he said, "At the last possible moment, when else?"

Dragon stared at him for a moment, then threw back his head and laughed. "Marriage has taught you prudence, brother."

Wolf grinned ruefully. "It's trying to, at least. But I've been thinking, she may not really mind. In fact, she might be relieved."

Dragon's look was bluntly skeptical. "How so?"

"You know what it will be like—hundreds of men staying up all night, feasting and drinking, singing, telling war stories, making free with the whores. Most of them will get falling-down drunk, there will be at least a few knife fights. Cymbra wouldn't enjoy any of that."

"Don't know why not. Sounds like a fine time to me." Dragon grinned again at his brother's look of reprimand. "But you're right, that sort of thing isn't for a lady. Unless, of course, the lady in question thinks she's worked her fingers to the bone to bring it all about and doesn't appreciate being told she can't come."

"Well, she can't," Wolf said sullenly, "whether she *appreciates* it or not. Odin's breath, brother, you know how men react to her! I've called the jarls here to talk, not make slobbering fools out of themselves."

"I did wonder if you'd thought of that when you came up with this idea. For all that I don't mind provoking my sweet sister-in-law a bit, she really does need protecting, if only from herself." He shook his head in wonder. "She still doesn't seem to have any idea of the effect she has."

Wolf sighed. As day had passed day and he saw how very hard and well his wife was working to make the feast a success, his feeling of guilt had grown. Yet he did not waver from his decision, recognizing it as the only one he could make.

"I think what she wants most is what she can never have," he said quietly.

"What's that?"

"A normal life. Just to be an ordinary woman doing ordinary things. In her heart, I believe she's always yearned for that."

Dragon leaned back against the mossy bank. "The gods are capricious. They withhold their gifts at will, yet do they sometimes lavish them so greatly as to be burden rather than boon."

They pondered that in silence for some little time but soon enough the respite ended. Both men rose, dressed, and armed themselves. As Dragon went to see to the horses, Wolf sought his wife to say a brief farewell.

He found her in their lodge, bent over as she tried to pull a chest out from under the bed where it had been stored. Wolf stopped just inside the entrance and stared. His wife was so intent in her efforts that she hadn't heard him come in. He had a very pleasant view of her firm little bottom wiggling back and forth as she tried to get a better hold on the chest.

"Need some help?" he asked pleasantly.

Cymbra jumped at the sound of his voice and looked over her shoulder, but didn't let go of the chest. "No, I've almost got it. All I have to do is—" She gave it one more good hard tug and . . . Too hard. The handle slipped out of her hand and she was flung backward by the force of her own efforts, landing hard on what he had so lately admired.

Before she could try to rise, Wolf was lifting her, setting her gently on her feet, and looking at her with concern until he saw that she was more irritated than hurt. Then he laughed and drew her to him. His big hand lightly rubbed the offended portion of her anatomy through her gown.

"You should take more care," he said. An imp of mischief prompted him to add, "I prefer that my property not be damaged."

"I didn't damage the chest. It just slipped out—" Abruptly, she realized what he meant and her eyes flared. "Property, Wolf? Are you sure you want to claim that when I'm not even wearing your—what did Dragon call it—your mark?"

He laughed and held her against him despite her attempt to resist. "Do you wear nothing at all, I claim you. Indeed, especially then."

This deliberate provocation earned him a glare but he was well pleased by it. Dragon wasn't the only one who found his wife teasable. Wolf did, too, and he was in a much better position to take advantage of it.

Her cheeks were flushed and she was glaring at him so fiercely that it was all he could do not to laugh again.

Instead, he tipped her back against his encircling arm and took her mouth. For just a moment, she resisted but quickly enough her lips parted to admit the thrust of his tongue. He went slower then, stroking and savoring her until she gave a little moan of frustration and began tugging him toward the bed.

They had lain there entwined, in the soft hours of the morning, making the most of what little time they had before the preparations for the feast drew them apart once more. Now Wolf had thought to say his farewells quickly but that plan was gone from his mind as though it had never been. Yet he realized full well that the hunt was already assembling—men, horses, and dogs waiting—with every available hour needed for their task.

But he had other, more personal needs, and if his wife's urgent efforts to get them both to the bed were any indication, so did she. Abruptly, he made up his mind. He bunched her skirts in his hand and pulled them above her hips. She gave a little gasp as he touched her intimately but that was drowned out by his groan of pleasure at finding her already sweetly pliant.

Moving quickly, mindful of each fleeting moment, he maneuvered her to the bed, turning her and gently but firmly urging her down on her knees on the mattress. She stiffened a little in surprise but he soothed her with a touch.

"Easy," he murmured huskily. "You'll enjoy this, I promise." Pulling her gown out of the way, he bared her lovely bottom. Moving behind her, he freed himself quickly.

"Spread your legs a little more, love."

When she complied, he bent his long, powerful body over the graceful curve of her back and moved carefully between her thighs, rubbing her lightly, letting her adjust to him. Her hips swayed, pressing back against him. He slipped one hand around to her front, stroking and kneading her, and heard her cry out softly. Only then, with the hot drumbeat of passion surging through his veins, did he thrust into her hot, slick sheath. She gave a little sob of pure relief and tightened around him. He reared back, seizing her hips between his hands, and held her fast as he plunged into her again and again. As he felt her begin to quiver around him, he leaned forward again, laying his mouth against the softly vulnerable spot between her neck and shoulder. Without warning, he let her feel his teeth.

She climaxed with a scream, her pleasure going on and on, drawing him with it as the seed of life poured from his loins. His heart hammered against his ribs, his lungs labored like bellows. So intense was his release that he collapsed over her, carrying them both down onto the bed.

Long moments later, the Norse Wolf revived enough to remember that his men were waiting. With a groan, he adjusted his clothing and levered himself off the bed. Cymbra lay on her side, her flanks gleaming softly white in the light filtering through the shutters, a smile curving her luscious mouth. She was deeply asleep.

Reminding himself that he was the strong, indomitable male, the Scourge of the Saxons stumbled back out into the day. Breathing deeply, he took a few moments to steady himself before joining the several dozen men mounted and waiting by the gates.

Dragon was holding his horse for him. As Wolf swung up into the saddle, his brother grinned. "That was certainly quick." The words had just penetrated his dazed state and Wolf was just turning his head to react to them when Dragon added, "Very wise to make no long farewells, brother." He smiled innocently. "Always best to leave them wanting more."

The Wolf laughed as he lifted his head to a sky so blue as to be an ache behind the eyes. Pleasure still resonated within him but he felt something far beyond that, a vast, all-encompassing delight in the world itself simply because it included one remarkable woman.

He grasped the reins in his powerful hands and dug his heels into his mount's sides. Over his shoulder, he said, "I promise you, my wife wants for nothing."

Dragon's laugh followed him out through the gates and down the hill. Wolf gave the horse his head and the powerful animal quickly leaped to the gallop, long legs stretched out, hooves throwing up clods of earth. The wind streamed by, the ground flying beneath them. Horse and man raced on, one with a world that was open, wild, and free.

Chapter

EIGHTEEN

C YMBRA MADE A FINAL COUNT OF THE BAR-
rels laid up in racks in the storage shed, added
it to the other tallies she had taken, and nodded. "I think we are finished."

Beside her, Brita's shoulders sagged with relief. The
half-dozen women with them exchanged weary smiles
that bespoke the same emotion.

It was near midnight on the last day before the guests
were due to begin arriving. Rarely had any of the women
been up at such an hour, for the deep of night was a time
when spirits roamed and sensible people kept to their
beds. The darkness made them uneasy yet they had done
their best to ignore it. Cymbra was grateful for that and
much else.

She and many others had labored long and hard at a
mammoth task that should more rightly have taken a
month rather than a mere week. Yet it was done. Everything was in readiness.

"Go to your beds," she said after hugging each woman
and offering her thanks. They stood just outside the

storage shed, cooled by the freshening breeze from the sea. The sky appeared as a helmet of stars. A few stray wisps of gray smoke rose from the banked fires always left burning in the kitchens and the great hall. Slumbering birds rustled in the thatched roofs while an owl hooted nearby.

"Rest well, for truly no one has earned it more. I wish I could tell you all to just sleep for the next few days but alas, there will be yet more to do before we may have fair respite."

"Do not concern yourself with that, my lady," one of the women said. "All that remains now is to prepare the food, serve it, keep the drink flowing, and clean up. Beside what we've already done, that seems easy enough."

The other women nodded their agreement. They went off to get what sleep they could, comforted to know that at least now the end was within sight.

Brita walked with Cymbra partway across the hill top before taking her own leave. She slept in the women's hall, set apart for the unmarried women and strictly off-limits to the men. So it would remain in the coming days as well. The women, including Brita, had let her know how much they appreciated that. In the past, misunderstandings had been known to occur especially when the mead and ale flowed freely.

Alone, Cymbra paused for a moment and looked up at the star-draped sky. The night was a little cooler than it had been, the first faint reminder that summer would end soon. She wrapped her cloak more closely around herself as she picked out the familiar shapes above. Her eyes were drawn to the Great Bear, standing astride the heavens.

She caught herself wondering if perchance Wolf was also looking at the stars and smiled at the thought. It amazed her that even with miles separating them, she was able to feel his presence so clearly. It was almost as though if she only closed her eyes and reached out with her heart, he would be there.

She hoped he was resting, for judging by the sheer quantity of game that had flowed back into the hill fort, rest was much due. They had enough meat not only for the feasting but for the winter as well. Although what she was going to do with that bear, she didn't know. At the very least, it would need heavy seasoning. She preferred thinking about that rather than of her husband challenging such a deadly creature.

With a little sigh, she glanced toward the berm, seeing there the dark, looming shapes of the men posted at guard. Unlike at Holyhood, they were all awake and alert, hard men keen of eye and swift of sword. Several had turned away from their scrutiny of the approaches to the hill fort and were watching her. She had no doubt they were following the Wolf's orders and would continue to do so until she was tucked up safely for what remained of the night.

With a last look at the stars, she went into the lodge. As always when she was alone, the bed looked very large and uninviting. She undressed quickly, folded her clothes and put them away, and on impulse took one of Wolf's tunics from the chest. She dropped it over her head, then giggled, for it came almost to her ankles and all but slipped right off her altogether.

Clasping it around her, she got into the bed and pulled the furs up over herself. Slowly, she touched the finely woven cloth, brushing it lightly with her fingers, imagining beneath it not her own body but the hard, powerful body of her husband. She felt his strength reach out to her, wrapping her gently. She snuggled farther down and let dreams of him carry her away.

·   ·   ·

S CANT HOURS LATER, ALMOST BEFORE THE FIRST hint of dawn, Cymbra was back at work. The baking had begun. There was endless dough to mix, knead, set to rise, knead again, and so on throughout what promised to be a very long day. Some of the dough was sprinkled with precious caraway and fennel seeds, and some had spices and herbs mixed right into it.

Cymbra made one of her own favorites that had become one of Wolf's, small round loaves of flour flavored with sweet, tangy cardamom. The scent of them lingered pleasantly on the air. She had just finished when a sudden shout drew her to the door of the kitchens. Several of the guards on the berm were gesturing out toward the sea.

Cymbra climbed up on the palisade wall, shaded her eyes, and looked in the direction they indicated. She could just make out a proud longship entering the harbor. From the emblem on its sail and the comments of the guards, she gathered the first of their guests would arrive within the hour.

Before she could even begin to worry about receiving any of the Viking lords in Wolf's absence, another shout from the guards drew her notice to the horsemen rapidly approaching the fort. The wolf's-head emblem was clearly visible on the banner carried in front. Greatly relieved, Cymbra gave hurried orders for water to be heated so her husband could bathe, then she herself saw to the laying out of his clothes.

As she was doing so, he strode into the lodge, a big, forceful presence seeming to bring with him the wild scents of forest and plain. She flew into his arms, embracing him with such strength that he laughed.

"Easy, sweetheart, I'm not fit company until I've bathed."

She laughed, ignoring the various, inevitable stains on his tunic that spoke of the fury of the hunt. When the women had brought buckets of heated water and left,

carefully concealing their smiles, she helped him off with
his clothing.

But when she took soap in hand to wash him, he
shook his head. Very seriously, he said, "I've been without
you for four days, Cymbra. Touch me now and Dragon
will be left to explain to our guests why I'm not there to
greet them."

With a smile that swept over her from head to toe, he
added, "I wouldn't mind that but they would and I'd
rather not have to undo the trouble it would cause."

Resigned to his good sense, yet flattered by his un-
concealed desire, she took his hand and placed the soap in
it. "All right, but promise me you will not be such a good
host as to remain at table with them too long. Let them eat
and drink and wench themselves into oblivion, but come
to me this night."

His quick but ardent kiss assured her of his intent.
She left him then and did not expect to see him again until
the feasting, but he surprised her. On his way to greet
their guests, he stopped in the great hall where she was su-
pervising the placement of drinking cups and the ornate
eating knives Wolf had ordered as a gift for each visiting
lord.

The women who surrounded her, receiving their final
instructions, saw him and flitted away like clouds before a
strong wind. Cymbra smiled, gazing at him with frank
enjoyment. His thick, ebony hair was still slightly damp
and drawn back from his brow with a golden band. So,
too, his tunic of crimson wool was intricately embroidered
with golden symbols of enduring strength. The same
symbols were embossed on the golden bands fastened at
his wrists. He wore the wolf's-head torque that was a
larger version of the one he had given her, the bloodred
eyes glinting in the afternoon light.

Frustration pinched at her when she considered how
many hours remained until they could steal time alone.

With a sigh for what must be borne, she went to him and laid her hand lightly on his broad chest.

"The garment suits you, my lord."

He inclined his head at the compliment but his eyes were strangely guarded. With a hand on her elbow, he drew her off to one side of the hall. Quietly, he said, "I thank you for all you have done. No one else could have managed it so well."

She stared at him for a moment, puzzled by the tension she felt in him, then let that go and smiled. "But you don't know what I've managed. You haven't been home long enough to find out."

"I need not see for myself. I trust you."

Cymbra's breath caught. She gazed up into his silvery eyes and felt a spreading warmth of happiness that seemed to blossom from deep within. She would have been delighted to tell him how he made her feel—or better, to show him—but they were being pulled in different directions. He had to meet their guests and she had to change before meeting them herself.

She contented herself with a quick touch of her lips to his and a smile. "Thank you. That means more to me than you can know."

He nodded and she saw it again—something in his eyes. Regret? His brows drew together. She felt his hold on her arm tighten ever so slightly.

"Cymbra . . . I do deeply appreciate all you have done. But now you must retire to our quarters and remain there until this gathering is over."

He spoke softly but audibly, the words were clear enough, yet they made no sense at all. Retire? Remain? She stared at him in bewilderment. "I don't understand." She shook her head as though trying to clear it. Her eyes met his and she saw his implacable resolve. "You want me to stay in our quarters instead of attending the feast?"

He nodded. "It is best this way."

Already, he was drawing her toward the doors. She saw Dragon waiting outside and realized with a shock that he was going to escort her back to the lodge while his brother went to greet their guests. Nor was he alone. There were other warriors behind him, their eyes carefully averted. She was to be well and truly guarded, it seemed, sealed away just like one of those women in . . . what had Kareem called it?—a harem. Say rather a *prison*.

"This council of the jarls is important," he said as he continued out of the hall with her in hand. "I cannot allow it to be disrupted by the temptation you present."

That she presented? As though it were her fault if men could not control themselves. The stinging unfairness of that burned through her. Though she wanted desperately to resist, pride prevented her from making a spectacle of herself before Dragon and the others. She knew with a sinking heart that Wolf would simply ignore her objections and do as he wished.

"Let go of me," she said under her breath. When he hesitated, she added, "I'll do what you want. It's not as though I have any choice." Without attempting to conceal her bitterness, she added, "But I want to know something first. You intended this all along, didn't you?"

He did release her then but stayed very close, his eyes never leaving her. She thought she saw a flicker of regret again but it was gone before she could be sure.

"Yes," he said simply, "I did. This is not merely a friendly meeting of the jarls. I called it to put to rest certain rumors."

Despite herself, Cymbra found her curiosity piqued. "What rumors?"

He hesitated but only for a moment before answering her bluntly. "Rumors that I am so besotted with my Saxon bride that my will is weakened, my power lessened, and my holdings ripe for the picking. Moreover, that such attacks are deserved because a Norseman enthralled by a Saxon can no longer be trusted."

When she would have spoken, he held up a hand. Curtly, he continued. "The men who attacked the settlement at Vycoff were not Danes as I originally believed. They were Norse. They thought they saw an opportunity and they seized it. Their deaths were intended to assure that no one else behaved so stupidly, but because I allowed them to die quickly, the rumors have only grown."

Cymbra pressed her lips together tightly as horror burst in her. He had granted the men a swift death for her sake, because she had insisted on being there, because he wanted to spare her pain. Never had she considered that his action might be interpreted thus. The color fled from her face as she realized the implications.

"I warned you," her husband said quietly, "this is a hard land and we a hard people. No man holds power who does not show himself willing to use it."

"And now you will show your power over your Saxon wife by imprisoning her?"

He made an impatient gesture. "Don't exaggerate, our lodge is hardly a prison. The jarls will understand what I do. They have heard the stories of your beauty and they will respect my prudence in guarding my property. They will take lesson from it and recognize that I will do the same for all that is mine. As for the rest, they will be left with no doubt where I stand."

Where he stood. She had believed she was coming to know this man, this *husband*, to know and to trust him. Yet she was not a wife he would have others see at his side, honored and respected. Instead, he meant to make an object lesson of her, to use her to display his power and ruthlessness.

Why was she so surprised? Why did her throat suddenly hurt so much with tears she would die before she shed? Had he not used her from the very beginning—for vengeance, for alliance . . . and for pleasure? She must not allow herself to forget that last part for all that it was a knife stabbing into her.

"I have been so foolish," she said faintly, her voice little more than a thin wisp of sound. It was all she could muster. "So foolish as to forget . . ." Her gaze turned inward toward a landscape both real and nightmarish, the beach beyond the berm, the bloodred sand, the savage promise he had made to her on their wedding day.

"You stand against the Saxon and for the Norse. *That* is where you stand, isn't it?" Despair threatened to choke her but she managed to speak her deepest fear. "Is that the real reason you've called the jarls here? To plan yet more attacks against helpless people, to plot my brother's death, to sate your bloodthirsty gods?"

A dark flush of color stained his high-boned cheeks. His eyes glinted dangerously. "I am Norse. If that displeases you, it is unfortunate for it is also unchangeable. And you know I want peace, elsewise none of what has passed between us would ever have occurred."

He cast a swift, hard look over her, lingering at her breasts and hips until it was all she could do not to squirm with self-consciousness. His mouth tightened. "I took you captive but made you wife. You have known only gentleness from me. Remember that and think well how different your fate could have been."

Before she could reply, he looked over her shoulder, saw the watch guard on the berm signaling urgently, and gestured to his brother. "Escort *my wife* to her quarters." To Cymbra he said, "You will have to bear your anger alone, lady, I have no time for it now."

Without another word, he turned and walked away.

CYMBRA FROWNED AT THE BRIGHT RED DROP OF blood on her skin. For a moment, it appeared to have blossomed all by itself. Only belatedly did she realize that she had pricked her fingertip. That small sensation of pain was scarcely noticeable beneath the far keener ache of the past three days.

Slowly, she lowered the length of finely spun blue wool she was fashioning into a tunic for her husband and stared at the opposite wall. She guessed the day to be very fair but she couldn't be sure. Nor could she know how the two days previous had been except that it had not rained, for she would have heard and smelled that.

The shutters had remained closed all that time, permitting only what sunlight could enter through the narrow slats. To see well enough to sew without tiring her eyes she needed the added light of braziers, but they also added heat to the chamber, which warmed enough as it was as the summer day passed. The air was very still, she could hear the hum of bees just beyond the windows. When the door opened to admit Brita with a tray of food, the sudden bolt of bright light was so intense that Cymbra had to look away from it. But not before she caught a glimpse of the guard standing just outside.

Brita set the tray on the table, glanced a little anxiously at her mistress, and smiled. "I've brought some of the cardamom rolls, my lady, your favorites, and there's a wonderful stew made just as you like with chicken and rosemary."

Cymbra shrugged, disinterested. She had no appetite. The trays Brita brought thrice daily went back scarcely lighter than they arrived. Indeed, she had eaten so little that the serving girl was growing anxious.

"I can fetch something else," Brita said. "Perhaps you'd like some goose liver spread on warm bread?"

Cymbra shuddered at the thought. Her stomach was uncertain these days. She ascribed it to the stressful circumstances. "I'm really not hungry. How goes the feast?"

"They are bottomless pits, these jarls. It is fortunate you planned so generously for they consume everything in sight. Their hunger is exceeded only by their thirst."

"They rode out again today. I heard them go." The pounding of their horses' hooves had sounded like thunder shaking the walls of the lodge.

Brita nodded. "Drunk or sober, they love to hunt. Fortunately, only a few have fallen off their horses and those have hard enough heads to bear it."

"What about the man who was knived last night?" Brita had told her about that when she brought breakfast. It was the only kniving so far, something everyone considered a sign of how well things were going.

"Ulfrich says he will be fine but thanks you for the salve all the same."

Cymbra set her sewing aside and stood up. Her neck and shoulders felt stiff from lack of movement. Despite having done almost nothing for three days, she felt oddly tired. But then perhaps it was not so odd after all, for she had slept poorly when she slept at all.

"And the rest of it?" she asked, looking at Brita.

The Irish girl shrugged. "I think it safe to say there will be no such thing as a poor whore left in these parts, only rich ones."

That was no surprise. The noise coming from the feasting halls late into the nights included the bold laughter of women floating above the beat of drums and the lilt of pipes. Nor was it confined to the halls. Those seeking a bit of privacy had often stumbled past her lodge. One pair had fallen to coupling right up against the wall, only to be shooed away by whoever happened to be on sentry duty at the time.

No man stood post outside her lodge for more than a few hours. She wondered if that was Wolf's way of making sure the guard was always alert and fresh, or if he thought longer contact might cause a hapless male to fall victim to her wiles. Did he imagine she would try to escape, and if so, where did he think she would go?

She might have asked him had she been given the opportunity, but since their angry confrontation in the great hall her husband had absented himself. He had not returned to their lodge that night or the next. Lying awake, listening to the ribald sounds of merriment, she tormented herself with thoughts of how he was amusing himself.

"I heard some of the whores complaining," Brita said, eyeing her mistress. "The most beautiful of them vie for the attention of the Norse Wolf but he ignores them all."

Cymbra wished heartily to believe her. The pain of imagining Wolf with some other woman—or women— was so great that she could scarcely bear it.

When Brita left, still urging her to eat, Cymbra glanced at the food on the tray but could not bring herself to taste a morsel. It was growing too dark to sew, she did not wish to play her lute for herself alone, there were no medicines that needed making. She had read her precious scrolls over and over until every word was imprinted on her memory. There was nothing left for her to do.

Night came and with it the steady increase of sounds from the feasting halls. The warm, still air of the lodge seemed to press in, smothering her. She jumped up suddenly and paced back and forth across the room but the activity gave her no ease. Too soon, she slumped again in the chair beside the table. A flicker of movement barely visible through the slats of the shutters drew her eye. She leaned closer, peering out, even as she prayed that no one would notice her. To be caught in such a humiliating pastime would shame her even further.

By the light of torches set up at intervals around the hill top, she saw Brita walking toward the women's hall. It looked as though she was retiring for the night, which Cymbra was glad to see for surely Brita needed her rest.

But wait . . . there came three stumbling louts, so drunk they could scarcely walk upright. They saw Brita, stopped for a moment, then continued toward her eagerly.

"Jus' wha' we need, a whore ready to hand," the largest of the three said. He was tall, with the lanky strength of youth, dark haired, and well dressed for all that his clothes were in disarray.

Another—shorter by a few inches and stockier—agreed. "Sthupid to leave the hall without one."

"No mind, she'll do." The third was between the two others in height and perhaps a few years older but still very much a youth. He spoke not just with lust but with a note of cruelty that made the fine hairs on the back of Cymbra's neck rise.

Her hand flew to her mouth as she tensed with anger. Was this how they repaid the hospitality of the jarl of Sciringesheal, by assuming that every woman within his domain was a whore available for the taking?

She stood up quickly, intending to call a warning to Brita, but before she could do so she heard the young Irish woman scream. The sound was terrified and terrifying, sending Cymbra scrambling to yank open the door. She all but fell through it and almost tumbled into the guard, who whirled at her sudden appearance and stared at her with mingled disbelief and wariness.

"My lady . . ."

Brita screamed again. The three youths had hold of her and were dragging her around a corner of the women's hall.

"Go to her!" Cymbra screamed at the guard. Vaguely, she recognized the young man as one of those who had been at Holyhood with Wolf and afterward on the ship coming to Sciringesheal. He was a good sort, always

smiling, but he had watchful eyes. His name was . . . ?
"Magnus, you can see she needs help!"

The young man hesitated. He glanced over his shoulder to where Brita was struggling desperately. Already, the top of her gown was torn, almost exposing her breasts, and the veil over her hair had been knocked off. He turned back to Cymbra.

"Go back inside, my lady."

She stared at him in disbelief. How could he possibly take even a moment to tell her that when—? "Help her!"

To her horror, he shook his head. "I am forbidden to leave this post." He took hold of the door, as though to close it in her face.

"Stop! You can't just stand here, you can't!"

He did look again toward where Brita had now disappeared from sight but he remained implacable. "The jarl was clear in his orders, my lady. Do I move from this spot, it is worth my life."

"What of her life?" Cymbra cried. Horror rose in her. She could still hear Brita's frantic struggles and pleas for help. Abruptly, she made up her mind. She couldn't get past Magnus; he had clearly anticipated her trying to do so and had the door well blocked. But she could—

Without another thought, she darted back into the lodge and slammed the door, shoving the bolt into place. She heard him call to her as she raced for the back window. Tearing the shutters open, Cymbra yanked up her skirts, climbed through the opening, and jumped to the ground.

She landed hard but regained her balance at once and ran around to the front of the lodge. The moment she came within Magnus's sight, he yelled at her to stop. She ignored him and sprinted toward the women's hall and the dark corner where Brita had disappeared. As she intended, he had no choice but to follow her.

Beyond the women's quarters stood the long, peak-

roofed stables. The startled nickering of horses drew
Cymbra in the right direction. There were no further
screams from Brita. Cymbra came upon her, sprawled unconscious in an unused stall. Blood dripped from a blow
to her forehead. Her gown was pulled up around her waist
and her legs were yanked apart. Already, one of the attackers was kneeling between her thighs as he fumbled
with his trousers.

"Scum!" Cymbra shouted. "Filth! Rapist!" She threw
herself at him with all her strength, knocking him side-
ways as she kicked and clawed at him.

"Bitch! Get her off!" He reared up, trying to get away
from her but Cymbra held on. She was fueled by rage
greater than any she had ever known before and determined to inflict as much damage as possible. Her fingers
were going for his eyes when he managed to get hold of
her shoulders and throw her against the stable wall. Her
head struck a wooden pole and for a moment her vision
dissolved into splinters of light. As it cleared, she saw
Magnus, his sword drawn, look at her in horror.

Time itself seemed to slow. In the pace of a heartbeat
that went on and on like the distant echoing of a drum,
Cymbra saw what that moment of distraction cost him.
Drunk though they were, the three assailants were trained
warriors. They had their weapons out and were advanc-
ing. Too late he saw them coming and had no time to prepare before they attacked as one.

Cymbra screamed. She lurched away from the wall,
frantically looking for something, anything to use as a
weapon. When nothing came to hand, she flew at the attacker in the middle, pounding his back with her fists. He
flung her off with a curse. She struck the floor, pain lanc-
ing through her shoulder, and looked up in time to see the
blades converging on hapless Magnus. The air left her
lungs in a soundless rush as he was slashed first in his
sword arm, then in his thigh. Blood poured from both

wounds. He collapsed onto the floor, his eyes locking on hers for a moment before unconsciousness claimed him.

"Tie him up," ordered the lanky youth.

The stocky one made to obey but hesitated. The struggle had stunned them all out of their drunken haze yet left them disoriented. "He's bleeding bad . . ."

"Let him," said the oldest, the one Cymbra had instantly thought cruel. It was he who had been kneeling between Brita's thighs but now he glanced at the Irish girl with scorn. His gaze shifted to Cymbra and with a surge of horror she saw the rapacious fire ignite in his eyes.

He recognized her fear and his mouth twisted in cold pleasure. "Forget that one." He jerked his head toward Brita. "This bitch needs lessoning."

The other two hesitated only a moment. They stared at Cymbra, disbelief at her beauty dissolving swiftly into mindless lust.

She managed to scramble to her feet but there was nowhere to go except back against the wall. It took all her courage and pride to refuse to yield to the stomach-churning terror that seized her. She lifted her chin and spoke with forced calm. "I am the Wolf's wife. If you harm me, he will kill you."

To her horror, the oldest merely laughed. "He will have to know who did it first. Mayhap we will not leave you alive to tell."

Before she could even attempt to reply, he reached out, seized hold of the top of her gown, and tore it from neck to waist. As she clutched at the garment to keep it from falling open, he knocked her backward onto the ground and came down hard on top of her.

"Grab her legs," he yelled to the other two. Cymbra made to scream but he clapped a hand over her mouth. When she tried to bite him, he reared back and struck her hard across the face. Lights danced before her eyes again. As though from a great distance, she heard him snarling,

"Bitch! Saxon whore! You're not fit for anything but this. Dammit, get her legs open!"

Someone was pulling at her ankles. She fought with all her strength but a dark cloud seemed to be sucking her down. She smelled the rank stench of ale and sweat mingling with rampant lust. The attacker slammed his hand over her mouth again, his fingers pinching her nostrils closed. She couldn't breathe; her lungs screamed for air. A last thought like a soundless sob welled up in her—*Wolf*.

NINETEEN

BRIGHT LIGHT MOVED BEFORE CYMBRA'S
shuttered eyes, so bright that she flinched from
it. She heard voices but they seemed to be far
away. A hand touched her brow and she jerked
weakly in response.

"Be easy, my lady. Everything is all right. You are safe
now."

Ulfrich, very close to her, his voice husky with concern. Slowly, she opened her eyes just enough to peer at him,
closed them instantly against the light of flaring torches
that seemed to fill the stable, then opened them again.

"Ulfrich . . . ?" Was that her voice, so faint and reedy?

His worn face creased in a smile of profound relief.
"It is I, my lady, and glad I am that you know it." He
slipped an arm behind her shoulders. "Here now, I'm going to help you sit up just a little. If it pains your head too
much, tell me at once."

Her head did throb but not overly so. She held on to
him as he lifted her with the utmost gentleness and steadied her. She smelled sweet hay and oats and realized she
was still in the stall.

Her eyes were adjusting to the light. She could make out the shapes of men, some very close, many more just beyond. A torch flared suddenly and she caught a glimpse of Dragon, his face very hard and tight. He looked at her then, met her eyes, and for a moment she thought she saw surprise mingling with the greatest relief. Then he was gone and she tilted her head back against the wall, her eyes beginning to close.

"Lord . . ." Ulfrich again, sounding cautious . . . worried.

There was movement beside her, a sense of over-whelming strength and power. She reached out a hand and it was caught fast, pressed against a rock-hard chest.

"*Wolf*—"

He said nothing but drew her to him, cradling her in his arms, his big hand stroking her hair so gently as to bring tears to her eyes. Instantly, as she felt his touch, the sweet balm of relief flowed through her. She gasped, surprised by how quickly she could feel safe again, yet in another way not surprised at all. Her solitude was gone; she was joined to this man in a way she would never have believed possible. In truth, she would have feared it, believing as she had that she could exist in the world only when sealed off behind walls of her own making. Now she knew that was not true, and in the discovery she rejoiced.

Off to the side, Ulfrich spoke quietly. "There are bruises and scratches, lord, but otherwise she is un-harmed."

Memories surfaced like sharp, painful shards of ice yet seen as though from a distance, no longer having the power to hurt her. She tried to sit up only to be prevented by her husband, who continued to hold her with carefully measured strength.

"Brita . . . Magnus . . . ?" Her voice quivered.

"They will both be fine," Ulfrich said quickly. "The lass took a blow to her head but she's already regained consciousness. She'd be here fussing over you herself if we let her. Magnus lost some blood but not so much that he won't recover."

Cymbra offered up a silent, fervent prayer of thanks for the mercy shown this night even as the means of it remained inexplicable. "How did you . . . ?" She twisted slightly, looking up into her husband's hooded gaze. "How did you find us?"

He stared down at her, his expression inscrutable. Only the jagged beating of a pulse in his jaw revealed the emotion he was keeping in savage check. "I heard you scream."

She frowned, thinking she misunderstood yet knowing she had not. The stable was much too far from the feasting halls for anyone there to have heard anything, even without accounting for the noise of the feast itself. There was no possible way he could have known she was in danger. Yet he had known and he had come, otherwise she would not have been there now, safe in his arms, unhurt but for a few bruises.

A tremor raced through her, and another, as the meaning of his words became clear in her mind. She was suddenly shaking so badly she felt she might come apart. He held her as the storm broke, murmuring to her softly, his arms her shelter from the world.

Dimly, she was aware of him lifting her, carrying her from the stable. The murmur of voices fell silent as they passed, picked up again behind them. Cool night air touched her. She nestled her head against his chest and refused to let herself think of anything at all.

A large tub of steaming water had been prepared inside the lodge. Wolf set his wife down carefully on the bed and knelt beside her. He gazed for a moment at the torn gown but said nothing as he eased it over her head. To his great relief she did not protest or show any fear of him. He sensed the still watchfulness that had settled within her, guessed that she was carefully and cautiously trying to come to terms with what had happened. Her trust in him was one more blessing among all those for which he would give proper thanks in due time.

But first he had other matters with which to concern himself.

His big, callused hands were gentle as he caught her hair up and secured it at the top of her head with the pins he had seen her use for the same purpose. That done, he lifted her again and carefully lowered her into the bath.

As she sighed deeply and settled into the water, he had his first real chance to observe the damage done to her. His eyes glittered with deadly rage as he saw the rapidly darkening bruises on her arms and legs, and along her back. There were thin red scratches near her breasts where her gown had been torn, and one cheek was already swelling where she had been struck.

Slowly, methodically, he took note of each injury. Only the knowledge that it could have been much worse—indeed, would have been had he not arrived when he did—allowed him to suppress the red-hot, churning sea of rage that threatened to consume him. That and the cold, steel-edged resolve that had already determined how this would all end.

He lathered her lavender-scented soap between his hands and began stroking them over her silken skin, going most carefully where she was bruised. She made a soft murmur of contentment and let her eyes close. Beneath his touch, he felt her relax further and knew that to be yet more evidence of her trust in him.

When she was clean, he lifted her from the tub and, still with greatest care, dried her. She stood silently, allowing him to do as he would even when he knelt and gently patted the cloth over her buttocks and between her thighs. She shivered delicately at his touch. The shadows beneath her eyes and her unaccustomed passivity meant that the first wave of relief had come and gone, leaving her to cope with the shock of the attack.

When she trembled again, he knew she was remembering, reliving fragments as he himself had done in the aftermath of battles. Experience told him that would happen to her over and over, possibly for years to come.

Rage at the men who had done this surged so powerfully that for a moment he could see nothing but a red mist, hear nothing but the drumbeat of his warrior's heart. Only the overwhelming power of his will coupled with the vast love he bore her allowed him to force it back down and concentrate on what had to be done.

Just then, he would have given almost anything to be able to take Cymbra to their bed, to hold her chastely and protectively throughout the night. But this time the wishes of the man and the husband had to be subordinate to the duty of the jarl.

He saw the flicker of surprise in her eyes when he dropped a fresh gown over her head and helped her draw her arms through it. Saw, too, the dawning awareness that this matter was not over yet. Indeed, could not be until punishment had been rendered. He went swiftly then, finishing the job, hoping she had not yet realized what he and most likely every other resident of Sciringesheal already knew, namely that the jarl's Saxon bride had disobeyed him yet again.

Standing before her, aware of how very small and delicate she was in comparison to himself, he breathed in the warm, womanly scent of her skin as he loosened the pins holding her hair. As it fell, he caught masses of it in his hands, trailing the chestnut tendrils through his fingers.

He thought of the first moment he had seen her, coming down the stairs to the dungeon at Holyhood, the torchlight gleaming in the glory of her hair, her slim and supple body so graceful, her expression determined despite the fear he knew she must have felt. Never had he known a woman to show such courage. He prayed she would find that now.

"Come," he said, and taking her hand in his, he led her from the lodge.

A CROWD TOO LARGE TO FIT INTO THE GREAT HALL had assembled just outside it. Torches set on poles in the ground defined a large circle in which firelit shadows danced ominously. Dragon stood just inside the rim of light, waiting.

Wolf gave Cymbra into his brother's care, strode to the center of the circle, and stood for a moment looking at the several hundred people gathered there. Many were his own people, warriors, merchants and their wives. Others were guests come from throughout the Vestfold. Without exception, their faces were tightly drawn with shock and anger, yet were they riven by conflicting loyalties. What had been intended as a feast of reconciliation threatened suddenly to become the beginning of all-out war.

Wolf stood unmoving, his feet planted firmly apart and his fists resting on his narrow hips. The summer tunic he wore revealed the massive breadth of his chest and shoulders. Torchlight rippled over the powerful muscles of his bronzed arms and legs. Inches taller than every man there save Dragon, superbly honed by a life of battles, he exuded an aura of power and command that none could mistake. What little sound there had been—the rustling of those still maneuvering for better position—died away. Into the silence, he raised an arm toward a point along the circle. "Bring them."

The crowd parted. Guards led in the three attackers. Their weapons were gone and their hands were shackled behind their backs. The short, stocky one was plainly terrified; the taller, lanky one almost as much so; but the third, the one Cymbra thought of as the ring leader, wore an air of sneering bravado.

Wolf saw it, too. The mane of his ebony hair swayed against his shoulders as he bared his teeth in a feral snarl.

Looking from her husband to the attackers and back again, Cymbra saw several men she didn't know standing near Wolf. One was genuinely grieved although he struggled manfully to conceal it, while the others seemed more angry than sorrowful. Moreover, their anger appeared to be directed at the assailants. They barely glanced at the three before looking away in disgust.

She stiffened when she realized that Brita, too, was being led forward to stand before Wolf. Brother Joseph was beside her, lending his quiet support, but the Irish girl looked strong and composed. She stared directly at the would-be rapists, her head high and her gaze unflinching.

Next, Magnus was carried in on a litter. He was very pale, and the arm laid outside the blanket that covered him was wrapped in a bloodstained bandage. Ulfrich walked beside him, scarcely taking his eyes from his patient.

When they were all assembled, Wolf looked at Brita. Gently he said, "Tell us what happened."

She did, succinctly and clearly, describing how she had been on her way to bed when the three attacked. She remembered being dragged behind the women's quarters and into the stable.

"Then one of them, I don't know which, hit me in the forehead. I lost consciousness and remember nothing further until I came to in the stall when it was all over."

Murmurings spread through the crowd but were quickly hushed when Wolf turned his attention to Magnus. The young man struggled to rise from the litter, but Wolf quickly gestured him back into place as Ulfrich

knelt with a word of admonishment. His voice weak but
his words clear, he told what he, too, had seen and done.

"Then I explained to the Lady Cymbra that I could
not leave my post. She went back inside and for a moment
I thought she intended to do nothing further." His mouth
twisted at the memory of his foolishness. Wolf shot him a
sympathetic glance that gave him the courage to continue.
It was no easy thing to report on the behavior of the jarl's
wife to the jarl himself.

"However, I quickly discovered my error when she
climbed out a window and ran past me toward where the
girl had been taken." He looked directly at Wolf, his expression obviously apprehensive yet resolute. "I followed
at once but when I entered the stall, they—" he paused,
taking a breath that obviously pained him, "they struck
the lady, and when I saw that happen I was so shocked for
a moment that I hesitated. Thus were they able to gain the
advantage and attack before I was properly prepared for
them." He hung his head, shamed by his failure. Softly, he
said, "I beg your forgiveness, lord."

Cymbra pressed her lips tightly together lest she cry
out that the young man deserved no blame. The blame
was her own for involving him.

Before she could declare that, Wolf went down on one
knee beside the youth. He touched his brow lightly and
said so that all could hear, "You were one against three.
There is no need for apology; you fulfilled your duty."

The young man's look of profound relief and gratitude brought tears to Cymbra's eyes. She was still blinking them away when she realized that her husband had
summoned her to speak next.

No, not her husband. The hooded-eyed man who
gazed at her without expression was not the man in whose
arms she had lain, whose body had joined so passionately
with hers, whose very heart had beat in unison with her

own. She knew with sudden, stark certainty that she stood before the mightiest and most feared warlord ever to come out of the northlands. The man whose plans for accord among the Norse were threatened with ruin because of the choice made by one disobedient Saxon bride. Not for a moment did she doubt that he would judge her without mercy.

As she stepped forward into the circle, she was aware of the sudden stirring among the crowd, almost all of whom were seeing her for the first time. Men looked and looked again; their eyes widening at what they beheld. Many nodded to themselves, as though in sudden understanding.

She took a breath, painful against the band of tension constricting her chest, and said simply, "I left the lodge because I knew it was the only way to get help for Brita." She turned to Magnus. "I am truly sorry for your injuries."

At this unexpected apology from the wife of the Norse Wolf, who was observing them both, the young man paled yet further. Careful not to look at Cymbra directly, he mumbled, "There is no need for that, my lady. I wish I could have done more."

Silence descended. Slowly, before the avid eyes of all assembled, the jarl of Sciringesheal walked across the space separating him from his errant Saxon wife. Slowly, he raised his hand. Cymbra had to draw on all her courage to stand unmoving. When his fingers closed on her chin, she stiffened but met his gaze without flinching. The silver fire of his eyes stole her breath and set her composure to flickering like the torchlight.

"You knew you were not supposed to leave the lodge."

It wasn't a question but she answered all the same. "Yes, I knew."

"And you knew why."

"I knew you believed my appearance would cause trouble among your guests." She paused. "You were right."

"Yet did you disobey."

"Yes, I did. To save my friend, I would do so again."

She heard the sharp intake of breath that ran through the crowd, the quick murmurs of disapproval, but that was as nothing to her. There was only his touch, firm yet oddly gentle, and his gaze that seemed to look directly into her soul.

As though there were only the two of them alone in the world, she asked softly, "Do you think I was wrong?"

A faint smile flickered at the corners of his mouth. She had a moment to realize that he was a man who admired courage. He dropped his hand but continued to look at her. "It is true I require obedience but I recognize there are circumstances in which there may be a higher duty. Protection of a friend is one such."

The crowd murmured again, this time united in agreement. It was wisdom indeed that a man of such strength and power could recognize when even his own laws must be exceeded.

"You made the right choice," Wolf said. Relief sped through her but before it could reach very far, he added, "Yet even a right choice has consequences."

He glanced at the three men, then again at the crowd. "Had the servant girl, Brita, been abused, it is our way that wergild would be paid. That she is in service to my wife and the insult therefore done to my house, the fine would be steep. A man could be ruined by such payment and left to hire out his sword as best he could to earn his bread. Yet would his life still be his own."

He said what everyone already knew, and even if there were those, like Cymbra, who thought it grossly unjust that men could escape true justice for such a crime merely by paying for their offense, they kept silent.

His voice cut through the night like the great walls of ice that slashed the sea far to the north where the sky rained fire. "But that is not all that happened here. These—" He turned to the assailants and as his gaze settled on them, an unholy light flared deep within his eyes. "These animals laid hands upon my wife. *My wife.*"

Between one breath and the next, steel sang. Bathed in the bloodred glow of the torches, the sword that was as legendary as the man who wielded it moved like a living extension of Wolf's mighty arm to point directly at the miscreants.

Flatly, he declared, "Your lives are forfeit." He looked at the youngest of the trio. "Thus does your father agree." His gaze shifted to the other two. "As do your uncles. You have shamed your houses as you attempted to shame mine. For that you will die."

Even as the attackers reacted variously, two stunned and disbelieving, the third still arrogantly defiant, Wolf continued. "Yet out of respect for your families, I will not deny you the chance to enter Valhalla." He gestured to the older men who stood nearby, watching and silently agreeing to what must be. "Arm them."

The crowd roared its full-throated approval. Here was a tale as great as any told of the gods themselves! One man against three. One man claiming justice and vengeance at the point of his blade. One man settling his right to primacy in the only way that ultimately mattered, in battle.

Feet stamped against the hard-packed earth, hands clapped in unison, cheers rose to heaven. Amidst it all, Cymbra's was an unheard scream.

"*Nooo!*" Oh, God, please no, let him not fight three men at the same time because she had disobeyed. She had sought only to help a friend, surely that was not deserving of this. Surely God would not be so cruel. She would wake, discover all this to be a dream. This couldn't be happening . . . it couldn't. . . .

Dragon wrapped a steely arm around her waist and held her fast as he drew her back toward the edge of the circle. When she struggled, so desperate that she hardly knew what she was doing, he bent down and said into her ear, "You will not leave this place until this is done, sweet sister, nor will you interfere. So has my brother ordered and so it will be."

She subsided against him but only because of the creeping numbness that made everything seem both unreal and hopeless. With stomach-churning horror she saw the grim-faced older men come forward, saw the flash of steel as they cut the attackers free and returned their swords to them, saw the mingled shock and hope in three faces. Saw, too, the calculation and craftiness as they assessed the situation.

Three against one. Even one so mighty as the Norse Wolf. They might yet emerge from this night alive, and for any who did the rewards would be beyond calculation. To smite the mightiest warrior would be to elevate them instantly to his stature. They would be as giants among men.

But first they had to live. And the Wolf had to die.

The one who was the ring leader shouted an order and the other two fanned out. They advanced together, coming at Wolf from the front and both sides. Three blades flashed high.

Another scream bubbled up in Cymbra's throat but she had no breath for it. To her horror she saw that her husband stood and watched the attackers come, his sword held almost loosely at his side, his huge, powerful body seemingly at ease. Incredibly, he looked coldly amused. Closer and still closer they came. When they were scarcely a blade length away, he raised his sword arm,

threw back his head, and emitted a blood-chilling cry to
the sky.

The howl of the Wolf, loose in the land. While yet the
air reverberated, he moved. The hilt of his sword clasped
in both sinewy hands, his huge body flowing with deadly
grace, he slashed once, twice, thrice. So swift was he that it
was done before any of the three could react.

They stared in bewilderment at the thin spurt of
blood blossoming down each of their chests, a strange
wound, not grave for all that the same motion could have
split a man in half. Perhaps they considered that, for they
hesitated momentarily. The ring leader recovered first and
moved to attack but Wolf easily parried his thrusts, as he
did those of the other two. In the process, he delivered
three more blows, as meticulously calibrated, cutting
open the right cheek of each.

Cymbra gasped as she suddenly realized what he was
doing. The scratches between her breasts, the blow to her
face, he was marking each as they had marked her. While
they were intent on killing him, he but toyed with them.

Twisting in Dragon's hold, she pleaded, "*Stop him,
don't let him do this! He's wasting his strength, they'll
kill—*"

But Dragon's attention was over her shoulder.
Abruptly, his big hand closed on the back of her head and
he pressed her face into his chest. "Don't look just now,"
he said gruffly.

"*Wolf . . . !*"

"No, no, he's fine, just wait—"

She was too frantic to heed him. Squirming loose, she
searched desperately for her husband only to see him
standing upright, sword in hand as he faced the two attackers—

Two? Then that bloody heap there on the ground
must be . . . "Oh, God," she whispered as bile rose in her
throat. Yet could she not bring herself to look away. This

was a Wolf she had never seen before. Not husband or
lover, not jarl, not even the threatening stranger he had
first been to her. In the light of the torches, his eyes aglow
like the animal whose name he bore, this was a figure out
of a nightmare.

The chiseled planes and angles of his face stood out in
harsh relief. His body moved with power that seemed
more than human. Again, he raised his head to the dark,
smoke-smeared sky and again his battle cry resounded.
Again, steel sang.

Blood spurted and another man crumbled. Only one
was left, the ring leader. He looked at Wolf with raw ha-
tred in his eyes, crouched in a fighting stance, spittle dripping from his chin. Cymbra felt a wave of malevolent
energy move over and through her, reeking of violence
and death, of twisted cruelty and festering rage. She
choked on it, unable to breathe.

With a scream that sounded like devils pouring out
upon the earth, the man leaped at Wolf. So swiftly did his
sword slash that it seemed to Cymbra's terrified gaze
nothing could elude it. Yet more swiftly did the Wolf
move, a dark, remorseless shadow, one with the night itself.

"Close your eyes," Dragon ordered and, lest she not
obey, he clapped a hand over them. Yet he could not shut
out her hearing. There was a sickening sound of bone and
flesh parting, followed by more of the same, and a voice so
tormented as to be almost beyond understanding, begging for death.

One final time, the sword descended. Then there was
silence.

Silence that lasted less than the space of a heartbeat
before the crowd exploded in blood-maddened cheers. As
one, the people swarmed around Wolf, hailing him as
their own and proclaiming their loyalty to him. Before
their savage joy, the world itself seemed to tremble.

Dragon relaxed his hold on Cymbra but she made no attempt to move. It was enough that her legs held her and that her stomach had no contents to vomit up. The terror of the dead men still reverberated within her. She felt it as keenly as if it were her own blood sinking into the earth.

Dragon steadied her with a hand. She felt his concern, too, but could not bring herself to turn her head and look at him. There was nothing in her sight or her mind save the brutal, barbaric figure who stood, blood-drenched sword still in hand, lit by flame against darkest night. Their gazes met and held. Even as she watched, he shrugged off the acclamation of the crowd and walked toward her.

He said something to his brother but she didn't hear it. So, too, did he speak to the crowd, but again the words were lost in the screams echoing in her mind. He took hold of her arm but did not draw her close to him. The stench of blood enveloped her. Her senses swam and for a horrible moment she feared she would faint.

When next she was fully aware, the lodge door had shut behind them. She was alone with the Wolf.

Chapter

TWENTY

THE WATER IN THE TUB MUST BE TEPID. SHE should offer to fetch hot water for him, or to send someone for it, or . . . something. But Cymbra could not move or speak, could not do anything save stand where Wolf had left her and watch.

He said nothing, merely went over to a chest and withdrew a cloth along with a small vial of oil. These he used methodically to clean his sword before returning it to its leather sheath. Having laid both on the table beneath the window, he kicked off his boots and in a single, lithe motion, pulled the blood-drenched tunic over his head.

Still without acknowledging her presence, he stepped into the tub, sat down, and proceeded to wash himself with the same efficiency as he had used to clean the sword. He even dunked his head under the water and soaped his hair. When he was done, he rose, water streaming from him, his body glistening, and toweled himself dry.

The towel joined the discarded tunic on the floor. Naked, he came to her. His hand brushed the curve of her uninjured cheek.

"You need to rest."

Her husband's voice. *Her husband.* She stared up at him, seeing the concern in his eyes—and the caution. Seeing, too, firelight and blood, anguish and death, justice and revenge.

He had won. She knew beyond question that no one would ever again make the mistake of questioning his power. But far more, he was alive. And whole. And with her.

Thinking only of that, she caught his hand. Holding his gaze with hers, she touched her lips gently to his knuckles, let them drift over his fingers, and lightly bit the tips. Before he could react, she pressed a kiss into his callused palm.

His eyes flared in surprise and something else—relief? No, not merely that. Hope. What had he thought he needed to hope for? The answer came to her in a ripple of understanding as her lips lingered against his skin and her gaze held his. Hope that she would not be so disgusted and frightened by what she had just witnessed as to turn from him in revulsion. Hope that they could recover what had existed between them before all this. Hope that she would accept him for all that he was.

Tenderness filled her. This was a part of him she knew instinctively he had never shown to others—not the indomitable warrior or mighty leader but the man with all the yearnings that she herself shared.

Still gazing at him, she drew his hand back and joined it with her own so that their fingers met and intertwined. As she did, she noted the contrast between them. His hand was so large as to easily engulf hers, hard and sinewy, the skin burnished, the palm callused. Yet this same hand that wielded death touched her with consummate care, as though she were the rarest and most delicate of flowers.

Rising on tiptoe, she touched her mouth to his, softly coaxing his lips apart. When her tongue met his, he groaned deep in his throat, loosed her hand, and made to catch her in his arms. But she caught his wrists instead, though her fingers could not close around them. With a smile his dazed mind thought must surely be goddess-born, she drew him to their bed.

He did not take his eyes from her as she gently urged him down with a light but urgent touch to his massive shoulders. When he was seated on the edge of the bed, she stepped back a little. Although she trembled inwardly, Cymbra did not hesitate. Slowly, watching him every moment, she removed her gown, drawing it down first one arm and then the other. Driven by desperate needs—to banish his concern, to celebrate his life, to give thanks for all they had—she gathered her courage.

For a moment she held the fabric so that it continued to conceal her before letting it drop. It made a soft, slithering sound as it slipped over her breasts with their high, peaked nipples, past the indentation of her narrow waist, and down her sleek flanks. When it pooled at her feet, she stepped out of it and shook her hair so that the silken mass tumbled around her like a veil.

She saw his unmistakable response and was emboldened by it. He followed the direction of her gaze and grinned. The gesture stole years from him and made it seem as though the barbarian warrior of so short a time before was little more than illusion. Even as Cymbra knew he was not, she couldn't help but laugh when her husband said wryly, "Men are so subtle."

Gracefully, she knelt before him and ran her hands over his calves and thighs bulging with muscle, the palms of her hands tingling with the teasing sensation of fine, dark hairs and warm, taut skin. Her body stirred hotly. Gently, she urged his legs apart and moved between them.

Caressing him with her eyes, she murmured, "The last thing I'd call you is . . . subtle." Magnificent, fascinating, thrilling, she could think of a good many ways to describe him but just then she didn't want to think at all.

She lowered her head, the fall of her hair drifting over them both. Scant moments passed before Wolf moaned. He tried to draw her to him again but she resisted. "Let me," she murmured, half demand, half plea.

He hesitated only briefly before falling back across the bed. His arms stretched above his head, his big hands grasped the wooden posts as he fought the nearly overwhelming urge to halt her love play and take her at once. Three days of feasting and before that four days at the hunt, a week in all since he had lain with her. His need was immense, his body ravenous. He wanted to bury himself deep within her silken heat, to feel the pulsating ripples of her pleasure that drew from him his own.

Yet, too, he wanted her to continue exactly what she was doing even if it damn well killed him. Her boldness delighted him, filled him with immense relief and passion that knew no bounds. Sweat shone on his burnished skin, his breath came harshly, muscles leaped in his arms, down his rock-hard chest, and along the ridged expanse of his abdomen.

When her tongue swirled around the tip of him, he moaned again, his control teetering. When she took him fully into her mouth, he all but came up off the bed, only to fall back with a sound of pure rapture. She brought him to the very brink before slowly drawing away. With a last, lingering stroke of her tongue, she slipped up his body to join him on the bed.

"I love being able to touch you," she said huskily. "You're so strong, it amazes me that you have never hurt me. I love the way you can make me feel so helpless yet so protected, too." She dropped light kisses around his navel, up over his chest, and along the hard curve of his jaw. Lying draped half over him, she slipped a hand down to caress what she had just savored. "I love being under you, feeling all the power you command as you thrust into me, but I love being like this, too."

She smiled down into his taut features. "I wonder if I'll ever be able to make up my mind which I enjoy more."

"Feel free," he rasped, "to take your time deciding."

MUCH, MUCH LATER, CYMBRA MANAGED TO LIFT her head off the pillow and gaze at her husband. He appeared to be asleep—finally. The man was astounding; he had more stamina than she would ever have believed possible and the devil's own determination. Deep within her, she still felt the echoing pulsations of the wild pleasure he had driven her to again and again.

She turned onto her side, lightly tracing the contours of his mouth with one finger. He was such a beautiful man, so perfectly formed in body and spirit. She gloried in their intimacy, felt reborn through their love. Never would she have thought it possible to be so blissfully happy.

On such exaltant thought, she was drifting into sleep when a rumbling sound startled her. She stared at her stomach and suddenly recalled how very little she had eaten in the past few days. And realized at the same instant how very hungry she was right then.

Right then. If she didn't eat soon, she suspected she'd be gnawing on the nearest piece of wood. With a grimace, she rose from the warm comfort of the bed and found her discarded gown. Slipping it on, she tiptoed soundlessly across the room and oh so carefully eased open the door.

Two things happened at once: Wolf awoke, swung his legs over the side of the bed, and rose in the same instant as he demanded to know where she was going; and she almost tripped over the tray left directly outside the lodge.

Brita, she thought with a smile, certain who had been so considerate—and so practical. "Just getting this," she said, picking up the tray. As she turned back into the room, laughter broke from her. Her husband stood there stark naked, fists on his hips, managing to look fierce and sleepy at the same time.

"You may not be hungry," she said with a grin, "but I'm starving."

He muttered something about satisfying one appetite only to have another come along and got back into the bed. But he made no attempt to return to sleep. Instead, he propped himself up against the pillows, the expanse of his bare chest gleaming in the lingering glow of the braziers, and watched her with amusement.

She all but swooned with delight when she took the cover off the tray and beheld what was there. Brita had remembered all her favorites—the cardamon-flavored rolls, the apples in cinnamon, the little rounds of ripe yellow cheese so soft as to be spreadable, the slices of cold chicken with mustard, the pickled red and green cabbage, even her favorite sweet cider that she much preferred to ale or mead. Although to be fair, a pitcher of ale was included along with slices of rare beef seasoned with peppercorns such as Wolf enjoyed.

"There's enough food here for four people," he said as she brought the tray over to the bed.

Wiggling out of her gown, she smiled at him boldly. "You think so?"

He was forced to reconsider as his slender, delicate wife proceeded to tuck into the largest meal he had ever seen her eat. She ate with gusto, savoring every bite and drop. The apples vanished first, followed swiftly by the chicken and most of the cheese. Had he not made a grab for the beef and some of the rolls, he had no doubt she would have devoured those, too.

When she shot him a chiding look and licked her fingers, he said, "Would you like me to get more food?"

She appeared to consider that seriously, but shook her

head, settled back against the pillows, and patted her stomach. "No, I'm finished." She cast a glance toward the remnants of the beef. "I think."

He sighed and passed her the plate. When she had finally finished, he said very seriously, "You haven't been eating, have you?"

She focused her attention on the far wall. "I wasn't hungry."

"Why not?"

"I just wasn't."

He sighed again, a very male sound of patience being sought, and gathered her into his arms. She tried to stiffen against him but that was a futile effort. Quickly enough, her slender form molded to his.

"I'll try again," Wolf said. "Why haven't you been hungry?"

"Because I had nothing to do so no way of working up an appetite?"

His arms tightened a little around her, warning that his patience was running out. "Because you were confined?"

Damn the man, he insisted on getting to the heart of it, didn't he?

"All right, because of that. I hated having to stay in here. I hate confinement. When I was a child, Hawk tried keeping me away from everyone so I wouldn't . . . hurt. He realized after a while that it caused as many problems as it prevented."

This was the first time she had seemed willing to talk about her strange abilities and Wolf seized the opportunity. "How old were you when you realized that you were different?" he asked gently.

She felt a moment's surprise that he had used that word—*different*—for people tended to steer away from it. The few who really knew the truth about her spoke of her "gift" and she supposed it could be seen that way. But what was blessing was also curse and weighing everything in the balance, she thought "different" was as close to the full sense of the truth as it was possible to come.

"I don't know exactly," she said quietly. "I cannot remember a time when it wasn't there so it must have started very young. I have only fragmented memories of the period Hawk remembers all too well, and I suppose that is to the good. For a while, it was so bad that he drugged me with opium in order simply that I might survive but he knew that couldn't continue."

"So he tried to seal you away from the world?"

"Yes, as much as that is ever possible to do. He told me later that he hoped that if I could be kept safe behind strong walls, I might learn to build such walls within myself. In that he was very wise, for that is exactly what I finally managed to do."

"Does he have a touch of this gift himself?" Wolf asked, wondering about the man with whom he must shortly communicate.

Cymbra hesitated. "He is a very wise and capable leader, and I think at least some of that must come from his understanding of people. I see the same ability in you. So, yes, I suppose it is the same in kind, but the degree is greatly different."

"Did you resent being sent away?"

"Not resent precisely, only regretted. But Hawk came often to visit especially while I was still very young. When he saw that I was better, he allowed me to visit at Hawkforte."

"But he never took you to court?"

"No, he seemed to think that would be borrowing trouble." She raised herself on her elbow, smiling at him wryly. "In that, as well, the two of you seem to think alike."

She waited, hoping that he would respond to her mention of her brother, that they might even talk further about Wolf's delay in sending word to him. But instead her husband said, "I know this wasn't easy for you. It was a difficult decision for me to make. I'm still not sure if it was the right one."

She looked up at him, surprised. "You can say that after what happened?"

He shrugged. "It worked out for the best. There won't be any further problems."

If he thought it strange to dismiss the savage execution of three men in such terms, he didn't show it. Instead, he looked down at her again and smiled. "Sleepy?"

"I should be," she said ruefully, "but somehow I'm not."

"Neither am I." He let go of her, rose from the bed, and held out a hand. "There's something I want to show you."

"STOP!" CYMBRA CRIED, LAUGHING AS SHE KICKED AT the green-foamed spray, showering Wolf with fine droplets of water. He grinned and bent over, scooping up handfuls to toss at her. Still laughing, she ran down the beach, well aware that her husband followed.

She had never before been on a beach at night, never imagined how beautiful it would look beneath the stars. When he told her where they were going, she was surprised yet curious. Her hand secure in his, bundled in the cloak he insisted she put on over her gown, she went eagerly.

If the guards on the berm thought their lord's behavior unusual, they said nothing of it as they obediently opened the gates. So, too, they would have the good sense to keep silent about the sight of the mighty jarl of Sciringesheal playing in the surf by starlight with his beautiful Saxon wife.

Her eyes took longer to adjust to the dark than did his. He found his way with the easy grace of his namesake. When he jumped down onto the sand and held out his arms to catch her, she laughed and leaped without hesitation.

She was still laughing as they played at the water's edge and even as she ran down the beach. When he caught her, she turned breathlessly in his arms, tilted her face up to the star-draped sky, and said softly, "I could stay here forever."

He dropped a quick kiss on her lips and grinned. Her pleasure delighted him, yet did he take due note of how very much she needed freedom. Truly, she was as a caged bird suddenly released to soar.

"What would you do if it rained?" he asked teasingly.

She arched a finely drawn eyebrow and gestured at her clothing damp from his splashing. "Get wet?"

"Ah, but you'd need a place to shelter." Seizing her hand, he ran up the beach. "Come on."

Beyond a curve of the shore, where grouse bushes grew against a proud cliff, he drew her toward a dark cleft in the rock. When she hung back a little, uncertain, he tossed a grin over his broad shoulder. "I found this place years ago. You'll like it."

Even as he spoke, he moved seemingly right through the rock and drew her with him. Cymbra found herself standing in a small cave the contours of which were just visible in the starlight filtering through the opening in the cliff. Near the entrance, the walls were covered with fragrant moss. Farther in, she caught streaks of light and shadow that glistened as though embedded with countless tiny stars.

Wolf gestured toward the pool of darkness at the farthest edge of her sight. "It goes so far back I've never been able to find the end."

"You searched for it?" she asked, more than a little

concerned. There were caves near Holyhood where it was said people had become lost, never to be seen again.

"I used a torch. There are magnificent chambers back in there, some the match of anything I've seen in palaces."

Even so, she had no wish to see them for herself, or to even think of him venturing into them again. "What if the torch had gone out?"

He laughed and caught her hand to his lips. "I also took tinder and a flint. Do you always worry so?"

"No," she admitted, puzzled by her uncharacteristic concern. Softly, she added, "I just can't bear to think of you being hurt."

He gazed down into her eyes for a long moment before gently gathering her to him. She worried for those she loved. Recognizing that confirmed Wolf in the decision he had made. Whenever she spoke of her brother, her love for him was clear. Moreover, it was evidently well de served, for Hawk had acted toward her with great care and compassion. Loath though he was to do it, Wolf could not help but feel a spurt of gratitude for the enraged Saxon he must shortly face. Face, too, the wife he had kept unknowing lest she fear for them both any longer than absolutely necessary.

"There were times," he said quietly, "when I came to this place simply because I needed to be alone for a while. Never before did I want to bring anyone with me."

She touched his cheek in silent thanks and leaned her head against his broad shoulder. Suddenly, she was very tired. The events of the past few hours seemed to crash down on her. Despite her best efforts, she could not contain a delicate yawn.

"I shouldn't have brought you out," he said remorsefully.

"Oh, no! I'm glad you did. It's so beautiful here."

"Still, you need to rest." Swiftly, he removed his cloak and laid it on the floor of the cave. Gathering her into his arms, he drew her down beside him and pulled the edge of the garment up over them both, creating a warm cocoon of safety and comfort.

Cymbra made a soft sound of contentment and nestled against him. There was so much she wanted to say— how much she loved him, how glad she was that they were together, her hopes for the future . . . so much. But thought fled as easily as dreams came.

She woke to a warm, freshening breeze and light pouring in through the entrance to the cave. Her husband stood just outside, looking at the sea. When she went to join him, brushing sand from her cloak, he held out an arm and drew her close. He said nothing, merely gestured out over the blue-gray water in which small waves chopped and seals played.

She followed the direction of his gaze and saw the vessel coming up rapidly over the horizon. For a moment, she thought only that the oarsmen must be rowing unusually fast, so swiftly did the ship move over the water. Then a sudden gust of wind filled the sail and she saw there, against the dazzling sea, the sign she had both longed for and dreaded.

The hawk, talons curved to seize its prey, flying fast and sure toward the lair of the wolf.

TWENTY-ONE

S UNLIGHT GLINTED OFF THE SHIELDS OF THE
men of Wolf's personal guard, two dozen in all,
who stood in ranks on the stone wharf. Their
swords remained in their sheaths but they were
close to hand if, as the grim looks on their faces indicated,
the trouble they were expecting occurred.

Behind them, the streets and lanes of the town were
deserted. Word of who was arriving had spread on the
wind and the good folk of Sciringesheal had made themselves scarce. Only a few well-fed dogs ambled about. In
contrast to their happy ease, the guests were departing
with speed, urged on by Dragon, who had remained at the
hill fort to see to a task made easier by unanimous desire
not to irk the Wolf.

Cymbra's breath caught as she realized that the Saxon
vessel was not slowing even as it entered the rock-strewn
channel guarding the entrance to the port. Wolf, too, took
note of that and smiled grimly.

"Either your brother is an expert seaman or he'll
never make it this far."

He was about to say a word to the captain of the guard regarding preparations for a rescue mission when Cymbra stopped him with a hand laid gently on his arm. Her eyes still on the approaching ship, she said, "I've been told that Hawk took a rudder for the first time when he was three years old. Supposedly, he was so delighted by the experience that he talked for days afterward about making the boat fly."

Watching the smooth tack of the vessel as it rounded a boulder-strewn islet, Wolf said grudgingly, "He sails well for someone who isn't Norse."

She smiled and squeezed his arm but did not take her gaze from the proud, hawk-emblazoned vessel now near enough for her to make out the men on board. Even this close to the wharf they were still rowing hard, until, at a single, shouted command, they upped oars at the same time as the sail was dropped. Smoothly, confidently, the ship settled beside the stone quay.

Cymbra took a quick, tight breath. She was distantly aware of the metallic rasp of the anchor being dropped, the stiffening of the men behind her, the fluttering of birds overhead. But all that was as nothing compared to the sight of the man who strode across the deck and leaped gracefully onto the quay.

The motion, and the freshening wind, ruffled the edges of the short, dark gray tunic he wore and sent a curl of thick, chestnut-hued hair tumbling across his brow. His eyes were the same vivid blue as Cymbra's, and his features were sharply chiseled, the bones strong beneath taut skin. His expression was achingly familiar for all that it was hard set with anger and resolve.

Hawk. Her dearly loved brother, whom she had not seen in half a year since his last visit to Holyhood but who looked exactly as she remembered him. He was as tall as Wolf himself, with the same broad sweep of shoulders and chest, the same long, lithe torso and powerful legs. He wore the same air of command, exuded the same aura of relentless will.

A will perfectly expressed in the taut set of his square jaw and his gaze lit by cold, deadly rage. Cymbra swallowed against the lump of fear in her throat and stepped forward quickly.

"Hawk! How wonderful!" She threw her arms around his neck, hugging him fiercely as at the same time she tried to slow his remorseless advance. Her welcome diverted him only long enough to express his relief at finding her alive and whole.

"Cymbra," he said with husky gentleness and returned her embrace, sweeping her around in a wide circle as he gazed down lovingly into her face. Lovingly and ominously. Slowly, he set her on her feet and carefully touched the bruise beneath her right eye.

She saw his conclusion and reached out frantically, but too late to stop him.

"Hawk, no!"

The solid thud of his fist connecting with Wolf's jaw seemed to echo off the surrounding hills with the force of a thunderclap. At once, the men of the guard drew their swords and advanced. So, too, did the men on board the Saxon vessel leap onto the quay with their weapons at the ready.

A bloodbath was heartbeats away when Wolf shouted, "Hold!" His superbly trained men froze where they were, but Hawk's kept right on coming until he, too, raised a hand. "Wait." His sword in hand, he advanced on Wolf, who had not drawn his. A blow that would have knocked most men unconscious had scarcely fazed him. Yet did he rub his jaw thoughtfully as he regarded the enraged Saxon.

"You thieving bastard . . . you Norse scum . . ."

Cymbra's stomach plummeted. Desperate to intervene, she threw herself between the two men, but before she could plead for them to stop they both made a grab for her, intending to pull her to safety. She found herself yanked in two directions at once as the two fierce—and fiercely protective—warlords vied with each other to get her out of harm's way.

Wolf let go first and took a step back, though his eyes never left his wife. Hawk shoved her behind him but he was surprised and it showed.

Moving quickly to take advantage of that, Wolf said, "Cymbra has suffered no injury at my hands, and the men who did seek to harm her are dead."

The enraged Saxon lord cast a quick glance over his shoulder to where his sister stood, pale but seemingly with no fear for herself. Though he could scarcely credit that, he had to ask, "Is this true?"

She nodded quickly but before she could say more, he turned back to Wolf.

"Who killed them?"

Flickers of firelight seemed to dance in the eyes of the Wolf, carrying memories of blood and vengeance. "I did."

As Hawk considered this, Cymbra wasted no time. She stepped forward, commanding his attention. Her voice soft and husky, she said, "Sheathe your sword, brother. I am very happily wed. Truly, everything has happened for the best. If you will but give us a chance, my husband—" she held out a hand to Wolf and smiled at him, "my husband and I would welcome you properly." With a bright if anxious glance at the hovering Saxons, she added, "And your men, too, of course."

Hawk looked at the couple standing together, his sister so seemingly delicate and fragile beside the mighty Viking, the selfsame man whose savage death had been uppermost in the Hawk's mind since the message arrived scant days before, revealing Cymbra's whereabouts.

He noted how his sister's hand nestled in the far larger, scarred hand of the Norse Wolf. How she instinctively moved closer to him as she spoke. How even now she glanced quickly at her husband as though for reassurance and comfort.

Her husband. It didn't seem possible. In his heart, he still thought of her as the little girl whose safety and welfare had been his first concern since he was hardly more than a boy himself and they were orphaned. Though he knew full well that she had grown into a woman—and a woman of stunning beauty at that—he had long ago decided that he would never compel her to marry. Since she had never brought it up herself, he simply hadn't thought of it.

Until now. After all the weeks of dreading her fate the agonizing visions of her abused and suffering, perhaps even dead—to find her seemingly safe and even happy required more of a change in his thinking than he could swiftly make.

Yet he could take some time and consider at least the possibility that, as she had said, everything had happened for the best, unlikely though he still thought that was.

"All right," he said, his gaze on Wolf, who was also regarding him steadily. Slowly, he did as she had bidden, returning his sword to its scabbard. Yet did his hand linger on it. Raising his voice so that his men could hear, he added, "We will tarry here awhile." He shifted his attention to Cymbra. "And see for ourselves this happiness of which you speak."

She heard the doubt—and the challenge. Rather than acknowledge either, she smiled and, linking one arm through her brother's and the other through her husband's, led the two mighty warriors back to the hill fort.

Wolf's guard followed along with the Saxons. They made an odd procession—two war bands primed for battle following with seeming docility in the trail of a beautiful woman even as they exchanged glares with one another and fingered the hilts of their swords.

"And the people here are really wonderful, Hawk," Cymbra was saying as they passed through the gates at the top of the hill. "Some come from as far away as Russka. Nadia and Mikal, who live in the town, just had a baby son. I helped deliver him. And we had a visit from a Moor who lives in Constantinople, can you imagine that? He brought the most incredible spices and fabrics. Oh, and you must meet Wolf's brother, Dragon. He knows the most fascinating stories, he can hold you spellbound for hours. And—"

Over her head, the two men exchanged glances.

"She didn't used to talk this much," Hawk observed grudgingly. Had he not been so struck by the change in her, he would not have been driven to mention it.

Wolf raised an eyebrow. "Really? You mean she may quiet down eventually?"

Cymbra stopped in midstep and looked at them both. When she saw the smiles tugging at their hard mouths and the teasing gleam in their eyes, she laughed with relief so great as to be scarcely contained. Yet did she inform her husband chidingly, "Don't count on that happening anytime soon. Everything is still so new here and so interesting, I'm bound to comment on it."

Wolf sighed but he didn't look displeased. On the contrary, he regarded her so lovingly that warmth flooded her cheeks. None of that escaped Hawk's notice. Yet did he remain unconvinced. He still wanted to hear much more about how that bruise had happened. It was all well and good for the Viking to kill the men who had sought to harm his wife, but what about keeping her safe in the first place? And why were her clothes wrinkled and water-stained with bits of sand sticking to them? Did she have no proper servants to see to her?

So, too, he noted the shadows beneath her eyes, hinting at lack of adequate rest. At the thought of the demands the Viking, as her husband, was no doubt making on Cymbra, Hawk's anger surged anew with raw, primitive force, only to be counteracted by the glowing smile his sister was bestowing on that same Viking.

No, she was not a little girl anymore. Still, it remained to be seen if she was truly a happy wife or simply trying to convince him of that to avoid bloodshed. Not for a moment did he doubt that Cymbra would willingly sacrifice herself to save others. As her brother *and* her lord, the latter still very much in force while he considered whether to accept her marriage, it was up to Hawk to protect her even from herself. With such thought in his mind, he took due note of the high walls surrounding the hill fort, the watchtowers and the men stationed in them.

His keen interest did not elude Wolf, who said dryly, "Perhaps you would like a tour of the defenses?"

Cymbra held her breath, fearing her brother would take that as sarcasm. But instead he nodded assessingly. "Perhaps I would. It was brought to my attention recently that my own defenses were lacking."

Wolf nodded with some sympathy. "I made a study of fortifications some years back. It convinced me that the highest walls are only as good as the men standing on them."

"Something I thought I knew," Hawk said. His face was grim as he added, "Unfortunately, the man I trusted to lead those men turned out to be an incompetent clodhead."

The look in his eyes as he said that was so chilling that Cymbra could hardly bring herself to speak. Yet did she have to know. "What happened to Sir Derward? Did you hold him responsible? I mean . . . did you . . ."

"He hanged himself," her brother said curtly. At her look of shock, he added, "It was the more merciful end for him."

"More merciful? But suicide . . . he doomed his soul—"

"There's no reason to dwell on this," Wolf said quickly. He cast a warning glance at his brother-in-law. "Obviously, Rooster Brain's . . . uh, Sir Derward's life was forfeit. The details don't matter."

"Rooster Brain?" Hawk repeated. He shook his head wryly. "That's a perfect description."

How nice that they were in such accord, Cymbra thought tartly, but she had other concerns. "What about the other men? Wolf said he left them tied up. You didn't . . . ?"

"They're fine," Hawk assured her. "There was only one man guilty of failing in his duty and he paid for it." He turned his attention to his host. "And since we're on the subject, I'd like to know why all this happened. Why you came to Holyhood, why you saw fit to remove my sister from there, why you brought her here. I want answers to all that and more."

"And you shall have them," Cymbra said before Wolf could respond. "But in due time. First, you must be shown to your quarters and your men also made comfortable. I'm sure you'd like to bathe, and while you're doing that, I must see to a proper welcoming feast. We've just had quite a few guests but they've departed." The relative calm of the hill fort compared to recent days had not escaped her notice. "How nice that we can just be together as family."

The two men looked at her with twin gazes of such incredulity that she was tempted to burst out laughing. Only the extreme seriousness of the situation—with life and death hanging in the balance—stopped her.

"Family," she repeated firmly just in case either of

them had not gotten her point. "And speaking of that, here's Dragon."

She smiled warmly at him. "My brother has arrived. Isn't that wonderful?"

"Wonderful," Dragon repeated dutifully, his keen eyes surveying Hawk. Abruptly, he shifted his gaze to his brother. "Is it wonderful?"

"So far," Wolf said carefully. The three huge, fierce warriors stood in a semicircle around Cymbra, seeming to dwarf her. She wondered for just a moment if they could possibly be aware how similar they were not merely in size but in stance—hands resting on the hilts of their swords, feet planted firmly apart, gazes alert—and in manner as well. Each was a warrior and a leader to the very marrow of his bones, accustomed to danger and death. Yet was each also a protector, caring and compassionate to those who were weaker or in need. She was convinced that given the right circumstances, they could be the best of friends. Resolve like finely honed steel swept through her. They damn well would be before she was through.

Deciding this was not the moment to mention that, she laid her hand lightly on Hawk's arm. "If you will come with me, I will show you to your quarters."

He was about to agree, eager to get her alone so that he might question her without hindrance, when Wolf stepped between them. He did it so smoothly that Cymbra didn't even see her hand removed from her brother's arm and placed instead in her husband's.

"That won't be necessary," Wolf said. "You have the feast to see to. Dragon will show Hawk and his men to their quarters."

Smiling, or at least showing his teeth, Dragon moved smoothly between his startled sister-in-law and her brother at the same moment as Wolf drew her back, separating her further from Hawk, who scowled and looked about to protest.

Before he could do so, Cymbra said, "Yes, of course, you're absolutely right. I'll see you shortly, brother."

Without giving him a chance to object, she turned away quickly and hurried to the kitchens. Her heart was beating very fast and she murmured a prayer that Hawk and Dragon would not come to blows. Or Hawk and Wolf. Or any of the Norse and Saxon. That all those superbly conditioned warriors would refrain from using their savage skills to brutalize one another at least until she could get a good meal into them. *And* a sufficient quantity of ale to improve their spirits or, preferably, knock them out altogether.

"My lady," Brita said anxiously when she caught sight of her mistress. "My lady, we heard—"

"Yes, yes, my brother is here. It's wonderful, I'm thrilled. Now quickly, there's a great deal to be done."

The dozen or so women gathered in the kitchens hurried to obey. They were as mindful as Cymbra of the urgent need to soothe male tempers and were joined in determination to keep the peace in any way they could. Work-worn hands clasped quickly at amulets that had hung from the sacred tree. These same hands also sketched the sign of the cross, just to be sure. The wise woman knew that when dealing with the uncertain temperament of men, it never hurt to have all the help one could get.

S O IT PLEASE ALMIGHTY GOD," BROTHER JOSEPH SAID solemnly, "we give thanks for His bounty and rejoice in the unity of family gathered beneath one roof, at one table, to break bread together."

With a glance at Cymbra to see if this was what she'd had in mind when she requested a special blessing before the meal, the monk received her nod of thanks. He smiled and sat down.

As only a tense silence greeted what she thought was a very nice prayer, Cymbra said a firm "Amen," which, perforce, required the Saxons—good Christians all—to do the same.

When Hawk hesitated to join in, she shot him a look and said pointedly, "Did I mention that Wolf was so kind as to have Brother Joseph officiate at our marriage, along with Ulfrich, too, of course?" She nodded at the holy man, to whom Hawk had already been introduced.

"Amen," her brother intoned with a sardonic glance at the newest addition to his family. He lifted the drinking horn a servant had just filled but refrained from partaking of its contents as his piercing gaze shifted to the monk. With feigned pleasantness, he said, "I presume, Brother Joseph, that you are aware of the Church's prohibition against vows given under duress."

Having just taken a sip of his own ale, the young cleric looked in danger of choking but he recovered quickly. Despite facing one of the most feared warlords in the known world, he managed to reply with his usual equanimity. "Most certainly I am aware of it, my lord. Be assured, I would never consecrate in marriage anyone who gave indication of being unwilling."

"I'm very pleased to hear that. Tell me, how exactly do you determine whether a party is unwilling? Did you, for example, take counsel with my sister prior to these *joyful* nuptials?"

At the obvious, indeed biting doubt underlying his words, Brother Joseph blanched slightly. But he held firm and said with gentle humility, "I had no opportunity to meet with the Lady Cymbra beforehand, my lord. However, she in no way impressed me as unwilling. Indeed"—he looked at Cymbra kindly—"she impressed me as a woman of rare courage and virtue."

"How perceptive of you," Hawk drawled. "Perhaps you aren't aware that such nobility of character may lead one to put aside personal interest—even personal safety—in pursuit of a higher goal."

"That is true," Brother Joseph said quietly. "But then are not we all supposed to be in pursuit of such a goal? I would hardly be much of a monk if I denied someone their chance to attain it."

"A neat bit of reasoning," Hawk allowed. "Very convenient to your case. Perhaps too convenient." Abruptly, he shifted his attention to Cymbra. "Were you willing? Did you go to your marriage without duress?"

She hesitated, turning cold inside at the thought of lying to her beloved brother. Yet how could she tell him of the threat Wolf had made? The moment she even hinted at it, swords would clash.

Choosing her words with care, Cymbra said, "There was not a shadow of doubt in my heart but that I wanted this marriage."

Hawk stared from her to Wolf and back again. His hand tightened on the drinking horn but still he did not raise it to his lips. "How extraordinary. A man you did not know, who had taken you from your home by force. Yet you suddenly decided that he was the one man you wanted to marry?"

Cymbra bought herself a moment before replying by signaling to the servants to begin bringing in the food. Silently, she regretted not having drugged it. At the rate things were going, there would be full-scale war before they finished the first course.

Under the circumstances, there was really only one thing to do. Lowering her eyes, she said softly, "You embarrass me, Hawk. Surely, you don't insist that I explain why I was so eager to wed?" She cast a warm gaze at Wolf, who was sitting directly beside her and who raised an eyebrow at her strategy. A becoming flush suffused her cheeks, never mind that it came not from womanly modesty but from pure fury at stubborn, provoking males.

That, at least, silenced her brother long enough for the food to be served. But he wasn't done yet, far from it.

Wolf had just speared a succulent piece of goose on his knife and was about to carry it to his mouth when Hawk said, "You know in England we have a quaint custom. When a marriage is first considered, there are discussions between the various parties. Next a contract is drawn up to which everyone agrees. Then—and only then—the marriage is blessed by the Church, in the presence of the bride's family. Funny thing is, I thought you Norse did it pretty much the same way."

Wolf put down his knife and made a small gesture to his brother, who had half-risen from his seat. Dragon subsided but sullenly. He continued to scowl at Hawk.

"As a matter of fact," Wolf said pleasantly, "we do have a similar custom here."

Hawk nodded. His jaw was so tightly set that Cymbra feared it might snap. Abruptly, he plunged his eating knife hard into the table and rose. "Then why, Lord of Sciringesheal, did you see fit to ignore the ways of both our people and take my sister by force?"

"I did *not* ignore them. After you rejected my offer of marriage to your sister to form an alliance between us, I—"

"What? What offer? There was never any—"

"You know damn well what offer. You said she'd never wed a filthy Viking savage. In fact, you made it sound as though she had said it, which is why I went to Holyhood intending to punish her for her arrogance and selfishness, only to find that—"

"Punish her?" Hawk roared the words even as he wrenched his dagger out of the table and grasped it purposefully. "My sister? You insufferable bastard. How dare you—"

Wolf too was standing now, dagger in hand. Nor was he alone. Every man at the table was on his feet and armed. Cymbra smothered a cry. She jumped up, shoved back her chair, and glared at them all in fury.

"Stop it! Stop right now! Obviously there's been a huge misunderstanding, but you are not—*not*—going to make it any better by killing each other!"

In desperation, she looked from her brother to her husband. "You both claim to care for me and want to protect me. How will shedding each other's blood do that? For pity's sake, just talk to each other—and listen!"

When still they remained, glaring at each other, she said, "Sit down, both of you! Or I swear, the next meal you eat will be flavored with emetine."

The two men exchanged baffled looks. Cautiously, Wolf said, "What does that do?"

"Why nothing, dear husband," Cymbra replied scathingly, "save cause you to vomit up everything your stomach may hold until such time as you pray it will never hold anything again!"

"Sounds delightful," Wolf muttered. He sat down.

"May have been a mistake educating you," Hawk grumbled, but he too resumed his seat. The other men swiftly followed suit.

Cymbra caught Brita's eye and motioned for the drinking horns to be filled again. She was more resolved than ever that the sooner they were all insensible, the better.

With forced calm, Hawk said, "You mentioned a marriage offer. I never received any such. Why should I believe it ever existed?"

"Because of this." From within his tunic Wolf withdrew the scroll he had shown to Cymbra in the hold of his vessel. He passed it to Hawk, saying, "Your sister tells me you can read and she's already identified this as your seal. What explanation do you have for it?"

Hawk took it slowly, studied it carefully. His dark,

slanted brows drew together. "This is not my hand, nor did I authorize this."

"Yet it is your seal?"

He looked more closely, holding the parchment up to the light to study the wax imprint. With great reluctance, he nodded. "It appears to be."

Returning the scroll to Wolf, Hawk looked at him thoughtfully. "You really did propose an alliance between us?"

"I did. The man who carried that message to you has never returned. His fate is unknown to me. I presumed him dead at your hand. This reply—" he gestured at the scroll, "was brought by a Cornish trader who frequents these waters and who claimed to have been paid to bring it."

"Paid by whom?"

"A man in your service, wearing your colors."

"I sent no such man, nor do I know anything of your messenger." Hawk's frown deepened. "Something is very wrong here. Someone has deliberately intervened to prevent an alliance between us."

Wolf nodded. "Any idea who?"

"Our mutual enemy, the Danes? But I don't see how they would have had the opportunity." Silently, he resolved to discover precisely what had occurred as quickly as possible. "An alliance between us has much to recommend it," he admitted. "Yet, too, I must be certain this is best for my sister."

"It is," Cymbra said quickly. With husky urgency, she added, "Surely you can't believe there is any reason for me to mislead you about that?"

Her brother smiled gently but his eyes remained dark with concern. "I can think of an excellent reason. You have always sought to heal even at great cost to yourself. Mayhap you are doing that right now."

"No! You must put such thought from your mind. Wolf and I are very happy together."

Hawk did not reply to that although he did look from one to the other of them thoughtfully. He turned his attention to the superb food. Shortly, the conversation moved off in other, safer directions.

Chapter

TWENTY-TWO

"TELL ME ONE GOOD REASON," CYMBRA SAID, "just *one* why men are necessary." She slammed the dough she was kneading so hard that the worktable shook. Around her, the women didn't even pretend to be concentrating on their own tasks. They exchanged tolerant glances and waited to hear what the jarl's bride would say next.

Brita stifled a giggle. "Well, I can think of *one* use they have but I'm quite sure you're already aware of it."

Cymbra waved a hand dismissively. "Oh, certainly, and with that they think to so dazzle and confuse us that anything else they do will pass our notice. I think not!" *Slam.* "I think they have not the sense of women." *Thud.* "I think they are stubborn, infuriating, mule-headed, and—" *Smash.*

"My lady—" Brita yanked the dough to safety. "Perhaps you'd like to gut the fish instead?"

The idea had appeal, if only because it would put a sharp knife in her hand, but Cymbra declined. With a sigh, she left off abusing the dough and went over to the window. In her mind's eye she saw not the children

scampering across the hill top but the scene she had witnessed shortly after dawn as the men rode out. "They're
hunting again."

Brita and all the other women already knew this, yet
did they cluck their tongues sympathetically. "Only boar,
my lady," Brita reminded her. "I heard the lord Dragon
say the jarl was in no mood for anything else. Boar we can
always salt. It will not go to waste."

There was already such quantities of food stored for
the winter, even after all the feasting, that real thought
had to be given to decide what to do with more. A week
now had Saxon and Norse hunted together, vying for the
fiercest kills. Daily they pounded back into the hill fort,
dripping blood and heaven knew what else, leaving to the
women the task of coping with the carcasses while they
went off to the sauna to see who could endure the most
heat, tell the most outrageous stories, and drink the
most ale.

That was when they weren't wrestling, throwing
javelins, or testing their skills in every conceivable manner. Just that morning, a fight had almost broken out
when one of Wolf's men claimed he could *piss* farther than
any Saxon.

It had to end soon, Cymbra thought wearily. Some of
the older, more experienced women had said this was just
how men got to know each other and it had to be tolerated
because it was their way. But she was worn out with waiting to discover whether they would decide they were good
friends or deadly enemies.

Moreover, there were ripples, undercurrents she
sensed but could not seize. Some of the Saxons—her
brother's lieutenants in particular—seemed to be exerting
themselves to be friendly. They were down in the town
frequently, spreading their coin about, talking to people.

"Very nice men," Nadia had pronounced them when

Cymbra came to visit her and the baby. "Mikal says everything will be all right. He says not to worry."

Cymbra wished she could feel the same way but she knew Hawk too well. He had not risen to be one of the mightiest lords in England, sworn directly to the great King Alfred himself, by leaving anything to chance.

Several times now he had tried to get her alone but always Wolf or Dragon intervened. When her brother was about, she was watched constantly. Even when she asked Hawk simple, innocent questions about people at Holyhood—Miriam, for instance, who thankfully was well—she could feel her husband listening to every word they exchanged.

She resented that, knowing it to be completely unnecessary, yet she was hardly about to challenge her husband's will just when she was trying to convince everyone of how very *happy* she was. Worse yet, Wolf seemed to realize her quandary and didn't hesitate to take advantage of it.

Only the preceding evening, as they all sat at table, he had announced that more Norse should consider acquiring Saxon brides because Saxon women were so amenable, so agreeable, so—and here she had almost choked—*biddable*. He'd all but congratulated Hawk on raising a sister who knew her proper place. Worse yet, she'd been forced to smile through it all rather than upturn a vat of ale over his head as she more properly should have done.

And Hawk had just sat there nodding at this apparent bit of male wisdom. Cymbra snorted scornfully. If for one moment they would try thinking with what was between their ears rather than between their legs, perhaps they would—

But no, that wasn't fair. The problem was that Wolf and Hawk—and Dragon too—all thought far too keenly and deliberately. Soon now, very soon, they would come to conclusions about each other. She could only pray that the outcome would be as she wished.

Pray and seek to do everything she could to bring about the alliance they all claimed to want.

That evening, as they supped, Cymbra waited for the lull in the conversation that came inevitably when the men were feeling well fed and content. It was always about then that Wolf summoned the skald to weave his tales. Before he could do so, Cymbra asked innocently, "Do you think you might be done with hunting for a while?" She glanced around at the men, as though the thought had just occurred to her.

Wolf leaned back in his chair, surveyed her tolerantly, and voiced their mutual puzzlement. "Is there any reason why we should be?"

"Only that we have enough food to feed everyone here and in the town many times over throughout the winter and beyond. I just thought you might like to do something different."

"Such as?" Hawk asked.

Such as decide to stop continually testing and provoking each other, but it wouldn't do to say that. Instead, she suggested brightly, "I thought we might go sailing."

"Sailing?" Dragon repeated as though he had never heard the word.

"Sailing," she said firmly. "Hawk loves boats and so do all of you. I thought it would be nice to see more of the coast. Coming here, I was struck by how beautiful it is and I thought—"

"A race," Wolf said as though he had finally understood what she meant.

Hawk nodded. "My vessel against yours. Excellent."

"No!" Cymbra protested. "That isn't what I intended. Haven't you tested each other enough by now? Wouldn't it be possible to just relax a little and enjoy yourselves?"

Husband and brother both looked at her as though she'd spoken in some foreign tongue neither understood.

Dragon laughed. "Give it up, sweet sister. Testing each other *is* how we relax and enjoy ourselves. But a race is a splendid idea." He grinned at Hawk. "How much of a head start do you think you should have?"

"Head start? Why would I want that?"

"Well, you don't know these waters, and after all, you're only Saxon and it wouldn't really be fair to—"

That did it. The challenges—and the wagers—flew fast and furious. Cymbra resisted the temptation to throw up her hands but only barely. At length, when they finally noticed that she was still there, Wolf strove to make amends.

"*Elskling,*" he said, "why don't I have one of the servants fetch your lute? You can play for us."

"By all means," Hawk agreed. "I haven't heard you play in months and I've missed it."

Pleased, if surprised, that they would choose so tranquil a pastime over the fierce tales of the skald, Cymbra was happy to comply. But after she had played the first few tunes, she noticed Hawk frowning.

"That isn't your lute," he said, "What happened to the one taken from Holyhood?"

She welcomed this opportunity to tell him of her husband's thoughtfulness. "It was damaged. Wolf very kindly got me this one to replace it."

Hawk sat back in his chair, smiling at her pleasantly. With no warning whatsoever, he asked, "Was that before or after he *kindly* dragged you away from the man who was whipped?"

"How did you—?" Hurriedly, she looked to Wolf. "Did you tell him that?"

Her husband was silent for a moment, regarding Hawk steadily. At length, he said, "No, I didn't. Where did you hear about it?"

Hawk shrugged. "You know how it is, people talk."

"Especially to visitors with coin to spend and a willingness to listen?"

"Perhaps. At any rate, Cymbra hasn't answered me. Was it before or after?"

"Before," she said, not waiting for Wolf to reply for her as she was certain he would. "And I think perhaps you misunderstood what happened with that man. He was a thief. His crime was great for he tried to rob two families of their livelihoods. It's true that I wasn't allowed to care for him after he was punished, but Ulfrich did."

"Then you suffered no distress from what happened?"

She hesitated, both unwilling and unable to lie. "You know I was . . . sheltered from such things and you know why. But my husband's rule is just. It is his responsibility to maintain order for the protection of his . . . that is, our people."

"Absolutely," Hawk agreed. "I'm very relieved to know you can . . . accept such things, especially as they seem to be very common around here. But tell me, how did you feel about witnessing the executions of those men who raided the settlement?"

Cymbra pressed her lips together tightly and shot another quick look at Wolf. He was lounging in his chair, long legs stretched out in front of him, a horn of ale held lightly in one powerful hand. With a sardonic lift of his brow, he said to Hawk, "You have been busy. Or should I say, your men have."

Hawk also appeared completely at his ease. He even went so far as to chuckle. "Just taking an interest. Nothing wrong with that, is there?"

"Of course not. Did your interest extend to finding out how those men died?"

"As a matter of fact, it did. Personally, I would have

gone for something a little more likely to stick in people's minds."

Wolf nodded pleasantly. "Now there we can agree. I actually had intended . . . I suppose you could call it an object lesson. But I decided against it at the very last."

"Really? Why?"

"Cymbra was insisting on being present, something about feeling it was her duty as wife of the jarl. I didn't want her upset so we just lopped their heads off, made a quick job of it."

"Very *kind* of you. I take it then that those men you fought together—and by the way, I'm sure that was very impressive—became the object lesson?"

"You could say that."

"And you insisted Cymbra witness it. She was actually forced to do so by your brother"—he glanced in Dragon's direction—"acting on your orders."

"No!" Cymbra exclaimed, "That isn't what happened. In fact, Dragon made sure I didn't see the . . . the worst parts." Dismayed by what Hawk had learned, and how he interpreted it, she blurted, "I don't think it's a good idea to have your men listening to gossip."

"Oh, really? What do you think they should be doing?"

She stared at him, momentarily at a loss, then seized on the first thing that came into her head. "Sailing. That's why I suggested it. They should be sailing."

He gave her a most peculiar look, combining tenderness, perplexity, and suspicion. She ignored it and picked up her lute. They'd wanted music; they'd damn well have it.

And they would go off the next morning, after telling her she couldn't come along because the sailing would be so fast and rough that she wouldn't enjoy it. She managed to smile through that and continue smiling when they returned hours later, tunics stiff with salt spray, faces wind scoured, seeming in high good humor.

"A tie," Wolf said with some amazement. "We raced four courses, I won twice, Hawk the same." He clapped his brother-in-law on the back, a blow that would have leveled a lesser man but which Hawk appeared not even to notice. "Not bad at all. How about we give it another go tomorrow?"

So they did, and the next day and the next. Grateful though Cymbra was that the parade of bloody carcasses had stopped, she chafed at having to remain in the hill fort, seeing to her *womanly* tasks, while the men amused themselves.

Almost a fortnight after Hawk's arrival, she sat ignoring the sewing in her lap and struggled to come to terms with the fact that she felt neglected. It was absurd, really, and even admitting the truth to herself was embarrassing.

She was surrounded by people who cared about her, most particularly a husband and a brother who were both determined that she should be happy. She had a household to run as well as her work as a healer. Her days were full and her nights . . .

Although she was alone, color suffused her cheeks. Regardless of his exertions during the day or what hour he finally retired, her husband never failed to make passionate love to her, often rousing her in the early hours of the morning to do the same again. She existed in a cocoon of sensual satisfaction, gentle care, and safety.

And she chafed. Really, she must be the most contrary woman ever born.

Wistfully, she looked out beyond the shore. Sunlight sparkled on the water. Seals played in the waves near the islets that guarded the approach to the port. Farther out, where sea and sky blurred together, she could make out the sails of proud longships speeding so swiftly that they seemed to fly.

Even as she watched, they turned landward. She set aside her husband's tunic, still to be mended, and went to greet the returning men.

"SO SOON," CYMBRA MURMURED. THE MOMENT THE words were said she regretted them. She sounded like a petulant child, always wanting more instead of being glad of what she had.

"It's been almost a fortnight," Hawk reminded her with a smile. "I do have to get back to Essex." He touched her cheek gently. "You can understand that, can't you?"

"Yes, of course, I'm very glad that you've stayed this long. Certainly, you have responsibilities at home. I know that."

Beside them, Wolf said, "Your brother is always welcome to return, *elskling*."

"And you are both always welcome at Hawkforte. But now I must carry word of all this to King Alfred. He will be most interested to learn of it."

Time seemed to speed up then, moving far too quickly as her final hours with her brother dwindled to nothing. Too soon, the farewell feast was done, the last embraces given and loving words said. Standing beside Wolf on the wharf, she watched the proud, hawk-emblazoned vessel vanish into the mists beyond the rocky islets. As it did so, a gull called long and hauntingly out over the water.

On the cusp of that eerie sound, Cymbra recalled her brother's words and belatedly realized why they had stuck so oddly in her mind. King Alfred would be *interested*. Wouldn't *pleased* have been a better way to describe the monarch's likely reaction to news of a Norse/Saxon alliance?

She puzzled over it for a moment, then shrugged and told herself she was fretting over trivials. Hawk's departure saddened her for she loved him dearly and would miss him. Yet it was also a relief, for now she could stop fearing the nightmare that had haunted her since the very beginning of her marriage. There would be no confrontation between her husband and her brother. Indeed, far from being enemies, they showed every sign of having become friends.

The wind picked up just then and she was glad to snuggle closer beside her husband. Wolf had an arm around her shoulders. He squeezed gently and smiled down at her. Together, they walked back up to the stronghold.

Cymbra woke the next morning to a strange sense of calm, almost like that which presages a violent storm. Yet the cloudless sky and sparkling sun hinted at nothing of the sort. Her first thought was that her brother was gone and she missed him. But she took such longing firmly in hand and turned her mind to her duties.

Now that all the feasting was over and the food well stored for the winter, there was time for the women to relax a little. But only a little, for the weaving had been neglected and must be resumed. So, too, Cymbra wanted to be sure she had gathered every possible flower, seed, grass, and bark that could be useful in the coming winter. Her garden was well begun and she looked forward to expanding it the following spring, but wild plants would always be necessary to add strength to the tamer variety.

She went in search of Wolf and found him just coming off the training field. Her sheer pleasure at the sight of him made her smile. Although she missed Hawk, she felt as though in some ways her marriage was only now beginning, free as it was from doubt and fear.

With love shining in her eyes, she went to her husband and laid a hand lightly on the bulging muscle of his upper arm. "I trust you have not overstrained yourself, my lord."

He raised an eyebrow but already his smile came, drawn by her own. "Surely you've noticed, my lady, that I am only given to excess when I am with you?"

She blushed, which made him laugh and caused her to swat at him in playful reprimand. He reached out teasingly to grab her even as she danced away, laughing in her own turn. Around them, Dragon and the other men made a show of seeing nothing even as they observed the merriment of the jarl and his wife with tolerant grins of their own.

"You wanted something?" he asked when he had caught her and drawn her close against him. She inhaled the heady scent of leather, horses, and man, and momentarily forgot everything else. Only with effort did she recall her purpose.

"Oh, yes, I need more wild plants for the garden and to dry for the coming winter. Brita will go with me and Olaf, too, if you will kindly give your permission."

She said the last lightheartedly, a teasing bow to his rule, but to her surprise he considered it seriously. She was astonished to see him hesitate. "Wolf—?"

He stared at her silently for a long moment during which she had the uncanny sensation that he sought to look into her very soul. Slowly, he took a breath and seemed to relax. He even mustered a faint smile as he said, "Of course, go but don't linger too long." His expression changed again, becoming sensual. "I would we had some time together before supper."

It was on the very tip of Cymbra's tongue to suggest they take that time right now. She well remembered her one trip to the sauna and would not be at all reluctant to repeat it. But Brita and Olaf were waiting, as were several traders who hovered nearby, hoping to speak with the jarl.

With a sigh, she promised to return promptly. Before she could move away, Wolf caught her hand, raised it to his lips, and pressed a light kiss into her palm. Again she was tempted to change her plans, but she only laughed and fled, aware of his warm gaze following her.

With Brita and the ever-watchful Olaf, she spent a pleasant morning in the hillsides and groves just beyond the town. Toward midday, they ventured down to the beach, where Cymbra found seaweed useful for clearing the chest and treating disorders of the skin. Olaf looked especially skeptical when she told him this but he already had some experience with her treatments, having the benefit of an ointment that eased the aching of his joints, and wouldn't entirely dismiss anything she said.

"If there is worth to be found in that," he said, looking down at the pile of seaweed she had collected, "you'll be the one to do it, my lady."

She thanked him prettily for the compliment and a short while later they made their way back to the fort. With the sea lanes soon to be closed by winter, Sciringesheal was thronged with traders, many of whom were passing back and forth through the gates in the berm. It seemed to Cymbra that the guards on the watchtowers were more numerous than before but she wasn't really sure of that and thought little of it in any case.

The day lengthened and soon enough she was busy with preparations for the evening meal. Having seen the women well started at that task, she left the kitchens and was walking toward the lodge, intending to bathe and change before seeking her husband, when a ripple on the edge of her awareness drew her up short.

A man was coming toward her. A very tall man wearing a long, brown cloak that enveloped his head and face. She had a moment to be surprised that any man would approach her so directly when he walked straight past her without slowing. Under his breath, yet with each word distinct, he said, "Come with me, Cymbra."

Hawk.

Disbelief roared through her. She had seen him leave,

he could not possibly be here. Yet he was and like this, concealed, come by subterfuge to seek her out and—

The realization of what her brother had done chilled her to the very marrow of her bones. Not for a moment did she mistake the meaning of his presence. For all her effort and all his seeming acceptance, he did not believe that she was happily wed. He thought the opposite and he had come to correct it.

Come right into the heavily guarded hill fort, right past the guards, into the very heart of the Wolf's lair to take from it that which the Wolf claimed as his own.

He would die. She knew it as surely as she breathed. Her brother would die and she would be the cause.

On legs that scarcely felt able to carry her, fearful that at any moment someone would realize what was happening and raise an outcry, she followed the cloaked man around a corner of the stables and out of sight.

Concealed from the guards and with no one else to be seen, Hawk tossed back the hood covering his head. His gaze swept over Cymbra, finding her pale, wide-eyed, and trembling. Instinctively, he reached out, taking her into his arms and reassuring her gently.

"It's all right, there's nothing to fear. I'll get you out of here, I promise."

"No!" She pushed free of his arms and stared at him in horror. "Oh, Hawk, what have you done? I thought this was all settled, that you had accepted my marriage. Why come you now like this when you must know how it will anger Wolf?"

His face darkened. "Aye, that damn Viking mustn't be angered, must he? You'll say anything, do anything, to prevent that."

"Yes . . . No! That isn't what I meant. He is my husband, I love him, of course I don't want him to be angry. But I have told you the truth, Hawk, I swear it!"

He stared down into her pleading eyes for a long

moment. Slowly, he said, "Speak those same words to me on the deck of my ship, where you are no longer in the Wolf's power, and I will believe you. Until then, I will not."

"I cannot go with you! I cannot!"

He shrugged his massive shoulders. "Then must I remain here, for I will not leave you."

What a fool she had been to think he had done exactly that. What a ridiculous, absurd fool! This was the man who had held the child Cymbra in his arms through solid days and nights when she screamed with the pain of others. The man who had wielded his power and authority to create her sanctuary from the world and, by so doing, given her the time and place to grow into the woman she had become. The brother who had also been both parents . . . and friend . . . and guardian . . . and lord—

And she had believed he would simply sail off and leave her? Fool! Stupid, idiotic fool!

"You cannot stay here," she said, her voice thick with tears she dared not shed. "You know what will happen if you are found."

He sensed his advantage, her deep and abiding love for him, and pressed it home. "Then come with me, Cymbra. Come right now. This can all be settled before the next hour is done."

The enormity of what he demanded did not escape her. She would have to leave the hill fort without Wolf's permission and with no escort save the brother who had violated the rules of hospitality to come by subterfuge into his erstwhile host's domain. If her husband found out—

She pushed that thought aside. Hawk was right, it would take only a short time. She could yet convince him that all was well and see him depart without anyone else knowing what had happened.

"Where is your ship?" she asked, anxious not to waste a moment.

"In a cove not far from here." He smiled mirthlessly. "All that sailing had its use. I now know this coast as well as I do that of Essex. It was an easy matter to double back and find a concealed anchorage."

So he had been planning this all along, probably from the first day he came and heard her claims of marital happiness. Again she silently berated herself for thinking the matter so easily settled.

Desperation edged her voice. "All right but we must go swiftly. I would prefer Wolf does not know of this." At the look he gave her, she amended, "*Not* for the reason you think. Only that no damage be done to the friendship that should exist between you."

Her brother had no comment on that beyond an eloquent raising of his brow. He pulled the concealing cloak over his head once again and handed her a second, equally voluminous cape that he drew from beneath his own. "Put this on then and let us make haste."

They joined the stream of traders heading through the gates. Hawk drew her between two heavily laden wagons that offered them further concealment. Almost before Cymbra knew it, they were beyond the berm but she could not relax until they reached the bottom of the hill and veered away from the main road that led into town. Instead, they followed a narrow path of trodden-down grass and dirt that wound around the hill and vanished out of sight of the watchtowers.

Only then did she catch her breath and feel her heart slow a little. A swift and largely silent walk brought them several miles north of the town to an area where Cymbra had not been. There, in a secluded cove, she saw her brother's ship riding at anchor.

With a worried glance at the sky where the sun was

arching earthward, she hung back a little. "Surely this is far enough? You can see I am under no duress. Won't you believe me now when I say I never have been?"

"I will believe you when you stand on the deck of my ship," he said stubbornly.

A sudden, terrible thought occurred to her. She dug her heels into the soft ground and stared at him, refusing to move. "Hawk . . . you meant what you said, didn't you? That when I have convinced you, you will let me go? You would not just . . . sail off even knowing that I want to stay?"

He looked surprised at the very thought, as though her fear that she would be forced to leave made him realize for the first time that she might well and truly wish to remain.

"I will respect your decision," he said with gruff reassurance, "once I am certain of it."

Convinced that she had no choice but to do whatever was necessary to satisfy his concern, Cymbra followed her brother down the verdant hillside fragrant with late-blooming wildflowers and into the secluded cove.

His men greeted them with eager relief. No doubt they had not been pleased by their lord's insistence on going alone into what they regarded as an enemy stronghold.

The sail was unfurled for a quick sprint to open water and the anchor was being raised as Hawk and Cymbra reached the shingle beach. He was just about to lift her onto the deck when the thunder of pounding hooves froze them both.

Chapter

TWENTY-THREE

THE NORSE WOLF CAME OFF HIS HORSE LIKE a vast, turbulent storm rolling down a mountain. Before his feet touched the ground, his sword sang from its sheath. He advanced on Cymbra and Hawk, his features set in a rigid mask of rage from which all reason and control were banished. His eyes glittered like the cold, hard steel he wielded. His mouth was drawn in a hard, taut line. Corded tendons pulsed in his neck and rippled down his mighty arms.

Cymbra gasped at the sight of him. In that moment, she truly understood how terrifying he could be and why men quaked at the mere thought of challenging him. His transformation into a being of raw emotion and instinct stunned her, and filled her with primitive fear. Yet nothing could change her deep and abiding love for him. Though her throat closed so tightly she could scarcely breathe, she still tried to reach out a hand, driven by the desperate need to comfort and reassure him.

"Wolf . . . don't—!"

Hawk, too, was driven by his instincts, and they

screamed to protect at all cost. Ignoring Cymbra's protest, he pushed her behind him and drew his weapon. He spared a glance for the men pouring down the hillside behind their leader, then concentrated all his attention on the deadly foe who continued to come straight at him without pause.

"*Hold, Viking!* Or the peace you claim to seek ends now!"

Wolf's mouth twisted in a sneer that revealed the depth of betrayal tearing at him. "Peace is for deluded fools! There is only war . . . only this—"

He attacked without hesitation and so swiftly that Hawk's superb reflexes alone saved him from instant death. Silence descended over the beach, broken only by the savage clash of steel as two mighty warriors battled without quarter.

On both sides, Norse and Saxon looked on. No one moved to intervene or to join the fray. Locked in single combat, Wolf and Hawk went at each other with such savage fury that Cymbra could only stand frozen in horror. The scream trapped in her throat reached to her very soul. Shock roared through her like fingers of icy fire. This was her worst nightmare come true, the two men she most loved intent on killing each other.

A black pit of despair opened up inside her. One of them would die and how then would she live, knowing it was because of her? How would she get through the long years ahead, every moment made agony by pain she knew would never end?

She had to stop them . . . *had to* . . . but her strength was as nothing against theirs. They were both blood-maddened, enraged, consumed by the lust of battle.

She gasped as Wolf raised his sword and brought it down within inches of Hawk's head. Her brother only just managed to escape what would surely have been a death blow. He attacked in turn, slashing and stabbing, only just missing severing Wolf's sword arm—

Around them, the men pressed in, pulled back, moving to the rhythm of the battle, as absorbed in it as the contenders themselves . . . oblivious to all else . . . including the woman who stood at the heart of the conflict itself.

At the heart . . . in her heart, loving them both . . . desperate . . .

"*Stop!*" Steel gleamed in the light of the setting sun, not the steel of warriors' swords but of Cymbra's own dagger, drawn from the sheath at her waist.

The dagger clasped firmly in both her hands.

Aimed directly at her own heart.

A mortal sin . . . eternal damnation . . . She gasped back tears, swallowed terror, and prayed as she had never prayed in her life.

"*Stop!*" she screamed again, her voice echoing against the verdant hills. "I love you both! If one of you dies because of me, I cannot live. Rather I would end my own life right now!"

For a seemingly endless moment, Hawk and Wolf stood unmoving, weapons locked. Only the dawning horror in both their faces told her they had heard—and seen.

"I mean it! Put down your swords! Step away from each other! I *will* do this, I swear it!"

A mere flicker of Wolf's eyes and Dragon moved. But she was prepared for that, knew the brothers were so close they could understand each other without words.

"Get back!"

Dragon stopped in midrush, staring at her with the same disbelieving shock that riveted every man on the beach.

Heedless of the tears streaming down her ashen cheeks, she tightened her grip on the dagger and pressed the point of it just below her breast.

"No more! This has to stop, right now, right here! *Put down your swords!"*

Gasping for breath, having run all the way from the stronghold, Brother Joseph pushed his way through the mob. At the sight of Cymbra, all the color fled from his face. He fell to his knees in the sand and made the sign of the cross.

"Child," he pleaded, "don't do this! You know what it means. Your soul—"

"I am damned either way," she sobbed. "I can't let one of them die . . . not because of me—"

Wolf stepped away from Hawk, breaking the death lock of their blades. She gazed into his anguished face, seeing it blurred by her own tears. She loved him so much that she would gladly trade her life for his, as she would for her brother's.

Wolf took a step toward her, his back turned to Hawk, whom he suddenly ignored as though they had not been doing their damnedest to kill each other mere moments before. His eyes never left Cymbra as he began walking toward her. Quietly he said, "I'll put down my sword but you put down the dagger. We'll do it together, all right?"

She forced her gaze past him to Hawk. To her brother she said, "You, too. Both swords . . . *down.*"

Hawk nodded quickly. Slowly, his gaze on her, he bent to lay his sword on the sand.

Wolf moved closer. Hawk still held his sword. Dragon closed in from the other side. Brother Joseph got to his feet and also moved forward.

Cymbra's breath came in pants, her heart beating so rapidly she thought it would break through her ribs. Eyes on her husband, she slowly began to lower the dagger from her breast.

Everything happened at once. Wolf dropped his sword and lunged for her. Hawk, startled by the sudden

movement and uncertain what it meant, straightened
with blade still in hand. Dragon drew his sword and
moved to protect his brother's back. Cymbra looked from
one to the other in confusion even as she continued to turn
the dagger away from herself. Momentarily distracted,
she did not realize how close her husband was until—

"*Noooo!*"

Gray eyes met hers in surprise. He made a faint
sound and stared down at his hands closed over his chest.
Blood flowed between his fingers, around the protruding
handle of the dagger, dripping down his tunic and flowing
away into the sand.

"No!" Cymbra screamed again and tried to reach
him, but Dragon was there first, thrusting her aside.
Instantly, warriors surrounded Wolf, who staggered but
fought to stay on his feet. Hawk made a grab for Cymbra
but it was too late. He, too, was surrounded, disarmed and
hurtled to the ground.

"Take them!" Dragon roared. In moments, the
shocked Saxons were stripped of their weapons, bound,
and led back up the hill to the stronghold.

CYMBRA WRAPPED HER ARMS EVEN MORE TIGHTLY
around herself and stared at the far wall of the cell.
She was shaking so hard she could scarcely stand. She
needed all her self-control to keep from breaking down
entirely.

In the adjacent cell, separated from her by thick
blocks of stone, she heard Hawk and his men. He had
called out to her, to determine if she was all right and reassure her that he would not let her come to harm. The
words, meant to comfort her, had only filled her with even
greater dread.

Hawk would die rather than see her hurt. She knew
that beyond doubt. The moment the opportunity arose,

he would do or say something to shift all the blame onto himself. She couldn't let that happen.

Neither could she still her anguished thoughts of Wolf. Since being brought back to the stronghold, she'd had no word of him, no idea how he fared. Ulfrich must be with him but she was desperate to care for him herself, even as she knew she would not be allowed to do so.

She could only wait as the long, seemingly endless hours wore on. Outside, twilight turned the world to shades of gray. She could just make out a few stars shining through the iron bars cemented into the small window. From the window she could also see the great hall ablaze with light, so crowded that people spilled out onto the field beyond.

Standing on tiptoe, she curled her hands around the bars and strained to see as much as possible. She heard angry voices but the words were indistinct and gave her no news.

Finally, just when she thought she could bear it no longer, the crowd parted. Dragon emerged from the hall and strode toward the cells. Hawk saw him, too, and shouted, trying to draw his attention, but Dragon didn't so much as glance in his direction. Instead, he ordered the door to Cymbra's cell unlocked.

He strode into the dank chamber, grasped her firmly by the arm, and pulled her outside. He said nothing, not even when she frantically pleaded. "Tell me how Wolf is! Has the bleeding stopped? Did Ulfrich stitch the wound? Did—?"

She broke off when the single, contemptuous look he shot her made it clear he would not answer. Forced to run alongside him to keep from being dragged, she had only a fleeting glimpse of the crowd pressing in around them, faces distorted, jeering.

Dragon pushed her into the hall. There were more

people in it than she had ever seen before, filling the space with their turbulent, roiling emotions. They fell silent the moment she appeared. A path opened up from the door down the length of the hall to the high table.

Cymbra gasped with relief when she saw Wolf sitting there. He looked somewhat pale and his face was clearly strained, but the bloody tunic had been replaced by a fresh one and he sat upright without obvious pain or difficulty. Her instinct was to run to him but his cold, implacable gaze stopped her.

Dragon let go of her arm and stepped away. She swayed slightly and for a moment feared her legs would not hold her. Pride drove her to draw deeply on reserves of strength she scarcely knew she possessed. Slowly, her eyes never leaving his, Cymbra walked the length of the hall to stand before her husband and her lord.

And, too, her judge.

Firelight glittered in the torches set in brackets along the walls, casting shadows onto the high, peaked roof like brooding spirits gazing down on the scene. Smoke curled ghostlike from the remnants of the fire dying in the hearth. A few dogs skulked around, heads low, seeking the way out. The crowd stirred uneasily but no one spoke. That was left to the Wolf.

"Do you remember," he said without preamble, "that I told you there are circumstances in which a higher duty must come before any other consideration?" His voice was flat, lacking any expression, but Cymbra was not misled. The pain he fought to conceal washed through her, pain not merely of the body but of the spirit. Pain so great it struck her like a mighty wave, leaving her dazed and confused.

Yet still did she understand what he had asked of her. Because of that higher duty, he had accepted her disobedience when she went to help Brita. Another man would not have. Another man would not have held her so tenderly in his arms, brought her to such pleasure, talked and laughed with her, given her so very much while asking . . . what? Only for her trust despite all that stood between them, Saxon and Norse, seemingly destined enemies seeking however fragile a path to peace.

She straightened her shoulders and looked at him squarely. "I remember."

"When we married," he went on, "I made promises before my gods and yours to protect you as my wife. But I am not just your husband. I am also jarl and I am responsible for the protection of all my people."

She knew too well that he had set aside those responsibilities on her behalf when he granted a swift death to the attackers of Vykoff, and that he was given ample reason to regret such leniency.

In the hush of the vast hall, Cymbra said, "I would never wish you to forget your duty to your people."

"Then you will answer what I ask of you." A muscle twitched in his jaw. For just a moment, his guard dropped enough to reveal the bleakness behind the mask of his imperturbable control. She had to press her lips firmly together to keep from crying out against it, knowing how very much he would want no one to know of his anguish. A moment later it was gone, concealed in an act of relentless will.

"Did you want your brother to take you from here?"

Cymbra hesitated. If she told him the truth—that Hawk had come back without her knowledge and had refused to leave until she accompanied him to his vessel—she had no doubt of the outcome. Her brother would be judged to have violated the alliance he had given every evidence of accepting. Wolf would have every right to claim his life for such an act of treachery and betrayal. His people would demand it.

But if she took the blame upon herself instead, she

would also take the punishment. At least then there was a chance that Hawk's life would be spared. Clinging to that thought, she gathered her courage and gazed into the eyes of her husband.

Wolf had asked for her trust and in that moment she gave it fully. She trusted him with her love, her loyalty—and her life.

"I went with him willingly."

Savage pain rippled between them as Wolf absorbed the impact of her words. He flinched like a man struck and his face tightened further. She felt his last, faint hope die and the steel-cold resolve of the warrior take its place.

"A woman who seeks to leave her husband violates our laws." He stared at her. "This is also the way of the Saxon, is it not?"

She nodded, not trusting herself to speak. Desperately, she fought back tears. She could not make this harder for him by revealing her own terror and anguish, yet neither could she let him believe the worst. "I never meant to stab you. It was an accident."

He said nothing for a moment, then merely shrugged, as though a wound that could have killed him was of no consequence. "You are not accused of that."

She knew he was sparing her a charge that would surely have meant a death sentence. Knew, too, that there must be many among the crowd who disagreed with his decision even if they would not dare to challenge it.

Slowly, Wolf rose. For just a moment, he pressed his hands on the edge of the table to steady himself, then stood unaided.

His voice was low and hard, filling the hushed great hall where it seemed nary a person so much as breathed.

"You sought to leave your husband without his knowledge or permission. That is a violation of our laws. So, too, you sought to leave here without the knowledge or permission of your lord. That also is a violation. For both those offenses, you will be punished."

Fear filled her. She fought to conceal it, clinging to trust, remembering love. No one moved for a long moment. Then Dragon stepped forward again and took her arm. He said nothing, only led her from the hall. Outside, they turned not back toward the cells but in the opposite direction—toward the punishment post.

CYMBRA STOOD, HER CHEEK RESTING AGAINST THE rough wood. Leather ropes bound her wrists. A slight breeze warmed by the multitude of torches touched the bare skin of her back. Wolf himself had opened her gown, cutting through the laces and spreading the fabric as far as her shoulders, no further. She heard his breath shudder as he did so and closed her eyes against the anguish that continued to come from him like molten waves.

The crowd was quiet yet she knew it was there. She could hear the shifting of many bodies, feel the confusion of their emotions—anticipation, vengeful pleasure, yet also bewilderment, regret, and dread. Of a certainty, none of them had ever seen the wife of a jarl whipped, never even imagined such a thing could happen. Yet this was a wife who had betrayed her husband, and the law was very clear about that.

Cymbra, too, was afraid. Yet she felt oddly separated from herself, as though she stood apart and watched it all happen to a different woman.

A sudden thought occurred to her and she frowned. Would Wolf do it himself? He could tear his wound open. She should warn him—The absurdity of that hurtled her back into the moment. She was suddenly, vividly aware of what was about to be done to her. She pressed her head against the pole, closed her eyes tightly, and prayed for courage.

Hawk was not praying. He was at the cell window with a clear view of what was happening. If he didn't wrench the bars out of the stone, it would not be for want of trying.

He had shouted himself hoarse, first insisting the blame was his and demanding he take Cymbra's place, then making murderous threats.

Brita, too, had tried to intervene, only to be dragged off by several of the women who were her friends and no doubt worried what her fate would be if she drew the attention of the Wolf.

Brother Joseph remained and Cymbra could hear him praying softly nearby. She turned her head and saw not the monk but the man who had wielded the lash against the thief. For just a moment, her eyes met his. He started and looked away hastily, but not before she saw the measure of his own dread.

Saw, too, what he carried coiled in long black loops dangling from his hand. Her stomach heaved. She clenched her teeth and tried again to pray.

W OLF FELT THE TOUCH OF HIS BROTHER'S HAND ON his arm and emerged from the numbness into which he had fallen since returning from the beach. He was vaguely aware that his wound ached and that he was weak from loss of blood, but that was as nothing compared to the far graver wound he had suffered.

She had gone with Hawk willingly.

Until Cymbra herself said that, he had retained some hope. She would avow her innocence, swear she had never meant to leave him, and pledge her love and loyalty. He wouldn't have to hurt her, at least not physically. He'd be left with the problem of Hawk as the one responsible, and he had no idea how he would manage that without breaking Cymbra's heart, but at least he could have tried.

Now there was no chance. She was condemned by her own words. Distantly, he knew he should be enraged by her betrayal of him. Had she ever meant anything she said, any soft word or gentle touch? Had it all been a sham from the very beginning? Anger surged in him but he couldn't sustain it. Anguish overcame all else.

He couldn't remember hurting so much since his parents' death and even then he had been so focused on what was needed for survival that he'd had little time to grieve. This was different. He felt a sense of loss so shattering that he could not begin to imagine how he would ever move beyond it.

Yet the world waited for no man. Dragon's silent reminder awakened him to the realization that time was passing. Further delay would change nothing. Indeed, it was cruelty of another kind.

He had a sudden, overwhelming need to be done with this. But how? Knowing what must be, he had not thought of the actual doing of it. The possibility of taking the whip himself filled him with such crawling horror that he discarded it immediately. Nor could he bear to put such a burden on his brother.

He was caught, unable to find his way out of a trap at least partially of his own making, when Olaf suddenly stepped forward. Quietly, the older man said, "You charged me to protect her, lord." He held out his hand. "Let me do so now."

Wolf took a long breath, heedless of the pain that stabbed through him. He looked into the grizzled face of the man he was about to trust as he had never trusted anyone. Olaf's eyes were filled with understanding and compassion.

Slowly, not taking his gaze from him, Wolf gestured for the whip.

•   •   •

SWEAT TRICKLED DOWN OLAF'S BROW, OVER HIS WEATH-
ered cheeks, and into his thick gray beard. He stood
some twenty paces from the post, the long black snake of
the whip uncoiled in his hand. The crowd was silent. No
one moved or made so much as a murmur.

Cymbra braced herself as best she could. Above all,
she did not want to appear a coward, no matter how terrified she felt. Pride was involved but so too was the need to
spare Wolf as much as she possibly could.

Bile rose in the back of her throat. She said a final
prayer that it would be over soon and squeezed her eyes
shut.

Olaf raised his arm. Still-powerful muscles flexed.
Face taut with concentration, he flicked the whip through
the air. It fell inches short of Cymbra's back. A ripple ran
through the crowd, not of disappointment or anger but
rather of sympathy, as though man and woman alike un
derstood his difficulty.

He wiped his brow, inhaled deeply, and took a measured step forward. Again the whip darted. This time the
very tip of it touched Cymbra's back. She jerked more in
surprise than pain. Indeed, she was startled by how very
little she felt. Again, Olaf raised his arm. Again the whip
touched her but only barely.

Incredibly, insanely, the thought occurred to her that
at this rate her punishment would take all night.

"Enough," Wolf said, his voice low and guttural,
wrenched from the very depths of his being.

Olaf gave a shuddering sigh of relief that was picked
up by the crowd and let his arm fall.

Wolf stepped forward. Cymbra's breath caught as he
carefully drew the fabric of her gown over her back. As he
did so, he very lightly traced the two thin red marks that
were the only evidence of the whip's passing.

"As the law requires," he said hoarsely, "punishment
will end at dawn."

So she was to remain at the post through the night. It was warm, the sky clear. While hardly the most comfortable way to spend several hours, neither was it anywhere near as terrible as it would have been had she truly been whipped.

As she realized that the whipping was over almost before it began, gratitude flowed through her, not merely for having been spared pain but for the trust in her husband that had not been misplaced. He had set aside his own pain and anger to administer justice tempered by mercy. Had there ever been a nobler, more honorable man? No wonder she loved him so completely and no wonder she would do anything she had to for his sake.

The crowd dispersed quietly. Wolf said a few words to Olaf but too softly for Cymbra to hear. Then they left, along with Dragon. Only Brother Joseph remained, having secured permission from Wolf to stay with her.

He did not attempt to speak with her, for which she was grateful, but took a seat on a rock some little distance away. His silent presence faded quickly from her awareness. Cymbra was left alone.

Tentatively, she tested her bonds in the hope that they might have loosened enough for her to wiggle out of them. That was not to be, nor had she really expected it. She glanced over her shoulder at Brother Joseph, who sat with his head bent and his hands folded.

With a pang of guilt for disturbing him at his prayers, Cymbra moaned. She closed her eyes when she did so and didn't see his reaction but an instant later she heard a footfall just beside her.

"My lady . . . ?"

Again she moaned, and let her weight sag onto her arms as though she could no longer stand upright. That was all Brother Joseph needed. He picked up the hem of his robe and ran for help.

Scant moments passed before he was back and not alone.

"I'm afraid she may be ill, my lord. She moaned, and then when I tried to speak with her, she didn't respond." With a sigh, the good monk added, "Women are very delicate after all."

Obviously the dear man had never witnessed childbirth, Cymbra thought. She only just managed to hold very still as Wolf touched the side of her face gently.

"Cymbra . . . ?"

The deep worry and regret in his voice brought tears to her eyes. Only with the greatest difficulty did she restrain them. In less than a heartbeat, he cut through her bonds and lifted her into his arms. Her pretense almost did shatter then, for she was struck with fear that he would reopen his wound. His swift, powerful stride to their lodge reassured her just enough to remain silent.

With great care, Wolf laid her on her stomach on the bed. He spoke her name again softly. When she didn't respond, he drew her gown from her back. She felt his gaze on her. He moved away from the bed but returned almost at once. With gentle strokes, he applied a soothing ointment to the two thin red marks.

His touch almost undid her. She yearned to turn over, hold out her arms to him, and reassure him that she was fine. Only the image of Hawk in the cell, still facing an unknown fate, stopped her.

Though she loathed the need for it, Cymbra moaned again.

Wolf sighed raggedly. He straightened away from the bed and gently pulled a cover up over her. A moment longer, he stood looking down at her. His hand lightly touched her hair. Then he was gone.

Alone, she was free to cry out the turmoil of emotions plaguing her these many hours and did so, her tears soaking the pillow. At length, she quieted and raised her head. There was no sound from outside the lodge, no indication of a guard or anyone else nearby.

Quickly, before her resolve weakened, she rose, threw on a cloak, and opened her medical box. It was the work of moments to find what she needed.

The guards in front of the cells received a ration of cider and food several hours before dawn. Slipping from the lodge, a gray shadow concealed within the deeper shadows of the night, she made her way cautiously to the kitchens. The barrel of cider was just within, near the door. Carefully easing out the plug, she shook in a finely ground powder. It was the same drug she had given to Dragon to make him sleep.

With the plug back in place, she shook the barrel lightly, then quickly concealed herself behind the door to the root cellar. A short time later, the senior guard came to fetch the food and drink. Cymbra held her breath until he was gone, then moved to the window looking out toward the cells. From there, she had a clear view of the men as they ate and drank, talking quietly among themselves. Quickly enough, their conversation gave way first to silence, then to snores.

With a final, careful look in all directions, Cymbra left the kitchens and ran across the field to the cells. Her heart pounded wildly and her hands shook so badly she feared she would not be able to hold the key even when she found it. But the moment her fingers touched the cool metal, she calmed.

The heavy lock made a faint screeching sound as it gave way, causing her to flinch. A quick glance over her shoulder reassured her that the guards in the watchtowers had not heard.

When she turned back to the door, Hawk was at the grille, his hands closed so tightly on the bars that his knuckles were white. He stared at her in mingled hope and disbelief. "Cymbra, thank God! Are you all right?"

She nodded quickly. "You must promise me something."

"What?"

"You won't kill the guards. Wolf didn't at Holyhood and you mustn't either. Can you promise that?"

He looked down and saw that she was about to release the lock. Saw, too, the men slumped unconscious outside the door. Understanding came swiftly and with it admiration.

"You are a brave woman, my sister."

Although his praise warmed her, she shook her head. "Only a desperate one. Promise?"

"Promise," he agreed even as he motioned to his men.

Cymbra opened the door to be caught in her brother's arms. He held her with great care but she felt his fierce joy all the same. Still holding her, he gave a few murmured orders. Barely were they spoken than the men were in motion, flowing out of the cell, hugging the darkness as they headed for the towers.

The guards, taken by surprise, fell soundlessly. The gates to the stronghold were eased open.

Cymbra hugged her brother close. She had no idea when, if ever, she would see him again and the thought tore at her. But she managed a weak smile. "I love you. With all my heart, I thank you for everything you did for me." Her voice caught. She gathered herself and rushed on. "Now go quickly and in safety."

Hawk gazed down at her. His eyes were unusually gentle. He touched her cheek lightly. "So brave, Cymbra. Always the healer, always willing to sacrifice yourself for others."

She started to say again that she was not and again that he must go, but she had no chance. His arm slipped around her even as his hand closed on her mouth. As shock roared through her, he said, "But never would I leave you here after this."

Too late, she realized his intent and her own terrible mistake. She tried frantically to struggle but her brother's

strength was as great as her husband's. He lifted her effortlessly, muffling any sound she made against his chest.
Swift as the wind that murmured around them, he carried
her from the stronghold of the Norse Wolf.

In the shadows beyond the great hall, a lone man
watched them go. He stood with his fists clenched at his
side, fighting his own fierce urge to keep what was his. But
she wasn't really, was she? She had been taken by force
and compelled to marry by threat of death. In his arrogance, he had presumed he could keep her safe, but the
memory of her tied to the punishment post would haunt
him all his days.

He loved her as he had never dreamed it was possible
to love. So much so that he could do nothing less than set
her free.

Wolf watched the shadowy figures vanish through
the gates. For a long time after that, he did not move.
Starlight shone on the tears in his silvery eyes.

Chapter

TWENTY-FOUR

DRAGON SHOOK THE SNOW OFF HIS CLOAK as he came into the hall. He handed the garment to a servant, then nodded to Ulfrich, who was himself just entering.

"How is he?" Dragon asked as they walked to the hearth together to warm their hands. Winter had struck weeks earlier than expected, interrupting an autumn that seemed to have come and gone in a night. Already, snow covered the ground and more was falling steadily. The last vessels that weren't wintering in Sciringesheal had left a fortnight before.

"Better," Ulfrich replied. "There is no sign of the fever returning."

They exchanged a look of relief. The fever that had struck Wolf in the aftermath of his wounding by Cymbra was not entirely unexpected. But it had raged so fiercely and lingered so long that the seriousness of his condition had been concealed from all but his closest followers. So far as everyone else was concerned, the Norse Wolf was content in his ice-bound lair, all the more so for being rid of his troublesome Saxon wife.

Privately, Dragon had come to the conclusion that the fever's grip on his brother was at least in part because Wolf had no will to fight it. Fear of what that would mean had prompted Dragon to linger in Sciringesheal when he would otherwise have returned to his own holdings farther to the west or perhaps ventured south again to pass the winter in gentler climes.

Instead, he had stayed, determined to fight whatever demons raged within the Wolf. Yet in the end he had to credit his brother's own vast strength for bringing him through the crisis whether he had truly wanted to survive it or not.

That was a grim thought and Dragon was still frowning over it after Ulfrich had taken his leave. Servants moved about the hall preparing for the evening meal but none disturbed the man brooding by the fire. None, that is, until a slight movement beside him alerted him to the presence of another.

He looked up, surprised to see the Irish girl—what was her name? The one who had served Cymbra and who helped Ulfrich now.

"What do you want?" Dragon asked.

He saw her take a breath and sensed she was nervous. Her face, framed by brown hair, was very pale. More kindly, he added, "Sit down."

She hesitated only briefly before doing so. As she settled herself on the bench across from him, he said, "You're Brita, aren't you? The healer?"

She looked at him in surprise. "Hardly a healer, lord, though I have some small skill." She paused, then said in a rush, "Thanks to the Lady Cymbra, who taught me and who was always so kind to me."

Dragon grunted. The girl's audacity startled him. He was willing to wager a considerable sum that she was the first person to dare mention Cymbra's name since her departure. Dragon himself had spoken of her only very briefly with Wolf within hours of the Saxons' escape. His brother had made it extremely clear that he would never speak of her again.

"Yes, well, what is it you want?"

Brita bit her lip. She looked down at her hands clasped in her lap, looked up at him again, and swallowed. "Lord Wolf has healed, in his body at any rate."

Dragon's gaze narrowed. He spared a moment to wonder exactly how much she knew. Ulfrich had tended to Wolf alone except for Dragon's own help. No one else had been let near him. "The jarl is fine. Is that what you wanted to know?"

She shook her head. "I don't want to know anything. That is, it is you who should know." She stopped, clearly reluctant to speak yet driven to do so. "Not you, exactly, Lord Wolf."

He looked at her more closely. "Lord Wolf should know something?"

Brita nodded. Her eyes were very wide and he could see her hands tremble. Dragon was expert at soothing women, albeit usually in very different circumstances. This one was clearly frightened or at the least unsure. Schooling his voice to gentleness, he said, "All right, there's something you'd like Lord Wolf to know. But perhaps you'd like me to tell him?"

She nodded again, more vigorously. "I don't really know . . . that is, I'm not sure what to say to him . . . how he will feel . . ."

"Because this is about the Lady Cymbra?"

Her voice fell to a whisper. "I do not wish to anger him but neither do I think I should keep silent any longer."

Dragon stiffened inwardly but he didn't let her see his reaction. The last thing he wanted was any sort of news that would upset Wolf, yet he also knew that nothing would anger his brother more than being kept in ignorance.

"You're right to do this," he told Brita. "Give me the information and I'll take responsibility for telling the jarl."

She looked at him with gratitude. "Thank you, my lord. Please understand, I wish only what is best . . . for everyone."

"That is to your credit. I'm sure we all appreciate your hard work and loyalty—"

"Not just everyone here. Everyone."

He thought about that for a moment, then nodded. "You mean Lady Cymbra as well."

"She was very good to me. Without her, I don't know what my life would be today. So, yes, I do want what is best for her, too." She looked very directly at Dragon. "I care about Lady Cymbra and Lord Wolf and—"

"And—?"

Brita took a breath, and Dragon had the sudden, clear impression that she was praying. When she spoke again, her voice was very low and urgent. By the time she fell silent, he was slumped back in his chair, his face drained of color and his eyes blank.

WOLF LOOKED TOWARD THE STALL DOOR AS HIS brother entered but did not stop currying the large black stallion who stood calmly beneath his hand. Despite the grip of winter on the land, the stable was warm, made so by snug walls and the heat of the animals who occupied it. Fresh straw lay over the ground and the feed troughs were full.

Dragon glanced from man to beast. "How's his fetlock?"

The horse, Wolf's favorite, had slipped on ice the pre-

ceding week and gone down hard, but he was recovering
well.

"Healed, I think," Wolf said. "Is it still snowing?"

"It is and looks set to continue through the night."
Dragon propped himself up on an overturned barrel and
studied his brother. Despite his recent illness, Wolf appeared as powerful as ever. Yet there was a new haggard-
ness to his face that spoke of painful thoughts behind eyes
that these days were always shuttered.

"You seem healed, too."

Wolf shrugged. "Too much fuss was made of that."

Deliberately, Dragon matched his show of uncon-
cern. "Perhaps. We didn't used to pay much attention to
such things." He waited until Wolf was concentrated on
the horse again, then said, "Until Cymbra came, that is."

At the sudden mention of her name, Wolf stiffened.
He shot his brother a single piercing look before returning
his eyes to the stallion.

Dragon was not discouraged. "So what I want to
know is, what do you think the odds are that she was
telling the truth?"

Wolf did not reply, nor did he look at his brother
again. Enough time passed for Dragon to think he would
not respond at all. But finally he emptied the pail he'd
been using, set the currying brush inside it, and straightened. His voice was hard despite the edge of soul-deep
weariness. "What are you talking about?"

Doing his utmost to hide his elation at getting a response, Dragon strove to show only the mildest interest.
"You remember what she said on the beach, that she
couldn't let one of you die because of her?"

He felt a stab of guilt when his brother flinched but
reminded himself that this was all for the best.

Wolf hung the pail on a peg and began forking fresh
straw into the stall. "I remember."

"She also told you she went with Hawk willingly."

"Is there some point to this?"

The bite of barely suppressed anger only encouraged Dragon further. He'd be damned if he'd let his brother bury his love for that Frigg-blessed Saxon in the grave of his own heart.

"Well, if she cared so much about *both* of you that she would have taken her own life to keep you from killing each other, what sense does it make that she would have wanted to leave here?" Without pausing for an answer he knew Wolf didn't have, Dragon went on. "What if she only said that she went with Hawk willingly to keep you from blaming him? After all, it's one thing if he came back to get her because she asked him to. Then it's just a matter of family loyalty; anyone can understand that even if we wouldn't necessarily like it. But if he did it on his own, he violated your hospitality *and* the alliance. How would you have handled that?"

"I don't know," Wolf admitted. He had given up the pretense of working and was focused on his brother. "I wondered about that myself."

Dragon nodded. "I think Cymbra might have, too. She must have feared you'd kill him. She'd seen you try to do just that on the beach."

Again, Wolf flinched at the memory of those horrible moments when Cymbra had stood with the dagger pressed to her breast. Again, Dragon felt a moment's guilt. He shoved it aside ruthlessly.

"Maybe she trusted that however you punished her, it wouldn't be anything as bad as what you'd do to him. And she was right about that, wasn't she?"

Wolf's only answer was a curt nod but he continued to look at his brother.

"And maybe," Dragon went on, "she wasn't really lying. She could have gone with him as far as the ship but intending to go no farther."

"That doesn't make any sense."

"Doesn't it? Hawk was here for a fortnight. Cymbra made every effort to show him that she was happy but they were never allowed to speak alone during that time. Perhaps he needed to hear her say that everything really was all right, with no possibility of her being pressured into it. The only place that could have happened was on his own ship."

Wolf snorted. "You have the imagination of a true skald, brother. Your stories are better than many I've heard."

Dragon resisted the urge to knock him up against the side of the head. "What if you or I were in Hawk's position? Wouldn't we have wanted to make sure she wasn't under any kind of duress?"

Long moments passed as Wolf wrestled with these questions. Finally, he said, "There's one problem with this tale you're spinning."

"What's that?"

"She's not here anymore. If she didn't intend to leave with him, how do you explain that?"

Dragon sighed. "I admit, that's the hard end of it. I can't explain it, not really. But think on this: Hawk had seen her whipped. He didn't have any way of knowing what would happen to her after he was gone. Whatever *she* may have wanted, under those circumstances how could *he* have left her behind?"

Wolf didn't reply. He looked at his brother in silence. At length, he resumed spreading the straw. Dragon left the stables a short while after that but he was not discouraged. If nothing else, he had set the Wolf to thinking.

As snow pelted him, he paused and looked out to the sea, where deadly rivers of ice now flowed. Until the year turned and the grip of winter was broken, thinking was just about all anyone could do.

•   •   •

"M Y LADY, COME AWAY FROM THAT WINDOW!"
Cymbra jerked guiltily and quickly pulled the
wooden shutter closed against the winter night, dropping
over it the ox-hide cover intended to further keep out the
chill. She turned around with a smile for the old woman
who glared at her sternly.

"I was just getting a breath of fresh air, Miriam. It
seems a bit warmer tonight."

"Night air of any sort is the worst thing for you." She
bustled over, seized Cymbra's hand, and drew her toward
the circle of iron braziers set up on tripods. They cast light
and warmth over a pair of high-backed chairs softened by
heaps of colorful cushions. Nearby was a large bed hung
with embroidered curtains and piled with pillows. There
were several carved chests, some brought from Holyhood,
and numerous other small touches that bespoke luxury
and comfort but Cymbra seemed scarcely to notice them,
occupied as she was with other matters.

"I don't know what you're thinking of," Miriam continued. "You hardly ate anything at supper and now here I
find you practically dangling out the window when it's
cold enough to freeze the drip off the end of Dreadful
Daria's nose—"

Miriam caught herself. She looked abashed. "Forgive
me, my lady, I'm an old woman and I tend to ramble."

Cymbra tried hard to suppress her laughter but she
just couldn't manage it. A very unladylike guffaw broke
from her. "*Dreadful Daria?* Is that what people call her?"

"I'm sorry, my lady, I know she's your half-sister
but—"

"You don't have to apologize," Cymbra said softly.
She sat down and urged her elderly nurse into the chair
next to her. "I've only really known Daria since I came to
Hawkforte. She is the child of my father's first marriage
and much older than either Hawk or me. By the time I was
born, she was already grown and gone. Apparently, when

our father remarried, she was glad enough to get her own household."

"It's a shame her husband's not still alive," Miriam grumbled, "and keeping her occupied elsewhere. Of course, going against the king isn't likely to guarantee a long life."

"A very poor choice," Cymbra agreed. One that proved fatal for Daria's husband, who had died years ago in a thwarted rebellion against the sovereign whom men were already calling Alfred the Great. It was in that very rebellion that a young thane called Hawk had risen to prominence, fighting beside the king he believed was the best hope of peace. "I suppose Hawk felt compelled to bring her back here once she was widowed. I was already at Holyhood and thus did not become acquainted with her." An omission for which Cymbra had learned to be grateful since living at Hawkforte in close proximity to her half-sister.

"She runs his household well enough from what I can see," Miriam said grudgingly. "But if she ever smiled, I swear her face would crack."

"I'm glad you're here with me," Cymbra said. Softly, she admitted, "I'd hate to have to depend on Daria."

"And so you shall not," Miriam declared emphatically. "Have no thoughts on that score and no worries either. Everything is going to be fine. Now can I coax you into eating a little soup?"

Although she really wasn't hungry, she agreed for her nurse's sake. Poor Miriam had been through agonies of worry after Cymbra was taken from Holyhood. Hawk's return with his sister had earned him the old nurse's eternal gratitude, but she still reserved her greatest loyalty for the woman she had raised from infancy.

"You were such a beautiful baby," she said a while later as Cymbra sat on the edge of the bed, braiding her long, chestnut hair. There were times when she thought of cutting it but then she remembered how much Wolf had liked her hair and couldn't bear to part with it. She had little enough left of him save for—

"And you were so bright," Miriam went on. "Right from the beginning, always looking around at everything. You smiled all day long."

"It was probably gas," Cymbra said with a grin.

"It was no such thing! Don't you believe that nonsense, my girl. Babies know, oh, yes, they do."

The two women fell silent, Cymbra lost in her thoughts and Miriam watching her with gentle concern. Long after the old nurse went to her bed and the fires burned low in the braziers, Cymbra remained awake. Her head resting on her knees, she listened to the wail of the wind beyond Hawkforte's strong walls and felt her spirit take flight.

As she did whenever sleep proved elusive and the hours wore long, she tried to imagine what Wolf was doing. She prayed he was well and could not bear to believe otherwise. And, though she tried hard not to dwell on the matter, she prayed that he was sleeping alone.

So, too, as she always did, she took refuge in memories of their time together. She remembered him in so many ways—coaxing her into the mineral bath on the way to Sciringesheal, carrying her through the town to the stronghold, comforting her on the night of their marriage when she was so afraid. And there were other memories as well, when she pelted him with food in the kitchens and he replied in kind, the sultry night of passion in the sauna, his laughter and gentleness, his determination to achieve peace, his rage on the beach when he believed she had tried to leave him.

Did he rage at her now, believing her a false wife and betrayer? Or had he put her from his mind so completely that she might never have existed?

With a moan, she turned over in the bed, hiding her

face in the pillows. The wind grew stronger. The wooden shutters creaked and the faint light left in the braziers sent up shadows that writhed and twisted against the walls.

She got up once to better secure the ox-hide curtains, then hurried back to bed across the cold stone floor. Huddled beneath the covers, she fell asleep finally with her cheeks damp and her arms wrapped protectively around herself.

In the morning, the memory of the night seemed unreal. It had no existence in the brilliant blaze of the cloudless day. The snow that had ebbed and flowed for weeks had finally stopped, although piles of it remained on the ground with drifts as high as a man along the walls.

Miriam clucked and tried to discourage her, but Cymbra dressed warmly in a long-sleeved wool gown of blue so deep as to be almost purple. Over it, she donned a cloak made of wool she had dyed herself to produce a rich green hue. Thus arrayed in colors that hinted of the spring for which she yearned, she ventured out into the brittle day.

The servants were busy in the great hall but several nodded to her as she passed through. Just outside, she paused to allow her eyes to adjust to the brilliant light reflected off the piles of snow. Pathways had been cleared between the keep and the outbuildings. People were hurrying about their tasks only mildly inconvenienced by the weather.

Off to one side, small children rolled in the snow like exuberant puppies. Cymbra laughed at the sight. On impulse, she went to join them. They quieted respectfully, managing to bow their heads without taking their eyes from her.

"Good morning, my lady," one of the bolder among them murmured. He was a boy of perhaps six with dark, curling hair and inquisitive eyes.

"Good morning," she said with a smile. "Isn't the snow wonderful?"

They all nodded, continuing to look up at her like so many grubby-faced, wide-eyed angels. A sudden thought occurred to her. "Do you know how to do this?" Before any could answer, she plopped down in the snow, stretched out to her full length with her legs together and her arms at her sides. As the children watched in astonishment, she moved her limbs back and forth in the downy flakes. With great care and just a little awkwardness, she stood up again, managing not to damage her creation. When she stepped out of it, she left the clear impression of a winged creature.

With a wave of her hand and a smile, she said, "A snow angel. Think you can do that?"

The children hesitated scarcely a heartbeat before leaping to the challenge. Cymbra helped the littler ones until they, too, had the idea. Soon that side of the keep was festooned with snow angels of varying sizes and shapes. The boy with the black locks even thought to try making one while turned on his side. She applauded his efforts, then attempted it herself while the children, who had thrown off their shyness, stood in a circle and encouraged her.

Cymbra had finished and was just getting up again when a shadow fell over the little group. She looked up to see the dour face of her half-sister frowning down at her.

"*What* do you think you are doing?" Daria demanded.

Reluctantly, Cymbra got to her feet. Although she gave the children a reassuring smile, they scattered like so many flakes before the wind. She frowned to see them go but contained her annoyance and addressed the older woman. As always when confronted with her half-sister, she found it hard to conceal her distaste. Daria roiled with emotions—anger, resentment, bitterness—and beneath them all, something else, something Cymbra instinctively shied from as from a chasm. Even now, her half-sister radiated tension, every inch of her too-thin form proclaiming rage.

"Just playing," she said quietly. "There's no harm in that, surely?"

Daria stared at her scornfully. Her long, narrow face twisted in a sneer of derision. "No harm? Of course there's harm. What sort of example do you think you set by cavorting like a hoyden? I have a hard enough time as it is getting these people to respect authority. When they see someone like you completely forgetting her position, what do you imagine they think?"

"That I'm human?" Cymbra suggested softly. She truly did not want to dislike Daria; they were family, after all, and she realized that her own presence at Hawkforte was upsetting to the woman, who seemed to have a frantic need to control every aspect of her own life and anyone else's who was foolish enough to accept her interference. Yet even as she strove for patience and tolerance, Cymbra had to admit that her half-sister made it extremely diffi cult to find either.

"Don't you be glib with me," Daria snapped. "Save that for our brother, who believes you can do no wrong. What he was thinking of bringing you here I can't imagine. We'll be lucky if we don't all end up murdered in our beds."

Cymbra repressed a sigh. Ever since her arrival at Hawkforte, Daria had been prophesying doom and destruction. She seemed to enjoy envisioning the most lurid scenes filled with rampaging Vikings who would attack without mercy, commit the most unspeakable atrocities, and leave no man, woman, or child alive. No one at Hawkforte paid much attention to her histrionics, and that seemed to drive her to even greater excesses. Yet her predictions were a constant reminder to Cymbra of how much she longed for one particular Viking and how greatly she feared that he had torn her from his heart.

"Your concerns are misplaced," she said quietly. "As for playing, you might want to try it yourself. It lifts the spirit."

Daria stiffened and drew herself up so straight that Cymbra worried her spine might snap. "Do not tell me about my concerns. *I* have far more important things to do. *I* am not a spoiled child always indulged and pampered."

That was too much for the woman who had been kidnapped from her home, married under threat of death, introduced to incandescent passion, gifted with profound love, and driven to risk her own life in a desperate gamble to make peace between two peoples.

With aloof disdain that Frigg herself would have envied, Cymbra said, "And I am not one to tolerate your rudeness any longer, Daria. Stay from my path as I will stay from yours."

Her half-sister was taken aback by such cool defiance. She looked about to respond but could not find the words. With a snort, she turned on her heel and stomped away.

Cymbra put her from her mind almost as soon as she was gone. The day was much too fair to be spoiled by thoughts of one such as Daria. Instead, she spent several cheerful hours in the kitchens. The servants welcomed her warmly. Despite their initial surprise when she had first begun to come there, they were accustomed now to her working beside them.

She had just completed assembling a pie of apples, raisins, and cinnamon that she knew Hawk liked when a clatter from the bailey yard drew her attention. Dusting off her hands, she looked out the window to see her brother returning.

After almost a fortnight away, attending the king's court at Winchester, he appeared somewhat weary and deep in thought. Cymbra went to him with a smile. His mood lightened when he saw her. He handed the reins to a stable boy and held out an arm to her, drawing her close.

"Are you well?" Hawk asked. His voice was very gentle when he spoke to her and the hard lines of his face eased, yet did his eyes remain shadowed by concern.

In both their minds lingered the memory of the conflict that had raged between them throughout the voyage from Sciringesheal and for many weeks thereafter. Cymbra had lashed out at her brother, decrying his betrayal of her trust and pleading to be returned to the husband she fervently claimed to love.

Hawk had resisted believing her with all his might, insisting that such love was an illusion and her judgment disordered by events. Only when he saw the depth of her anguish did he reluctantly begin to acknowledge that she might truly be in the grip of an emotion he had hitherto thought not to exist.

But by then they had reached Hawkforte and the swift onset of winter had closed the sea lanes. Slowly, reluctantly, driven by deepest concern for her well-being, he had drawn her out on the subject of her Viking husband and in the process discovered that Wolf was not at all what he had believed him to be. Honest to the core of his being, Hawk had finally been forced to the realization that he had made a terrible mistake.

One he desperately hoped to find some way to undo. But first he had to see to her safety and welfare even as he gave thanks for the generosity of her nature that had led her to forgive him.

"I'm very well," Cymbra said as they walked together across the bailey, "and you?"

Hawk grimaced. "Considering where I've been, fine. Alfred apparently does not need to sleep and forgets that anyone else does. The tables groan under the efforts of cooks vying to produce the richest food imaginable. All the while, the talk swirls from politics to fashion to music and back again."

"Poor Hawk," she teased, "if you thought you had escaped, you are mistaken. You must tell me all about what the ladies are wearing and if Alfred's physicians have any interesting new remedies. Did you bring back any books?"

"Four, all copied out by Alfred's own scribes. He sends thanks for the medical treatise you provided. Indeed, he was disappointed that you had not brought it yourself."

"Did you explain to him why I prefer not to travel just now?"

Her brother nodded. He glanced down at the swell of her abdomen visible even through the loose cloak and sighed. His arm tightened around her gently. "I told him. We agreed to speak of it again in the spring."

In the spring, when the sea lanes would reopen. When the waiting would end. When she would discover whether the love she nurtured within her heart as she nurtured the child within her womb would ever again know the man to whom they both belonged.

She mustered a smile and turned her face to the sun. Stray flakes of snow fluttered on the wind but there was no cloud to be seen. Over by the stables, where icicles hung from the eaves, a few sparkling droplets of water began to fall.

Chapter

TWENTY-FIVE

THE RED-BREASTED ROBIN LANDED ON THE edge of the nest to be greeted by the squawking of his hungry young. He darted food into their eager mouths before setting off at once in search of more.

Cymbra watched him go, then she stood up slowly. The small of her back ached. She pressed a hand to it as she glanced around the solar. The windows were thrown open to admit air fragrant with the scent of damp, fertile earth.

Below in the bailey, rays of sunlight cascaded through the mist still lingering from the night before. Although small piles of snow tarried in the most shaded parts of the keep, the grip of winter was broken. As swiftly as it had come, so had it gone.

Daria and several of the other ladies, wives, and daughters of Hawk's lieutenants, were gathered at the far end of the spacious chamber. They were busy at their sewing—and their chattering. Cymbra had no wish to join them.

Indeed, she had no wish to do anything save walk

slowly to and fro, rubbing her back. The ache had begun the night before but she had paid it little mind even when it kept her from sleeping much. Now it seemed oddly persistent.

"Does it hurt more?" Miriam asked. For several days, she had rarely strayed from Cymbra's side, even insisting on sleeping in the same room with her.

"It's nothing," Cymbra assured her. She rested her hands on the mound of her belly and looked down at herself ruefully. Somewhere under all that were her feet but she certainly couldn't see them. After carrying very small and high through most of her pregnancy, the last few weeks had seen a startling change.

"You are near your time," Miriam said with a smile.

Cymbra looked surprised. "Oh, I don't think so. That would have to mean that I—" She broke off, flushing slightly, but reminded herself that as a healer she should entertain no such foolish modesty. "It would mean that I conceived right away and I don't think I did."

"You don't think," Miriam repeated. "But you don't know either, do you?" Her brown eyes sparkled with amusement. "I'll warrant you weren't paying much attention."

"I suppose not," Cymbra admitted. "I've never been exactly regular and I just thought . . ." She shrugged, still embarrassed by how surprised she had been to realize, shortly after reaching Hawkforte, that she was with child. A healer might be expected to know such a thing before other women but not, apparently, in her case.

"You can sense the feelings of others so strongly," Miriam said. "I wonder if it doesn't make it more difficult to sense your own."

"That's possible," Cymbra admitted. It was as good an explanation as another. "But I really don't think this baby is coming anytime soon. It will be weeks yet."

Miriam nodded but her smile only deepened. She resumed sewing the tiny shirt she was making. The morning wore on. Beyond the high walls of Hawkforte, out toward the sea, the mist continued to lift. Cymbra saw gulls circling as they, too, hunted food for their young on the incoming tide.

She was distantly aware of Daria and the other ladies but paid them little mind. At least not until she suddenly became aware that one of them, a young girl Cymbra liked, was gazing open-mouthed out the window at something that had just caught her attention.

"W-what is that?" the girl asked.

Another of the women followed the direction of her gaze and frowned. "I don't know. It . . ." She gasped and pressed her hand to her mouth.

"There are more of them," the girl said even as her eyes widened in disbelief. "Many more . . . oh, my God . . ."

Daria pushed her way between the women to get a better view. She froze, her dour face rigid with shock. A moment later, her shrill scream reverberated off the walls.

"Vikings! Devils of the north! Thousands of them! We are doomed!"

Cymbra gasped but not because of what her half-sister had said. She was gripped by a sudden clawing pain that reached clear around from her back to center in her belly. So intense was it that she doubled over. At the same moment, she was suddenly drenched by a shower of water from between her legs.

Her soft cry of surprise momentarily distracted the women, who stared at her in blank amazement. "What is it?" Daria demanded, resenting the intrusion on her terror.

Miriam stood up slowly. She spared a glance out the windows where the mist was parting to reveal the fierce dragon prows of a dozen or more Viking war ships cutting through the water at high speed, aimed straight for the strand beneath Hawkforte. So close were they that the men could be seen straining at the oars, their powerful backs flexing rhythmically as if to a single will.

Already, the signal horns were sounding from the watchtowers. Men and women were streaming through the gates, dragging their children and animals with them. Hawk was in the bailey, buckling on his sword and conferring with his lieutenants.

With a shrug, the elderly nurse said what she thought ought to be obvious to all. "The Norse Wolf comes." She turned her attention to Cymbra, who was gasping again and looking very startled. "As does his child."

Pandemonium erupted. The women were torn, drawn to help Cymbra yet riveted by what was happening just beyond their walls. Most simply fluttered about, trying to do something useful but accomplishing nothing.

Miriam took matters in hand. She shepherded Cymbra out of the solar while giving instructions over her shoulder. "One of you take word to the Lord Hawk. Tell him his niece or nephew will be born this day. Then send to the kitchens for hot water, clean blankets need to be fetched, there is much to be done."

Reminded that the great doings of men notwithstanding, a child was coming into the world, the ladies calmed and hurried to their tasks. All save Daria, who continued to stare out the windows with satisfaction so great she was hard-pressed to conceal it behind the mask of false fear.

Now the wrath the fools so richly deserved would surely strike them. Now there would be retribution for their failure to exalt and honor her, she who was superior to them all. She should have had *everything*—marriage to a man wise enough to do as she directed, courageous enough to seize the power that had gone to Alfred instead, grateful enough to set her above all women, to make her the *queen* she was born to be.

Instead, she was supposed to think herself fortunate

for the charity of her brother's sufferance, for she knew well what Hawk thought of her, knew and hated him to the very marrow of her being. Now, at last, blood would run and the undeserving would die. But she would survive, her plans for escape being long laid. And she would reap the rewards promised to her in return for preventing the alliance of Norse and Saxon. Happy day when she had thought to intercept the letter sent from the Wolf to her brother! And even happier that in her skill and cunning she had managed to steal Hawk's seal long enough to forge the reply intended to provoke not peace but war.

So did she proclaim, but no one was left there to hear, neither her words nor the mad laughter that accompanied them. They had all gone elsewhere, ignoring her—yet one more crime for which she swore they would pay.

W HAT CAN YOU SEE?" CYMBRA ASKED. CLAD IN A fresh night robe, she had agreed reluctantly to get into bed but was determined to know what was happening. A steady stream of women came and went. They were pale and tense but so eager to help that she could not send them away.

Miriam set aside the swaddling clothes she was folding and went to the window. She glanced out with little interest. "Your husband is here."

Cymbra felt a surge of joy so intense as to rob her of breath. She had to clutch the covers to keep from leaping out of the bed and running straight to him. Although, to be truthful, probably the best she could have done was to waddle.

"What is he doing?"

Miriam's frown silenced the woman who had been about to answer. "He's talking with the Lord Hawk. They're having a nice conversation. Now you forget about them and tend to your own task."

The fierce pain that suddenly took Cymbra made the good sense of that advice all the more apparent. Miriam hurried to her side and clasped her hand. "There, there, sweetheart, it will be all right. Just breathe when they come and try to relax in between."

"Sweetheart," Cymbra murmured as the pain receded. She blinked back tears that had nothing whatsoever to do with her labor. "He called me that."

"Called you what?" Miriam asked.

"Wolf, he called me *elskling*, 'sweetheart.' "

"What a dear man," the elderly nurse said, forgetting that she had rained down a thousand curses on his head when she learned he was responsible for taking Cymbra.

"He is dear," she gasped as another pain seized her. "Dear and kind and gentle . . . and always so reasonable, so understanding."

Miriam murmured consolingly, gently wiping the sweat from Cymbra's brow as the contractions continued to come hard and fast.

Meanwhile, down below on the open ground in front of Hawkforte, the dear man had a few things of his own to say.

Armored and helmeted, his sword gleaming as it slashed the air, the Scourge of the Saxons roared, "Stone by stone! Plank by plank! I will leave nothing standing. Send her out *now*!"

From his position on the parapet, Hawk looked at the enraged warrior who had just threatened to demolish his keep and could not repress a surge of admiration. Behind Wolf, drawn up in ranks ten deep, was a veritable Viking army. He estimated at least a thousand men, and there might be more. His own garrison matched them in strength and he had the additional advantage of high walls. But not for a moment did he doubt that the Wolf stood a damn good chance of doing exactly as he threatened.

Nor could he blame him for seriously considering it.

Fortunately, they were closer to accord than Wolf had any way of knowing. It was now up to Hawk to convince him of that. Leaning over the wall, he gave his answer. "Cymbra is busy right now. Come in and we'll talk."

Hearing this, the Viking array shouted in derision and drummed their sword hilts against their shields. But Wolf did not answer immediately. Instead, he spoke quietly with his brother, who stood at his side.

"Strange answer; what the hell does he mean she's busy?"

Dragon shrugged and didn't meet Wolf's eyes. "It's not as if he said no."

Wolf glanced back up at the parapet, noting that Hawk was watching him with interest but no apparent concern. He didn't look like a man who wanted to fight, but then it wasn't always possible to tell.

"Hell of a risk," Dragon said cheerfully. "Just you and a thousand Saxons. You're good, all right, but maybe not *that* good."

"What choice do I have?" Wolf muttered. "If I try to take the damned keep, Cymbra could be hurt in the process. Odds are Hawk's already figured that out."

Dragon nodded. "Sounds like he's got you." He patted his brother on the back encouragingly. "Don't worry. I'll handle things out here."

Sparing a moment's thought for Dragon's odd willingness to see him walk into the jaws of death, Wolf nodded. When all was said and done, there was little else he could do.

Hawk shouted down an order and the gates were opened just enough to admit one lone Viking. Wolf strode into the bailey yard to find himself the target of all eyes. The Saxon warriors glared at him but kept their distance, well aware that they were in the presence of a legend.

Hawk was more forthcoming. He jumped down from

the wall and walked over to Wolf. Both men were armed but Hawk had not drawn his sword. He stood before his "guest," took a deep breath, and said what he knew both honor and reason demanded. It wasn't easy but he managed it with more grace than he had thought possible.

"I made a mistake when I took Cymbra from Sciringesheal. I was wrong to do it and I ask your pardon."

Wolf stared at him, dumbfounded. Never had he expected that the proud Saxon warrior would admit guilt and apologize. A great knot of tension began to ease in him, just a little. Still cautious, he said, "Then she will come to me now and we will leave."

Hawk hesitated. "First there are other matters we should discuss, bearing on the alliance. That's what you wanted in the beginning, isn't it? Have you changed your mind?"

Scant moments before, Wolf would have sworn that he had. The very notion of an alliance with the Saxons seemed an evil joke. But now he wasn't so sure. Hawk had apologized and invited him into his home. Honor demanded that he put aside old enmity and at least try for a new beginning.

"I am willing to consider it," he said grudgingly.

Hawk smiled broadly. "Excellent!" He began walking toward the hall, Wolf beside him. As though they were engaged in no more than the most ordinary conversation, Hawk asked, "Did you have difficulty getting here?"

Silvery eyes blinked. "What?"

"You're a little earlier than I expected. There must still be ice in the sea lanes."

Wolf shrugged. "We steered around it." So did he brush aside a feat of seamanship that would become legend in its own right.

"Very sensible," Hawk said and led the way into his

hall. He gestured to the servants, who, despite their terror, hastened to bring forth refreshment.

"Let us dine together," Hawk said, "and talk over our differences."

"I will see Cymbra first, then we will talk all you like."

"Alas, I regret she truly isn't available at the moment. Let us talk first."

Hawk had already taken his seat and was waiting for him to do the same. With a spurt of impatience, Wolf yanked off his helmet, tossed it down on the table, and made himself as comfortable as he could be while fighting the lingering urge to hack his host to bits. As for Cymbra, he could only conclude that she was being recalcitrant about seeing him again. All things considered, he couldn't blame her. With an inner sigh, he contemplated how he might win back his wife's favor. Not killing her brother was probably a good first step.

A pasty-faced servant poured mead. Some of the liquid spilled onto the wide wooden table but neither of the warlords noticed. They drank eyeing each other over the rims of their goblets. Food followed. Wolf ignored it. Abruptly, he demanded, "Why did you take Cymbra from Sciringesheal?"

"Why?" Hawk shot back. "How could I have not done so after you *whipped* her."

"She wasn't hurt," Wolf insisted, though he flinched at the memory. "You must know that by now."

"True," Hawk admitted, "but I didn't then."

Slowly, Wolf nodded. The first faint stirrings of hope began in him. Lest they grow foolishly strong, he asked, "What about before then, when you pretended to leave and came back? Did she ask you to do that?"

Hawk looked at him in surprise. "No, of course not. She had no idea I was coming. She only agreed to go down

to the ship because I told her that was the only place I'd
believe she was speaking freely."

Hawk watched with interest as all the color drained
from his guest's face. "Something wrong?" he asked
pleasantly.

Dazedly, Wolf said, "That's what Dragon thought.
He's only her brother-in-law and he didn't lose faith in
her, whereas I, her husband . . . I believed . . ."

"Believed what?" Hawk asked more kindly.

Wolf took a breath, let it out slowly. "I thought she
was lost to me."

With a moment's fervent gratitude for being spared
the tortures of true love, Hawk said, "That's for the two of
you to settle between yourselves. But first, I am charged
by King Alfred to work out the details of the alliance between us."

Reluctantly, Wolf dragged himself back to the matter
of great issues. "He knows of it?"

Hawk nodded. "I told him when I went to court a few
months ago. He is strongly in support of this and prepared to do everything possible to make it succeed."
Because he did not want any diversion from the matter at
hand, he refrained from adding that he had also told King
Alfred of the false message sent in response to Wolf's
original proposal of the alliance. Britain's monarch had
agreed that the Danes were most likely at fault, although
how exactly remained to be discovered.

Thus encouraged, the two men buckled down to
work. Parchment and ink were sent for, more food arrived, torches were lit as the sun angled westward.
Outside in the bailey yard and beyond the walls, two
armies waited to learn if there would be peace or war.

And upstairs, in the high tower, new life struggled to
be born.

Cymbra gasped as yet another wave of pain struck
her. The contractions were coming so fast now that she

had no chance to recover between them. She was consumed by the fury of birth, striving with all her might, yet desperately afraid that her strength would not prove equal to the task. For all that she had assisted many women in childbed, she had never truly understood the experience. Now she did. Deep within her, she felt the ancient, absolute imperative to bring forth life overriding all else, even the instinct for her own survival. Again, her womb contracted. Again, pain devoured her.

After all the hours of anguish, for the first time, Cymbra screamed.

In the hall, Wolf heard. Shock roared through him. He leaped from the table on which the draft of the Norse-Saxon alliance lay and raced for the stairs. Two men-at-arms foolishly stepped into his path. He tossed them aside like so much chaff before the wind and took the steps two at a time. Behind him, still seated, Hawk reached for his goblet and took a long swallow, trying to ignore the fact that his hand shook.

On the upper level of the keep, Wolf paused for a moment, uncertain which way to turn. Another scream told him. He raced down the corridor and thrust open the door at the far end just in time to see—

"Cymbra!"

In the grip of the most intense contraction yet, Cymbra was stunned to see her husband suddenly appear. After all the months of longing for him, he seemed like an apparition. One armed for war, to be sure, but still wonderfully welcome.

Trembling, she held out her arms to him. "Wolf . . ."

He was at her side in an instant, one quick, shocked glance enough to tell him what was happening.

"Help her to sit up a little, lord," Miriam directed calmly. Wolf had the great good sense to do as he was bid even as his mind reeled from the stunning discovery. Cymbra clung to him desperately. He bent over her, a huge, powerful presence seeking with all his might to add his strength to hers.

"Push!" Miriam ordered. Cymbra did . . . and again . . . and once more . . .

A baby's lusty squall announced her success.

Moments later, Miriam smiled broadly. She straightened from the foot of the bed, cleaned the infant swiftly, and held him out to his stunned father. "You have a son, lord."

Wolf's knees felt so weak that he thought it wise to sit down before accepting the precious burden. He looked from the baby lying in his arms to the woman on the bed, and felt such all-encompassing love that for a long moment he could not move, or speak, or indeed even breathe.

Finally, he said the only thing he truly could when confronted with such a miracle. Gazing into the eyes of the woman he loved more than life itself, he whispered, "Thank you."

Cymbra blinked back tears. Weary though she was, she was also exultant. Raising herself a little on the pillows, she touched her husband's face with gentle awe. "Thank you," she murmured.

Miriam turned away from the tender scene, giving the three their privacy. She ushered the other women from the room and went downstairs to inform the Lord Hawk that he was uncle to a fine little Viking.

That same uncle waited a discreet time before knocking on the door of Cymbra's chamber. She was asleep and did not stir but Wolf came to admit him. He had removed his sword and armor and wore only a simple tunic. His son was nestled asleep in the crook of his arm.

"How is Cymbra?" Hawk asked.

"Good," Wolf said, all his infinite relief in that single word. Softly, he added, "She has great strength."

The two men were silent for a moment, dwelling on the unknowable mystery of women. At length, Hawk smiled. He peered at the baby, who yawned broadly but did not open his eyes. "Sturdy little fellow."

Wolf grinned with pride. "A good combination, Saxon and Norse."

Hawk nodded. "You might tell your friends outside that. I think they're getting a little restless."

Only then did Wolf realize that he had been inside the Saxon stronghold for hours. He was amazed that Dragon had been able to hold the men in check so long. Quickly, he wrapped the baby in a warm blanket and followed Hawk down the steps.

The Viking array stirred when the gates of Hawkforte were thrown open. Men looked up, blinking in the fading light of day. The sun was going down in glory. Already, a few stars could be seen.

The Norse Wolf stood in full view of his men and of all those who were gathered on the walls of Hawkforte. He stretched his powerful arms high above his head, holding his child to the heavens, and shouted for all to hear.

"I have a son!"

High up in the tower room, the full-throated roar of warriors proclaiming their approval drifted through Cymbra's dreams. She turned over against the cool linen of the pillows and smiled contentedly.

Chapter

TWENTY-SIX

THE SCREAM WOKE WOLF JUST AFTER DAWN.
He was out of bed, sword in hand, before he
realized he confronted not the demented enemy he had momentarily assumed but only a
woman. A very dour-faced, shrill woman.

"*Viking!*" the creature screamed again. "Save us!
We'll be—"

"What on earth . . . ?" Cymbra murmured sleepily.
She sat up, looking from her irate husband to her frenzied
half-sister. Softly, she said, "Daria, this is my husband,
Lord Wolf Hakonson. He is a guest here. Pray treat him
as such."

Daria's eyes glazed over. Tiny flecks of spittle shone
at the corners of her mouth. She had told herself this could
not be, not even her despicable brother could go so far as
to make peace with Vikings because the contemptible cow
lying before her had spread her legs for one and gotten a
son in the process. It could not be, yet even through the
twisted darkness of her rage she saw that it was and knew
she had failed. But only for the moment, only that. She

was better than they were, smarter, more deserving, superior in every way. This was only a setback; she would prevail in the end if only because any other possibility was utterly unthinkable. But to win, she must survive, and to do that, she must hide herself quickly from the too-keen gaze of blue eyes focusing on her now in belated but growing puzzlement.

"A guest?" Daria shrieked. "In here? It isn't bad enough that there are thousands of them outside, they are to be allowed in, too?"

Cymbra summoned patience, finding it easy to do when she was filled with such joy. Her gaze was drawn irresistibly to Wolf. Vaguely, she remembered him returning to her the night before and laying their son in her arms. He had made to go then but she called him back with a soft word. After so long apart, she could not bear to be without him. He stayed gladly, sleeping in his clothes beside her on the bed, waking in the night to bring her the baby to nurse. Still dazed and weary from the exertion of childbirth, their first tender hours together as parents touched her deeply.

But now the world intruded and she was resigned to it. "They will all be in here soon enough," she told her half-sister gently. "Hawk plans a feast to celebrate the birth of his nephew as well as the alliance."

"Vikings within our gates! I cannot believe it. What can he be thinking of? And a feast—it's impossible, absolutely impossible, we could never manage." Her small, flat eyes glared at Cymbra. "You've caused all this, it's your responsibility. How long do you mean to lie there? Surely you can get up and—"

Whatever Daria would have said next was cut off by the infuriated Viking who pointed to the door and snarled, "Out!"

She skittered away but not without a look of pure

venom. Cymbra promptly forgot her. She leaned back against the pillows, regarded her husband, and smiled. "You do that so well."

He raised an eyebrow in question. Her smile deepened. "Remember that day in the kitchens?"

He did, and to her delight, he blushed. Cymbra laughed and held out her arms to him. He was just drawing her into his when Miriam bustled in.

"Enough of that. My lady needs looking after." She glanced at Wolf. "And if you don't mind my saying so, you could do with a clean-up yourself."

Far from taking offense at the old woman's directness, he rubbed a hand over his whiskered jaw and grimaced. Pausing only to drop a light kiss on Cymbra's brow, he said, "I'll be back when I'm more fit, *elskling*."

"That dear man," Miriam murmured as the door closed behind him. Smiling, she went to help her mistress.

SEATED ON A SMOOTH WOODEN BENCH, NAKED AND dripping sweat, Wolf studied the man across from him. Allowing for a certain tendency to provoke thoughts of murder and mayhem, Hawk wasn't a bad sort. For one thing, he had a sauna, which he claimed to be the only good idea he'd ever gotten from the Danes. Then, in all honesty, he'd only done what Wolf himself would have if their positions had been reversed. And lastly, he was Cymbra's brother; it was in their interests to get along for her sake and for the sake of both their peoples.

Reflecting on what they had accomplished so far as well as what remained to be done, Wolf said, "This alliance puts us in good position to withstand the Danes, but more is needed."

Hawk tossed a ladleful of water on the fire stones. He was amazed—and relieved—to find himself so at ease with his sister's abductor. Love bewildered him; up until very recently he would have sworn it didn't exist. Now he was willing to admit that in this one solitary case, it had worked wonders.

"Closer ties between our peoples," Wolf went on, "would strengthen our mutual security."

Hawk nodded. This was good sense. "We should look to trade more. That would help."

"That's true," Wolf agreed, "but I had something else in mind." He paused deliberately, then said, "You're not married."

Hawk's broad back stiffened. He moved quickly to quash any thought Wolf might have along those lines. "I was married many years ago. She died. That was enough for me."

"I'm sorry," Wolf said sincerely. "But even after such a loss, you must go on."

"You misunderstand. We were not close, on the contrary. The experience convinced me that marriage is not for me."

From a nearby bench where he was stretched out, letting the heat draw out the excesses of celebration that had followed news of his nephew's birth, Dragon raised his head briefly. "Don't let him persuade you otherwise," he warned. "He used to have a perfectly sane, sensible attitude toward the whole thing but that's all changed. If we're not careful, he'll be looking to get everyone married off."

"Not everyone," Wolf said. He glanced from one to the other, his silvery eyes alight with amusement. "Just both of you."

"Both?" That was Dragon again, truly caught by surprise and outraged. He'd assumed his brother's scheming extended no further than their host, who also was having none of it.

"Not likely," Hawk scoffed. "Once was more than enough."

Wolf refused to be deterred. The soul of patience—and ruthless determination—he asked, "What could be more reasonable? If Hawk takes a Norse bride and you, Dragon, take a Saxon bride, the alliance will be secured three times over. I have no doubt King Alfred would agree." He paused. "Indeed, that's why I've already suggested it to him."

Hawk stared at him. "What do you mean, suggested it?"

"I sent a letter to him outlining this plan." The Saxon's look of unbridled shock was, Wolf decided, ample recompense for the anguish Wolf himself had experienced over Cymbra's loss. Indeed, he could not have devised a better punishment. The best part was that it had only just begun. He would have months, possibly even longer, to savor the Hawk's twisting on the matrimonial hook.

"It's too late," Wolf said cheerfully as Hawk turned toward the door, clearly intending to send men to intercept the message. "It went this morning, you'll never catch them."

He did not mention, although he would tell them later, that in the same message he had asked for Alfred's help in discovering the identity of whoever had intercepted his own message to Hawk the year before and forged the response that set all in motion. Grateful though he was for the outcome, he was still determined to unmask the miscreant lest he be tempted to strike again.

Slowly, Hawk subsided but he continued to stare at Wolf in stunned disbelief. "Alfred may not like the idea. . . ." Even as he spoke, he knew he was grasping for hope where there was none. It was exactly the sort of suggestion the king would seize upon to further his own aims to defeat the Danes. Hawk had sworn fealty to Alfred. If the king ordered him to do so, he would have no choice but to . . . marry. And marry a Norse woman at that, a stranger he wouldn't even be permitted to choose for himself. Gloom over the prospect cast him into silence even as he grabbled for some way—any way—to escape the trap closing around him.

"Praise Odin I'm not beholden to any Saxon liege," Dragon said fervently. He swung his legs over the bench and sat up, the better to observe the other two. Hawk's plight was amusing, but his brother, Dragon decided, needed much more careful watching than he'd realized.

"You're not," Wolf agreed, "but Alfred isn't a man to anger." He looked at his brother pointedly. "Neither am I."

Dragon stared at him, incredulous. "That's the thanks I get? Not only did I plant the seed in your mind about what actually happened between Cymbra and this one"—he gestured at Hawk—"but purely out of compassion, I refrained from telling you she was pregnant so you wouldn't madden yourself waiting for the sea lanes to open. *This* is how you would repay me?"

Wolf was on his feet so suddenly he almost brained himself on a low beam of the sauna. "You *what*?"

"How did you know?" Hawk asked, vengefully pleased to see the scheming Viking discomfited.

Dragon shrugged his broad, bare shoulders. "That Irish girl, Brita, told me. She overheard you by the stable, telling Cymbra you wouldn't believe anything she said until you were sure she wasn't under duress. Brita tried to intervene later when everything happened, but some of the women dragged her off, thinking they were doing it for her own good. You can imagine how she felt since she was more or less certain Cymbra was with child."

Wolf sat down abruptly. He stared at his brother in disbelief. "You knew she was pregnant?"

"I knew there was a damn good chance, but Brita swore Cymbra didn't know. She thought that was really funny, Cymbra being a healer and all."

"Funny," Wolf repeated, stunned by what his brother

had kept from him. Yet in all fairness, Dragon had the right of it. As it was, he had scarcely been able to wait for the first thaw. Had he known Cymbra was with child, he might have been pushed into an act of madness that would have risked his own life and those of any who followed him. Dragon had spared him that, for which he would be grateful—someday.

"She thought that *until* everything happened, then she was worried sick."

"So she confided in *you?*"

Dragon smiled modestly. "Women like me. It's a curse, to be sure, but I bear it."

Hawk laughed but stopped abruptly when he caught sight of the Wolf's expression. Hastily, he said, "It all worked out for the best."

Wolf surveyed the pair. Slowly, his scowl gave way to a broad smile. He sat back on the bench, folded his powerful arms behind his head, and contemplated the future. "True enough it has—for me. We'll have to see what happens with the two of you."

Despite the heat of the sauna, Hawk and Dragon exchanged looks of frozen horror. That amused the Wolf even further. He was in high good humor when he returned to his wife.

H E FOUND CYMBRA SITTING UP IN THE BED, FRESHLY bathed and gowned, her hair in ribbons and her child in her arms. She looked up from her contemplation of the little one, bestowing on her husband a smile that would have stolen his heart had it not already been hers.

Her eyes widened as she beheld him. Gone was the fierce Viking warrior of the day before. He had bathed and shaved and was garbed not in armor but in a tunic of deep purple trimmed with bands of gold. His thick, ebony hair was secured at the nape of his neck, revealing more clearly than ever the harshly beautiful planes and angles of his face. Arm rings of gold glinted around his powerful biceps and the wolf's-head torque shone at his throat.

At the sight of it, her hand flew to her own bare neck. He saw the gesture and smiled. Drawing a small wooden chest from behind his back, he held it out to her. "Looking for this?"

She opened it to find her jewels, including the torque he had given her on their wedding day. With trembling hands, she drew it out. Wolf stepped closer to the bed. Gently, he took the torque from her and with great care placed it around her throat. The wolf's diamond eyes gleamed in the morning sun.

The baby woke then, opening eyes the same deep blue as his mother's yet surrounded by rims of silver. He looked up at his father solemnly. Wolf reached out to touch a hand so tiny it would have disappeared into his own palm. To his surprised delight, his son grasped his finger and held on firmly.

"Strong little cuss," Wolf murmured with a grin.

"And in need of rather a different name than that," his wife chided. Smiling tenderly at the two males she adored, she said, "What think you of calling him Hakon?"

Deeply touched that she would think to name their son for his grandfather, Wolf nodded. But a moment later he was grinning again as his son made his own opinion known.

"We may name him Hakon but I suspect he's more likely to be known as Lion. Surely that roar is worthy of the king of the beasts."

Cymbra laughed but didn't disagree. With just a little nervousness for a task still so new, she set him to her breast. He rooted around for a moment before finding what he sought. Silence descended, to the great relief of the besotted parents.

A MAZING," HAWK MUTTERED A FEW DAYS LATER AS
he stood in the chapel listening to his nephew's response as the holy water of baptism was placed on his
brow. The baby's bellow of outrage reverberated off the
stone walls, causing Brother Joseph to speed up his
prayers noticeably. To the intense relief of all assembled,
Norse and Saxon alike, the good monk finished quickly
and returned the child to his mother. He quieted after one
last howl that caused even his mighty father to wince.

"A fine set of lungs," Brother Joseph observed tact-
fully when the service was concluded.

From her husband's arms—Wolf having agreed to
her coming downstairs only if he carried her everywhere—Cymbra said, "And a fine service despite the ac-
companiment. Thank you for it."

The young monk smiled. He glanced at the fierce jarl
with a twinkle of amusement. "I am glad to have been of
use after all, my lady, and for a much happier task than to
try to persuade you to return."

Cymbra, too, was delighted that Wolf had insisted on
bringing Brother Joseph along, no matter what the reason.
She much preferred him to Hawk's house priest, the dour
Father Elbert. He was somewhere in the crowd, no doubt
in the company of Daria, for the two of them seemed of
the same ilk. On the excuse that Brother Joseph had
helped to officiate at her marriage, she felt no qualms
whatsoever about asking him to baptize Hakon.

As promised, Hawk seized that as an occasion to celebrate the unity of Norse and Saxon. Despite Daria's dire
predictions, the feast proceeded smoothly. Guests were
present in such numbers that the great hall could not contain them and even the bailey yard looked full to bursting.
Tables set up inside and out groaned under a bounty of

food scarcely seen in spring. That this was due in part to the provisions Wolf had brought along in anticipation of a siege was politely ignored.

Wolf placed her in a chair at the high table and took his own seat beside her. Hawk and Dragon were on either side of them. Scarcely had they settled than a steady stream of guests approached to offer greetings. They came from throughout Saxon England; Essex itself was well represented, so was the royal province of Wessex, from which Alfred had sent his own dignitaries, and even the Mercian lords, Udell and Wolscroft, were on hand. Vaguely, Cymbra remembered that the latter had been friend to Daria's late, unlamented husband and was therefore not surprised to see the two of them in conversation. But before very long, she had been introduced to so many lords and ladies that in truth she could notice very little and gave up all hope of remembering more than a handful of their names.

To her surprise, she realized that as eager as they were to meet the Norse Wolf, they were equally driven to satisfy their curiosity about his Saxon wife. From their asides to one another, she gathered they had all heard the stories about her seclusion at Holyhood and her abduction from there. Ordinarily, so much avid speculation would have left her feeling invaded and exhausted. But with Wolf beside her, she basked in his comfort and support, and found that she was thoroughly enjoying the evening.

Never more so than when she caught sight of Olaf and with a quick smile called him to join them. She had known for days that he too was with the Viking army, but he had managed to avoid her until now. The older man came reluctantly, starting with surprise when she reached out and took his grizzled hand. At once, she felt his dread and concern, neither of which could she permit to long exist.

"I am so glad you are here," she said softly. "I hope my son will have the benefit of your wise counsel as my husband has done."

Olaf stared at her for a moment as his eyes dampened. Gruffly, he murmured, "Thank you, my lady."

Wolf had been listening. He stood, and in full view of the assembly embraced the old warrior, calling for a chair to be brought that he might sit among them. The grateful look her husband gave her told Cymbra she truly understood that she bore no resentment for his punishing of her.

The feast lasted far into the night but long before then the Norse Wolf carried his beloved wife upstairs to their quarters. Though the revelry continued, he was content and more to remain with her. He lay on his side, his head propped in the palm of his hand, and watched Cymbra sleep. That she was there with him, loving him, was almost more than he could encompass. That they also had made a child together brought him joy beyond any he had ever known.

Since his own boyhood, when he found himself an orphan surrounded by the ruins of the only life he had ever known, a hard knot of anger and grief had existed within him. He had done his best to ignore it, driven as he was to seize the future rather than dwell on the past. Yet had it remained until now. There in the quiet of the room in the high tower, he realized it was gone.

He reached out a hand and with utmost care traced the soft curve of his wife's cheek, passing a finger lightly over the fullness of her lips and down along her delicate throat to where her life's pulse beat. Unbidden, he remembered his first impression of her, recalling how he had thought her something other than human. He knew the truth now; she was utterly and completely a woman endowed with all the mysterious power and grace that had been missing from his life.

She had come to him in an act of vengeance that became an act of redemption. With endless courage and generosity, she had banished the pain of the past and given him a future filled with hope. Cymbra the healer had healed him.

Now together in everlasting love, they would bring the blessing of peace to both their lands.